W
Kathern W
127 W No
Truro, IA

D1409680

Books by James Walker

Husbands Who Won't Lead and Wives Who Won't Follow

The Wells Fargo Trail

- The Dreamgivers
- The Nightriders
- The Rail Kings
- The Rawhiders
- The Desert Hawks
- The Oyster Pirates
- The Warriors

9703

THE WARRIORS

+ + + + + + + + + + + +

JIM WALKER

BETHANY HOUSE PUBLISHERS
MINNEAPOLIS, MINNESOTA 55438

The Warriors

Cover illustration by William Graf

Published by Bethany House Publishers
A Ministry of Bethany Fellowship, Inc.
11300 Hampshire Avenue South
Minneapolis, Minnesota 55438

Printed in the United States of America.

Library of Congress Cataloging-in-Publication Data

Walker, James, 1948–
The warriors / by Jim Walker.
p. cm. — (The Wells Fargo trail ; 7)
I. Title. II. Series. III. Series: Walker, James, 1948– Wells Fargo trail ; bk. 7.
PS3573.A425334W35 1997
813'.54—dc21 97-4734
ISBN 1-55661-702-X CIP

This book is dedicated to two intellectual warriors,
professors of mine in seminary,
who fanned the flames of my love for Scripture
and ignited the spark of my interest in western fiction:

Dr. Richard Rigsby
and
Dr. James Rosscup

JIM WALKER is a staff member with the Navigators and has written *Husbands Who Won't Lead and Wives Who Won't Follow.* He received an M.Div. from Talbot Theological Seminary and has been a pastor with an Evangelical Free Church. He was a survival training instructor in the United States Air Force and is a member of the Western Outlaw-Lawman History Association. Jim, his wife, Joyce, and their three children, Joel, Jennifer, and Julie, live in Colorado Springs, Colorado.

PART 1

+ + +

THE JORNADA DEL MUERTO

CHAPTER 1

✦ ✦ ✦ ✦ ✦ ✦ ✦

THE CANDLELIGHT FLUTTERED on the table, twisting like a dancer on a narrow stage. Its pale ooze of tallow trickled down the slender wax stick, forming a puddle around the square wooden block that held it upright. Julian lay in a corner of the adobe cell, watching the first gray hint of dawn splash gentle rays of light over the Animas Mountains. This was to be the promised day of his death. For what, he had no idea.

Turning on his back, he blinked his one eye at the ceiling. The blanched green paint peeled back from the surface in lazy curls. Refusing to fall, they hung like pea green icicles in the late spring. The cell was bare except for the blankets that had become his home in the corner of the dusty room, and the table and two chairs that had been brought in for his inquisition. The dew that formed a morning sweat on the walls and the position of the solitary window told him that much of the room was underground. Bars of iron ran from the ceiling to the floor, exposing his entire cell to the hallway beyond.

A fly crawled slowly on the wall beside him, lifting its emerald wings from time to time and meandering in what seemed to be a circle. Julian watched it. After crawling along the surface for a few minutes, it buzzed upward and out through the prison bars. Julian could only imagine why he was here, condemned to die. He could remember nothing. The side of his skull throbbed painfully from a near miss that had left him with what was now only a foggy recollection of what he was or who he had been. He knew his name only because the commandant had told him.

He heard the keys clang in the door that led to the hallway. They would be bringing him his last meal. Perhaps they would be merciful and include something that might appear as if he were the first to eat it. The sound of the boots on the floor was accompanied by the soft sound of a woman's dress dragging over the straw and debris that littered the walkway. That would be the nun Sister Mary Perizza.

The burly, half-dressed guard stopped in front of his cell and, rattling his keys, turned the lock and swung the door open. "Señor, the sister is here with your meal. You get up and stand beside the wall."

Julian wrestled himself to his knees, then slowly and shakily stumbled to his feet. He backed up, pressing against the damp, adobe wall. He watched the woman as she held the tray and plodded toward the table, dragging her lame and twisted foot. She set the tray down and motioned him forward. Backing up, she nodded to the guard. "Gracias, it will be enough. I will sit with him now."

The man backed up, closed the iron door, turned the key in the lock, and plodded away.

"I fix your breakfast myself, Señor Cobb, and I bring you some hot coffee."

Julian stepped toward the table, and dragging out a chair, he seated himself in front of the tin plate and cup. Several tortillas were spread with eggs, and a piece of fatty ham lay nestled on the side. He picked up the cup with both hands, allowing the warmth of the black liquid to radiate life into his fingers. He breathed in the steamy aroma of the coffee as it wafted past his black mustache. Holding it to his lips, he sipped slowly.

"I bring you a gift of mercy. It is all I can do."

"Thank you, Sister, I appreciate it. It's the first decent meal I've had . . . I can't remember when."

"Ahh, this memory of yours. It must return, señor."

"It keeps coming back to me from time to time, but mostly memories of me as a boy. I can't rightly remember anything of a recent nature."

"Señor, you must tell the commandant what he wants to know. Otherwise, you will be shot today."

"I wish I could. If he hadn't told me who I was, I wouldn't even know my own name."

"I hate to see any man shot, not for who he is, but for who he was and something he can't even remember, for something he has done that he can't find the words to express. How can you even confess a sin when there is no recollection of what that sin is?"

Julian raked a pile of the eggs onto one of the cold tortillas and curled the flat bread into a tube. He bit off the end and chewed slowly.

"Sister, I suppose I've sinned plenty of times, more than I might care to remember. I suppose I could just confess to just about anything and it might be true, sure enough."

"I cannot have you confess to what you cannot remember—and why should you die for something that isn't in your mind?"

"With all the things the commandant says I've done, maybe it's a blessing that it isn't in my mind. I don't recollect as how I could have faced death with any sort of innocence on my soul"—he reached up and felt the gash on the side of his head—"and now maybe I might do just that."

He stabbed a portion of the grisly ham with his fork and began to chew it. "'Sides, from what I can remember about my brand of Christianity, I'll be able to see with two eyes."

She reached over and, with a light touch on his black eye patch, smiled. "You are a special man. It is not every man, señor, that God blesses with the ability to get by with less. I was born a beautiful girl of a wealthy family. With the refinement of the education my family sent me to obtain in France, I seemed destined to become a woman of hospitality, a butterfly among the gentlemen of Mexico City."

"What happened to you? What made you become a nun? You're a beautiful woman."

Reaching down, she stroked her hand across her crippled leg. "The hand of God touched the horse I rode. He fell on me and crushed my leg. No gentleman desires to spend his life with a woman who skitters across the tile floor like a crab on the rocks at the edge of the ocean. Now I belong to God. He made me special. He made me His. You see, Señor Cobb, those of us who have endured some misfortune have been set apart from the rest. It is a gift, a special gift that very few can open. With it, we must make our way back into the sea of humankind, bearing the gift above our heads. To do so is to allow the world to know mercy, the mercy of the severe hand of God. To shrink back from this task is to allow our hearts to twist into a bitter and poisonous root, unfit to taste, unbearable to look upon."

Julian put down his fork and massaged the stub of his missing left arm. "I guess all I can remember of this is the hatred I feel for the Yankees that did it."

"But you are not a coward."

"No, I'm not."

"But you see, the coward abandons himself first of all. He recoils from the goodness he has been taught. He withdraws from hope. After that, all other acts of timidity and fear come to him in an easy manner."

"And you think I've done that?"

"I don't know what you've done, señor. All I know is what you are now. You remember very little, and perhaps that is good. You can begin once again." She paused. "But you must remember some things or you will die."

He picked up the tin cup and swished the remaining coffee around in a careful, circular motion. Holding it to his lips, he sipped it slowly, then put the cup down and pushed it back. "I suppose you're right, Sister—maybe it is good that I can't remember everything I've done. But I ain't got very long to be a new man with this clean slate you speak about."

"Then you must find a way to remember. This treasure of the emperor is not yours to keep. It belongs here in my country, not in some hole in the United States. It is soaked with the blood of the martyrs of the revolution."

The sound of the keys in the outer door brought both of their heads up. "That will be the priest and the men who will take you to the wall."

Julian smiled. "Guess they give a body a last meal without the time to digest it."

She reached out and took hold of his arm. "You must think, señor."

The old priest stood at the door with the guard. Several men in uniform hurried in and took their places beside them. The guard turned the key and barked, "It's time for you, Yankee."

Julian got to his feet and smiled at Sister Mary Perizza. "Can't say as I'll ever get used to being called *that*."

Moving out into the dark corridor, the men formed a line to the rear. Julian fell into his place behind the guard and the old priest. Bowing their heads slightly to clear the inner door, they moved along the dark, damp walls toward the morning light. The fresh, cool sunshine of dawn struck their faces, bathing them in a rosy hue.

The far wall of the compound was pockmarked by the evidence that Julian would not be the first to die standing beside it. The officer in charge of the small detail lifted his hand and motioned Julian into position.

Like a whipped dog being called by his cruel master, Julian ambled toward the adobe wall. He stopped suddenly and, lifting his head to the dawn sky over the Animas Mountains, watched the sun swim on the roof of the dark blue peaks. Straightening his shoulders and lifting himself with pride, he strode to the base of the high wall.

Captain Santiago, the officer in charge, drew his sword and followed Julian to his place. "Would you like a blindfold, señor?"

Julian shook his head.

The captain lifted his gaze to the balcony overhead. They watched the assembly of dignitaries take their places along the rail. Julian saw the general as he stood closest, his gold braids glinting in the sunlight. A woman in a full black gown took her place at the man's side. The four men who had escorted Julian from his cell were joined by eight others, making a full complement of twelve. They held their rifles at the ready.

Across the courtyard, a young girl who appeared to be about eight years old held a handful of freshly picked flowers. Her dark hair and shining eyes set off a clean white blouse and a black skirt decorated by a bright silver-studded conch belt. Santiago signaled to her, and she stepped forward, making quick strides to cover the distance of the yard. Standing in front of Julian, she held out the bundle of yellow daisies sprinkled with a spray of red Indian paintbrush flowers and curtsied. "For you, please."

Julian took the flowers and nodded his head. "Thank you." He held them to his face and breathed deeply. "They smell real nice."

Once again bowing, the girl retreated and made her way to the far side of the court, taking one last look at Julian before she ran inside.

"I guess this is it, then," Julian said.

The captain nodded. "Sí, señor. Unless you can tell us where to find what we seek, I am afraid so."

Julian shook his head. "I can't rightly say as I can remember my own momma's name, much less where some gold and jewels are buried that I ain't never seen."

"I am very sorry to hear that, Señor Cobb. Now you must die."

Julian looked at the firing squad. He motioned to the line of men with a lift of his chin. "Those fellers over yonder shoot straight?"

"They are very good."

"I saw a man executed once. Nobody really wanted to kill him, so all of them fired shots that were slightly off. Left him writhing on the ground like some stepped-on snake. The officer in charge had to finish him with his pistol. I wouldn't want that."

"Nor would I, señor."

Julian lifted his head to the sky. "You best get on with it, then. B'fore long them men are gonna be staring into that rising sun. I wouldn't want anything to draw their aim off."

The captain clicked his heels together, spun in an about-face, and marched to a position beside the line of riflemen. He held out his sword and looked up at the balcony.

Zac puffed on his pipe and rose to his feet to pull his carpetbag and saddle from the overhead rack. He liked to travel with his own saddle—it was already broken in and it fit him perfectly. Somehow that always made the going easier. The long blast of the whistle told him they would be in Santa Fe shortly, and he was anxious to meet up with Joe. The telegram in his shirt pocket contained nothing in the way of details, only that there was trouble with the family and that his presence was required. It made him anxious.

The brass lamps with their green shades swung sharply. He gripped the bag and saddle and pulled down the long, rawhide, beadwork bag that held the Sharps rifle. It might give him an edge if he needed to shoot from a distance, should that prove necessary. Tipping his hat to a lady, he made his way to the front of the car.

The big locomotive rattled to a halt, slamming cars into each other. Zac swung onto the wooden platform. Adobe walls were pockmarked and painted with the smoke of the coal-fired engines, which curled under the awnings when the wind was blowing from the south. Today the clear bright sky, as blue as a sapphire, hadn't a trace of a cloud overhead. The sun was low on the eastern horizon. It would be a hot day when it climbed overhead, but for now the coolness of the morning air was a refreshing change from the smell of sweaty passengers and strong cologne.

Zac's starched white shirt peeked out from his buckskin jacket and set off the soft brown corduroy trousers that made a comfortable traveling outfit. He'd long since abandoned the practice of traveling in his suit, unless the occasion called for it. On this trip he knew he'd have to travel light and wear only those clothes that could survive prickly scrub oak. The leather shotgun chaps in his bag would help plenty if he needed to go for a long desert ride.

He pulled his gray officer's hat low to avoid the beaming sun in the east. The gold braid on it tended to pique people's curiosity, sometimes in a way he didn't like. They would ask questions about a former Johnny Reb who'd obviously been a cavalry officer. He didn't much care to confront the obvious innuendos, but it was an ornament he couldn't part with, not just yet.

An old man sat with his back to the wall, his sombrero pulled low over his eyes. Several women waited patiently, surveying each man who stepped down from the cars. A lawman with his badge prominently displayed scrutinized the new arrivals, especially Zac. Any policeman worth his salt would brace himself for an incoming train. Trouble came from many directions, and questions along with it. A man alone, like Zac was, with no one to greet him, would arouse great curiosity. Just as the man turned in Zac's direction, a familiar voice rang out.

"Zachary Cobb. Over here."

The greeting stopped the lawman in his tracks, and from behind him, Zac could make out a familiar face. It was Joe. The lanky man strode past the crowd and held out his hand, grinning from ear to ear. His worn denim shirt was tucked into jeans, and a beaten hat was squashed down around an overgrown mop of brown hair.

Zac shunned the handshake and grabbed the man by the shoulders instead, pulling him into an embrace. "How the dickens are you, big brother, and how's that family of yours?" he asked.

"We're doing fine. Karen's in a family way, and we're making plans for the new Cobb come November."

Zac pushed him back and grinned, working hard to take in the sight of the man. "You're turning out to be quite the citizen."

"I guess I am at that. Marriage and decent work will do that to a man."

"I s'pose so."

"James is over at the De Vargas Hotel. He woulda been here, but he met up with a señorita who seems to be taking up all his attention."

Zac smiled and nodded. "Might have expected that. He's always been the romantic."

"He is, but I wouldn't say much about it if I was you. Since Emma died, and he's been looking after his daughter all by his lonesome, he makes noise like there will never be a replacement—but knowing him, his mind is working on the matter."

"Well, I won't say anything as long as he's entertaining a lady."

"More like a girl, but he's entertaining her all right. All he needs is two big eyes watching him and someone to laugh at the right times and he's good all day."

The two men walked side by side down the boardwalk, and Joe pulled a telegram from his shirt pocket. "I got your telegram. Wouldn't have come and left Karen if it hadn't have been you that sent it."

Zac stopped in his tracks. "I didn't send you a telegram. Fact is, I've got one here from you."

"From me?"

Zac pulled the worn message from his shirt pocket and handed it to Joe. "There it is. It's got your name at the bottom."

Joe read it. "Just like the one I got, only difference is it's got your name. James has one just the same, only with Julian's name fixed on it."

Zac quickly scanned the crowd, hoping to spot anyone who might have an interest in his arrival. Several men turned away quickly, but he didn't recognize them.

"I knew something was wrong when I came in and saw James, but I figured as how it might just have been some mistake," Joe said.

"Fact is, I wouldn't have come at all for anyone but you," Zac said. "I just got myself engaged."

"To Jenny?"

"Of course to Jenny. Who else would put up with me?"

"You're right about that."

"I suppose whoever it was that sent these things knew just what it would take to get us here."

"Why you reckon anybody'd do a thing like that?"

They started their walk once again. Zac was silent, lost in his thoughts.

"I suppose if we just bide our time for a spell, we'll find out soon enough," Joe said. "The three of us are gonna be hard to miss."

Zac silently nodded as they walked through the door of the hotel. The De Vargas was a new structure, adobe like much of the town and spread out over the length of a city block. The massive carved oak and iron chandeliers that dotted the ceiling were enough to attract anyone's instant attention. Indian rugs were scattered over a tile floor that was a baby blue mixed with the texture of brown artwork. Overstuffed chairs and settees dotted the huge great room, and a cave of an adobe fireplace set the place apart. Two shiny red leather loveseats flanked the fireplace. The skin of a giant bear spread out between them, its snarling but lifeless teeth glaring white in the dim morning light.

Seated on the far loveseat, a young woman with large black eyes and raven black hair seemed mesmerized by a man standing over her. The man, dressed in a fresh black suit, had his back to them, but Zac could tell at a glance that it must be James.

"That's James, I take it."

"That's James."

"I s'pose, then, we ought to go over and rescue his intended and very beautiful victim."

Joe grinned. "Let's do it. It'll serve him right."

Striding up behind the man, Zac cleared his throat.

Spinning around, James produced a broad smile. His cherubic, clean-shaven face would never have shown him to be thirty-five, not by a long shot. His creamy complexion clearly established the fact that he was a man unaccustomed to outdoor work. His brown eyes twinkled at Joe. "This is Zachary, I take it," he said.

"The one and only."

James smirked. "You have grown some since I went off to college. And you've shot up too. You must top six feet."

"A shade over six foot four, I reckon."

James shook his head slowly. "I left you a boy, and you've come back to me a Greek god."

Zac noticed the young woman eyeing him. He gave off a faint smile. "Aren't you going to introduce us to your friend?" he asked.

James stepped aside. "Where are my manners? Please allow me to present Miss Palmira Escobar. Palmira, you've met my ugly brother, and I regret to have to introduce you to the handsome and single sibling that I am forced at the moment to call a relative. This is our youngest brother, Zachary Taylor Cobb."

Zac bowed slightly. "Pleased to meet you, ma'am. I can understand why my older brother here would be reluctant to have you meet anyone who might see you again. I'm certain he'd like to have you all to himself."

"Precisely," James replied.

"Well, you needn't worry about Zac here," Joe chimed in. "He's just up and got himself engaged."

James laughed and began to pat Zac on the back. "That's wonderful news." Looking back at the young woman, he grinned and added, "You don't know how wonderful."

"I am pleased to meet you, señor," she spoke the words in a smooth, almost liquid voice that bore a hint of her Mexican upbringing, "even if your name does bear bitter memories for my country."

"I don't suppose there's anything I can do about that, Miss Escobar. It's a war my father fought—it wasn't mine."

Palmira looked up at James. "All of your brothers are quite handsome. I can believe it to be a family trait."

"Well, I couldn't say much for the eldest of the group," James said. "I was expecting to see him, given the fact that he sent for me."

"You've always been partial to him," Zac said. "Comes from all that coon hunting you two did with Daddy before the war."

James stroked his chin. "I suppose you are right there. I know he's run afoul of the law, and I guess I always saw it as my duty to lift his sights."

"From what I know of Julian," Zac said, "I'd say if he isn't here, then it's his doing that got us this far. Trouble seems to follow him, but I don't expect he'd like to see me, all the same."

"Yes, Joe here tells me you work in some aspect of the law."

"More of a private law," Zac replied. "I work for Wells Fargo."

The young woman wagged her fan, even though the air was quite cool. Her hands were small and delicate. She looked to be a woman quite capable of reaching into the neck of a small pickle jar and extracting a briny cucumber in one precise motion. "You do sound like a man of adventure," she said.

Zac watched her eyes dance. There was a flirtatious nature to them, dark and beautiful. Her high cheekbones and the hint of an oiled complexion showed that she took great care in preparing herself for the day. The cream-colored dress had a swooping neckline, and Zac was careful to keep his eyes riveted to hers.

"It's a job."

She continued waving the fan. "A modest man too. How becoming."

James wrapped one arm around Zac's shoulders. "As a boy, he had much to be modest about, except his love of books—a characteristic we both share. Miss Escobar here has an interesting proposition for the three of us, one which may allow me to see the country and, given our sudden quandary about why we were all asked here, one which both of you may find compelling as well."

CHAPTER 2

JULIAN STOOD AT ATTENTION as the firing squad took aim. The young girl who had given him the flowers watched sorrowfully from beside the red vines that crawled up the side of the church. The deep magenta colors of the blossoming vines glinted with the fresh light of the dawn. He'd seen men shot before and could well imagine the sight of his shirt when he fell to the ground after the order was given.

A woman hustled out from the mission, took the child aside, and pulled her back into the doors of the great church. Birds flitted toward the bell tower of the massive structure and a hummingbird seemed to pause before taking a drink from the blooming vines. It was a sight Julian wanted to keep in his mind—the birds, the flowers, and the child. Nothing could be better for a man to capture in his thoughts before dying.

The captain looked once again at the man in the shadows of the balcony. Julian couldn't make out the officer's face, but the ornate buttons and medals on his chest caught a glint of sunlight and winked at him from across the courtyard. The man cleared his throat. "You have something to say?" he growled.

Julian paused and thought the matter over. "I'd just like to thank that little girl for the flowers, that's all."

"You still insist that you remember nothing?"

"I'm makin' my memories right now—at least all I can recall."

"You still have a moment for the truth, señor. One word of truth from you can stop this."

"You just tell them men over yonder to shoot straight. I wouldn't want to wallow around here and have that captain have to use his pistol."

"Have it your own way, señor." With that the man in the shadows nodded toward the captain and, turning aside, walked into the upstairs room.

Julian stared at the squad of men. The captain held his sword high. "Listos," the officer shouted. The men's eyes were trained down the barrels of their rifles. "Apunten." He could see them tighten their grips. "Fuego!" At the shout of the final command, the men squeezed their triggers. Julian heard the rapid, staccato sound of the hammers falling on empty chambers, with the rippling sound of small plows drug over a plate of steel. The guns were empty.

The captain motioned suddenly at the men and several of them hurried toward where Julian stood, his knees weak and buckling. Two of the men grabbed his arms and marched him back toward the small door that led to the dungeon below the church. Minutes later, after dragging him through the smoke-stained corridor, they opened his cell door and threw him to the floor.

The next morning in Santa Fe found James rolling over in his hotel bed. Joe was shaving. "Where's Zac?" James asked.

"More'n likely he's already eatin' or leastwise havin' coffee down at the bar."

James swung his legs out of the bed and fumbled for his pants. "Guess that boy don't sleep well on the floor."

"I spect it's what he prefers. He seldom gets the city comfort you're used to. Most of the time I reckon he feels mighty thankful he ain't beddin' down on some scrub or cactus."

James scratched his head and, swinging his arms widely, yawned with a growl. "I suppose he always did fancy himself as being tough."

"Well, I figure he never did take to all that babyin' Momma gave out to him. Always made him feel like he had to prove himself to the rest of us Cobb men. If you ask me, he's done a fair job of it so far."

James got to his feet. "I reckon he has, at that. Personally, I don't think I'd do well at all leading his kind of life. I think I'll hang on to my classroom and home for a while yet."

Joe splashed water in his face and rubbed the remainder of the soap off with a towel. He grinned in the mirror at James. "From what I've seen of you, I think that would be wise. Words always seemed to be your strong suit."

James pulled his shirt on. "Back East where I come from, words are often more lethal than bullets." He raised himself to his full height and pointed his finger in the air. "The man who makes his way in the world with symbols and words will be the man who makes his mark on the world to come."

Joe turned around and laughed. "Then, I think you're well armed.

Let's hope you get a chance to use them words of yours while we're out here."

The cafe in the hotel was filled when Joe and James came down the massive, sweeping stairs. Bright paper draped over the chandeliers, the orange, red, and green colors filling the room with an air of excitement. It was plain to see there was a holiday underway in Santa Fe. In the cafe, vases filled with colorful flowers sat on each table and the maître d' wore a bright red sash, wrapped around his ample waist, giving a flair to his black cutaway suit and starched white shirt. He grinned at them, bowing slightly and showing off his carefully waxed mustache. "Buenos días, señores. I am at your service."

"Why all the hoopla?" Joe asked.

The man swung his hand in the air, as if to emphasize the decorations. "Tonight we have the burning of the Zozobra. It is a fiesta."

"What, may I ask, is that?" James inquired.

"All of the bad luck of the city is placed on the hated demon. The people dance and shout and we burn him. It is a good thing, señor, to have your bad luck burned away, so we celebrate with a fiesta."

"Sounds like a good thing to me," James added.

"Humph," Joe murmured. "Superstitious gibberish."

The man swung his head around. "A table may be hard to find, señores."

"We're looking for our brother," James offered.

"Ah, the gringo with his book and coffee."

"That would be him," Joe said.

They wound their way past the crowded tables to a spot in the corner where Zac sat with his back to the wall. He nursed a cup of coffee as he stared busily at a leather-bound volume. "What you reading there, little brother?" James asked.

Zac closed the book and dropped it into his pocket. "Tennyson seems to clear my head from time to time."

"A fine poet," James said, taking his seat.

The men's cups were filled with steaming coffee. They ordered eggs and tortillas. It wasn't long before they spotted two finely dressed women. One of them was the young Palmira; the other, an older woman, obviously her mother, followed close behind her. The woman had dark hair and a full but attractive face. Her eyes were dark with sparkles of light that seemed to radiate confidence. She gazed at them with a soft but firm determination.

James got to his feet and motioned them toward their table. "Ladies, why don't you join us?"

"We couldn't impose." Palmira smiled.

"No imposition here, is it?" He looked down at Zac and Joe, who seemed uncomfortable with the women's presence but rose to take new places. "You can take your breakfast with us and tell us about this need of yours."

Palmira stood and allowed Zac to seat her mother. "This is my mother, señores, Rosalyn Donna Matrice de Escobar." The men nodded. "Pleased to meet you, señora," Joe said.

The woman gave off a subtle smile, eyes dancing. "The pleasure is mine, señores. My daughter has told me much of you and your family. I've looked forward to meeting you."

After the women had taken their places, Palmira began to relate her story. "We are in need of an escort, gentlemen. My father is a planter and soldier in Mexico. Neither he nor his men can come this far north. They are all soldiers of Mexico, and this land now belongs to the United States. We hear the Apaches are between us and the border, and we are afraid. We can pay you, and we have several men with us as well."

"We're here on family business," Joe said, "but right now we're not quite sure what that is."

"I suspect a few days more may just tell us how free we are," James added. "After that, I'd love to see the countryside, especially in such pleasant company."

Palmira flashed her eyes at the quiet Zac. He sat taking it all in, sipping his coffee. "And what do you say, Señor Zac?"

"You plan on going through the Jornada del Muerto?" Zac asked.

"What's that?" James asked.

"The way of the dead," Joe answered.

Zac sipped his coffee. "It's a place filled with Apaches, snakes, scorpions, and dry water holes. It saves three days travel headin' south, but only a fool goes there if he doesn't have to. I've been through it once, chasin' a man, but I wouldn't hanker to make the trip again."

"You seem to have made it through," James offered.

"That was my job, this isn't."

Señora Rosalyn hunched forward and spoke in a low tone. "I am not supposed to make this known in Santa Fe, but my husband has some of his men waiting for us there in an abandoned army fort. He specifically chose that place because no one would look for our soldiers there. It is not a place gringos would go."

"So he would be there to meet us?" James asked.

"Sí, señor, and accompany us to our hacienda. We would be very grateful and entertain you in a most hospitable fashion. We just need your guns and the appearance of strength to take us to Fort Craig. It is no more than four days' ride."

"Is that right?" Joe asked Zac the question.

"Four days of agony and no water, watched every step of the way by the Mescalero Apache."

"I am prepared to pay you five hundred dollars," Rosalyn added.

"Why choose us for this favor?" Zac asked. "You'd find plenty of men round here willing to do that for the sum you offer."

Palmira smiled, batting her eyes at James. "I'm afraid it's my selfishness, señor. You see, I've grown quite fond of your company."

Rosalyn spoke up. "And we fear strangers. You men seem like such gentlemen, men of good family and breeding, not a usual thing for Santa Fe."

Joe tried to break the tension, saying, "I can't speak for my brothers here. We're here on what might be a wild-goose chase, but we need to wait it out for a few days, all the same. All of us are away from our homes and families. We're not exactly men on the drift, looking for work. I've got a wife with child in Texas, and James here has a little girl back East. People would miss us if we never came back."

"I can understand your concern about the danger, señor," Rosalyn said. "It is a hard journey and not one to be taken lightly."

James cleared his throat. "Madam, you see before you men who are not unaccustomed to hardship, men who see opportunity in danger. We have been in war and do not shy away from an opportunity to accommodate such ladies as yourselves."

After some small talk, the men left the ladies to finish their breakfast while they strolled outside into the plaza. Booths were being erected to sell all manner of refreshments to the expected fiesta crowd. Indians were scattered along the walkway, holding up jewelry to onlookers passing by. An old man, dressed in shabby clothing and limping as he leaned on a makeshift crutch, hobbled up to the three men. He held out a shaky hand. "Un peso, señor, por favor."

James dug into his pocket and extracting several small coins, dropped them into the man's gnarled and quivering hand.

"Gracias, señor," the man said, repeatedly bowing at the waist. "Muchas gracias."

They watched as he hobbled off, counting his newfound wealth. "You beat all," Zac said.

"Why? Because I gave a few coins to that old man?"

"No, because you've got us chasing off over this miserable desert just because you've taken a shine to that señorita in there."

"We made no decision. I just thought it was the chivalrous thing to do."

"The foolish thing to do. You best stick to that college teaching of yours and leave traipsing off over the desert to other people, folks with sense." Zac's eyes drifted across the plaza to where a man dressed in a black suit stood, watching them. He wore a white shirt and string tie and had a flat black hat pulled down over his blond hair. At Zac's sudden attention, the man looked away. Zac could see him take his hand off his waist, dropping his coat below where he had a gun tied down.

"I suppose the adventure attracts me," James added.

"The adventure nothing," Zac replied. "We know what attracts you." Zac nodded in the stranger's direction. "Either of you seen that man before?"

"Which man?" Joe asked.

"That one over there in the dark suit."

With the attention of all three brothers drawn toward him, the man quickly walked away.

"I may have seen him at the hotel," James said.

"I saw him when I first got to town," Joe said. "I thought he looked me over kinda careful like. Didn't care for it, either."

"Do you think he knows something about why we're here?" James asked. "Would he be the law?"

"Don't think so. I'd say, though, that he was plenty interested."

In the early evening, the sound of firecrackers ripped through the air. The hotel was almost deserted when the brothers finished their supper. After paying their bill, they strolled out into the plaza to watch the festivities. Children danced to the sound of a brass band, the lively music blasting along the walls of the shops and government buildings that surrounded the grassy park. A large throng of people milled about in the square, their eyes riveted to the central figure, a large white doll with black face and hollow eyes. Several men held the figure aloft on a pole.

"Fuerzas, fuerzas!" The crowd shouted at the men. "Fuerzas a Zozobra!"

Joe leaned against one of the pillars that held up the hotel balcony. "I reckon this is where the show starts," he said.

James glared at the people as they danced around the figure on the pole. The women's brightly colored dresses glittered in the semidarkness, and the loud music continued to be punctuated by the noise of the fireworks. "Quite a sight, I'd say."

Zac nudged Joe and motioned back toward the hotel. The man in the black suit was standing at the window, his eyes fastened on them. "I think we should pay our respects to that fella," Zac said.

"I think you're right," Joe said.

Joe took James's arm, pulling him along with them. As the three of them walked though the door of the hotel, the man turned and began to walk away.

"Hold on a moment," Zac said.

The man turned around, an impish and quizzical smile on his face. With his thin face, boyish smile, and blue eyes, he looked nothing like a lawman. His weren't the rugged features of a man accustomed to the desert of New Mexico, and he looked out of place. Had he not been dressed the way he was and had he not been wearing a tied-down revolver, he could easily have been mistaken for a women's sundries drummer.

"You seem to have taken quite an interest in us," Zac said.

The man slouched forward, looking almost apologetic. "I'm sorry," he said, wringing his hands and frowning with discomfort. "I have been wanting to talk to you, but I've just been waiting for the right time."

"Well, you're starting to be a bother," Zac said, "so I'd say this was the right time."

"I wouldn't want you to miss the burning of the Zozobra."

"We ain't here to see that," Joe added.

Sheepishly, the man looked around the room. "What I have to tell you is extremely confidential."

Zac looked out the window at the increasing pandemonium. "Everybody in town is out there in the plaza. I'd say this might be as private as you're gonna get."

"You might be right." He pointed toward a collection of chairs gathered around a red leather couch. "Perhaps we could sit over there."

The four men took their places where they could see one another. Outside the hotel, they could see the flames of the Zozobra, accompanied by the wild screams and shouts of the mob. The man nervously looked out the window. "I never cared for crowds."

"We're in agreement there," Joe said.

The man scooted forward in his chair, dropping his voice. "My name is Michael Delemarian. I work for the Secret Service."

"You have identification?" Zac asked.

"Yes, yes I do." He fumbled in his coat pocket and produced a leather case. Opening it up, he passed around the shiny badge.

"All right," Zac said. "Suppose you are who you say you are. What does that have to do with us?"

"We've gone to a great deal of trouble to get you all here."

James produced his telegram. "Did you send this?"

"Yes, we sent the wires. We had to attach different names to them. We knew you'd never come otherwise. Zac and Joe, we figured each of you would respond to the other."

"You know us?"

"We know all three of you very well." He looked in Zac's direction. "Of course, some people are easier to trace and know than others are."

"Why us?" Zac asked.

"It's your brother Julian."

Zac sat back and frowned.

"He is being held prisoner in Mexico, and we would like to see him freed."

"I thought he was dead. He's a wanted man in Arizona. If he's in prison anywhere," Zac said, "that's exactly where he belongs."

"Yes, we figured that's exactly the way you'd feel. However, it's extremely important to your government that he be freed."

"Then, why us?" Zac asked. "Why not just send your own men?"

"I'm afraid that freeing your brother and getting him to cooperate are two different matters, and the way he feels about the federal government doesn't help in the least."

"Those are sentiments he and I share," Zac added.

"That may be, Mr. Cobb, but at least you wouldn't steal from it."

"So you want us to bring him back so you can hang him?" Joe asked.

"Mercy no." Delemarian laughed. "Quite the opposite. If he cooperates, we plan to give him complete amnesty. I have the papers with me, signed by the President himself."

"And how do you expect him to cooperate?" James asked.

"We have reason to believe that your brother has knowledge of the whereabouts of a vast treasure. It belonged to Emperor Maximilian. The emperor attempted to smuggle it out of Mexico and through the United States, and had he accompanied it, he would not have faced the firing squad that killed him." He scooted closer. "It is imperative that this gold not fall into the wrong hands. We believe there are powers in Mexico that are attempting to force your brother to tell them of its whereabouts in order to finance a revolution."

"He wouldn't tell them anything," Zac said.

"Perhaps not, but we can't be sure of that."

"We have families to care for," Joe said. "What if we decide to just leave things be and let Julian stew in his own juices? The government's problems are of no concern to us."

"We do have a contingency plan for that eventuality."

"And what would that be?" James asked.

"My orders are to send operatives to Mexico to have your brother killed. We can't take chances that what he knows will bring down the government of Mexico and President Diaz."

"We can't allow that." James looked at his suddenly silent brothers. "Can we?"

Joe and Zac looked at each other, each refusing to say what was on his mind. To tell one's mind to a stranger was something neither had ever been accustomed to doing.

"We may be going to Mexico in any event," James went on. "There are two women here who want us to accompany them."

"You are referring to the Escobar women, I take it."

"Yes, you know them?"

"It is General Escobar who has your brother as his prisoner. Not everything we do can be kept totally secret. Somehow, General Escobar found out that you would be here. I think he hopes to use you as leverage."

CHAPTER 3

IT WAS CLOSE TO MIDMORNING when Julian heard the doors leading to the downstairs corridor open. He lay on the mat, watching a fly creep across the wilting paint on the wall. The fly had been joined by two others, one in flight and the other surveying the same side of the peeling green pigment. It amused him somewhat that these flies were in the same prison as he was. The difference was their mindset. They wanted to be here. They were not here to have someone get something from them. They were here to get what they could. Perhaps a man's state of being was in the mind, after all. To be a man content with wherever he was would be the ultimate revenge on any jailer.

There was something, though, about a man coming to terms with his death and then having it snatched away from him. The memory of the firing squad crawled through his head and left him sick to his stomach. The man on the balcony was obviously someone who delighted in twisting a man's emotions. The notion of a subtle killer in the shadows—someone who toyed with his prey before dispatching it, like a cat with a mouse—left him with the feel of icy fingers groping up his back.

The guard turned the key in the lock, and Julian looked over to watch the nun rake her foot over the stones in his direction. Taking a step with her left leg, she dragged the right one behind her. She was not a slight woman—too much inactivity had left her rather plump. Wrinkles around her eyes testified to her lost youth. She had broad shoulders, but there was a sense of femininity about her that the limp and the robe couldn't hide. Her smile beamed and radiated a confidence in who she was on this earth. Her hazel eyes reflected different colors, and a bronze hint of curly hair blossomed beneath her headwear.

Julian slowly moved his legs off the mat and struggled to his feet. The nun reached down to help him up. "Oh, señor, you are alive. I am so grateful to God."

"I'm alive for now, I reckon, at least until that man finds a new game he wants to play—with me as his toy."

"I think the general showed you mercy."

"That ain't mercy, Sister. That's torture."

"He may believe you now—believe that you are telling the truth when you say that you no longer remember."

Julian struggled to get into the wooden ladder-back chair. The red, weather-beaten wood was gnarled, and the straw matting that had once formed the seat was ragged and held together by wires. "Maybe he just figures me for being bullheaded and plans on some new way to break me down. He might not be too wrong at that." He swatted at a buzzing fly that came close to his head.

The nun reached into her cassock and pulled out a jug and silver goblet, placing them on the rough table. "I have some brandy for you, señor, something to make you warm inside. It is one of the few things the French left in my country that we appreciate."

Reaching out, he took the bottle and removed the cork. Slowly, he let the liquid chug out several jiggers into the silver goblet. Setting down the bottle, he replaced the cork and pulled the goblet across the table toward himself with both hands. Lowering his head and holding it to his lips, he took a sip. His eyes closed with the feel of the amber brandy seeping down his throat. It burned. He felt strangely warmed as the liquid moved deeper into his body.

She reached out and placed her hands around his as he held on to the cup. "Tell me about you as a boy, anything you remember."

Julian's head swam. "I recollect pecan trees, me climbing up them and standing on the branches. My ma and pa would stand down below, and I would jump on the branches to knock them nuts off. When they hit the ground, it would happen all at once, all them things fallin' when I jumped up and down. I'd hang on to some branches overhead and while I jumped and stomped, I'd shake them things like a man fightin' to latch on to a runaway horse. I can still recall the sound they made when them nuts hit the ground, kinda like a thunderstorm overhead, right over you but with the lightning a ways off." He leaned down and, with her hands still on his, took another swallow.

"This is good. You remember this well. Maybe the rest will soon come back to you."

"I hope so. Things are still in a fog for me. I . . . I know I was in the war. I can recall a mite of the field where I lay with this arm and eye gone. I remember the wagon."

"The wagon? What wagon?"

"The wagon they put me on. Most of the men were dead. Some hollered. Some screamed out with each jolt of the wagon on the road."

"But you did not."

"No. I didn't want them Yankees to have the satisfaction."

"There, you see, there are some things that you do remember."

"Not much, I'm afraid, just some of the hard stuff in a body's life—the pain, the loneliness, and some of the best parts of being a boy."

"Well, this is something, señor. Soon I think that you will remember the rest."

"Somehow, Sister, I think there's lots that I don't care to recall."

"There is much about each of our lives that we would like to rub out. At times I think of the beauty of a blank page. It lies before us all white and clean and beckons us to write anew. We long to hold the pen in our hand and make new meaning, new words that will tell us how clean our souls are, something that would make us soar like the eagle and never come down to the ground again. But of course, that is not possible. Only God himself can give us this clean page. It is not a matter of the mind. It is a thing of the cross."

Julian lifted his eyes to hers. He knew that he had known many women. Right then, however, he couldn't think of a single one. For all he knew, he was married with children waiting for him somewhere. But right now, all he saw was this not-so-young nun. There was a tenderness to her that appealed to him, a soft manner of speaking that revealed an even more tender heart. He couldn't remember much of what he thought about religion, but the woman's warmth made him nervous. "You ever thought about turning a new page?" he asked.

She bowed her head slightly. "Of course, señor, many times." Looking back up into his eyes, she parted her lips in a soft smile. "But I have too much writing on this page of mine. As a girl, I saw the world of the hacienda with money. Now I see the peon and the hard labor of the poor. I see their suffering. I care for the sick and those without a friend."

"But what about you? Can't you have a life?"

"This is my life."

"Sounds to me like it's other folks' life, not yours."

"I have made them my life."

Julian reached his hand up to her face, gently stroking her cheek with the back of his hand. "I believe you to be a beautiful woman, inside and out."

She pulled his hand away, placing it back on the goblet. "You mustn't say such things. It would be a sin even for me to think it."

"You must have thought about it."

"We have no mirrors here. Such things are vanity."

Dropping his hand, she scooted back in her chair, trying to put some distance between them. "I cannot allow myself to think such thoughts. Silly girls think only about how they look in a man's eyes, but I belong to God." She tapped her chest. "It is only what He sees in here that means anything."

"I'm sorry. I suppose you're the one fine thing that my recent memory can find any space for. You have a way about you that I haven't known before. Here I sit in this jail—and only half a man to speak of. But when I see you I feel whole again."

"I am afraid, Señor Cobb, that you may have mistaken any personal feelings of mine for my duty to my people and my country."

He could see her shift nervously in her chair. She bit her lower lip. "I am here to help guide your memory and to see to any needs you may have. My ministry is to the friendless, and just at this moment, you are among the most friendless."

Julian held the goblet to his mouth and once again took a swallow. "I do count you as a friend, Sister, and I'd like to be your friend too. Fact is, I'm mighty grateful for that. Ain't been much in the way of a kind word here for me, 'ceptin' you. I don't know where or even exactly who I am. All I got to go by is the name that the guards keep calling me and what they say I've done, but I don't rightly have no memory of either of it."

"You will, señor. Of that I am confident. I have heard of your injury before. That narrow miss to your head has caused you to forget, but your thoughts will return in time. They will be back—and not just the memories of you as a child or your injuries, but all of them. I have told the general this, and I'm sure he will be patient."

Julian's face hardened. "I have seen my death. I saw it this morning. When a man visits his own grave and walks away, he dies to himself. If my memory ever did come back and I thought it was in the best betterment of anybody not to say what I know, I'd never tell. He could shoot me or put me on some torture rack, but I'd never give out a grunt."

"This is most unfortunate, señor. The general wants only what is best for Mexico. That mind of yours holds the key to the future, as he sees it. He will never let you leave knowing what you know."

"Then, you and I are gonna see lots of each other, Sister."

The morning after the burning of the Zozobra, the plaza was still crowded with people. This would be the day of the blessing at St. Francis Cathedral. When Joe's eyes popped open, he found Zac sitting on the balcony of the room, smoking his pipe. Joe rolled off the cot and pulled on his pants. "You been up for a while?"

"A couple of hours. Already had my breakfast."

Joe scratched his head and rubbed the sleep from his eyes. "I must really be slipping. At the ranch I'm up before the cows."

"The rest will do you good. Myself, I just wouldn't be able to sleep past the rise of the sun out there."

Joe took his seat next to Zac and propped his bare feet on the iron railing. "What you reckon to do about Julian?"

"I never did cotton to being used, by the government or anybody else. And as far as that brother of ours is concerned, the last time I saw him I was on his trail for robbery and murder. That ain't changed in the least."

"He is our brother."

"Maybe so, but he's a murderer, all the same. There's orphans and widows out there on account of his hatred."

"I count it, then, that you're not goin'?"

"You count right. We all go our own way, though. You and James are free to do just what you like." Zac pulled the pipe from his mouth and pointed at Joe with the stem. "If you do go, you'd do best to just go along with the women. They and that general of theirs would get you there. You might not make it on your own. Once you do get there, you'd best find a way to get Julian out. Don't let that man use you. You use him."

When the brothers left the balcony to roust James, they saw the corner of a note shoved under their door. Zac pulled it out and read it. *Cobb, meet me at the depot at noon. I have sent for help and want you to meet the man.* It was signed by Michael Delemarian.

An hour or so later, when all three brothers were ready, they went down the stairs. There in the lobby, the Escobar women sat talking. Beside them stood a tall Mexican in a large black sombrero. His drawn face was marked with a scar that meandered down his cheek and ended at the tip of his chin. He wore brown trousers and a vest with a six-gun sitting lazily on his hip. Large bushy eyebrows sat over two piercing black eyes. The Cobb men were obviously the topic of conversation because when Rosalyn saw them on the stairs, she put her hand to Palmira's arm. They looked up and smiled.

"Good morning, ladies." James swept his hat off his head and bowed. "I trust you both slept well in spite of the revelry in the streets."

"I'm afraid our concern for this trip made our rest very difficult," Rosalyn replied.

"Then you'll have to find yourself some time for a nap so you can go refreshed." James gave out a broad grin. "My brother Joe and I will be most happy to accompany you."

"And what of Señor Zac?"

"I guess he's a moonstruck calf," James said. "That woman of his has him wanting to get back home."

Rosalyn bit her lower lip. "I see. Well, Mr. Cobb's reputation will make him missed. We had hoped—"

Zac interrupted her. "Joe here's better with a six-gun than I'll ever be, and he's got most of the savvy in the family."

"I'm sure we will do just fine," Palmira said. "Won't we, Mother?"

"Yes, I suppose we will. Please let me introduce you to one of our stockmen. This is Gaucho. He and three others accompanied us from Mexico."

"Well," Zac said, "if you two ladies wear pants and keep your hair under your hats, the sight of the eight of you ought to keep the Mescalero at a respectable distance."

"Given where we'd be goin'," Joe added, "we'd be best advised to do most of our ridin' at night. Saves on the water and horses and makes for a less temptin' target."

"That sounds like a good idea," Rosalyn agreed. "Don't you think so, Gaucho?"

The man silently nodded.

"I think we'll do very nicely with this brother of yours." Palmira laced her arm into James's. "Should we start tonight?" she asked.

"No," Joe answered. "We still have to get James here an outfit. He's armed only with poetry. We still have a mite of personal business to attend to and wires to send home. Nothing much will be open with this fiesta and all. Zac here leaves on the train tomorrow afternoon, and we'll want to say our good-byes."

"That will be fine," Rosalyn said. "My husband's men will wait at Fort Craig for as long as it takes for us to get there."

"Zac and I have something to attend to," Joe said. "James, can you wait here and keep the ladies company till we get back this afternoon? We'll join you all for a late lunch and palaver a mite about the trip."

"There's nothing I'd like better," James said. "Entertaining beautiful women has always had a strong appeal to me."

"Truer words were never spoke," Zac added.

"We won't be gone for long," Joe said. "Zac here's gonna show me a few stores and we may get into one if it's open and see about some personal supplies."

"Don't buy any weapons for me," James said. "I think I'd prefer to pick them out myself."

"Rest easy, big brother," Zac said. "A man has to have a feel for his own hardware. You'll know what you want by the heft of it."

With that, the two brothers said their good-byes and headed out the door. "Let's take a couple of sightseeing turns around the plaza first," Zac said. "I'd like to make sure we're not being followed before we go to join that federal man."

"Sounds like a good idea."

The two of them slowly strolled through the crowds of the plaza. They stopped frequently at the stalls that dotted the street, inspecting the wares and handmade jewelry that were laid out for gawking. It was some time later when Zac sprang open his watch. The locket Jenny had given him still dangled from the chain. The sight of it made him miss her all the more. "Guess we'd better make for the depot," he said. "We'll take the side street."

About twenty minutes later, they strode onto the wooden platform of the depot. The noon eastbound train had already come and gone, and standing at the edge of the platform was the lanky Delemarian. Beside him stood an Indian, dressed in trousers and a white shirt. Rawhide-laced moccasins came up above his calves. His long, jet black hair was tied by a blue bandana. Zac recognized him and his bowed legs even at a distance.

As the two of them approached the standing men, Delemarian gave off a subtle smile. "Nice to see you," he said. He looked at Zac. "I thought you'd be coming along, though."

"This party's Joe's," Zac said. "I'll be on the afternoon train tomorrow for home."

"I'm sorry to hear that," Delemarian said. "As you can see, we've gone to a lot of trouble for you."

"I can see." He extended his hand to the Indian. "Didn't think I'd be seeing you again, Chupta. This here's my brother Joe."

The man shook Zac's hand with a powerful grip. He nodded at Joe.

"Chupta here's a White Mountain Apache," Zac said. "He knows the desert, and more important, he knows that brother of ours pretty well. Tracked him with me in Arizona."

"Pleased to meet you," Joe said.

"I was counting on you to be on this expedition," Delemarian said.

"Has no appeal to me. I do this often enough when I have to. Never do it when I don't have to."

"I just figured this being your brother and all, you'd want to go."

"You figured wrong. Fact is, that's reason enough not to go. I wouldn't want to see a cold-blooded killer freed up, especially Julian. The man's poison. I also don't hanker at being used by that badge of yours. A man ought to do his own killin', not hire or force folks to do it for him."

"You don't share these sentiments?" He questioned Joe.

"Plain truth of it is, I do. I suppose I ain't quite as jaded as this little brother of mine, though. I ain't seen Julian in many a year. We spent time together in a Yankee prison during the war, so I reckon I got myself a little bit more of an attachment to him than Zac here does. I also think he'd be more likely to go along with me. There doesn't seem to be much love lost between the two of them."

"He's got that right," Zac said.

"Perhaps you're right, then. We brought this Indian—"

"Chupta," Zac interjected. Zac always hated the notion of talking about a man as if he were not a person. "The man has a name."

"Chupta." Delemarian replied. "We brought Chupta into this with the understanding he'd be going with you."

Zac motioned to Chupta to step aside so they could talk alone. The men turned and walked to the end of the wooden platform. "Look," Zac said, "I know you work for the army. I also know this government man is paying you and telling you about how easy this is going to be, but frankly I wouldn't trust the man with a dead horse. Far as he's concerned, the folks he involves in this government scheme of his are nothing more than pawns on a white man's gameboard. You living or dying won't bring one tear to his eye."

Chupta watched Zac as he spoke. Chupta was the type of man who often said more with no words than many men did in a lifetime of talking.

"Nobody will think less of you if you just go back to your woman and those children of yours."

"What you want Chupta to do?"

"I ain't sure I want to say."

"You tell me go home. This what you want?"

Zac looked back at Joe and Delemarian. "My brother there is a good man. He's got himself some common sense, and that's rare for a man. He'll respect you and follow your advice. He's good with a gun and handles horses well. He's a fair tracker in his own rights—not like you, but good for a white man."

"What you want me to do?"

"If I was you, I'd turn around and go home. This ain't your fight."

"This what you want?"

Zac looked back at Joe and then turned and looked Chupta in the eye. "No. There ain't a better man on the desert than you, and no one has more experience at getting where he needs to go. I'd feel a right smart better with you alongside Joe and James, that other brother of mine. With you along, they might just make it back in one piece."

"I go with them."

Zac looked at him, a look of respect. He put his hand on his shoulder. "You have my thanks."

CHAPTER 4

+ + + + + + +

THE GENERAL SAT BACK in his soft leather chair behind a massive mahogany desk. He was nursing a thick black cigar. A lazy blue haze of smoke swirled over his desk and meandered toward the large open door that led to the balcony. On the walls, several paintings depicted scenes from Mexico. Racks from longhorn cattle adorned the doorways, and Zapotec rugs were spread out over the black tile. Beside him, a row of portraits seemed to cast dead eyes over his shoulder. Each of them bore a family likeness, their dour countenances glaring down at him. He studied each paper in his hand, one by one, picking them up and placing them in a stack as he turned them over.

At the light knock on his door, he scarcely took his eyes off his work. "Enter," he shouted.

The carved door swung open softly, and the general lifted his eyes to watch Sister Mary Perizza rake her foot through the doorway, closing it behind her. "Am I interrupting you, General?"

He got to his feet, motioning her toward a spotted cowhide chair. "No indeed, Sister. I want to hear your news. How did our prisoner react to his death this morning?"

"It was most convincing, General."

"Bueno, I am glad to hear that." He paced the room as the nun took her seat, watching him carefully. He wrung his hands slightly. "If we had heard what was in the man's mind, the rifles would have been loaded."

General Escobar was a large man, though not all that tall. His chest was barrel sized with a girth to match. The red sash around his belt was visible through his open, metal-speckled jacket. A blazing white shirt contained several scorched pinholes from errant cigar droppings. His jet black hair was slicked straight back; streaks of baldness that were beginning to show with his age gleamed through the black hair. His protruding mustache drooped down the sides of his mouth, giving him a perpetual frown. "This is a man who must be reminded of his fate. Es mal intencionado. He is evil-minded."

"Right now, my general, this man has very little mind at all. He remembers nothing of his evil deeds. Whatever evil lived in his mind before has been changed to nothingness. It is almost as if the man has become a boy in a man's clothing."

"He sold himself to the emperor. He must remember that."

"I am afraid not. If he did, I would know it. He thinks back and can recall certain things from his childhood along with how he received injuries in his American Civil War. Apart from that, he remembers nothing. Had we not told him his name, he could not respond when called."

He pounded a fist into his open hand. "Perhaps the end of a whip will jar his thinking."

"At this time you could beat him until he dies of the lash, and he would be of no help to you, whatsoever."

Striding back to his desk, the general picked up the papers and waved them at the nun. "Do you see this? This is a list of the equipment that I must have to become the president of Mexico. Now it is just a dream, a dream gone like a vapor in the night air. This American can make this dream become real. Locked in his mind is the means to power, power that can be used for good."

Dropping the papers back to his desk, he slammed his fist down. "I must have this gold. Mexico must have it. It belongs to us, not in some hole in the land that used to belong to us."

Sister Mary had seen him this way before. She didn't flinch. A calm voice had always had a soothing effect on the man. "You need not worry, my general. I have heard of this injury to the brain before. He will remember, and when he does, he will tell what he knows to someone whom he trusts."

"And does he trust you?"

Mary nodded. "Yes, he trusts me completely. I am his only friend. Just now I believe he was going to ask me to join him. I am a nun, but I am sure he doesn't see me that way. The man is not religious. He sees me only as a woman who is his friend."

Escobar crossed his arms and sat on the corner of his desk. "And how do you see him?"

"I serve the friendless, and this man is truly that. I also am loyal to the people of Mexico. You know that. You have known me since I was a girl."

Escobar moved to the chair in front of her and sat down. He took her hand, holding it and watching her knuckles turn pale. "Yes, Mary, I have known you for so very long. There was a time . . ."

She dropped his hand. "You have said enough. That is all behind me now. I left my old life and the ease of the hacienda. I have a place here now, a place where I can be crippled and still serve people."

He blinked at her, unable to understand why she was reluctant to acknowledge her past. "You have changed much."

"Yes I have. In the past I thought only of my own pleasure and girlish notions of a soft and pretty life. I was silly."

Escobar sank back into his chair. "You do amaze me. I have seen you laugh and play and dance. I have held you in my arms as a young man, even though you were little more than a child. Now I watch you pray at the altar. I see you live this hard life. I have heard such soft words from your lips, and then at times I hear only your thoughts about the revolution. There are many men who are zealous for blood and for the bodies of our enemies to be trampled under the hooves of our horses, but I have seen none who can match the zeal I see in your eyes."

"I am committed to justice. Whatever else I am, I am a soldier."

"That you are. I would feel perfectly safe with you in command of the army. No matter what you may say about love and mercy, I believe you would show none when confronted by the guns of our enemies."

"It is a sin, but I hate the puppets in Mexico City, and I hate the gringos who hold their strings."

Escobar got to his feet. His tight, polished, knee-high boots clicked over the surface of the tile. Coming to a halt at the open window, he looked toward the mountains. He pivoted on both heels, facing her from across the room. "I suppose we all choose our forms of sin. Mine may be passion"—he pointed his finger at her—"but yours is passion too."

"Yes, Roberto, but yours is a passion of the flesh and mine is of the spirit."

"That may be." He took several steps in her direction. "But we are both slaves to our passion. We do not control it. It controls us."

He held his hands out in front of him, crossing his wrists as if bound by rope. "Like the most terrible criminal in the darkest prison, we are bound. There is no escape for either of us."

"See to it, Roberto, that you do not allow your passions to keep you from serving Mexico."

He dropped his hands to his sides. "What is good for me is good for Mexico as well."

"That may be true, now, though I truly wonder what would happen if a time came when what was best for Roberto and what was best for Mexico were two different things."

He took her words to heart. They stung, and she could see it. Turning around, he once again faced the window, drinking in the sight of the desert plains with long, slow swallows. He turned slightly, looking at her over his shoulder but refusing to face her. "That time is not now. When I am president, I will serve the people."

"And I will serve God and the people."

Marching back to his desk, he took his seat. Lifting his chin, he did his best to look official, forgetting all claims to a relationship with the nun. "Then you must serve the people by getting this gringo to tell you where this stolen gold is buried."

She nodded. "I will do my best. It is a delicate matter, however. The velvet glove will bring more fruit than the iron fist. What of your other plan? Have you heard from your wife? Were the reports about the gringo's brothers right?"

Shifting through the suddenly strewn papers, he produced a yellow telegram. "I received a wire this morning. The reports were correct. The gringos believe they are working for the American government and are coming to the hacienda with Rosalyn and Palmira."

"Good, this is good. And what of the Americans?"

"The Americans plan to kill our prisoner so that he won't talk." He smiled. "I am more merciful. I want him to lead us to the gold, then we will kill him."

The day after the fiesta, Santa Fe was a sleepy town. Chickens and dogs picked through food that had been dropped in the plaza. The sun rose lazily in the sky, warming the bricks on the street. The three Cobb brothers made their way to the general store behind the plaza. Zac had gone out earlier by himself. Joe figured the man was getting restless, anxious to get back home. He'd been watching Zac since he arrived in Santa Fe. Zac had always been private with his thoughts, even as a boy. He'd tell you something only after the thoughts had been polished. James, on the other hand, thought best when he was talking. It was as if by hearing the words come out into the open, he could perfect his ideas with the next sentence or the next or the next.

They strode up the boardwalk toward the store and, opening the glass-paneled door, stepped inside. Tables were topped with blankets and clothing, and the walls were strung with traps, furs, and beaded ornaments. Barrels of flour and dried fruit were stacked and the smell of the peppers hanging on the walls jelled in the room with the scent of the fresh flour and the aroma of gunpowder.

A bald, portly man leaned over the counter, his meaty fists mashing down a stack of Indian blankets in front of him. "Can I help you gents?"

Zac pointed to the rifles behind the man. "We need to outfit this brother of mine. Can we take a look at one of those new model Winchesters?"

"I don't get as much practice with these things as you do," James said, handling the Winchester. "But I've always been a pretty fair shot."

"Coming from where we come from, most boys grow up cuttin' their teeth on a squirrel rifle. I don't spect even that classroom back East can drive you far from that."

James hefted the Winchester and held it to his shoulder. He squinted down the barrel. Looking over to the rack, he put the rifle down and pointed. "What about that rifle with the tapered barrel?"

The shopkeeper swung his head around. "That Remington magazine bolt action?"

"Yes, let me see that one."

He held up the long, military-style rifle, eyeing down the cold blue metal barrel. "This has a nice feel to it. Does it shoot straight?"

"Straighter'n an arrow. Some folks find it hard, fumbling with the bolt. Ain't used to it, I reckon. But people swear by its aim."

"Good, I'll take this and three hundred rounds with it."

"You always seem to go your own way," Zac said.

"Just like you, little brother."

The shopkeeper began to rub the rifle with an oiled cloth. The man mumbled, "It's a mite bulky to heft around, some folks would say."

James watched him. "That's precisely what I was thinking. I'd like you to cut it down for me."

"Cut it down?"

James took the rifle from the man and held his fingers up to the spot. "Right about here, take off twenty-four to twenty-six inches, I'd say."

The man scratched his head. "Ain't never done that afore."

"Good, then that puts us on an equal field. Make me a good sight on it too."

"Might take me an hour or better to get 'round to it, and I couldn't hone that stock down none."

"That will be fine."

Zac shook his head. "You do have your own brand of thinking. Now just what do you suppose you'd feel comfortable using in the way of a handgun?"

James looked at the Shopkeeper Special Zac carried under his arm and the Peacemaker slung on his side. "I can see you favor the Colt."

Zac nodded. "Yes, I do."

"Personally, I don't think of myself as much of a gunman. I see these things as a means of last resort, desperation in search of a solution."

"That they are."

James pointed into the glass case at a shiny, nickel-plated revolver. "Why don't you let me have a look at that one."

The man shrugged his shoulders. "That's one of them new Smith and Wesson D. A. revolvers. They carry them new .38s. Don't have much kick or much in the way of knockdown either."

"Fine." James grinned. "Then I shall be able to fire in rapid succession. I'm not the best shot with these, and with several rounds fired quickly in the general direction I'm aiming at, I just might hit something."

"You might at that," the man said, slipping the revolver out from its showcase.

Joe listened to his brothers at the gun counter and smiled. There was something about their talk that reminded him of how they both were as children—James with his own mind, and Zac always trying to show he had done his homework on whatever was being discussed. He had found two serviceable pairs of sailcloth Levi's that appeared to be James's size, along with a pair of boots. He held them up. "You might want to try these on when you finish with your toys over yonder."

James held the revolver in his hand. It was light to the feel and snug in his palm. "This is good. I'll take it and three hundred rounds of the ammunition. I'd like a holster too, something that rides high on my hip."

"You may be armed," Zac said, "but I wouldn't call you dangerous."

James bounced the revolver in his hand. "Oh, I don't know about that. A man with brains and determination is plenty dangerous." He sighted down the short barrel of the pistol. "I don't think any man would be seeking to place himself in the way of this thing."

Zac chuckled. "You just keep looking like the innocent that you are and you'll see soon enough. Those shiny guns along with the new pants and boots you're getting will mark you for sure." He pointed to a jar. "Maybe you'd like some of that striped candy to go along with them."

"I just might at that." He pointed the peppermint sticks out to the shopkeeper. "I'll take a bag of those and some of that fudge for two lady friends of mine."

The shopkeeper filled two bags with the candies.

Less than an hour later, the three men emerged from the store. Canteens slung around them and arms full of supplies, they waddled their way back toward the hotel. "You didn't buy much, Zac," James observed.

"You forget, I'm not in your party."

"Oh, that's right, you're going home. Why the peaches and the canteen, then? And why all that extra ammunition?"

Zac cast a glance at Joe. "I figure I might need extra water for the train ride, and the dried peaches seemed too good to pass up." He didn't bother to rationalize the extra two hundred rounds of ammunition. Joe noticed it but said nothing.

Two hours later they stood on the platform beside the westbound train. Rosalyn and Palmira had offered to accompany them, and Zac had agreed, hoping it would satisfy their curiosity to see him get on the train.

Chupta was there to greet them. Instead of his suit, Zac had dressed in his khaki jeans, rough-cut boots, and buckskin jacket. His white, collarless shirt was clean but wrinkled.

Zac watched as a dun horse was loaded onto the stockcar. Zac had always been a good judge of horseflesh and this was a fine animal, one that would attract any man's attention. The animal was a big one, sixteen hands high and broad at the chest. He looked to have a lot of bottom to him, able to go all day on short water and feed.

"You say this Indian fella will work for us as a guide?" James asked.

Zac took his eyes off the horse and raised his voice so they could all hear. "Yes, and the best one you'll ever find, too."

James pushed back his hat, looking Chupta over at a distance. "He is small, isn't he?"

"Don't let his stature fool you. Dynamite comes in little bundles. That man can lick his weight in wildcats. He's built low to the ground and knows every inch of it too."

"My men know the way," Rosalyn interjected. "This Apache may not be welcome among Gaucho and my men. The Apache is a traditional enemy of my people."

"Chupta is White Mountain Apache," Zac said. "It was just fortunate luck that we ran into him here in Santa Fe."

"I believe a man makes his own luck," Rosalyn responded.

Zac braced at the woman's response. "Your men may know the way, but Chupta here knows the Mescalero. Before you get too far, you'll be thanking whatever luck you have that he's volunteered to go along for the ride."

"The Apache do not frighten us."

"They should," Zac said, "especially the Mescalero. You're riding through their nation, and they'll be watching you all the while, night or day. They can sit for hours on end just watching and waiting for a wrong move. A white man, he gets restless, wants to move, and the first thing you know he does—and he dies." Zac nodded in Chupta's direction. "You'd be best advised to follow that man's every word. Out there I wouldn't spit lest he told me to."

"Chupta goes or I stay," Joe interjected.

Palmira took James's arm. "Then I think he should go," she said. "He will provide us with another gun and perhaps one that shoots straight." She looked up at James, blinking her eyes and smiling.

"Now, here here." James grinned. "You shouldn't reach any premature conclusions about my ability with firearms. I'll do quite well with this new Remington of mine, and if anyone gets close enough"—he patted the stubby holster at his side—"they will find a hail of lead heading their direction. Swift and sure is the destruction of the wicked."

She tugged on his arm and laughed. "I'm sure you will be wonderful."

He placed his hand on hers, patting it softly. "I am always wonderful, my dear. It comes from a lifetime of consecrated practice."

"Very well, then," Rosalyn said. "The Apache can go with us."

Chupta was standing at a distance that may have indicated he was out of polite earshot, but Zac could tell he had heard every word spoken.

"My men will find this a difficult thing, however," Rosalyn added. "Many of them have had family killed by the Apache."

"No more than we've lost to the Mexicans," Joe pointed out. "Our father lost a leg in Mexico with Zachary Taylor, and we had an uncle die at the Alamo. Time for hating's long since past. Best thing for a body to do is put old wounds aside and get on with the business of living. We've got some in our family that ain't done that yet, and they've suffered for it." Zac and Joe exchanged looks. They both knew Joe was talking about Julian. "A man's wounded spirit will never heal as long as he nurtures it with the notion of satisfaction. For men to get on past their hurts, they must practice a purposeful forgetting."

Zac swung his saddle up the steps that led to the railcar. He set his bag on top of it but chose to hang on to the buckskin rifle bag. "Well, I guess this is it," he said. Reaching out, he took James's hand. "You take care, teacher man. Keep yer head low. You're not exactly heading into that college classroom of yours."

"No, but I'm quite certain I will learn."

"I'm sure you will."

Joe gave Zac a hug, slapping his shoulders as he backed away. "You keep yourself in touch with us. We wouldn't want to miss that upcoming wedding."

"You'll find out in plenty of time, and we want to hear about the baby," Zac said. He nodded to Chupta as he spoke to both Joe and James. "You listen real careful to that man over yonder. He'll save your hide. Sometimes you have to watch his eyes and drag the words out of him, but you do it, all the same."

"We will do that, little brother," James said. "I may have my own mind, but one thing an education has taught me is to listen to my teachers."

"See that you do just that." Zac swung aboard the train. He nodded at the women and watched the group from the doorway as the train got up steam and pulled out of the station. It was no more than ten miles down the line, with Santa Fe safely out of sight, when Zac reached up and pulled the emergency cord.

CHAPTER 5

+ + + + + + +

THE TRAIN GROUND TO A STOP, pitching passengers back into their seats. Zac braced himself at the door. He looked up to see the conductor scrambling past passengers on his way toward the back of the crowded car. The man's dark blue suit still looked fresh, and his cap was pulled low over a flushed face. "You can't be pulling on that thing. What seems to be the problem?" he asked.

"No problem." Zac threw the saddle off and onto the ground. "I'm just getting off."

"You just got on."

"I know—and this is where I get off." Zac pulled a bridle from his bag. "I'm getting off, and so is my horse."

"We can't allow that. We have a schedule to keep."

Reaching into his pocket, Zac produced the small case that contained his Wells Fargo Special Agent badge. He flipped it open. "I'm afraid you don't have much choice."

The conductor bit his lower lip. "All right." The words came out in a guttural growl. He took out his watch and, springing open the lid, took a look at the time. "You're putting us behind, though. You better make it quick."

Zac jumped off the coupling and strode toward the stockcar. Grabbing on to the latch, he cranked it open and slid the heavy door aside. He climbed up and picked his way through the animals tethered to the sides of the car. Finding the dun, he slipped on the bridle and untied the halter rope. He scrambled to the ground and pulled on the bridle, forcing the big horse to jump off. Swinging the animal aside, he waved at the conductor.

He had bought the horse the day before, when he managed to get a little walk alone. He had liked the looks of the animal at first glance, and the man had agreed to load him on that day's train along with a small sack of oats. The oats would be good to have, going over the ground they would travel. Grazing might be slack, and whether he ate or not, the dun would need to keep moving.

Zac threw the blanket onto the horse's back and slapped on the saddle. Cinching it up, he could feel the big dun take a deep breath. Many horses did that to ease the pull on the cinch. The problem was that once a man was aboard, that same horse would just as easily exhale, allowing the saddle to slide to the side. A man might find himself staring up at the horse from between his legs, a mighty dangerous place to wind up.

Zac forced his knee into the dun's ribs and cinched the saddle up tight. Watching the animal exhale, he drew up sharply and then backed off a mite. *That ought to do it.* He watched the train pull away, many of the passengers now with their faces at the windows as it passed, working hard to see the man who had caused all the commotion.

Zac slid the Sharps from its case and stuffed it into the saddle boot. He tied his bedroll to the rear of the saddle and stuffed his ammunition and food into the saddlebags. Pulling out a spare shirt, a couple pairs of socks, and sundries, he crammed them in as well. He heaved the carpetbag over the edge of the rail bed. Perhaps someone who needed the things he had left in it might find it. Things he didn't need at the moment were never of importance to Zac. Right now he couldn't put up with anything more than he already had.

Sticking his foot into the stirrup, he swung himself onto the horse. The dun stamped and bucked, kicking up his rear legs, then bouncing and jumping. The animal hadn't had a saddle on him for some time and it showed. It might take him a few days to get the rodeo out of his system. Then again, he might never straighten out. It was fine with Zac. He liked a spirited horse.

Zac slapped his spurs to the dun's ribs, and the big animal bolted back down the line. Zac would find a spot to wait. When night came, the group heading south would pass, and he'd fall in and keep a respectable distance. He had no desire to be a part of anyone else's plans, neither the government's nor the Mexican women's. Zac always liked making his own plans and going his own way. For all he knew, that federal man would be following them with his own group of assassins, and if that was to be the case, Zac wanted to be the first to know it.

It did make him feel bad that he hadn't taken Joe and James into his confidence, but the less they knew right now, the better. Sometimes when a man knows something he shouldn't, his eyes give him away without a word being spoken. It might be bad for him if that happened, and it certainly wouldn't go easy on his brothers. He could have told Chupta, but when Joe and James found out what he was up to, having

Chupta know about it when they didn't wouldn't go over well. No, this was the best way.

The day passed slowly in the bowels of Julian's cell, with nothing more to do than watch the growing number of flies crawl across the surface of the semigreen wall. He was thankful for the breakfast, even though it was given under the guise of a last meal. If that's what it took to get a decent meal, he might just look forward to dying tomorrow morning. He'd been thankful as well for the brandy that Sister Mary had brought, but just now, he'd trade it for something to read.

His mind buzzed with a conscious effort to remember, remember anything of his life outside these walls. He tried various names on himself, but Julian Cobb seemed to fit best. He could see a little boy in his mind, someone he imagined as himself. It was hard to make out the features, though. He saw a creek and a farmhouse. He saw the trees, especially the row of pecan trees alongside the house and their curly leaves piled up in the fall of the year. One of the things he had liked best was scooting the brown leaves into an enormous pile and running for them, jumping into the soft, billowy crush of brown. He remembered the other children, his brothers and sisters, he guessed. They'd play together in a gang, and he would always be the leader.

There was a picture of his father that floated into his mind. The man was standing on the porch, watching them as he leaned against the support beam. He could remember his father's soft brown eyes, which always seemed to follow him. Maybe that was the price of being the eldest and the leader. The man would hold on to the beam as if he were hugging a woman. Why was he leaning? It was a puzzle, as if the man were trying to say something to him, something he couldn't remember.

He heard the outer cell door, keys were being turned. Getting up from his cot, he moved to one of the chairs. If the sister had come to see him, he wanted to be upright. Several guards came to the door of the cell. It was unusual to have more than one accompany a visitor. He waited as they turned the key. There was no visitor. Would they be executing him again?

"Vamos!" The guard motioned him forward.

Julian rose to his feet and ambled across the room. The guard shoved him roughly into the corridor. He stumbled, but steadied himself. Moving down the dark hall and then into the sunlight brought a tear to his eye. The afternoon sun was warming up. It was something he missed in the coop down below. The men showed him the stairs and followed him as he tramped up them. He was weak and each step seemed like a labor.

Walking through the door that led from the balcony, he was taken down a long hallway. Two massive hand-carved doors stood at the end, and a guard pushed one open. Julian stepped inside.

The large room, furnished in cowhide and oak, was studded with paintings on the wall. Large walk-through doors led onto an upstairs balcony. Seated behind the desk was a man of obvious great importance. The man raised his head and glowered at him, his drooping mustache accenting his frown. Beside the desk stood an officer in polished boots and ornate decorations. The man was unusual looking, blond with glassy blue eyes and a well-trimmed blond mustache. The guards walked Julian up to the front of the desk.

The blond officer waved them off. "This vill be all. You may go now."

The men reluctantly backed away and, turning around, left the room.

The man behind the desk drummed his fingers on the polished mahogany. He stared at Julian, then pointed to a chair. "You can seat yourself, señor."

Julian took the arm of an oak chair. It was in front of the desk and had obviously been set aside for him. Gingerly, he sat down, raking the bottom of his boots on the thick rug in front of the desk.

"I am General Escobar, and this is my adjutant, Major Manfried Hess."

Julian stared silently.

"Do you know why we have brought you here?"

"I figure you set yerself up another execution time."

Escobar lifted his chin, making an attempt to stare down his Romanish nose. "That may come, in time. You are a convicted criminal."

"So I have been told."

Hess circled around and paced behind Julian's chair.

"You served with the emperor's elite guard."

Julian shook his head. "I don't know nothing about no emperor."

"The Emperor Maximilian. You former Confederate soldiers were always a favorite of his. He promised you gold and land."

"I ain't got no gold, but if this here is my land, I'd thank you to get off."

The major pulled the gloves from his belt and slapped the back of Julian's head. "Impertinent American!"

Escobar raised his hand. "That will not be necessary." Scooting forward, Escobar leaned over his desk. "This land has been in my family for over five hundred years, this land and all that you could see for a five-day ride at a gallop. You, sir, are a mercenary, a trader in death."

Julian remained silent.

"I am a patient man, señor, but my patience wears thin." Escobar waved his fingers at Julian, circling them in the air as if stirring a cool drink. "Somewhere in that head of yours is the knowledge of the emperor's stolen gold and jewels, treasure that he was attempting to steal from my people and my nation. The man who was with you when you were shot was part of the escort that was taking those assets to Galveston. We know it was to be loaded on a ship bound for France, but something happened, something that led to the burial of the gold in your New Mexico. We believe that you alone know the whereabouts of this buried plunder."

"Right now, I ain't even terrible sure 'bout my own name, much less some gold of yours. Things are moving right slowly in my head."

"Then, you would do well to speed them along, señor—otherwise you will never live to see beyond these walls."

"Why don't you ask the man you say was with me?"

"He is dead," barked Hess. "It is by less than an inch that you are not in the same hole as he now lies in."

Escobar folded his hands. "The aim of my men was slightly off target."

Julian raised his hand to the side of his head, fingering the bandage wrapped around his skull. "I'd say that was a lucky thing for me."

"Maybe so," Escobar agreed, "but maybe not. Perhaps your own death will be much slower and far more painful, unless you see yourself cooperating."

"Like I said, I don't recall a blame thing. I recollect how I lost my arm and my eye or at least after it. I can make out a few things with me as a boy, but I don't remember your emperor or that gold of his."

"This is most unfortunate, señor," Escobar said. "If you did think about these things, I would set you free. You could accompany Major Hess and some of my men, and I would reward you with fifty thousand Yankee dollars and send you on your way to spend it as you choose."

"Sounds like a handsome offer."

Hess broke in. "But if you should fail to remember, ve vill be forced to use bullets in our next firing squad. My men ver disappointed, but they vill not be the next time."

Julian swung his head around, watching the man as he ran his bright yellow leather gloves through the palms of his hands.

Escobar sank in his chair. "I am afraid the next time they will have to strap you to a stretcher before the firing squad. You see, the major here is anxious to experiment with methods of forcing you to tell what you know, and I'm afraid his methods will be very painful and quite debilitating."

"I can't rightly tell what I don't know."

"Perhaps it will come back to you."

"It might come back a little bit quicker if I had some better vittles and maybe a little exercise. Things like that tend to make a body think somewhat better." Behind him, Julian heard Hess give out a low guttural growl.

Escobar looked up at the man to silence any comment. "I think we can see to that. We still have some patience left—not much, but a little."

Julian pulled at his shirt. "It might help to have a bath and a fresh change of duds to go along with it."

Escobar nodded. "We can do that as well." He got up and walked around to a spot directly in front of Julian. There, he sat on the edge of the desk. "You see, we are agreeable men. You are a mercenary and a murderer. You are a thief. Your efforts and those of your comrades helped to keep a foreigner in authority in my country and yet, in spite of all that, I am a merciful man."

Julian stared at him and blinked slowly.

Escobar leaned toward him. "However, I will not always be so indulgent. A man in my position can be charitable with an enemy for only so long." He straightened up. "But I can see that whatever else you are, you are an intelligent man. Here in this place, only pain and death await you. If this mind of yours returns, however, you can have a fast horse under you and more money than even you can spend. Now, what more could a man want?"

Julian was once more silent.

"Very little, I should think." He looked up at Hess. "Call the guards back in. I think the gringo here knows our mind on this."

Hess turned and walked back to the door.

"You see, Señor Cobb, I am a fair man. I have given you my word on the matter. You must also realize that I have given you my word on the alternative to this choice. We will not wait long."

The guard came back into the room and, standing beside Julian, waited silently.

Escobar waved his hand. "You may go now. We will do as you ask. Now you must do what we require."

Near the ridge that overlooked Santa Fe, Zac pulled rein. He had circled south of the city and found a spot to wait in the trees. The ground was sandy, orange-colored clay, and rocky outcrops were dotted with ponderosa pines. The trees were small and rather spindly, but they offered shade and a good place to see the trail as it stretched below.

Stripping the saddle and blanket from the dun, Zac picketed the animal near some grass. The horse began to crop the green growth, stamping his feet as he moved from side to side to get a better taste.

Zac mumbled to himself as he set the rest of his gear beside the saddle. It bothered him not telling Joe about his plans. He'd grown accustomed to keeping his own counsel in the years since the war, though. He'd never been one to think while his mouth was moving. James did that—he'd always done that. It was as if the words hanging in the air would reveal the wisdom of how they'd been formed. Maybe that was all right for James, being a teacher and all. But for Zac, the notion of seeing his own wrongheadedness at the same time everyone else could spot it sent a ripple of fear down his back. The greatest fault any man could have was a weakness in the mind. He'd stayed alive until now by making sure that whatever shortcomings he had were kept from anyone who might have a cause to use them against him.

The shade was pleasant, and he stretched out on the rough blanket, pulling his hat down over his eyes. It would be hours before the group left town, and if he was lucky, he'd have had his nap by then and be ready to ride until morning. He pulled a dried peach from his jacket pocket and bit off a piece. It reminded him of home. Just the idea of home gave him another reason not to go along with the group.

His father had gone off to the war with Mexico on other people's say-so, and although he'd been born after the man's return, everyone had always told him that his father had never been the same. It was more than just losing a leg. His mama had said that something died inside the man while he was gone. When Zac saw the brothers leave to fight for the South, he'd watched his father shake his head with each departure. When he at last had left, his father had taken him aside and told him that there was no glory in doing another man's killin' and dyin', no glory at all. At the time he hadn't understood the words, but now he did. Working for Wells Fargo, he took each job on his own say-so. He could just as easily tell them no whenever the fancy took him. When he said yes, it was always his idea to say so. This was different though. Joe and James were being used, by the women and by the government. There was no way he was going to be used by the federal man, no way at all.

He looked down the side of the hill. He was far enough above the trail to stay out of the way of any passersby, and he was sure the dun would warn him if anybody happened to get close. Zac was a very light sleeper, especially when the sun was high overhead.

It must have been at least two hours later when his eyes blinked open. Rolling off the blanket, he began his search for some dry wood. The dry stuff would keep the fire hot and the smoke almost nonexistent. He prepared a small fire under the branches of a young pine. The boughs of the tree would sift what little smoke there was, breaking it up so it wouldn't be so obvious against the blue sky.

A small stream trickled nearby, and Zac hunkered down beside it while the fire cooked down to coals. He had a small string and several hooks, and with worms he dug, he soon had produced two fish. In no time at all, he had them gutted and turning over the hot coals. What he didn't eat would carry well and make a nice breakfast when the sun rose over the desert.

Below him, he could see where the Rio Grande turned slightly to the west. The river was not hard to follow. It created a trail of cottonwoods, an olive green path that cut its way south through the desert. The Jornada del Muerto went straight south, not along the river. It would save three days, but only the desperate or men on the dodge followed it. It was some of the meanest country he'd ever been across. He pulled one of the hot fish apart and considered his plan of action. The women must be very anxious to get home to attempt to go through it. Of course, if there were Mexican soldiers in disguise waiting for them there, there could be no better place for them to slip in and out of the United States undetected. No one but the Mescalero would see them, and anyone who did would ask no questions.

He spotted the group three hours later. Chupta was in the lead, and the rest followed two by two. The first of the night stars had come out. They hung in the air like lanterns suspended in velvet.

Slowly and deliberately, he saddled the dun. He would follow a ways off. The moon was full, a bright harvest moon, and tracking them would be easy, even in the dark. Only Chupta or Joe would think to check their back trail, and he wouldn't be close enough even then to present much worry.

He filled his two canteens with fresh water from the stream. More than likely that little amount would have to last both him and the dun the better part of a week. There weren't many men who could go that long on what little he had, but he'd done it before and he could do it again.

He mounted up and spurred the horse down the steep hill. They would travel slowly, deliberately. It wasn't who he was following that worried him. It was who else might be following them.

CHAPTER 6

+ + + + + + +

SMALL COOKING FIRES DOTTED the hillside to the southeast. They were well hidden and most, if not all of them, would be out before the sun went down. The women had gathered dry wood to burn; there would be little smoke. The huts were branches woven into cavelike structures, leaves and dry brush stuffed into the cracks to offer shade from the heat of the day. The hills behind them caught what little breeze there was and raked it through the camp, making the perspiration on their backs cool to the touch.

By the standard of the white man's army, the band of Mescalero was not a large one, numbering fewer than forty braves. Of course, just over a dozen hostile Apaches had kept the cavalry and much of Mexico's army on the hunt for years. A half-dozen such men could create havoc in the territory. No farmer would feel safe, and every traveler would ride looking over his shoulder with a hand on his gun. Nani was determined to make this stand a strong one. He would make sure that the fear of his band would keep the white man from the desert.

With the women and children, their numbers swelled to more than a hundred and twenty, with a few of the old ones who refused to let their grandchildren out of their sight mixed in among them. The families' presence would keep the foolish hotheads at bay. The sight of the old ones and the little children would make the men brave, but at the same time make them want to go home and not die at the hands of the white man's rifles. Nani had taken them away from the white man's eyes in Warm Springs to the place of the hot sand. Here they could be free to live on what land could be seen. No one would follow; there was no reason.

The occasional white who stumbled across their path would be killed, his horses and supplies taken. No questions would be asked, and no prisoners would be held. There were none of the troublesome white farmers to cut up the earth with their iron earth axes and plant their seed in the ground. The men who failed to return from their ride through the desert would be a warning for the others to keep their distance.

Nani was content as he watched the hawk soar near the cliffs above them. The bird was alone and he was free. There was no one to answer to and no one to disturb his nest in the rocks. There was no soldier and no Indian agent holding out a hand filled with spoiled meat for the bird. If the hawk were to begin to take food from the hand of a man, he would cease to be a hawk. He would become a crow, a feeder of the discards of man. Nani watched the bird sail higher on the evening wind. The beaked hunter of the sky was alone. He needed no one, no one to lift him to the sky, no one to hold out a morsel of already dead meat.

Lowering his eyes, Nani watched his own youngest child play near the cliff, his eyes following the boy's every move. Someday, being alone would no longer be possible, even in this place. His muscles tightened at the thought. When that day did come, the boy would have no memory of his father standing in the white man's line to get a small amount of rotten beef. There would be no shame in his memory as a man when he thought of his father. The boy would remember this place and his father on his painted pony. The idea made Nani smile. His hard lips creased slightly as he watched the boy pick up stones and begin to throw them. The young boy's eyes would grow sharp and his muscles and aim steady.

The women pulled several strips of meat from the hot rocks beside the fire and motioned toward two young men who stood nearby. The meat sizzled and the braves bounced them from hand to hand, cooling them to the touch. Then they began to tear at the food with their teeth. Nani watched the women smile as the hungry recipients eagerly gnawed the meat. There was a pride in watching the braves enjoy what they had prepared. Nani caught the eyes of the men and motioned for them to join him.

His signal stopped their dinner. Dropping their hands to their sides, they ran up to him and waited for their orders. They were to be the night wolves, the eyes and ears of the village until the sun came over the cliff. The larger of the two squinted his eyes at the chief.

Nani pointed due south to a group of stars that had yet to make their full appearance. "You will ride to the Great Bear." He circled his hand to the west. "Go to where the sun dies."

The taller of the two nodded.

The younger brave was a slight man, not over a hundred pounds, even dripping wet. His scrawny legs were muscled, and he put on his hardest face, as if to scare any adversary who might try to take advantage of him. Puffing up his chest, he held his head erect, as if suspended to the sky by a string. Bending his eyebrows down and narrowing his eyes, he listened.

"Little Stone"—Nani pointed at the setting sun—"you will ride with the sun. When it dies, you will go to where the great cliff lies down and sleeps with the desert."

The boy nodded. It was a slight nod, not meant to give away the eagerness he felt at such an important job, but just enough to show he understood his orders. Nani watched him, looking through the windows of his eyes. He liked the boy for his enthusiasm and for his subtle self-control at such a young age. Nani seldom saw a man for what he was, but took great pains to see him for what he was to become.

"You will both ride to where I say and then walk your ponies back to the places where you start. There will be no stopping, only to watch with your eyes and taste the air with your ears."

Both of the young men nodded.

Nani struck his hands together, and the newly appointed scouts scampered away. The taller of the two went back to the hot rocks for more of the goat meat, but Little Stone made his way straight to his spotted pony and rode off. Nani's smile grew larger as he watched the boy ride away. It would be a good night to sleep in the coolness of the desert sky. He could watch the stars and think about the time when he was once a young man such as this. Once he had dreamed of a world where he proudly walked the earth. There had been no fear in him. Now there was only fear of what the earth would become without him.

Little Stone rode hard to get out of sight of the village. To be away from the village, alone, was to be a warrior, one that Nani trusted. Several small hills kept the huts out of sight from the grassy sand. Rounding them, he slowed the animal down to a walk. The pony was still eager to move, but he kept him back. It would be a long night, and the hills and the grassy sand would be his and his alone. The lizards, the snakes, the birds, and the coyotes would be his tonight.

He blinked his eyes at the setting sun, trying to get accustomed to the glare from the sand. A feeling of unsettledness came over him. A man riding near the sun would be almost invisible to him now, while he would be clearly seen. He wound the pony around a small hill. He would take care to keep the sun from his eyes. As long as it stayed up, above the desert sand, he would weave in and around the hills.

He had dreamed of this many times. The knowledge that the rest saw him as no longer a boy sent a rush of excitement through his veins. Often he had sat around the evening fires and listened to the stories of the old men. They would tell of the counting of coup on their enemies and how screams of joy would come when they could see fear in an enemy's eyes. It was a feeling Little Stone wanted more than anything. Up ahead, he caught a small movement in the brush. It was a quail, perhaps more than one. He slid off the back of the pony and, reaching down, picked up several small stones. Tossing one with his left hand, he cocked his right arm and waited. The bird skittered out of the brush, flapping his wings in useless motion. Little Stone flung the rock, aiming it straight and true. It bounced off the body of the small bird, sending it into a nervous frenzy on the sand.

Little Stone bounded forward like a cougar hungry for a kill. He was on the bird in a matter of moments, grabbing its feet and wrenching at its head, leaving it motionless. Dropping the dead quail into his shirt, he walked back proudly to the standing pony. The bird would make a good breakfast for his mother and sister in the morning. He liked the warm feeling of the feathers against his belly.

Gathering the reins, he slid onto the back of the pony and trotted off toward the swimming sun. It would be a long night, but already he felt better. He would come back to the village tomorrow and see the smile of his mother.

The setting sun cast a soft glow on the grass and the rocks seemed to glow with a light all their own. It was a land virtually without water and rarely visited by the white man. Roamed by the Mescalero Apache, for whom it had become a last stronghold, this was the final place for a last stand against the encroaching foreigners from the east.

Beyond the broken sandy land, peaks rose, casting a soft haze over the playa, purple in the distance—cool, remote, lost. Here and there in scattered spots there would be water. The marauding bands of the Apache knew the wells and high tanks where the cool moisture collected. The occasional whites who stumbled across them seldom survived to tell about it.

Overhead, vultures circled in lazy loops. Their swinging passes dropped lower and lower over the distant playa as they waited for the last breath to leave the dying target.

The riders in the lonely line were well armed, but in the Jornada del Muerto they would be hunted prey. Regardless of the preparations and care taken, there was a feeling of vulnerability. They were the strangers here, watched and waited for. With each stride of the horses they rode, the feeling of being scrutinized crept across them. Picking their way over the sandy rocks, they made their way south like a band of lean wolves surrounded by lions.

Joe watched Chupta ride on ahead of them, thankful the man was with them. Knowing the man had a keen set of eyes and an acute sense about what they were seeing was a great comfort. The scout rode silently, moving his head from side to side with deliberate determination as he took the lead in the front of the group. Like a hawk sailing over the night sky, Chupta rounded the hill in front of them, taking care not to skyline himself on the top of the hill.

Joe pulled rein and trotted back toward the rear of the column. James was holding forth with the women, animated as usual. Joe brought his horse up beside them. "We have to keep ourselves kinda quiet like. Voices carry in the night air and ears can have eyes of their own."

James smiled and looked at the two women. "My brother here is a very conscientious man. He leaves little to chance, even our conversation." James grinned at Joe and nodded. "We'll behave ourselves, little brother."

"I got myself little desire to have this hair of mine, or yours either, hanging on some lodgepole here in the desert." Joe looked at the two women. "You ladies would be a special prize, I'd think."

"Well, we have no intention of becoming mere casualties out here," James replied.

Joe looked at the silver stirrups on the women's saddles, noticing the way their spurs rattled against the shiny metal. "Before we go much farther, I'd like to nudge you womenfolk to take them things off. Either that, or tie some cloth around them. Folks will be able to hear us coming for some distance off with them things rattling like that. Pays to be real careful."

Rosalyn straightened up in her saddle. "Señor, no one travels this land, day or night. It is an empty place."

"And that's exactly what I want us to sound like—no one." He spurred his horse and rode back to the front of the meandering line of horses.

"I'm afraid my brother is right, ladies," James said. "It will make for a dull ride, but right now Joe is simply concerning himself with our safe arrival. A man who is prepared for the worst might never have to encounter it."

"But, señor," Palmira said, "you are the eldest of the two of you. Is it not so?"

"True enough, my dear. My brother Julian was the oldest of the boys, and I'm next in the line."

"Then why do you feel it necessary to take his orders?"

"Suggestions, my dear. Although I do know that when Joe's certain about something it may come out sounding like an order. In my classroom, I'd be the one to give the orders." He waved his right hand toward the desert. "But this place is his classroom, his and my brother Zac's. I find myself a student here." He leaned over toward the young woman. "Of course, where the fairer sex is concerned, I find no need to receive instruction from any man."

"You American men are a strange breed," Rosalyn said. "In my country an older brother would never listen to a younger one, and if he did, he would pretend to never have heard."

"I find the exercise of pretending to be a man often keeps one from becoming a man," James replied.

Rosalyn shook her head and trotted toward the front of the line to talk to the men from her ranch. James beamed, enjoying the chance to talk in private.

"My mother is right," Palmira said. "In my own country a man would find it very hard to take words this way from a younger brother."

"I suppose, my dear, that once a man knows his strengths and his weaknesses and has arrived at a place of graceful and wise ignorance—at that point, instruction from anyone comes quite easy. It is the mark of maturity and intelligence to receive it."

"You are a strange man, señor."

"I am a learned man, señorita. An English poet, William Shakespeare, once wrote in one of his sonnets: 'When, in disgrace with fortune and men's eyes, I all alone beweep my outcast state, and trouble deaf heaven with my bootless cries, and look upon myself and curse my fate, wishing me like to one more rich in hope, featured like him, like him with friends possessed, desiring this man's art and that man's scope, with what I most enjoy contented least: Yet in these thoughts myself almost despising, haply I think on thee—and then my state, like to the lark at break of day arising from sullen earth, sings hymns at heaven's gate; for thy sweet love remembered such wealth brings that then I scorn to change my state with kings.' "

"These are beautiful words. What do they mean?"

"Men find many causes to be jealous of each other—their position, their wealth, their power. I may envy Joe's ability at knowing the right from the wrong thing to do in a place such as this, but if he had any eye at all he would know that the greatest prize of all tonight is mine, the opportunity to ride back here and survey your beauty."

The words and the meaning of what he was saying caused a blush to creep up her face. "Oh, señor, you say such beautiful things."

"No more beautiful than words you should have heard all of your life. You are a woman who should be adored."

"I am afraid no one has ever done that to me before."

"Surely that's not true. A woman of your radiance should attract men from all over the territory."

She stared straight ahead and rode. It was as if she held a secret that only she and the horse she rode knew.

"From a child, I should think you would have been praised for your beauty."

"You do not know my home, señor. There is room there for only praise directed at one."

Joe raised his eyes to look at Rosalyn in the distance. "Your mother is a very beautiful woman. You are much like her."

"Not my mother, señor."

"Then who?"

Palmira's face was filled with stony silence. She let the question lie as they continued to ride.

James was never a man to be denied. He let the question rest for what to him seemed like an eternity. "My dear, no one can deny your beauty and charm. You would be a sheer delight on the arm of any man. I can think of no one who could refuse you this."

"There is room in my house for only one, my father."

"Your father?"

"Yes. He must be the bride at every wedding and the corpse at every funeral."

The words stunned James. He said nothing in reply, replaying the sound of the strange words and the mystery of the thoughts in his mind. Several times he looked at her and fought to reply, but no words came to mind.

She broke the tension. "My father is a man of great purpose. He sees himself as a man of destiny and so must we all. The sun must rise when he wills it and can never go down until it accomplishes his purpose. All who know him fear him, and they fear him most when anyone gives recognition to someone else in his presence. Is this such a foreign thought to you?"

"Yes, I'm afraid it is. I suppose when I grew up I had the idea that my parents saw themselves as their children's helpers, lifting each child up to a greater life than the one they themselves had. The thought of holding down a child's natural abilities for fear of being upstaged would never have occurred to them."

"They sound kind."

"They were, very kind, two of the most gentle spirits I've ever known."

"My father sees kindness as weakness. To be kind to someone is to hope for the favor to be returned, and my father never places himself in the need for any man's favor."

"Kindness comes from a richness of the soul, not from poverty. When a man forbears from his own rights, it means he has risen above the need to demand them. Only a man who is truly powerful in his soul can do that."

"Is this why you allow your brother to give you orders?"

"Precisely. It is because I know who I am and have no need to find it in the eyes of others that I can listen to anyone. For me, to do otherwise would be a signal of weakness. Men can cover their weakness with great bravado. Like a wounded bull in the midst of wolves, they paw at the ground and snort to drive away their enemy. But the wolf smells the blood. The death of the bull is sure. It is only a matter of time."

"Don't you want to achieve great things? My father says that the greatness of a man is found in the legacy he leaves."

"A man's greatness is found in the measure of his soul, not in the land or wealth he leaves to others. When I see my Creator and He says, 'Well done,' that will be more than enough for me."

"I have met very few men like you, señor. You seem so content, and that is a most peculiar thought to me."

"I've lived a good life. I have had the best wife a man could have hoped for. I have a beautiful daughter who reminds me more of her mother each day. I use my mind and the words of my mouth to inspire the best in my students. It is more than enough for me."

James looked up ahead. He could see Joe's gaze and, even in the dim light of the sunset, the look of disapproval. He lowered his voice. "I'm afraid that brother of mine does not look with great favor on our continued conversation. We will speak of this again. I would love to hear more about your home. I'm only sorry you haven't grown accustomed to praise. Where you are concerned, it is most deserved."

Joe signaled the column around the hill. They would follow the route laid out by Chupta. The dying embers of the sun in the west gave out a last gasp, bathing the sandy soil with a pink hue. It would be a long ride in the silent darkness. The stars overhead blinked, telling them of the approaching darkness. Joe swung around in his saddle, looking back toward the north. In the distance he could see the soft cloud of light from Santa Fe.

The danger would come later, when they were away from any sight of the city and the surrounding farms. By morning, they would be on the merciless desert, surrounded by the heat, the snakes, and the Mescalero.

CHAPTER 7

+ + + + + + +

THE MULES IN FRONT of the wagon strained hard in the sandy soil, plodding ahead, their shoulders slumped forward. The animals had been without water for three days now, and it had been a week since they had left Tucumcari.

Oscar Rolfsrud was a disappointed man and old for his years. His wispy beard and soft, thinning hair were white, but by most standards he'd never have been called old. It was only lately, over the last five years or so, that his age had begun to set in. When his wife, Mollie, died, Ellie had been fourteen. He'd sold the farm only weeks after Mollie had been laid away and left Kansas. He'd been quick to take up the life of a peddler.

It was a life of forced optimism and silent regret. When the customers would come to the wagon, he'd put on his best smile to hawk his wares, but on the inside he knew he tried much too hard to be pleasing. He liked the traveling. Most of all, he liked being gone from Kansas. He liked the feeling that the next day would be unlike this one—different town, different people, different place. What he didn't care for was the fact that he would be the same.

Ellie watched him as he slapped the reins on the backs of the tired mules. She was twenty-five now—a full-grown woman and by some standards already past her childbearing prime. In the last eleven years of knocking around the country with her father, she'd been looked over many a time by young men of a marriageable notion. She'd be hard not to notice—blond hair the color of straw, penetrating blue eyes, and the firmness of a woman accustomed to work. She was pleasing to look on, and her face sported dimples in the cheeks on the occasion of a smile. It was mostly her appearance at the side of the wagon that pulled the young men in to look and see the wares she and her father were selling. The towns they stopped in, for the most part, already had stores. What they didn't have was Ellie.

She often found herself looking back when their wagon pulled out of a town, looking back at the promise of a life that wouldn't belong to her. But she'd already made up her mind. This was to be her last trip.

Oscar slapped the backs of the mules with the reins.

"I think they're all done in, Papa. They're laboring hard for mules with no water."

He muttered under his breath. "We ain'ta gonna be sellin' nuffin in Santa Fe if'n we turn up there. Dem folks back a week ago said there might be some farms this a way, but I think they wuz jes' wishin' in their heads."

"It would be safer in Santa Fe. We know nothing about this place, and I can't say as I like the looks of it."

To the north of them, a range of cliffs jutted up from the floor of the rocky desert. The setting sun bathed the rocks in a blushing shade of pale lavender. Like giant sentinels of the coming night, the huge rocks seemed to survey the sandy playa. To the peddler and his daughter, the small caves and cracks were like hundreds of dark eyes staring down at them. Pinon pine and juniper twisted their way up from the rocky outcropping. Each of the scattered trees seemed to turn their faces away from the sandy grassland below, a stretch of dry and parched ground that offered little hope for farming and no hope for the weary passerby.

"We'd better pull up, Papa. I know you want to go through the cool night air, but I just don't think those mules are going to make it for very long."

He hauled back on the traces, bringing the mules to a thankful stop. "Ellie, I thinks we got us jes' a might of water in the bottom of dat barrel. See if you can soak some of dat up and mop out their nostrils with a cloth. If there is more to spare, swish their mouths a mite. I'll take off the harness and try and find 'em some grass someplace where dey might feed."

"Yes, Papa."

Rummaging around in a trunk, Ellie found a swatch of cotton cloth. She scooted back out the rear of the wagon and lifted the lid on the water barrel. It had been a week since they had found any water, and that had been at the good graces of a farmer who was willing to part with some from his very low well. It hadn't been much, only half a barrel full, but now there was very little left. She pressed the cloth into the shallow water and, lifting it up, wrung it out slightly. Her father hadn't had any water all day, and she suspected he'd gone without the day before. It troubled her.

Moving to the mules, she swabbed out the nostrils of the first one. Old Elmer, as they called him, swung his head up at the feel of the cool cloth and shook it. She moved to Sassafras and repeated the procedure.

Returning back to the water, she made the trip back and forth to the two mules, each time running the wet cloth over their teeth and tongue. There just wasn't enough to give them a full drink. What little there was would have been devoured by the first one she allowed to drink, and the disappearance of the water would take only seconds. She felt sorry for them. It seemed cruel to tease them with the wet cloth and then give them nothing.

"I spied out a bit of a grassy area over behind dem rocks." Oscar strode forward in the twilight, pointing to the area he'd just explored. "We'll picket 'em dere for a spell and let 'em eat. What little moisture's in the grass will do 'em good."

They led the team of mules around the rocks to a flat area of sandy grass. Stretching out a rope from a nearby juniper, he drove a pin into the rocky ground and picketed Elmer and Sassafras. Then they turned and walked back to the wagon. "Are we going to have a cold camp tonight?" Ellie asked.

"Figure so, honey. We got ourselves some jerky and dried fruit." He stumbled on a small rock, weaving as he worked to gain his balance. Shaking his head, he plodded ahead. "Ain't got 'nuff water for to cook none."

"You should take a drink of water, Papa."

"I do myself fine till we find ourselves some."

"You don't look too good."

"I think we should turn for Santa Fe tomorrow or when the mules have rested tonight. We could find water there and rest."

"There's gots to be some farmers someplace in these parts or gold diggers in the least."

"Why not Santa Fe?"

"Them people's gots everythin' they need. I don't hanker to starve. Out here, folks is poorly and hurtin' fer supplies and things. We'd do right smart to stay away from town fer a spell. Dat purse of ours is ever bit as empty as our water barrel."

"That may be, but no one ever died from an empty purse."

He ignored the remark and, opening the back door to the wagon, pulled out a bag of dried apples. "Here, you go to chawin' on this some. It'll keep up yer strength."

Ellie ignored the bag and walked to the water barrel. Picking up a tin ladle, she opened the lid and dipped it down. She heard the ladle hit bottom and brought up a half cup of the stale water. Gently nurturing it with two hands, she brought it back to him. "Here, Papa, I want you to drink this, all of it."

He shook his head. "No, won't do it."

"You must. What would I do without you?"

"I'll be fine. I'll drink some when I needs it."

"And I say you need it right now. A man without water goes crazy first, and I need your head right."

"I is always been crazy, so it can't hurt me none to be without. Might just set my mind to flyin' right."

If there was one thing that Ellie had learned, it was that no amount of arguing would work with a full-blooded Norwegian. The man had hundreds of years of stubbornness built up into him and very little quit. She lowered the cup. "Then, you'll drink tomorrow?"

"I'll drink when I'ze good and ready, girl. Don't you go to worryin' that head 'bout me."

"Then we'll go to Santa Fe?"

He didn't answer her. He just picked up the bag of apples and, taking one in his hand, began to gnaw on it.

She sat down in a heap beside the van, collapsing more on the inside than out. Linking her arms around her knees, she began to rock back and forth. The rocking motion always seemed to have a calming effect on her, like her own personal cradle.

He turned away from her. "Yer gonna drive me plumb loco with that rockin' long before lack of water does."

"You just don't want me in Santa Fe, do you? That's it, isn't it? The thought of me being in any size town has you frightened, doesn't it?"

He pretended not to hear her as he rummaged for the jerky.

"You should at least talk to me and tell me the truth. I deserve at least that."

His head snapped back, staring at her. "I don't want you up and leavin' me. I needs you too much."

"You don't need me, Papa. There's more than enough company for you with that head of yours and Momma's grave back in Kansas. You're never far away from that."

He shook his head. "Yer all that's left of your momma, and now you want to take that too."

"She's gone, Papa. She's dead and I'm alive."

"T'ain't right. The Lord took her and left me. T'ain't right."

"That ain't quite true, Papa. I think when she died you died too. The Lord took you but left the shell you walk around in. You walk and talk but you aren't here anymore, not really here."

"Don't talk such foolishness."

"There's nothing foolish about it. I've been with you or what's left of you for eleven years now. You're like those two mules back there, alive in name only, just taking one step at a time and trying to pick your spot to drop. In the meantime, you're taking me with you. It's like the last sight you want to see on this earth is one that reminds you of Momma, and you're determined to have that no matter what it does to me."

"Maybe I just don't want to cut you loose in this here world. This place is wicked and cruel."

"No more cruel than walking around with a dead man, a man who won't live and won't even drink when he's thirsty."

"All right, carn sarn you. Give me that there water. If'n it'll satisfy you somewhat and keep the yammerin' down, I'll drink it."

Scrambling to her feet, Ellie once more lowered the ladle into the bucket. She drew up the half cup of water and handed it to him. Watching him carefully, she saw him lift it to his parched lips and drain the cup slowly.

He pushed the empty cup back at her. "There, will that satisfy you?"

"It will if we head north to Santa Fe."

"Girl, there's no livin' with or without you."

Little Stone watched. His eyes bored into them. He had seen the mules. There was nothing more tasty to his people than mule meat, and without them, the white eyes would go nowhere. From his position behind the smooth large rock, he watched and waited. The sun had just gone down, and the white eyes were not starting a fire. Perhaps they would try to sleep soon, and he could take the mules. He snaked his head slowly around the rock, working to see for sure if these two, the woman and the white-haired man, were the only ones in the camp.

If he could take the mules and bring them back to camp, Nani would send him out alone again and perhaps very soon. He would have proved his worth as a night wolf. To bring back meat and the report of people so easy to take would be a coup for him and hasten his manhood. He could have the mules in camp before the night was half over and bring back warriors to kill the whites. The wagon was loaded, and it would make great sport to take the things of the white man. Perhaps he would even find a rifle and Nani would let him keep the weapon.

His heart pounded and he smiled. Many times he had heard men talk of stealing horses. They would pound on their chests and speak of their bravery and the skill it took to venture into an enemy's camp. Now it would be him telling the story. The men would listen to him and not laugh.

He slunk down to the ground and sat peacefully, wrapping his arms around his bony knees. He listened to the sound of their voices. It was the first time he had been so close to an enemy. To hear them speak, even if he couldn't understand their words, excited him. The woman's talk was soft, like strange music in the night air. The words of the old man sounded like a dried goat stomach full of shaking rocks, harsh and with a tumble in it.

Tomorrow they would be dead, and it would be him the people of the village would celebrate. He cocked his head slightly to pick up the speech. Seldom had he viewed an enemy as human beings. They were strangers, foreign thinkers whose soldiers would murder his people, a breed apart, not truly humans who belonged to the earth.

It was some time later when he heard the two of them settle down. Unlike most white eyes, they had no fire. They were trying to stay out of sight, but he, one of the night wolves, had found them. In a short while, he heard the buzz of the old man's snore. Like the sound of a giant bumblebee, it floated over the rocks, a soft, muffled sleep sound. Little Stone smiled. Soon he would have the two mules and be walking proudly into the village.

He got to his feet and moved back into and over the rocks. His pony had continued to graze on the grass. He picked up the reins and patted the animal's neck. "You do good," he said. "You stay right where Little Stone leave you."

Leading the pony back around the rocks, he crouched near the place where he had seen the two mules. The animals were still tied to the picket rope and feeding peacefully on the grass. The people would eat well on these two.

Dropping the reins on the pony, he skittered over the ground, keeping low. When he reached the mules, he cut the picket line and gathered it in. Standing up, he tugged the two mules close to him and then led them back to his pony. Stealing the mules had been easy. The white eyes were locked into their own world—a small place, taking up only the ground on which they stood. This was a place that belonged to him and his people, a place he could call his as far as his eyes could travel.

Sliding up onto the back of his pony, he kicked its sides and led the mules away. Rounding the rocks to the playa below, he began a slow gallop. He held the lead rope with his left hand and waved at the starry sky with his right, hugging the pony with his narrow legs. He loved to ride free, his hands to the air. He had been taught to shoot the bow this way, and it made him feel free, a part of the pony he rode.

Sometime later he rode between the narrow rocks that hid the entrance to the narrow gorge. The steep valley had watchmen, two of his younger friends posted on either side. "Ah yeee!" Little Stone shouted in celebration. "I have meat to eat, my brothers."

The young men got to their feet high above him and waved him on.

He came out of the gap in the rocks and rode toward the low hills. Circling around them, he pulled rein at the foot of the smoldering fire. The coals glowed red hot, their fiery eyes winking at him as he slid off the back of the pony.

Nani stooped low as he came out of his hut, and Little Stone walked up to him and handed him the lead rope with the two mules in tow. "Here, Grandfather, I bring these as my gift." Little Stone always called Nani grandfather, even though the man was not his real grandfather. It was a mark of great respect. "There are two white eyes over an hour away who will be walking without these. One is a man and the other a young woman. They have many things to steal."

"You have done well, my son." He signaled several warriors who had come to see the noise in the middle of the night. "Come see what Little Stone brings us. Waken the men in the far wickiups and have them follow our night wolf here. He will lead you to the white eyes."

Little Stone's face beamed. Nani had spoken of him to the others with great respect, not calling him a boy. Tonight he had been the night wolf, and he had brought back much food and the news of a victory. It gave him great pleasure.

"These whites do not know you took the mules?"

"No, Grandfather, they are sleeping."

"You have done well."

To the north of the Mescalero camp, Ellie stirred in her bedroll. The cool night breeze revived her and made her sit upright. Overhead, the silent stars winked and filled the sky like lanterns hung by the hand of God, as if He walked through the streets on earth and held a torch to each one, slowly coaxing it to life. The rocks and boulders dotted the terrain, shoulders in the ground, strong and silent. The camp was peaceful and quiet, except for the sound of her father's snoring, but Ellie could tell that something was not quite right.

She kicked off the light blanket entangled around her feet and, rolling over, got to her knees. There was no sound, only the gentle blowing of a soft breeze from the west. Standing up, she straightened her dress and stepped into her boots. Scuffing the sand slightly as she stepped out, she made her way to where the mules were feeding.

Rounding the rock, she stared at the vacant patch of grass. A cold chill ran down her spine, giving her a feeling of being watched, stalked like a deer. She stepped over to the juniper tree and found the remainder of the line they had used to picket the mules. It had been cut.

Untying the remnant of the cord, she wound it around her hand. Picking up her skirts, she ran back to the van where her father still slept. She shook him violently. "Papa, Papa, wake up. The mules are gone!"

"Uh . . . mmm . . . what?" He sat upright, still groggy from too little sleep and the abrupt end to what might have been a pleasant dream. "The mules are gone?"

"Yes, Papa." She handed him the remains of the line. "Somebody cut them loose."

He fondled the cord in his hand, the evidence beginning to register in his tired and still water-starved brain. Jerking his head from side to side, as if looking for the thief to step forward and confront them, he continued to babble, "When? How long ago, girl? How long you figure we been a-sleepin'?"

"Several hours I think, Papa. I think it was Indians."

"Couldn't have been many of 'em, they of come over and ripped our throats open."

"If it was only one and he took the mules, then I'd say he'll be back and with more of them."

The thought got his mind to snap wide awake. He scrambled to his feet. "Where's my boots?"

Ellie reached over to the side of the van, and picking up the worn, knee-high driver boots, she set them down beside her father. He stumbled as he worked on getting them on, first the left and then the right. Cramming his shirt down into his Levi's, he lifted the suspenders over his shoulders. "We gotta go after them there mules of ourn."

She tugged on his sleeve, yanking it hard to jar some sense into him. "We can't do that. We start looking for the mules and we're going to run smack dab into the middle of them coming back this way. We've got to take what we can and get to Santa Fe and quick."

He looked at the wagon. It was a four-sided covered van, painted on the sides with wares being advertised for the passerby. It had served them well for eight of the eleven years they had been selling on the road. The mules and the van represented all that they were as a family, their livelihood and their home. "We can't leave that wagon, girl. It's got all we own on it. We stomp off and leave that thing here, and dem folks'll burn what they don't carry off."

"We stay here, Papa, and they'll leave our bodies beside it for the buzzards to feed on, if we're lucky." She pulled on his sleeve. "We got to go, Papa. We ain't got no choice."

Ambling over, he jerked the brass doorknob open on the back of the wagon. She watched him rummage through the remains of what hadn't been sold. He lifted up a large mantel clock.

"Papa, we can't take that. We can only take some food, some ammunition, a couple of the rifles, and what we can pour into a canteen of the rest of the water." Reaching into the wagon, she pulled out a metal canteen. "If you tip the keg over, I'll see the water into this. We have to move fast. We don't know how much time we have."

He shook his head, staring at the mantel clock. "It ain't fair. Havin' them thievin' Indians about ain't at all fair."

"Here, Papa." She held the canteen to the lip of the water barrel. "Lower it real easy like."

He loosened the ropes that bound the barrel to the side of the wagon and lowered it ever so slowly. The trickle of water rolled out of the lip of the oak in a skimpy rivulet and made a tinny sound on the bottom of the canteen. Ellie carefully kept the narrow opening fastened to the ever narrowing stream. In a matter of moments, her father held the barrel almost straight up, squeezing the last drop of water off the waterlogged oak bottom. It was as if he were milking the last remains of a precious fruit.

"I think that's it, Papa. There just ain't no more."

CHAPTER 8

+ + + + + + +

ZAC SWUNG THE DUN to the side, winding his way through the scattered trees. Knowing the direction the group was going made following them a simple matter. He could afford to take his time and fan back and forth across their back trail. If the group was going to be followed, he wanted to know by whom and how many.

The night sky was bright with stars. It was one of the things he loved about the desert. The daylight hours had little in the way to recommend itself out here, but the night was filled with beauty, and the cool temperatures made it easy to enjoy even the barren landscape. Large rocks dotted the floor of the draw, and the grassy sand rose up to a series of slopes, each one disappearing behind the last. Without the stars or the sun by day, anyone might easily get lost in a sea of sand and rock.

The range of mountains to the east made it easy to keep one's bearings, but they didn't run a true north and south course, and a man who decided to follow them would be days off and out of water. The rocky hills with the few trees scattered over the rise would give way to the sandy hills and then to the flat plateau area. The sand soaked up what little rain fell, leaving no water to collect and everything bone-dry just minutes after the rain stopped.

An owl swooped close to him, its wings beating a sudden storm of fury. Landing nearby, it wrestled on the ground momentarily with what Zac figured to be a mouse. Picking up its prey, the creature flew off, bending its wings into the low-hanging moon.

It was a startling sight. The moon seemed to be twice the normal size it appeared anywhere else on earth. The pockmarks on the surface of the great globe formed the familiar face his mother had called the man in the moon. Many was the time he'd lain in the grass back home and studied the features of the smiling face. It was as if the great moon knew him by name and held many secrets he wouldn't begin to tell no matter how nicely he was asked. There was much Zac wanted to know from it as a boy, mostly about himself and what life would be like as a man. Now that had become a subject he knew far too much about. There was little innocence left, only the harsh real world.

The mountains to the east were an indigo blue, dark and lonesome. They shadowed the land in the day with shards of welcome shade, and what little water might be found there trickled at the feet of the massive rocks and collected tanks in among them. Somewhere there, Zac imagined cool running streams with fish and trees. Many was the time he'd been riding down in the lowlands only to go up higher and discover another world, an island hanging thousands of feet in the air. Places like that were what men dreamed of when they thought of the beauty of silence.

The Mescalero no doubt were near the protection of the great cliffs. Like ants in a great ant hill, they would stay out of sight until a man was alone or in trouble, and then they would come in numbers. Like the carpenter ant, the Mescalero would tear an enemy to pieces and then cart the remains back to their village to feed on later. A man would be a fool to get too close, no matter how inviting the mountains might seem. He'd fight shy of that side of the playa. They'd have scouts fanning the area looking for someone alone like him. It would be best, Zac knew, if he saw them before they caught sight of him.

Zac moved cautiously down the hill, through the juniper and pinon. At one spot a pine leaned toward the desert below, pointing the way south. Like the mast on a great ship as it surged up a great swell in the ocean, the trunk of the tree slanted against the night sky. Several juniper trees surrounded a rocky outcropping, their branches hanging low, giving way to the parched land.

He heard the sound of the horses before he ever saw them. These weren't Indian ponies. He could hear the sound of the iron horseshoes clipping over the rocks in the draw below and the squeak of the saddle leather before he ever saw them. It was why he brought his own saddle with him. A man always sat better in his own saddle, and keeping it well oiled as Zac did minimized the noise of stiff leather.

Pulling up behind a tumble of rocks, Zac stepped down from the saddle. He led the dun quietly to the side of the rocks and waited. There below him a group of riders emerged from around a hill. They were traveling south and looking over the ground as they went. The man in the lead wove in his saddle, swinging low to get a better view of the ground in front of him. There were three of them, and by the looks of the men, they were traveling deliberately, not wandering about aimlessly.

The men appeared to be hard and well armed, saddle rifles and bandoleers of ammunition strung around their shoulders. Their coats were tied to the saddles, and bags of provisions flopped on the sides of their horses as they rode. This was no bunch of farmers, and if they were prospecting, it more than likely was for the two-legged kind of wealth. It was often easier to take the gold from someone who had already dug it than to find it on your own.

The group of riders cut the back trail of Joe's group and stopped. The man in the lead got to the ground and appeared to talk over what the sign on the ground told him. Zac couldn't make out the words, only the slow and deliberate murmur as the man explained what he was seeing.

Zac watched him at a distance. The light of the moon showed the heavy shadow on his face that indicated a pronounced beard. Zac spotted at once the two pistols he carried, butts forward in a crossdraw position. The ivory handles shone brightly, even in the moonlight. Very few men wore their guns this way, and the ones who did usually knew how to use them. Zac marked the men below as hard cases.

The man turned his head to look up the hill to Zac's position. It was as if by a sixth sense he could feel Zac's eyes on him. Zac was in total shadow with the large boulder between him and the moon; still it made him feel a bit uneasy to be stared at and not seen. The man held up his hand to the two on horseback, quieting them down. He listened to the silence. Zac could tell that the man could sense something. Zac had felt it many times before, and when a man felt the touch of another man's eyes on him, it made his senses sharper, kept him on edge. Zac would have to be careful, very careful.

Mounting up, the man motioned in the direction that Joe's group was traveling. They rode off at a slow walk, with the man in the lead craning his head around, as if he were trying to catch the movement of whoever had been watching him. They followed the trail of the group that had gone before. They seemed to know how long ago Joe, James, and the rest of them had passed by—and for a good tracker such a thing wasn't hard to see even at night. The more time that passed, the more the sand would shift over the tracks, but these were fresh. Dirt or sand that had been turned would not be baked by the sun, and these tracks would be darker than the surrounding sand. A blind man could see how fresh they were even in the moonlight.

Zac watched them ride away. The man in the lead hung over his saddle, closely following the trail, while the other two scanned the horizon, searching for anyone who might be watching them. Whatever the leader's suspicions were, he had passed it on to the men who rode behind him. Most folks who had any sense at all would be watching their back trail from time to time. These men evidently knew that. What they obviously didn't want was for Joe and James and the group they were following to double back and spot them. Zac smiled. If they knew they were being watched even now, they would be plenty nervous. As it was, they had a suspicion. He didn't know who these men were. What he did know was that they were following Joe and James, and they were trouble.

He watched them clear the hill and disappear. Mounting up, he started down the rocky hillside. He ducked his head under the sudden branch of the juniper and pulled rein. What he saw startled him. There was another traveler in the draw below him, someone on foot, someone who was evidently following the men on horseback. Zac sat his horse and watched, never making an attempt to move.

The traveler below was a small man, perhaps even a boy, shirt torn to shreds. He carried a large bag of water over his shoulder that banged against his waist. Scampering over the men's tracks, barefooted, the boy followed them like a coyote following the trail of a rabbit, a hungry coyote.

Had he lifted his eyes to the hillside, he might have been able to see Zac. There was no distraction to this one, however. Zac could see that. The boy was intent on one thing, and for now that one thing was following the three men on horseback. Bent low, he followed the tracks of the three horses as they mingled with the fresh trail underneath them. Like a barefoot land crab, he moved low to the ground.

Zac stepped the dun down the hill as he watched the boy skitter over the top of the rise, still on the trail of the bunch that had gone before. It was an interesting sight, the hunter becoming the hunted. The sight was a first for Zac. This last searcher was obviously no match for the men on horseback, but what he lacked in ability, he more than made up for in blind determination.

He pulled rein at the bottom of the sandy draw and stepped down from the saddle. Bending down, he inspected the tracks. The small imprints lay on top of the hoofprints, pressing them into the sand. *It was a boy,* Zac reasoned, *either that or a very small man.* Overhead, the pale moon glistened, sending a shimmering sheet of soft gold over the grassy hillside. He could clearly see the narrow print of the boy's bare foot as it dug its way up the sandy hill. It was no bigger than the size of his hand. Now, why a boy would be following such hardened men went beyond his imagination. He stood up and pondered the small impressions as they trudged up the hill. He shook his head. *Pardner, why you'd go to chasing those men is anybody's guess, but you're a determined cuss. I'll give that to you.*

Zac moved to his saddlebags. Reaching in, he removed a bag of jerky. He'd rest a mite and eat some. There was no sense in climbing on top of the train of stalkers following his brothers. That could wait. In the meanwhile, he'd just watch and see what developed. For a place seldom traveled by white men, the Jornada del Muerto was fast becoming a thoroughfare. It made him wonder who'd be coming next.

Chupta rode back. The desert alone was a forbidding place, but he felt at home on it and even more at home by himself. At one point he'd been more than five miles in front of the party; now he'd shorten up his lead. The last thing he wanted was for someone to slip in between him and the people following him. He needed to make sure the group's back trail was clear. He hadn't known Joe long enough to be sure the man knew what to do. Zac had great confidence in his brother, but for Chupta, trust was something to be earned. It must be proven by a white. All too often he'd seen them distracted by things that didn't matter much. All it took to draw their eyes away from what they should be looking at was a coyote, a fox, or some new sight they'd overlooked for their entire lives. The white man never emptied his cup. He always sat it down with water still in it and then he'd reach for another. His eyes were never full.

Chupta rode up to the group. Joe was in the middle of the pack, and the woman and her Mexican caballeros were in the lead. The man called Gaucho snarled at him. "Where you go to? You go off and sleep somewheres?" The burly, bearded man pulled out a mixture of tobacco and, opening the pouch, proceeded to sprinkle some of it onto a small piece of paper.

Chupta's face hardened. He would not answer craziness, and that from a man who seemed so desperate to be seen as a fool. There was a hatred in the man for the Indian, an insanity that crowded out thought.

Joe had spotted Chupta and rode up just as the Mexican struck a match on his thumbnail and held it to his newly made cigarette.

Joe jerked the smoke from Gaucho's mouth and crushed the glowing end onto the man's leather vest. "You tryin' to get us killed?" With that, he flipped the extinguished butt into the air.

Gaucho was livid with rage. To have his cigarette taken away was one thing, but to have it put out on his vest was another, especially by a gringo. He snarled, and his hand dropped down to his gunbelt. Before he could bring the revolver up, he found himself staring into the business end of Joe's Colt. He froze in place.

"Now just you slack on back and relax," Joe said. "You've been fool enough for one night. Don't go to makin' yerself a dead one. Anybody out there coulda seen that cigarette for ten miles and smelled it for five."

Señora Escobar kicked her horse forward. "My men are not children, señor," she said.

"They ain't my children, but they seem to be yours. You best be keeping a tight eye on them. Friends can kill you quicker than an enemy out here. Many's a time when a man will let a friend's weak-mindedness pass just because of misplaced compassion. That ain't my problem, and I don't intend to start now."

"I was lighting a smoke, señora," Gaucho said.

"You were livin' in nonsense," Joe replied. He turned to Rosalyn, whose eyes were dancing with amusement. "We came along with you to offer our protection, and now I can see why that was necessary."

Turning his head, he surveyed the big Mexican cowboy as the man slid his partially extracted revolver back into his holster. "We don't need no fire, no noise, no shootin', and very little talk. Am I understood?" Joe ordered.

"Perfectly, señor," Rosalyn said.

The two other Mexicans had gathered around them, forming a menacing phalanx. It was plain to see that the idea of a gringo giving out orders bothered them. "Who put you in command?" Gaucho asked.

"Somebody needs to be in charge. I've seen what you can do when given your head," Joe shot back. "With you on your own, you ain't gonna last outta tomorrow. This ain't your ranch we're riding over. It's a place where people die."

Joe holstered his revolver and, sitting forward in his saddle, stared directly at the beautiful Rosalyn. "Señora, it's your call. James, Chupta, and me can turn around and make our way back to Santa Fe. Probably should anyhow. But we ain't stayin' the course less'n I'm in charge. I ain't about to make my wife a widow 'cause of foolishness. So, you say your piece and we'll go on from here."

Rosalyn looked at the men surrounding them, tension in their eyes. The call was hers. "I am sorry for the misunderstanding, and I will take full responsibility. You are in charge, Señor Cobb, until we meet my husband's men. They are soldiers, and I think you should have no fear once we have found them."

"All right, fair enough by me. I don't cotton to being in command unless I have to be, and until we meet up with your husband's men I reckon I have to be. These men of yours understand that? Is it clear to them?"

"Gaucho?" Rosalyn looked at the man, expecting an answer.

"Sí, señora. The men and I will do as you ask, but only until we meet with the general's troops."

"Fine," Joe said. "Then no more smoking."

Chupta had remained out of the line of fire, and James and Palmira rode up to see the hullabaloo. "What seems to be the problem?" James asked.

"No problem," Joe said. "We just had to get ourselves fixed on smoking."

"I shouldn't think that would be a wise idea at night," James said.

"You think right." Joe turned his glance to Chupta. "You see anything we'd be wise to swing 'round?"

Chupta nodded. "We go west for a ways." He motioned with his hand toward the place the sun had set hours before. "It be best."

"Now why is that?" Rosalyn inquired. "My husband's men are waiting due south. If we ride out of our way, it will take us much longer."

"He must have seen something," Joe said. "What did you spot out there?" Joe was beginning to learn that the Apache scout was a man of few words. To get the whole story out of him, a man had to ask direct questions.

"Chupta see strange wagon and empty camp."

"Humph," Gaucho rasped. "If no one is there, there is no need to bother."

"Maybe the Indians have taken them off," James said.

Chupta shook his head. "Mescalero come."

"How do you know that?" Gaucho asked.

"I see tracks of Indian pony leading off two mules. Lone rider come, take mules, and he be back with more braves for wagon."

"What about the people?" Palmira asked.

"People walk west, try to find river."

"Then if those Indians follow them, we'll run right into them," James said.

"No, Chupta rub out tracks. They not see them tonight. Mescalero come and steal from wagon. Then they burn it. When sun come over mountains, they begin look for whites. If we ride fast, we can get around them before people found."

"We can't leave those people out here on foot," Palmira said. "They're all alone and defenseless."

"I think we'd better do as Chupta here reckons best," Joe said. "We might meet up with them yet, and we just want to make sure we don't come upon the Mescalero."

CHAPTER 9

+ + + + + + +

ELLIE WATCHED HER FATHER stumble in the sand and fall, spilling the rifles he held in both hands. It broke her heart to see him so helpless. "You all right, Papa?" All of her memories were of a strong, horselike man who endured great pain and came out still standing tall. He'd never been one to show pain or fear. A soul of steel, he had always defied the odds with nary a whimper. She knew his refusal to show emotion was partially the reason he lived with the anguish of her mother's death on a constant basis.

"By the blazes, some of dem rocks don't no ways show." He picked himself up and, reaching down, once again took hold of the rifles. They started walking southwest again.

Watching her father limp, Ellie could tell he'd banged his knee, but she knew he'd never admit to it, so it would do no good to ask. It was the way he was. It had always been his way. There had been times when she'd find him staring off into a sunset. She knew his mind was locked onto a scene with her mother, remembering back. Just to look at him a body could tell he wanted to cry in the worst way, but the tears would never come. He made it a habit of changing the subject whenever he spotted her watching him—usually to a topic neither of them cared much to talk about. It was just talk, words to hide his feelings.

"When do you think the sun will come up, Papa?"

Craning his neck toward the sky and then looking back at the mountains, he nodded. "I'd spect in a few hours. We gots to make us some time though, afore it does."

"Do you think they'll come looking for us?"

"I surely do. After they go and smash my clocks, put on dem women's undergarments, shout and scream 'bout dem rifles, and burn the wagon, they'll light out after us lickety-split."

"But they won't find us, will they?"

"I'm afraid they'll find us, all right. Dem folks is real good lookers. I seen one track a coyote 'cross bare rock afore." He shook his head. "They'll find us if'n they wants to."

"Then what are we going to do?"

"We got one of two options. We can keep on goin' and head as fast as we can for the river, might take us a day, and we'd be out in plain view in the heat."

"That doesn't sound good."

"No, it don't, and they'd be 'spectin' us to do that. Most white folks run like scared rabbits among 'em and fer good reason."

"What else could we do?"

"We can find us a spot to hide out when the sun breaks over the mountains back yonder, somewheres where there's some shade and a place for to die if'n they does find us."

"Well, I'm not ready to die yet, Papa. I haven't even started to live."

"Most folks don't got a lot of choice 'bout where they'ze birthed or where they drop."

"Maybe not, but just as long as it's God that does the choosing and not my own foolishness, then I'll be satisfied."

"Whether it's God, some disease, or your own boneheadedness, you're dead all the same."

The subject of death had come up periodically since her mother's passing, and her father had always treated it with philosophic pessimism. She knew full well that it wasn't just death he was talking about when he did. It was her mother's death. There was a constant brooding about the matter, even in his laughter—and if he could have, he would have shaken his finger in the face of God. He was a Christian man, but his familiarity with the Bible and with what he knew to be true served only to make him more bitter. To her father, her mother's death had been like the betrayal of a good friend, a never forgotten stab in the back by a trusted ally. No amount of preaching and no amount of reading and praying had been able to shake it, and she knew she couldn't.

"Papa, you make your own decision."

"All right. You be to lookin' fer a spot where we can settle in to, someplace we can get us a good field of fire. We might just be able to discourage 'em a mite if they do find us."

The night sky blazed with stars overhead, and the flat area they trudged over was marked by small plateaus in the distance. They were like tables of rock spread out on the desert floor. Each one could offer a commanding view of the playa, but they were hard for two people to defend alone. It would be easy for a group of attackers to circle around and come on them from the rear. No, they had to find a better place than that.

Ellie followed him at a distance. That was the way it was between them. There had always been a distance. She couldn't remember a hug or a kiss that had ever passed between them. Her mother always told her that it was the way of Norwegian men. They didn't show their feelings on the outside or express their emotions. Mother would say, "It doesn't mean he doesn't love you, dear. He shows you he loves you when he makes something for you. When he goes out into the fields every morning, he's telling us that he loves us."

It was Ellie's mother who hugged and kissed her. She was a Yankee—a Norwegian same as her father, but one born in America, not Norway. Her mother would tell her that the disease of consumption in Norway had taught the children there not to touch each other for fear of catching it. Mother had done her best to explain Ellie's father to her, but Ellie missed the hugging most.

They trudged forward across the sandy grass, each step making their feet heavier. Ellie watched her father as he deliberately picked up one foot after the other, his shoulders bent low as if a heavy load were crushing him underneath it. He had grown old before her eyes, no longer the strapping man of her childhood. Brush and creosote studded the desert sand, snagging their breeches from time to time as they waddled through it in the darkness.

"Do you think we could stop for a bit?" Ellie asked. "Some food would do me a lot of good."

"We dassen't stop, girl, not till we find ourselves a place. We got lots of ground to cover afore that sun comes up, open seeable space. We lose ourselves some time and get caught out in a spot that dem injuns can see and we're dead sure nuff."

She was much more concerned about him than herself, but she could never show it. To make him actually do something for his own good, she'd have to convince him it was for her. The man was stubborn as a bent nail, but he did love her. She knew that.

The flat area, that from a distance appeared to have no hills or valleys at all, was actually very broken ground when a person worked on crossing it on foot. They stumbled down the sides of a small draw, kicking rocks loose and sending a shower of loose sand down the hill in front of them. It was plain to see that anyone would be able to follow them if they knew the first thing about where to look.

"Papa, it's going to be easy to follow us. As tired as we are, we're not being very careful with where we're stepping."

They climbed out of the draw, scratching on the ground for any leverage to pull them up. The sand was soft, and the grass grew in bunches.

It made it easy to grab a handful of well-rooted grass, like taking hold of a man's hair in a wrestling match. They pulled themselves up from the draw and staggered out onto the playa.

He stopped at the edge of the long hole and, bending over, put his hands on his knees, panting. He was breathing hard now, and Ellie knew it was not the time for her to suggest a rest. To do so would mean that the man would go on until they both dropped.

He looked back at their path through the draw. "Nah," he gasped, "we ain't doing a very good job coverin' up our tracks. 'Course, we ain't zackly goin' where they'd be supposin' to look." He pointed behind them. "They'd figure us either to meander north to Santa Fe or direct west to the Rio Grande. What they wouldn't figure was on us going southwest. A man would be a fool to do that, sure 'nuff. There ain't no water out here and no place to go but that old abandoned army fort. We'll jes' hope they run off tomorrow lookin' in the wrong place, and that by the time they pick up our trail it'll be dark again and we can head back out."

Ellie reached out and took hold of his arm. "That's a good plan, Papa." She beamed at him, genuinely proud.

"I ain't gonna try and get us kilt. I still got myself some tricks up my sleeve." He pointed in the distance. "Let's head off to that tabletop and look around. We could hold up there. I could shinny up top and look about from time to time, and then we could hunker down in the shade. There ain't much of it 'round here, and if we're to find some, that'd be a likely place."

Silently, the two of them moved on into the night. A soft breeze with a hint of moisture in it blew from the south. The best they could hope for was a summer monsoon to blow up and catch them. That would be a blessed relief. Ellie was sorry that she had brought only one canteen. She hadn't been thinking. If it did rain, she'd have to find a way to drain some water down into the narrow opening. Trying to figure out how to store fresh rainwater was a problem she'd love to have. Water was precious, and they had so very little of it left.

They walked for over an hour before he stopped. They were getting closer to the tabletop hill they'd been making for. Her father, much to her surprise, had been walking much more quickly. It was as if discussing his plans had given him some hope. Ellie knew full well that hope was the thing that kept all people going when things looked bleak. When she walked up to him, however, his eyes were blank. He had turned and was staring back at the direction they'd come from. "What's wrong, Papa?"

Silently, he lifted his arm, pointing back.

Ellie turned. She could see a faint glow in the distance, a twinkling bright light. "What's that?"

He stood there stunned and took a deep, dry swallow. "That's our wagon, everything we have in the world."

Joe drifted back when the group started west. They were turning, following Chupta's idea of avoiding trouble with the Mescalero. It would be a good time to check their back trail and make sure they weren't being followed. Anyone who had been tailing them wouldn't need to keep much of an eye to the ground to keep heading south, but with them swinging west, he wanted to make sure no one would follow.

He walked the blood bay around the hill where they'd stopped to talk and gingerly picked his way around the hill to the north. Being skylined against the moon-soaked hilltop was no way to stay healthy. Pulling up near the bottom of the hill, he watched and waited.

From where he sat, the north star hung low in the sky and behind it lay Santa Fe, now more than a day and a night's ride away. The night was a lonely time on the desert, and he wanted to keep it just that way. It would be plenty easy for Indians to track them to a spot where they could start an attack, and with a group of Indians behind them, they'd be caught in the cross fire. That was a situation he didn't want to face. No, he wanted to make sure the land around them was lonely and bare.

Pulling the reins on the bay, Joe started around to the opposite side of the hill. It was the side the party hadn't taken, and anyone who might be following them would take their path. He just didn't want to be in the same spot they had already tracked across. When he reached the other side of the sandy hill, he dropped the reins on the bay and sat passively. He'd known how to be still since he'd been a boy hunting his first deer. His father had told him that deer were color-blind, and if he just froze when he saw them, they'd think he was a very strange tree. He'd stop and watch until they once again began feeding, then he'd move closer until they lifted their heads again. That way, if a feller was patient, he'd get the best shot he could and would take no chances of wasting a bullet. Ammunition was precious, and a body had better bring back game for each round spent.

He'd been taught well. There were things a boy learned that he never forgot, and staying still was one of them. Somehow, in times like this, he could almost feel his father standing next to him, watching. It gave him some comfort. If there was one thing a man always needed, it was the boy inside of him. Lessons taught when one was too young to know the cruelties of the outside world were so much more innocent and pure.

As he started to turn around and catch up to the group, he heard a noise. It was a slight noise, but unmistakable, the sound of a spur. Backing the bay up, he waited.

As he watched, three riders emerged from around the hill. They were obviously following the tracks laid down by the group. The man in the lead occasionally swung low to continue to pick up their path. Joe was in the shadow of the small hill, and he didn't think he could be seen, but in the bright moonlight he could see them very well. They appeared to be a salty lot and well armed.

Quietly dismounting, he slid out the Winchester from the boot of his saddle. Slowly and noiselessly, he cocked the rifle and hammered a round into the chamber. He moved discreetly around the back of the sandy hill. If they were going to follow the tracks laid down for them, he was going to make sure he was there to greet them when they cleared the other side. Finding a large rock, he waited.

Moments later, he watched them round the hill, counting them as they came into view. Their eyes were on the ground in front of them. They weren't expecting anything or anyone to be waiting for them.

Joe stepped out and held the Winchester straight. "That's far enough."

The men pulled rein, startled.

"I wouldn't make any sudden moves," Joe snapped, "or I'm gonna empty some saddles right here."

"Hey there, not so fast." The lead rider was jarred, and his hands went up. "We don't mean nobody no harm."

"You let me be the judge of that—the judge and the jury. Now who are you, and why are you following us?"

The man swallowed hard, and Joe could see he was searching his brain for an explanation. "Name's Torrie, and this here's Web and Yuma. We're miners headin' down to Silver City, and what with the 'pache hereabouts, we figured it'd be lots safer to travel with folks, that's all."

Joe watched one of the men, a man with an angry scar on his cheek, inch his hand down to his side. He lifted the rifle higher. "You just keep those hands on the pommel of that saddle and don't give me cause to bed you down right here."

"Easy, Yuma," Torrie said. "This feller 'pears to be an understanding sort. He'll see our case." Turning back to Joe, he let a mouth full of white teeth shine through his black beard. "We're jest looking to ride with some other folks. Pays to be careful out here."

The man called Web spoke up. He had large ears that stood out like the doors on a carriage and a nose the size of the Texas panhandle, and when he grinned, everything on his face stood to attention. "Mister, we sure don't mean you no harm. We gots our own grub and plenty of water too. We wouldn't be askin' fer no favors, just to stay alive a mite longer if'n we should meet up with them Mescalero."

There was nothing about these men that looked like miners. The guns they wore showed they made their living with them. Joe thought the matter over. If Chupta hadn't reported on the wagon and the sign of approaching trouble, he'd have turned them away right then and there.

"All right, we'll talk it over with the rest. I want you in front of me, though, all the way. My horse is on the other side of the hill. You just step lightly around me and ride on. Just remember, I hit what I aim at, and right now I'm aiming at you."

The three men walked their horses to the other side of the hill and Joe followed with the rifle aimed at their backs. These men were trouble, that was plain to see. It remained to be seen whose trouble they were, but at least until they met up with the promised troops at old Fort Craig, three more guns would come in handy.

Reaching the bay, Joe swung onto the saddle, waving the rifle in the direction of the three strangers. "All right, you're so good at following our sign, lead on."

The four of them trotted in the direction of the trail laid down before them, Joe in the rear. He could see at a glance that the horses they rode were of the expensive variety, not at all like miners heading off to a hole in the ground. They might or might not be who they claimed to be, but there was nothing about them that verified their story.

A short time later, the four of them caught up with the group. Chupta was out, scouting ahead, and right then Joe wished him here. He trusted the man's instincts. The sight of the four of them brought the entire group to a stop. The three Mexican riders who worked for the Escobars seemed wary. James glowed with a quizzical grin. He always liked surprises.

"See what I found following us," Joe said. "They claim to be miners riding to Silver City and looking for protection."

"Wonderful," James exclaimed. "With what this scout of ours reported, these men could be quite useful."

James's remark made the three strangers exchange glances and smile.

The three Mexican riders began an animated conversation in Spanish. "And what do you think, Señor Cobb?" Rosalyn asked.

"I think the only thing worse than an enemy outside the camp is one on the inside." Joe looked them over. "They look like no miners I've ever seen, and they were following our trail pretty close. This ain't no accidental meeting. They are well armed, but that's a two-edged sword. With what Chupta reported we could come onto a situation where we might need their help. It's a dicey deal, ma'am. It's your party, though, and your daughter riding with us."

Torrie spoke up, "I like a plain-speaking man, señora, a man who tells you his mind. We're well armed for our protection out here, and we certainly mean you no harm. A body does get a might nervous with what we've heard about the Mescalero 'round these parts. We'd have no cause to do you harm, though. That would leave us unprotected, now wouldn't it?"

"I say let them come with us," James said. "Might liven things up a bit."

Yuma took a long look at him. In spite of James's voiced support, it was plain to see an expression of contempt cross the man's face. Easterners often wore their welcome out with men from the West, and with one glance Yuma had evaluated the professor with the Southern dialect.

Rosalyn studied the men. "We will have no cause for worry once we find my husband's men, and every cause for concern until we do. I'm willing to take the risk."

"Why, thank you, ma'am," Web said, sweeping his hat off his head. "You won't be sorry."

"We keep to our own supplies and water," Torrie added. "We won't be a burden or a bother."

"Understand this," Joe added. "Until we find the men we're lookin' for, I'm in charge. What I say goes."

"I figured that." Torrie grinned.

The group began to move out, and Joe drifted back to ride with James. He spoke softly. "You just need to make sure you keep these men in your sight at all times. They aren't who they claim to be."

CHAPTER 10

SEVERAL HOURS LATER, the group ground to a halt. Chupta had ridden on ahead with Joe to survey the grassy plateau area. Visibility would be good there for quite some distance, and both of them wanted to fan out and make sure they weren't being watched. Such a large group of riders would be easily spotted, and they wouldn't be hard to follow, either, especially for the Mescalero. Once they joined up with Señora Escobar's waiting troops they'd be safe enough, but that wouldn't happen for some time yet.

James kept up a steady conversation with Palmira, pointing out the stars. "It may be hard for us to imagine, but the stars in the heavens are much different below the equator. It may seem like the same earth, but the heavens are unique."

"You have been there?" she asked.

"I have visited Australia and some of the islands of the South Seas. There is a mysterious beauty to the land and the people there."

"I would love to go to places like that."

"You would love it, my dear—trees with leaves as large as a woman's dress and nuts the size of a man's head."

Yuma grunted.

"It sounds wonderful," Palmira said.

"Travel broadens the mind. A man can tend to believe that the ground he walks on is the world as it exists, but it isn't. We are mere visitors here on this earth and small ones at that."

"Many times I've read books about places like that, but in my mind they seemed so unreal and so very far away. I would love to travel," she said.

"And you should, my dear, you should. Beauty like yours should be seen by men all over the world. Their admiration would merely add to the grandeur you would find there."

Gaucho held up his hand to stop the group in the foothills. He canvassed the flat area just ahead and, as Joe had instructed him, brought the group to a complete stop. "We wait here," he rasped in a loud whisper.

One by one, each of them struggled to the ground. James gently helped the young Palmira off her horse.

"Now, ain't we got us the gentleman here!" Yuma mocked.

Torrie and Web rumbled with laughter. "A body finds all kinda folk here in the desert," Torrie said.

"Maybe I can get him to pull off my boots and rub my feet for me," Yuma snarled. "I sure could use myself some tender touchin', couldn't you, boys?"

James ignored the remark. "Hours in the saddle can make one long for the ground." He smiled at Palmira. "A little rest will do us all good."

"Don't think the man heard you, Yuma," Web said.

"Oh, he heard me, all right. He's just trying real hard not to have himself showed up in front of the lady, ain't that right, Mr. Smarty Pants?"

James turned his head, staring at the man. "Are you addressing me, sir?"

"Yer the only smarty pants I see out here," Yuma said. "I been listenin' to your palaver fer over an hour now and I'm plumb fed up with it."

"Perhaps you should make an attempt to understand the words."

"I don't need no smart words."

"Ignorance need not be a source of pride for any man, I should think."

The man shot to his feet, his arms braced by his side. "You callin' me ignorant?"

"My good man, all of us are born ignorant. Fortunately for our society, few of us take pride in remaining there."

Torrie laughed, stretching out on the ground. "Yep, I think our teacher man here thinks you ain't got no smarts." The bearded man cocked his head and stared up at James. " 'Course, without that brother of his to back his play, I'd say he was the dumb one right about now. That right, teacher man? You gonna tattle on us to that brother of yours?"

"Sir, you forget. I am the one who insisted on your accompanying us. Had I any fear of you whatsoever, I wouldn't have suggested it. Given your situation and the pity I felt for you, I could do no less."

"Man's got a point there," Web smirked.

"Well," Yuma barked, "if'n I'da known I'd have to put up with all that yammerin' 'bout them stars and such, I wouldn't have wanted to come."

"Education is free to the ignorant, but costly for the fool."

"What do ya mean by that?" Yuma asked.

"Ignorant men can learn. It's the fool that shuns knowledge to his own shame and harm. When he does understand, he does so at the cost of bruises and bumps and usually at the hand of a man with greater intelligence."

Yuma took a step toward him. "Mr. Smarty Pants, I ain't about to learn nothing at your hand. You ain't man enough."

James chuckled. "Well, it does appear that the man who used that knife on your face taught you very little. Perhaps you need further instruction."

James unbuttoned his sleeves and rolled them neatly up his arm. Torrie got to his feet and suddenly blocked Yuma with his arm. He nodded in the direction of the dark plain in front of them. There in the darkness, they could make out the form of two riders. It was Chupta and Joe.

Torrie pushed the lanky man back. "Guess you're gonna haf to wait a spell to give the teacher here a lickin'. Seems like that brother of his is coming back."

James unbuckled his gunbelt and neatly folded it before he laid it down. "I shouldn't think that would bother you gentlemen. Lessons learned in public seem to be of a most permanent nature."

Yuma strained against Torrie's arm. "That be enough. Let me at him."

Joe and Chupta rode up and stepped out of their saddles. "What seems to be the trouble?" Joe asked.

"Ain't no trouble," Torrie said. "My man Yuma here was jest getting himself a might frayed with all them words coming outta yer brother's yapper."

Joe chuckled. "I'm afraid it's been a curse of the Cobb household as long as I can remember. There ain't much any of us have been able to do about it, though."

"Well, I sure can." Yuma spat out the words.

"You think so?" Joe smiled.

"That seems to be the man's problem," James said. "He supposes a matter without a great deal of thought."

Torrie held Yuma back as he hunched toward James.

"Well," Joe said, directing his gaze at Torrie, "why don't you just take the man's knife and gunbelt off, and then we'll just let you cut your dog loose. This might be an interesting thing to see."

Yuma quickly dropped his gunbelt and, drawing his knife out of the scabbard, threw it into the sand.

Palmira grabbed Joe's arm. "Please, señor, this is not a thing to do. Your brother is a gentleman, and this other man is a fighter."

Joe patted her hand. "Oh, in a fair fight, señorita, the professor here might just surprise you. 'Sides, if the stranger yonder has a burr under his saddle, might just be best that we settle it here and now."

James hiked his sleeves farther up his arms. He squared himself at the lanky man and held both hands up in a classical boxing position. "Let the lesson begin, sir. I am at your disposal and prepared to teach."

Yuma rushed at him, arms extended. James deftly moved aside, delivering a sharp blow behind the man's ear and sending him sprawling to the ground.

James danced around, facing his fallen foe. "The first lesson of the evening, my good man, is that a boxer can best a wrestler at will. The ancient Greeks discovered this in their Olympic games, and had you been paying attention to my first lecture, you would have discovered the truth of what I taught."

Yuma got to his feet, and James looked at Palmira, still clinging to Joe's arm. "Have no fear, my dear. Some men of wisdom learn their lessons vicariously, while others must absorb knowledge having passed through the fire."

Yuma moved closer. He took several wild Herculean swings, all of which James avoided by quickly moving his head back and then side to side.

"Now we begin lesson two," James said matter-of-factly. He started a series of left jabs into the tall man's jaw, snapping the man's head back with a succession of sudden impacts. Slowing the blows down, he began to talk in between each jab. "This," he snapped a left into the man's face, "is a left jab." He laced another swift, catlike punch into the surprised man's jaw. "It is designed to confuse a man with its suddenness. As you can see," he continued his series of strikes, "it doesn't require a man to telegraph his blows."

Yuma staggered back, fighting to keep his footing.

"And now we shall begin lesson number three." James smiled.

Joe patted Palmira's hand. "You see, James here is the boxing coach at his college. He does that along with teaching English literature. He talks a great deal, but unlike a lot of men, he knows what he's saying."

James signaled Yuma forward. "Come along, my good man. I wouldn't want you to miss a single lecture. The tuition is much too expensive for you to be skipping class."

Yuma stepped forward, his eyes filled with rage. He hadn't managed to land a single blow, something he planned to correct. "Why don't you just stand still and fight like a man, not some sissy."

"Why, sir, I don't think you understand. The *man* here will be the one left standing." With that he continued his barrage of left jabs, each one stinging Yuma with suddenness.

"Lesson three is much different," James passively went on. "When you have an opponent leery of your jabs"—he swung from belt level, delivering a swift blow to the man's solar plexus—"you take his wind away."

Yuma reeled backward, landing sharply on his bony backside.

James dropped his hands slightly, looking the man over. "For many a neophyte, such a beating would be more than enough. But I suspect our man here will require lesson number four. Pride combined with ignorance always seems to take a man much further than he should ever venture."

Yuma crawled in James's direction. "I think I'm through." He writhed closer. "You done got me beat."

With surprising speed, his hand shot out, sweeping James's feet out from under him. Scrambling to his feet, he ran toward James.

James braced himself on the ground with his elbows, watching the charging man. Suddenly lifting his feet, he caught the man's headfirst dive, pitching him overhead and sending him sprawling into the darkness. Getting to his feet, James dusted himself off. "Now where were we? Oh yes, like I said, a man of this nature requires lesson number four." Motioning to Yuma as he got to his feet, James's voice was calm. "Step forward, my good man. Class hasn't been dismissed quite yet, and you are not excused."

Yuma staggered forward into the semicircle. Torrie motioned him onward.

"I gotta see this here lesson four." Web smirked.

"First, we will need a quick review," James said. He motioned Yuma toward him. "Lesson number one was the prohibition against wrestling an opponent. You've just seen that demonstrated once again. Lesson number two was the jab." Once again, James sent a series of swift jabs into Yuma's face, snapping his head back with each blow.

"Lesson three was the body blow." With that James unleashed a sharp blow once again into Yuma's midsection. The blow made the man bow slightly forward. "Lesson three makes number four quite easy."

Uncoiling a wicked uppercut, James launched a right directly into the man's chin. The force of the blow sent a sound of bone and teeth into the air and dropped Yuma like a dead man in the middle of the group.

"And that, my friends, is lesson number four, the uppercut with the right. It is quite effective."

James backed away and dropped his hands to his side. "There are many other lessons in the sport of boxing, but I'm afraid my opponent here is not quite up to them. I believe class is dismissed."

"I think it is." Joe grinned. He motioned toward Torrie. "I think you better load your man onto his horse. We'd splash some water onto him, but we ain't got none to spare."

Moments later the group started off over the grassy plain. Clouds were forming overhead, and there was a smell of rain in the air. The mountains to the east took on a blackness, like the dark towers of some foreboding race of giants. They formed a surreal barrier, shadows of fear amid a vast expanse of silence.

Chupta rode on ahead, and Palmira trotted her horse up to James's side. "You were wonderful back there. Somehow, I never pictured you as a fighter."

"I'm not a fighter. I'm a teacher, and what I did back there was cruel."

"Cruel? I don't understand. That man desired trouble."

"True enough. He had it coming, too, but not from me. I know too much to be doing what I did back there, and the man was probably right. Had you not been there and were I not predisposed to impressing you, I wouldn't have given in to my vanity. I'm afraid it's a serious weakness with me and one I'll endeavor not to repeat."

She shook her head. "I'm afraid I'll never understand you Americans. My father would never hesitate to do what you did, had he been able, nor would any man I've ever known."

"I suppose that makes me quite different from the men you've known. Strength is something that need never be shown. It's enough in the mind of a man to know that he has it and needs never to use it, especially for his own narcissism and arrogance."

"You are very strange, señor."

James shook his head. "No, my dear, not strange. I am a moral man with a conscience. What I did back there was akin to whipping a large child for my own sport, not something to commend me. In that sense, you and I are much alike."

She looked puzzled. "I'm sorry, I don't understand."

James looked at her with a serious look on his face. "You are a woman of great beauty. Where men are concerned, that attractiveness is a weapon, and yet you choose not to use it. To do so would take unfair advantage of mindless men."

She bowed her head. "At times I hate my looks. I see men watching me, and it is all too easy to toy with them. I feel like a prisoner trapped by my own mirror. If a man truly cared about me as a person, I would never know it. For many I could simply become someone like my mother, an attractive ornament to own and show. Do you think I will ever know what it means to be loved for what is inside of me, the part that no man can see?"

"Yes, Palmira. The fact that such a thought enters your head shows your true beauty. Someday a man will come into your life who sees your value as a friend first. This is the man that you must love."

"Could you be that man, señor?"

James paused, a thoughtful pause that had the young woman waiting for the answer. "I might be. Heaven knows I would like to be. Friendship takes time, however, and it takes trust. It is like a flower whose petals you must watch open. It cannot be pulled apart."

"I want you to trust me. You know that I was sent here to attract you to come home with us. It didn't have to be you. It could have been any of you three brothers. It didn't matter."

"I know that."

"You do? How?"

"I may be many things, but I am not a fool."

Suddenly, Chupta came riding in a fast gallop back into the group, signaling them to dismount.

"What's wrong?" Joe asked.

"Mescalero," Chupta said.

The men gathered and watched Chupta point in the distance. There, along the horizon, a group of riders rode in spread-out formation. They were small dark shapes against the stormy sky, barely visible to the eye.

"They look for people of the wagon," Chupta said.

It was then that the first of the rain began to fall.

CHAPTER 11

"DID YOU HEAR THAT?" Ellie asked the question with an ear cocked in the direction of the opening. The place in the rocks they had found could have hardly been called a cave. It was simply a slice of hard-packed clay eroded into a deep gash in the face of the dry mesa. Boulders flanked the entrance, and the spots of heavy runoff were about six feet into the side of the tabletop plateau. They both had their backs to the darkened clay wall. Ellie's arms were wrapped around her knees, and once again she had begun rocking back and forth. Oscar lay stretched out, his feet almost to the entrance of the hiding place.

"Hear what?"

"That!" She perked up at the sound of the low rumble in the distance, rocking forward to her knees. "I think that's thunder."

"Yer just hearing stuff, girl."

The distant noise murmured once again, jerking him into a sitting position. "By jiminy, Ellie girl, I believe you're right."

At that moment, the first few drops of the approaching storm glanced off the rocks. They landed with small thuds on the packed and parched ground—first a few, then a smattering of drops. The beating of the sudden sprinkle broke the stillness of the night. With the sound of marching drummers, the drops hit the dusty ground outside the hideaway.

Oscar got to his feet. Stepping outside into the sandy grass, he held his hands up, arms outstretched. Ellie watched as he lifted his head skyward. A broad smile crossed his face as he blinked the rain back from his eyes. "Thank you, Lord." His voice was gritty, like a rake being drug across loose gravel.

He raised his voice slightly to speak over the falling rain. "We got to catch some of this fer that canteen of ours." Leaning back toward Ellie, he pointed to the wall behind her. "Maybe you could take in some of the runoff that comes down back yonder."

"Yes, Papa. You reckon this rain will wash out our tracks?"

"I suppose it just might at that, girl." He raised his hands to the sky again. "This here be the providence of God, sure 'nuff."

With those words he spun around, keeping his hands in the air. He was like a child at Christmastime, beaming a smile from ear to ear, delirious with joy. It amazed her to see him so thankful for such a simple thing as rain. There was emotion inside of him after all—deep, pent-up feelings surfacing in spite of his efforts to bury them. Getting to her hands and knees, she crawled out of the tight space.

"I think it will be a while yet before we see any runoff," she said.

He blinked his eyes at her. He was still much too happy to see anything but the joy of the moment. Given a simple rainstorm, he'd forgotten that he'd just lost everything in the world, everything that he'd given years to build.

"Won't it have to rain much harder to wipe out our tracks?" she asked.

The thought brought him back down to earth. He dropped his hands to his side and walked to where the mesa spilled out onto the plain. The darkness of the desert flashed with lightning, fiery fingers erupting from the dark clouds. In the distance, empty washes pockmarked the desert. The black mountains turned a deep purple with each flash of lightning.

The life of the sky made the desert seem even more lonely. This was a time the entire place waited for, a time of rainfall. Listening to the silence of the land, one almost got the impression that every creature waited breathlessly for the rain to fall, afraid to stir. They waited in holes in the earth, watching for the heavens to part and the life-giving rain to keep them alive. There was a tension to the land, a flexed muscle coiled to drink its fill.

He took a long look across the flat desert as the lightning flashed. He did a double take, leaning into the darkness with his whole body. Turning abruptly, he ran back to where Ellie stood. His eyes were wild. "I think I saw something move out yonder."

"Are you sure, Papa? The lightning can play tricks with your eyes, you know."

"No, I'm sure. I guess this rain didn't fall near soon enough."

The suddenness of the strike took them by surprise. They heard the gravel shift on the slope of the mesa first and then, like a bird of prey dropping sharp talons into the back of a frightened rabbit, an Indian jumped to the ground, knife flashing in his hand. The man was small with spindly legs. He had a powerful chest, larger than normal for a man of his height. His rifle was slung behind his back. He brandished the blade back and forth, his eyes riveted on Ellie and Oscar.

The rain came down harder. Oscar pushed Ellie behind him. "Get me my rifle."

Joe and his group heard the sound of the gunfire. The first shot startled them. The Mexican cowboys walked forward to get a better view. James and Palmira circled around the horses and stopped to watch the dark plateau where the shot had come from. Minutes later they heard the eruption of other shots, first a few, then many. Joe watched the flashes of gunfire light up the side of the blackened plateau with pinpricks of manmade lightning, while overhead the thunder continued to crack.

"Them people catching it down there," Gaucho said.

"Yes, I'm afraid they are," Rosalyn agreed.

Joe swung up onto his saddle. "Well, we can't just sit here and watch it. We got to go down there and get them folks' bacon outta the fire."

Rosalyn walked up to him, putting her hand on his leg. "Señor, this is their concern, not ours."

"Ma'am, if my brother and I had felt that way, we'd still be in Santa Fe, 'stead of here with you."

James was already in his saddle. He trotted up to Joe. Joe motioned to the three men who had joined them. "Okay, boys, let's go. We don't have much time to lose." He looked at the cowboys. "We could use you three hombres, too."

Rosalyn kept after him, shaking her head. "This is crazy. You will give away our position."

"Señora, Fort Craig is only a day off. We can drive the Mescalero off here and be halfway there before they regroup and figure out what they're up against. Now, if the eight of us men just fan out and ride down there shooting, we'd have them peeled off and running like scalded dogs before we got to within shooting range. If we sit here and do nothing they'll find our trail. Then they'll come up behind us and bring us down one at a time. Now you can do what you want, but personally I'd rather take things on noggin to noggin."

Gaucho looked at Rosalyn. "Señora?"

"Yes," she said. "Go ahead."

The men saddled up, accompanied by the sound of creaking leather. Drawing their rifles out, they rammed ammunition into the chambers, the rounds popping into place with an almost businesslike sound. Joe pointed down at the valley below. "Now, they don't know we're here, and they durn sure don't know how many of us there are. We keep spread out and fire shots in the air as we ride down there, and they just might figure us to be a company of Yankee horse soldiers."

The men grunted and nodded.

"You do plenty of shootin' and yellin' on our way down there, and they'll be hightailed out of there afore we ever get in range. Ladies, I want you to follow along. When we get about halfway, you light out behind us. I don't want you sittin' here in case they circle 'round us."

He slapped his spurs to the side of his horse, bolting forward into the dark stormy plain. Firing a shot into the air, he gave out a bloodcurdling Rebel yell. The formation of men on either side of him began a series of screams punctuated by shots into the air. They rode at a gallop.

The shooting near the mesa suddenly stopped, and in the distance Joe could see the disappearing figures by the glare of the blazing lightning. It was a fearful sight; men swooping out of the darkness, yelling at the top of their lungs, with rifle fire and the flash of heaven's anger overhead.

The sudden fury of the charge brought back memories of the war to Joe, who urged his horse into a frenzied run, fear racing through their instantly hot blood.

Minutes later, they pulled the horses up at the foot of the dark mesa. The ground was wet, with gathering mud forming a footstool for the pelting rain. Lightning flashed in the sky, lighting up the faces of the men. "Hello!" Joe called out. "Anybody here?"

Zac watched the boy at a distance. The youngster crept up over the sandy hill and lay facing the plain below. The rain had started to spread, and in spite of the thunder and flashes of lightning, he could hear the sound of gunfire below. It gave him a queasy feeling in his stomach. Zac was, after all, following them for a reason, and if they needed his help right now, he was too busy playing possum.

The boy lay still on the crest of the hill overlooking the grassy desert flatlands below. His legs were spread out, and he watched carefully the scene being played out in the valley.

Sudden movement in the flashing lightning caught Zac's attention. There, to his left, a lone solitary figure skittered along the crest of the hills. Whoever it was obviously had the place where the boy was lying firmly in mind. Zac didn't know for sure if the intruder had seen the youngster, but one thing was for certain—if he hadn't, he soon would.

Getting to his feet, Zac reached into his saddlebags and removed his moccasins. He wrenched off his boots and tossed them beneath the dun horse. Carefully slipping on his soft leather moccasins, he crept down the hill in the direction of the prone boy. Soon, he was looking up the slope at the youngster. Inching his way up the gradual rise, he crouched low and waited.

Moments later, he could see the head of the intruder peer over the crest of the hill. The man was bareheaded and wore no shirt. It was possibly a Mescalero scout, circling around the fighting below. Zac tensed his muscles, edging ever closer to where the man would emerge, stalking the prowler above him. Like any predator, the thought that he himself was being watched had probably never entered his mind. Like a coyote, he had his nose to the ground, following one and only one scent.

Zac crept closer. Every muscle inside him was tense. Reaching into the sheath at his side, he pulled out the sharp Greener knife. His long throwing knife was in a suspended thong between his shoulder blades. But this was his fighting knife, and its keen edge could send terror through any opponent. He wouldn't risk a shot. The Greener would do nicely.

Edging closer, he watched and waited. The rain fell in sheets, thumping the dry ground with heavy striking sounds, music in the thirsty land.

The slight man above him raised his head. He had spotted the boy lying on the ground and moved closer to the point where he could make a quick but silent dash.

Zac watched him get to his feet and begin his run. Raising up, he began a sprint to intercept him. The two of them met not five feet from where the boy lay. Zac struck the small man with both arms extended, and the two of them went sprawling over the edge of the hill and down the sandy side. Reaching the bottom of the hill, Zac tossed him like a stick, sending him flying through the air.

In an instant, the man was on his feet. He pounced in Zac's direction, his knife flashing. Their two blades met with the sharp sound of metal on metal. Backing away and swinging the blade, the man once again lunged at Zac. Zac caught his arm in midair and twisting it back, rammed the Greener home.

The wounded scout collapsed at Zac's feet. The man panted with short gasps, wheezing and coughing. Zac turned him over. What he saw shocked him. It was an Indian boy, a teenager, more than likely out trying to prove his manhood in battle. Whatever else he was, the Mescalero boy was a scrapper and a brave one, at that.

Zac got to his feet and looked back up the hill. There was no one there!

Scrambling back up the hill, Zac looked down and spotted the boy running in the direction of the dun. He gave chase. The boy struggled with mounting the tall horse, fighting to get his foot in the stirrup. Just as he swung up onto the saddle, Zac reached him, pulling him to the ground with a thud.

"Hey there! I saved your life and now you're stealing my horse?"

The boy lay on the ground, the wind temporarily knocked out of him by the fall. He grunted softly and rolled over.

Zac picked him up by the rope tied around his waist that was serving as a belt. A large Colt's Dragoon black powder cap and ball pistol fell from the youngster's pants. "See here," Zac said, picking it up. "This is a man's gun, an old man's gun. What you doing with this thing, boy?"

"Abajo!" The boy grunted. "Put me down."

"Sure thing, button. I was just letting you catch your wind."

Zac carried the boy a step away and then set him down. He held up the pistol. "Now, what were you planning on doing with this, starting a war?"

"Sí, if I had to."

Zac bounced the oversize pistol in his hand. "Son, with this thing, if you'd tried to pull the trigger, it would have taken all you were worth and knocked you down in the process. Might just as well have blown up in your hand and left it a bloody stump."

"I didn't want no war."

Crouching down beside him, Zac looked back up the hill. "Well, you were almost in one up there, and you'da been the first casualty, to boot. That other young fella was planning on slicing your throat, and if I hadn't met up with him first, he would have done it."

The boy looked back up the hill.

"Now just why are you out roaming around in the dark, with no horse and no shoes?"

The question got nothing but a silent stare.

"You should be at home with your momma."

"I ain't g-g-got me one no more." The boy stammered out the words with a twitch in his voice.

"You live close by?"

The boy shook his head.

"Then where's your home?"

Raising his hand, the youngster pointed to the east. "A day and a half that way."

"And you just decided to go exploring all on your own, I take it. I saw that bag of water you've got. You must have planned to be out awhile."

"As long as it took."

"As long as what took?"

"As long as it took to do what I come to do."

"And what would that be?"

"My own business. Ain't no concern of yours."

Zac nodded up the hill. "You following those men?"

"What I do or don't do is my own business."

Zac pushed his hat back. "Right now, button, I'd say whatever the reason, you being out here has become my business. I can't rightly leave you wandering about in this place. If the rattlers don't get you, then the sun or the Mescalero will. Now, how am I gonna sleep at night knowing I cut you loose out here?"

"I can take care of my own self."

"You like not to have made it through the night here, and I'd spect tomorrow won't get any better for you." He looked back up the hill. "We'd best be seeing to that other boy up yonder. He's losing blood, and it's gonna take some tending to."

The two of them got to their feet, and picking up the reins of the dun, Zac started up the hill with the boy. When they made it down to the bottom on the other side, they could see that the Indian boy was gone. The trail of blood on the ground was obvious, even in the dark. "He won't have gotten far," Zac said, "not with that hole in him."

They followed the trail to a spot behind some far rocks. There they spotted the unconscious boy at the feet of his painted pony. Zac mumbled. "Didn't even have the strength to get back on his horse."

Crouching down, Zac turned him over. "This fella's not a whole lot older than you are, button. He had a lot of fight in him, though." Glancing over at the boy, Zac added, "I spect you do too."

The boy had turned and was watching the far-off mesa intently, his eyes scanning the darkness. The desert was silent now. The lightning storm had passed, leaving behind a slow and gentle rain.

"I suppose they've managed to drive the Mescalero away for now, but they'll be back and bring more with them." Zac paused, studying the boy. "Of course, you weren't all that interested in those other folks, now, were you? It's those three hombres you're hunting down."

The boy looked at him and then dropped his head. He wasn't about to give away his intentions. Zac could see that. He pressed down on the Indian boy's wound. "This bleeding is pretty bad here. Reach up into my saddlebag there and find me some bandages. I carry a roll of it. What did you say your name was?"

"I didn't say."

"Well, I didn't say, I think you'll find those bandages on the left side."

The boy walked around the horse and, unbuckling the saddlebag, fished around for the roll of bandages. Pulling it out, he walked back and handed it to Zac. "It's Pablo. My name's Pablo."

Zac nodded. "Fine name, Pablo, mine's Zac."

He tore off a piece of cloth and then stuffed an edge of it into the open wound. Lifting the Indian boy up, he wound the bandage around him. "We can't move him tonight, but I'm afraid we have to take this boy somewhere he can be treated proper."

Pablo's interest became peaked. He squatted down beside the Indian, watching Zac work. "There is no place near here, señor."

"Well, there might be."

Cocking his head, the boy looked at Zac in a quizzical manner.

"We could bring the boy back to his folks, his village."

"Go to the Mescalero?"

"Exactly."

"You volverse loco, señor. You go crazy."

"Maybe, maybe not."

The boy shook his head in disbelief.

"Indians respect courage. A man with enough of it can ride right into their camp and back out again as an honored guest, especially if he's bringing one of their own."

"This is loco. You not get close enough to them."

"Well, we can't just leave the boy here to die. He's got too many years ahead of him to do that. You let me worry about getting us close to their camp."

"How we find it?"

Zac nodded at the painted pony. "We'll let him worry about that. We'll just give him his head."

"Why you do this, señor?"

"A man's got to play honest with the cards he's dealt. I'm no nursemaid, but right now I got you with no home to go to and this boy here who will die unless I get him some help. A man can do lots of things to get by on today, but he still has to face himself in the morning no matter what he does."

Zac watched the boy nod. He didn't completely understand the meaning of what was being spoken, but he understood the words enough to be able to ponder them.

CHAPTER 12

+ + + + + + +

THE RIDERS GATHERED in the rain near the foot of the mesa. Just as Joe had predicted, the Mescalero had melted back into the night air at the sight of the oncoming riders. It had obviously been a band prepared to hunt down and kill two people—not take on a group of armed riders or soldiers.

"Everybody make it okay?" Joe asked.

"That was quite the thrill, little brother," James responded. "Makes me feel sad that I was stuck in the artillery during the war and not riding with you cavalry types. It would have been a good sight better for my hearing too."

"Are the ladies coming on?" Joe asked.

Gaucho turned his horse and trotted back into the dark plain. "Sí, señor," he yelled. "They are coming now."

Several of the riders worked at picking their way through the rocks. One of the Mexican riders, Dom, called out, "Over here! We have dead Apache here."

The men walked their horses to where the dead man lay. Suddenly, Oscar Ralfsrud stepped out from behind a rock. He swung his rifle up to his shoulder. "Who are you?" he asked.

"We're just travelin' south," Joe said. "We heard the shooting and figured to lend a hand."

Oscar swung the barrel of the Winchester toward Chupta. "Who's the injun?"

"Chupta's our scout," Joe said. "If you're the ones who set out from that wagon back east, it was him who found it. He worked at covering your tracks up some, too; otherwise, those Mescalero would have overtaken you out yonder in the open."

Oscar lowered the rifle. "We're grateful then." Turning back to the rocks, he spoke in a loud voice. "It's fine, Ellie. You can come out now. These here folks are friendly."

The young woman stepped out from between the rocks. Her dress was torn and a streak of clay smeared her forehead. The dirt was only partially covered by the blond hair that cascaded over her face. She brushed it aside with the back of her hand. Even with the look of many days on the trail, she had a natural beauty that shone through. She wasn't a stunning looker like Palmira or Rosalyn, with their dark-eyed chiseled features, but she possessed a natural comeliness, all the same. She reached out and held on to her father's arm, relaxing the revolver she still carried in her right hand.

"You are a definite answer to prayer," she said, "like a part of the angelic host."

"Well, I don't know much about that," Joe replied. "We were just heading this way and heard the commotion."

The group's attention was rudely snapped to where the fallen Mescalero lay on the ground. Web had straddled the man and with drawn knife was proceeding to take his scalp. He pulled the long black hair from the man's head and, seeing he had the group's attention, pushed his hat back and gave off a sinister smile. "Ain't no need to leave this here to lay and rot. It'll fetch $200 in Silver City."

Chupta spat on the ground and turned away.

Web got to his feet, pointing at Chupta with the bloody knife. "I'm just surprised he didn't beat me to it."

Chupta watched the man as he walked to his horse and opened his saddlebag, sticking the fresh scalp down into it. "I can cure it in the sun tomorrow when we stop."

"We may not be stopping during the day tomorrow," Joe said. "We stirred us up a mess of trouble here tonight, and by daybreak we'll have the whole clan of those folks out looking for us. I'd just as soon see us put all the distance we can toward our destination, and that's going to mean some hard riding. What you just did," he directed his words at Web, "won't slow those people down, either. They won't quit and go home, not now."

Buckling the bag, Web turned back to the group and grinned. "Hey, if it had been us layin' there, they'd have done the same, and right quick like. Speaking for my own self, I'd just as rather see my hair hangin' on some war chief's lance than see it rotting in a hole somewheres."

Having said his piece, Web walked back and leaned up against a rock.

"In a society of law, we cannot allow ourselves to be lowered to the most unworthy standard among us," James said. "To do so drags us down as a nation under the Christian ethic."

"I ain't sure we see it that way, teacher man," Torrie said. "A feller finds a dollar on the ground, he picks it up. Don't much matter whose pocket it done fell out of, Christian or no."

James rocked back and forth on his feet. His lower lip protruded. "I don't exactly think we are discussing dollars here. What your friend did there was desecrate a human corpse. Dead or not, human beings are precious in the sight of God and not a thing to be trifled with."

"You folks get your things." Joe motioned to Oscar. "We're going to have to move out fast. I'll let the lady have my horse for a spell while I stay back on foot and watch our back trail." He held out his hand in the still falling rain. "It would be best if we did it in the rain. Might make us a little more troublesome to follow."

"We'll do that, by jiminy. Ellie here's filling up our canteen in some of the runoff back yonder."

James turned to Rosalyn and Palmira. "Are you ladies prepared to travel? I know riding in this rain will be most uncomfortable, but it must be done."

Quietly, Chupta had circled the men's horses. He unbuckled one of the saddlebags and, reaching in, produced a fistful of scalps. "They have more." Chupta raised his voice. "These men scalp hunters."

"Hey, get yer grimy injun paws off our stuff," Torrie yelled out. "You ain't got no call." He drew his revolver, but before he could bring it up, he found himself facing Joe's Colt.

"Just you hold on there, miner man," Joe drawled. "You travel with us, and we better know just what you're up to. You put that shooter away, and we'll just have ourselves a look-see."

Chupta walked over to Joe, holding out a fistful of scalps. He handed several to Joe. "These not Indian scalps. Indian grease hair. These three Mexican hair."

That word brought Rosalyn, Palmira, and the three cowboys to full attention. Rosalyn walked over to Joe. "Is this right? Let me see."

Examining the hair, her head jerked up, her eyes flashing at the three newcomers. "The Apache is right," she said.

Torrie and the two others backed off slightly. "There ain't no way you could know that," Torrie said. "We took all them things off Apaches we killed. We were savin' 'em for a grubstake when we got to Silver City."

Joe watched as Gaucho and the others settled their hands onto their guns. "Hold on there." He raised his hand to still the movement of the men.

Turning toward the three newcomers, he motioned toward their horses. "I'd say, boys, that it's time for a parting."

He could see the fear in their eyes. Web's lip was quivering. Yuma maintained a steely gaze, his hand flexing itself over the butt of his pistol.

"Where we're going there'll be plenty of Escobar's troops." Jerking his thumb back in the direction of Gaucho and the men, Joe went on, "And without worrying much about the Apache, along with plenty of extra shooting irons, I'd say you'd be sleeping with the scorpions."

Torrie backed up, raising both hands to his waist and waving them in a motion of surrender. "All right. You don't have to tell us twice. But you're gonna be needing us before this is all through, especially after tonight. If you're not about to take our word for it, then you best be able to pay the price. Where you're goin' three more guns will come in mighty handy."

James dropped Palmira's arm. "I should think that we would much prefer treachery outside the camp than inside. A man would rather die with his friends than live with his enemies."

"James is right," Joe said. "I'm afraid you boys have made your own bed and now, like it or not, you got to toss and turn in your own covers. You best just ride out."

Torrie stepped into his saddle, followed by Web and Yuma. "Have it your own way. We'll be sawin' on steaks in Silver City while your bones are bleaching out here."

"I'd head west," Joe said, "toward the Rio Grande. You go south and you're gonna run into Escobar's men, and with what you're carrying, I wouldn't advise it."

The three men turned their horses and rode off through the rain toward the west. The drizzle had blossomed into a steady downpour, and small streams of water poured off of each of the men's hats. Joe looked up at the black sky. "I'd say we'd best try and fill our canteens here while we can. You men take your hats off and turn them over. We need to dig a few ditches, too. We catch enough of this and we can give the horses their fill. They're gonna need it 'cause we'll be riding hard."

The men began to make trenches to catch as much of the rain as possible so the horses could drink. Rosalyn walked up to Joe, blinking back drops of water. "I would say, señor, putting you in charge was the right thing to do. You seem to have a way about you—a, how you say, balance between doing the right thing and for the right reason."

"Thank you, señora. That means a lot coming from you."

"I do not give out compliments to men lightly. Your wife must be very proud of you."

"Keeping her proud of me means doing the right thing."

She smiled. "With many men, señor, the right thing tonight is often the wrong thing tomorrow in the light of day. Some men see the big vision of what they want and the thing that seems right to them. The small indiscretions they commit are all set aside because they see only that thing. It consumes them. I see you as someone who looks at each small thing or each person and makes up his mind on that thing alone. This makes you trustworthy."

"You ladies seem to have made a great study of men."

"Of course. All women study the men around them. This is a man's world still. Men seem to fill up every part of it. A woman who is ignorant of men is a woman lost in the world. This is not so with men. They often see only one thing, and how a woman feels or what she is like on the inside is of little importance to them. Once a woman belongs to them, they can put her away and turn the key."

"That's a sad thing, ma'am. My own Karen wouldn't have any part of being treated like that. She'd hog-tie me and heat up her running iron. Believe me, she's a woman a man would be a fool to cross."

"All of us are, señor." She smiled. "It is just that a few of us have found more subtle ways to maintain a whip hand. Because we study men so well, we know how to best control them."

"I can see where a country boy like me would have much to learn."

"You have good instincts, Señor Cobb, very good instincts."

It was more than an hour later when the rain stopped and shortly after that when the first rays of sunlight painted the tops of the mountains to the east with a frosty pink haze. Zac had stripped off the saddles from the two horses and hobbled them to keep them from wandering away. He caught what little nap he could while keeping an ear open for any movements from the two boys.

Throwing back his wet blanket, he took his boots from underneath it and pulled them on. Standing up, he strapped on his Colt and the Greener knife. He had kept some dry kindling in his shirt and a few branches under the blanket. Quickly assembling the makings, he stuck a match and blew on the tender blaze, sending a few flumes of flame into the air. He took the small coffeepot he'd left open for the rain and sat it on a rock beside the fire. A short while later, he dropped a handful of the precious black grind he carried into the surging hot water. It rolled, a thick, foaming black broth. Unwrapping a brown paper filled with strips of bacon, he dropped them into a pan. The popping noise and the aroma of cooking meat soon cracked open the eyes of little Pablo.

"I see you're alive," Zac said.

The boy threw off his blanket and jumped to his bare feet.

Zac tossed him the moccasins he carried. "Here, put these on." He tossed the boy two strings of rawhide. "You'll be like a wooden duck floating in a pond. You can use this to keep them tight on you. At least it'll hold you for a while, and you won't go to dancing through the stickers out there."

Pablo pointed to the moccasins on the Indian boy's feet. "How about them? They might fit me just fine."

"They might, but they're not yours to wear, and if you notice, he's still breathing."

Pablo put on Zac's footwear and, lacing the thongs around them, tied them tight.

"Now come on over here, button, and let's put some food and hot coffee in that belly of yours. I have a few old biscuits in that bag of mine over there. They ain't exactly like your momma made, I'll bet, and they're hard to boot, but they'll go a ways to filling you up."

The boy ambled to the fire, stepping awkwardly in the sloppy footwear. Crouching down beside Zac, he proceeded to down four of the old biscuits and several pieces of bacon.

"Appears to me to haven't eaten in quite a spell."

The boy nodded, downing another biscuit.

"Now, why don't you tell me why it is you're out here chasing those men. They must have done something powerful wrong to send you out onto the desert with your pa's cannon. I might just be able to help. You know, I chase down bad men for a living, and I gotta say that if it was me, I wouldn't want you on my trail. What you lack in caliber, you make up for in sheer cussedness and determination."

"You won't do me no good." The boy's voice was muffled by the bread he had stuffed into his mouth. His cheeks bulged.

"I'd say I've done you plenty of good already. You can trust me. If I can't help you, I'll just send you on your way. I sure don't have any plans to keep you. Now just what did those men do? Did they steal from you?"

The boy nodded, his mouth full. He stared into the fire.

"Looky here. I'm sure it was more than that, but I'll just let you tell me in your own time. A man's got a right to whatever's inside of him." Zac glanced over at the Indian boy. "We better try and get some water into that boy yonder. He's lost a lot of fluid already. Then we'll scatter our fire and bury it and head out. I want to make plenty of miles before the sun climbs high. You up to this, riding into the belly of the beast?"

Pablo looked puzzled at the very idea. He shook his head slowly.

"Well, you'll do all right. I spect you'll manage a far sight better with me, even if it is into Mescalero country, than you will out here on your own."

Pulling out the canteen, Zac scooted over to the semiconscious boy. His eyes blinked open as Zac held the canteen to his lips. "Here, son, you take some of this. We're gonna take you back to your people this morning. They'll take care of you."

Later, when Zac had managed to bury the remains of the fire in the sand, he saddled the horses. "We're going to try something a little different, button. Hand me that blanket."

The boy shook the sand from the blanket and handed it over to Zac. Cutting off some short ends of rope, Zac secured the four corners of the blanket, leaving enough line at each corner to fasten it securely. "Now we're going to tie this blanket off between our two saddles. It will be a stretcher for the boy over there, a mighty precarious one, but it's all we've got. We'll put you on the boy's paint and give him his head. It'll be up to me to keep the dun here abreast. You think you can do that?"

Pablo nodded.

"You'll just have to wrap your legs around him and hold on. Don't try to make him go your way, we'll just go his."

The two of them got onto their horses and started off across the sand. The paint definitely had his own idea of where he was to go, and they let him lead. Zac worked hard at keeping the dun next to the paint, reaching out constantly to steady the Indian boy.

The sun climbed up over the mountains, and the rocks that dotted the edge of the playa grew larger as they approached the foothills. The grassy desert seemed greener with the water of the previous night, and several bees buzzed by them on their way to what few blossoms or what little standing water was left above ground. Winding their way around several hills, they came up to a narrow passage surrounded by towering rocks.

"Keep a sharp eye out here. It's a perfect place for an ambush. Just don't make any sudden moves no matter what you see. We don't want to spill this here youngster."

Pablo nodded sharply.

Up ahead, Zac noticed a movement in the rocks. "Look alive now, button. We're gonna find out plenty soon if we'll be enjoying our dinner or if we'll be dinner."

They rode into the narrow canyon. The rocks cast dark shadows on the ground, giving a coolness to the rocky gap. A hawk flew overhead. Zac had long since forgotten if the Indian viewed this as a good or an evil omen. It swept over the canyon, its wings barely moving. Like a sentinel of the spirits, the bird sailed over them and out the other end of the canyon. It was a strange thing to be watched, and Zac could feel the eyes of men on him now, measuring him up for size.

"Just keep your eyes forward. No matter what happens, you just keep looking straight ahead. We're gonna ride in here like the king's ambassadors on special business. There must be no fear in our eyes. Just think that in front of you is a thick glass wall that nothing can get through. Don't even look at me, and don't make any eye contact with anybody you might see. Just eyes straight ahead. You understand all that?"

"Yes."

"Good, 'cause we ain't got no time to rehearse this. We do it right the first time because there won't be a second." Zac pulled his gray hat down close to his eyes. It brought a sudden memory to his mind. He shook his head. "We do have a bit of a problem, though."

The boy looked over at him, his eyes widening.

"You see, back in 1861 there was a Colonel Baylor, I think, who tried to wipe these folks out. He was a Confederate officer, and he wore a hat like this one." He glanced over at the puzzled Pablo. "I should have thought that over, I suppose. No matter what, though, you just keep your eyes straight ahead."

It was only a matter of moments before they saw the first of the riders. More than a dozen Mescalero rode toward them, their faces fierce with hatred and their bare backs glaring in the noon sun. They shouted loud screams of anger, each designed to send panic into the heart of an enemy, and waved rifles and lances over their heads.

Zac rode abreast of the paint. Reaching out, he steadied the boy between them. "Remember what I said, button, eyes straight ahead, no fear."

The men wore breechcloths, their bare legs stuffed into calf-high moccasins. Several wore bone breastplates, studded with eagle feathers. Their shouts grew louder and, surrounding Zac and Pablo, they began to ride around them in circles, bellowing at the top of their lungs.

Zac and Pablo rode forward, ignoring the men who continued circling them. The men rode ever closer. Several waved lances and rifles in Zac's face, hoping for a look of panic or fear. There was none. Zac rode forward as if the Mescalero were only a rumor, one he didn't believe. He steadied the boy between them, drawing attention to the fact that this was one of their own. It was a movement of care that wasn't missed by the riders.

As they rode into the clearing on the other side of the cliffs, a village spread out in front of them. Woven wood and branches made up the structure of the wickiups. People ducked out of the openings to see this great sight.

Someone Zac imagined to be the leader mounted his horse in the distance and rode toward them. The man wore a feathered cap. It was pulled around his head, and short, clipped feathers covered the thing like a fur ball. He wore an orange gingham shirt, bloused at the wrists, and a red bandana to set him off. The man's face was sharp, with high cheekbones and a narrow nose. It was his eyes, though, that would have attracted anybody's attention. They were sharp and black, set into hollow sockets and flanked by his pudgy cheeks. He rode up in front of Zac and Pablo, stopping the parade in its tracks. "Who are you, white man, and why are you here?"

"I brought back a boy that belongs to you. He's hurt bad. I like to have killed him last night, and it's for sure he wanted to kill me. He's a brave boy, though, and he deserves to live."

The Indian studied Zac's gray officer's hat carefully. He then looked the boy over. Turning to one of the other riders, he spoke in a harsh voice. "Tell Nani Little Stone here. Little Stone here with a gray coat."

CHAPTER 13

ONE BY ONE THE PEOPLE emerged from their wickiups. The women of the village stayed behind, and the older men ventured forward out of curiosity. Zac watched as several of the young braves talked with them. There was a buzz of distant conversation, and several of the men became very animated. The one who addressed him was obviously a person of great importance. One steely look from him silenced any notion of independent thought. He started in Zac and Pablo's direction.

The man was squatty in appearance, with a large chest and frame on short, spindly legs. His face was piled with brown wrinkles, and his black eyes twinkled on either side of a broad and triangular nose. A bright blue bandana held his salt-and-pepper hair in place, and his white shirt with no collar shone in the sun. He walked up to the outstretched figure of the boy still hanging between the two of them and put his hand on the youngster's forehead.

"You bring Little Stone back to us," he said.

"Yes," Zac said. "Little boy like that, as brave as he is, deserves to live. I wasn't about to leave him out there."

The man motioned, and several of the older women scrambled over to lift the boy from the stretcher, gently carrying him away.

Zac untied the rawhide strips that held the blanket. He pointed to the painted pony. "The horse here belongs to the boy." He motioned to Pablo to get off. "My young friend here can ride double with me."

Slowly, Pablo slid off the back of the paint. He untied the blanket ends and folded it gently, making sure he stayed busy and didn't look up.

"I am Nani," the man said. "You are Rebel soldier."

"I was. I ain't no more."

"Mmm," Nani grunted. "Your people do us much harm."

"That was a war with a lot of harm to go around."

Nani nodded.

The younger man beside them on horseback began to plead a soft-spoken case to the older chieftain. It was plain to see he was unhappy with the presence of the two strangers in their camp. His eyes narrowed as he looked at Zac. There was no trust in them, only hatred.

"Redondo says you must die here," Nani said. "You know our place, and you must not ride out."

"And what do you say?" Zac asked.

"I say you must come and eat mule with us while I think on it. You are a brave man, and if you die, you must die like a brave man."

"If I'm to eat with you, I'd just as soon eat as a guest, not a prisoner."

"Come then. You will be Nani's guest."

For some time Zac and Pablo were allowed to walk around the perimeter of the camp. They had interrupted a game of hoop stick when they rode in, and now they watched the game begin once again. It was a test of skill. Rolling a hoop along the ground, a man would stop and throw a lancelike stick. He would try to see how close he could come to the moving hoop, preferably hitting it. They took the game seriously, assigning several of the older men to watch them play and act as judges.

It was hard not to become interested in the outcome of the contest. Pablo's eyes were fixed on the moving hoop and the lances as they flew through the air. Zac stooped down to the ground and began to scrawl in the dirt with his finger. He would lift his head and watch the game and then continue to write. Looking over his shoulder, he watched the three warriors who had been assigned to keep him in view at all times. Flashing his dark brown eyes at them and for the first time gaining eye contact with someone other than Nani, Zac grinned.

Getting to his feet, he pulled Pablo's attention away from the game. "Let's us take a stroll down by the stream. It's a rare sight around here, and I don't think we should miss it."

Pablo slowly followed Zac, looking back over his shoulder at the game from time to time. "They might just let you play once they get a little tired of it," Zac said.

"Do you think so?"

"They might. Everybody needs to do something from time to time to take their minds off the mess they get themselves into."

He pointed back to the guards who were trailing them. They had stopped at the drawing Zac had made on the ground and were obviously studying it. "They're as interested in us as we are in them."

"What did you write?" Pablo asked.

Zac smiled. "Oh, not much. I drew a couple of stick figures holding hands. One was a white man and the other Indian. They were both grinning from ear to ear."

Pablo and Zac watched the men look up at them and then back at the art in the soft dirt. "It would seem they're as curious about that as you were about the game."

"Why did you do that, señor?"

"I was just giving them a look at our humanity. You see, oftentimes folks never see an enemy as human. They only look at the outside of a person, never at what's inside their skin. Now there's some enemies, like those men you were following, who are so twisted in their souls that there's very little that's beautiful at all to look on. But many times an enemy is just folks like you are. In the war we used to go down to the river at night and yell over to the Yankees. We'd trade them tobacco for coffee and sugar and then the very next day try to kill them."

"This is very strange."

"Maybe, but it does a body good to know that every one of us was made in God's own image. Those Indians back there are no different than we are. They have hopes and dreams same as we do. In some ways we've pushed them all the way back here, and they've got no place else to run to and be free."

"Why did we do such a thing, señor?"

"Same reason those men you were chasing did what they did. We want things and land that don't belong to us—greed, pure greed."

Pablo hung his head and walked beside Zac. They followed the path that led to the stream. Rivulets cascaded down black rock, sending a thin flume of ghostly spray into the blue sky. It was a place of cool and calm quietness. Cottonwoods shaded the stream that cut into the sandy bank and the dark water pooled up beside the edge of the trail.

Zac looked up the imposing cliffs opposite the stream. "Don't look up too sudden like, but I want you to look at where that water is falling from. Take a good look at it. Do you think you could climb up that in the dark if you had to?"

Pablo sneaked a peek at the cliffs. "Sí, señor, I think I could."

"All right then. If we should get into trouble and have to make a run for it, I want you to come right here. You get here as fast as you can and don't look back. Climb up over those rocks and keep climbing. I'll either be right behind you or find you whenever I can. You understand, button?"

The boy nodded. He pulled on Zac's sleeve. "I no swim, señor."

"Well now, that could be a problem."

"You think we may have to do this?"

"I don't know if it will come to it, and I hope it doesn't, but I want you ready no matter what happens. Why don't we just take off our shoes and go see how deep it is?"

Zac and Pablo sat on the bank of the stream. Zac pulled off his boots, and Pablo untied the straps holding Zac's moccasins on his feet. The water was dark and flowing ever so slightly as they stepped into it. Moving steadily forward, Zac reached a point where it was over his knees. The water was at Pablo's waist. "I think this is as deep as it gets," Zac said. "Do you think it's going to give you too much of a problem?"

Pablo shook his head. "No, señor, I can make it."

Zac put his hand on the boy's head and tousled his hair. "I'm sure you can, you're a man with powerful motivation."

The notion that Zac would call him a man made Pablo smile.

"I think we'd best be getting back and check on that Indian boy. I wouldn't want them to think we were too fascinated with this place."

They strode back into camp a short time later, still trailed by their three shadow walkers. Zac spotted one of the women who had taken charge of the boy. "How's the boy? Where is he?"

The woman beckoned him and waddled off while he and Pablo followed. Moments later, they ducked into a low door and into one of the brown, leaf-covered wickiups. The light from the small door only barely illuminated the sparse interior. Lifting a gourd, the woman pressed it to the boy's lips.

Zac and Pablo scooted closer. Taking a torn and frayed but clean cloth from a pile near the boy's head, Zac dipped it into a bowl of water. He wrung the cloth out and pressed it on the boy's head. Knife wounds like this usually carried the danger of infection, and now a fever was raging through the boy. Zac looked down at the poultice the women of the village had applied to the wicked wound.

Sitting across from him, next to the boy, the woman watched Zac's eyes. She was what one would call a rounded woman, her cheeks bulging and a sparkle in her eyes. A leather latticework necklace hung loosely around her neck, and she folded her hands, knitting her pudgy fingers together. She narrowed her eyes as Zac inspected the wound and herbal dressing. The woman could very well have been the boy's mother. There was great care written in her eyes and a hint of anger at Zac. He had brought the boy back, but he had also inflicted the wound.

The touch of the wet cloth and Zac's firm hand behind it caused the youngster to open his eyes. "I hope you're doing better, boy," Zac said. "I'm sorry I did that to you, but you were something fierce out there." The boy swooned slightly, his eyes half closing. "We get you through this and you're gonna grow up to be a brave and fearsome warrior."

Once again the boy's eyes opened. Apparently it had taken some time for the boy's mind to register who it was who was saying the words, but

young men. They too were strangers like you are."

"My home was burned too during that war by strangers from a far place. I know. I did not come to you, though, as a soldier. I came because if I hadn't that boy would have died out there, that boy who is now your son."

Redondo spoke to Nani and the men next to him. Zac could tell the words were unfriendly. His speech was animated and spoken with subdued and respectful passion. Nani raised his hand and cut him off.

"This is what I say. You came as a friend and you can go as a friend. The men you follow are our enemies. If you join them, you too will be our enemy and your bones will bleach in the sun along with theirs."

The faces of the older men, along with Redondo's, were stone cold and rigid. They sat passively as Zac chewed his meat.

"You can take your horse, and we will give you water," Nani went on, "but you must leave our land. Your brothers will die along with the people they come here with. If you are with them, you will die too. This is fair, your life for the life of the boy."

The group riding south had stopped in the heat of the day to give the horses a rest. They had ridden hard all night and through the morning, and all of them were tired. One by one each of the men had reluctantly shared their horses with Ellie and her father. It was wearing on them, especially Gaucho and the Mexican cowboys. They sat at the side of the group as the party chewed on jerky, their eyes belied their hostility. There was muffled grumbling in Spanish.

James watched the men and got to his feet. He walked over to where Ellie sat with her father. "How are we doing over here?" he asked. "Are you both getting enough to eat?"

"We're doing fine," Oscar snapped.

Ellie put her hand on his arm. "Yes, thank you. We appreciate your help so much."

The old man got to his feet. "I think I'll take a walk," he said.

"That will be fine, Papa. Maybe it will do you good."

They watched him walk off. "I just don't think he's in much of a mood to hear conversation," Ellie observed. "He doesn't talk much anyway, and right now Papa's feeling useless and quite a burden."

James watched him walk away. "Very few men like to feel they aren't useful, but before we get to where we're going, both of you may prove to be very useful."

"He would like that. My mother died a number of years ago, and Papa hasn't been the same man since. I think he was much more attached to her than anyone ever realized."

James squatted down beside her. "We have quite a bit in common then. My own wife died four years ago, leaving me with just my daughter. The emptiness a man carries around inside goes on long after the funeral. People can be so sympathetic then. They bring you food and extend their condolences, but not long after that they begin to lose patience with your grief. No one likes to be reminded of their own death, and another person's loss only drives the point home to them. It's not their grief, and many of them chafe at having to put up with yours. Of course the loss goes on, in spite of the lack of continued sympathy."

"We moved away after my mother's funeral. He just couldn't stand to remember all the things he had built for her—to be reminded of them every day was too much to bear."

"That does seem to be the way of things. People don't seem to understand loss, but it's the absence of someone that goes on day after day."

Ellie's eyes brightened. "You do seem to understand. Are you a Christian, sir?"

"Yes I am. My mother and father raised us children to believe in God."

"We are, too, but the passing of my mother affected Papa's faith as well. He felt betrayed in many ways. It was as if his faith were a house of cards that depended on mother keeping them up."

James dropped his head, remembering feeling the same way. "I can recall that. For me it was like someone escorting me to the edge of the earth and kicking me off. I was totally alone for the first time in my life."

"But you had your daughter."

"Yes, and in many ways she is like her mother. I can see it with every passing year."

Ellie bowed her head slightly. "My Papa says that's true of me, and I can see it in the picture of her he carries. I'm afraid, however, that's of little comfort to him. In many ways it just reminds him."

James nodded. "I can see where that would be a problem. Over the years a loss has a way of melting away the hard times and leaving only the things in our hearts that we want to hang on to; the quiet walks, the special times. It makes us feel guilty, too, about what we could have done and refused to do because we were too busy with small and unimportant matters."

Ellie looked up at her father and watched him pace back and forth. "I think that's a problem with Papa. He was always so busy with the farm.

Work seemed to take him out of the house when most people would have stayed home."

Joe signaled for the group to mount up, and they straggled toward the horses. Starting out single file, they made for the direction Chupta had gone some time earlier. Joe circled around to carefully check their back trail. It would be nightfall before they hit Fort Craig and the Rio Grande. They would have to once again leave the river and take to the desert, but at least there they would have water for the horses and maybe for even a bath.

The day dragged on, and the evening shadows lengthened over the land. Occasionally they would hear the soft sound of a quail. They were getting closer to the river now. Even in the growing darkness, they could make out the shape of cottonwood trees that gathered at the water's edge. The dull shape of the olive green tree tops cut a swath through the desert.

Joe spoke to Rosalyn. "Won't be long now. Your husband's men will be waiting for us, and hopefully they'll have some fresh supplies waiting with them."

"Sí, señor. That will be good."

A short time later they crested the butte of a small hill. In the distance they could see the stones that marked the outer walls of the fort. The place was dark, no sign of light or life.

CHAPTER 14

IT WAS TWILIGHT BEFORE Zac and Pablo reached the mesa where the fight had happened the night before. They had ridden steadily. Zac lowered the boy to the ground. "We'll cook ourselves a mite of supper and rest up a spell before we go. Why don't we scour around and see what's burnable? There won't be much, maybe a little scrub brush and some droppings from the horses last night, but that'll do."

He slid off the back of the big dun and started to search along with the boy. Circling around the west side of the mesa, he came to the place where the group had gathered. He stooped down to read what signs he could find. Beginning a series of half circles, he counted the horses by some of the prints left. Moments later Pablo came around the mesa carrying a handful of dry sticks. He watched as Zac continued to inspect the ground. "What do you see, señor?"

Zac stood up. "I think we'd best get that fire started. I want it out before the darkness comes up on us," he commented without answering the boy.

He broke several of the twigs. Taking out his knife, he made shavings and fashioned them into a small pile. Striking a match to the shavings, he quickly had a small flame going. Setting the small cook pot on the fire, he emptied some water into it and shaved a few pieces of jerky into the water. "We'll have us some soup before long, or a least some beef-flavored water along with soggy jerky. It won't be much, but it will be hot."

The boy started prowling the edge of the area, looking to see what he could of the group and its makeup. Zac watched him as he bent down to inspect the tracks. "You best get my tin cup out of my saddlebags. I'll let you use it first," Zac said.

Rummaging through the saddlebag, Pablo found the cup. He walked and sat beside the small flame, holding it out. Zac took the pot and filled it, sitting back to watch the boy slurp the weak soup. Pablo downed it gingerly but eagerly, handing the empty cup back to Zac. When Zac filled the cup with the remainder of the soup and held it to his lips, the boy asked the question again.

"What did you see in the tracks, señor?"

Zac paused, sipping on the cup. "I won't lie to you, boy. Those men seem to have split off here. They went off to the west, and the rest of them went south."

"Then I must go west, señor."

"I don't see how you can do that, button. You have no horse, and you have my moccasins."

Pablo worked at untying the straps around the buckskins. "Then I go barefoot."

Reaching out, Zac stopped him. "That won't be necessary. I've got a feeling those fellers won't let the other group out of their sight. They were following them pretty close when I spotted them. No matter which way they pretended to go, we find one group and we're going to find the other."

"No, I will go west."

"You sure have a lot of cussedness in you, pardner. You seem dead set on a war with those men, don't you?"

Pablo nodded. "Sí."

Zac pulled the large black-powder revolver out of the boy's waistband. "And you plan on using this?"

"Sí."

"Son, you use this thing against those hombres and you better be close enough to smell their breath. Even then, you're just going to get off one shot, and that might even backfire." Zac waved the pistol in the boy's direction. "No, this is going to be much more dangerous to you than it is to them. You just better follow along with me."

Pablo looked off into the dying sun. "No," he said, "I go west."

"All right, all right, you sure are a stubborn cuss. If you're bound and determined to follow those men, then we'll both go west. If it's like I say, we won't be heading in that direction for long."

The boy smiled and nodded. "It is good then."

"Well, it's obviously good for you. I know where those other folks are going. They're going to Fort Craig. I'd suspect those men we'll be following won't be going west for long. If they do, they'll hit the Rio Grande and turn south along the river."

"Sí, señor, it is good then."

After dinner, which included a few more of the hardened biscuits, Zac began to stir the coals. "You dig us a hole here and we'll cover this up. I'll see to the dun over there and get him a bit of water. If we're going to the river, he'll have plenty of it there."

A short time later Zac mounted the dun and pulled Pablo up after him. The sun had set and the tracks the men would have made the night before would be hard to follow. Zac would just have to use his best guess as to where they might go and stop once in a while to see if he was right.

The night seemed to have eyes. The clear air and the blazing stars made any change in the shape of the ground stand out. In some ways a man could see farther at night. There was no glare to blind him and none of the sameness to lull him into wakeful sleep. A stillness following the storm settled on the playa. Here and there he could make out the quick movement of a rabbit or mouse. The small creatures would dash near them as they rode, veering off to the side and scampering over the rocky ground. The rabbits were almost comical to watch. The animals made for one heading, and then, as if some unspoken word had been uttered, they would bolt in a different direction, scattering loose rocks as they dug their feet into the sudden turn.

No matter how disapproving the land, life refused to give in to the relentless sun. The night would peel back the merciless cover of the daytime agony, and the creatures who hid their faces from the furnace overhead during the day would venture out. It was for them a time of life, and for some a time for death.

Zac watched a coyote pick his way around a rocky slope. With his nose to the ground, he followed the smell of dinner. Zac pointed it out to the boy. "If a man's not careful, he can follow tracks that way. Only problem is, he doesn't see much else. He doesn't see what's coming up on him, and he takes no care for his back trail. The real danger out here is not what you see. It's usually what you don't. Those men you followed had no idea you were on their trail. They were too busy following tracks of their own. They don't have a notion we're following them now, either."

"Can you follow tracks at night, señor?"

"Most of the time I can, especially if I know where they're going."

Zac pointed at the coyote. "See there, button?"

The boy nodded.

"That coyote knows where the rabbit's going. Critters like that are simple sorts. They have holes and they have places where they feed, and the coyote knows them all. He waits to get them into the open, and then he runs them down when they are. That's what we'll do. Those men are heading to the river and turning south toward the old fort. We'll cut them off and go southwest. With any luck we'll save us some hours and get there about the same time they do. I don't expect them to be pushing themselves too hard. They just ain't the sort."

The fort stretched out below the mesa, a massive dark shape like a giant sleeping snake curled around the rocks below. Stone buildings dotted the interior of the long gone gates, and the round bastion of what had once been a busy place stood like a stony mushroom on the dry and hard ground. Joe signaled the group to a halt. Somewhere below, Chupta had gone to scout the place. There would be no going into it unless he viewed it as safe. It was one thing to be caught out in the open, and it was quite a dangerous thing to be trapped by walls where they knew little about the way of escape.

"We better hold up here a ways until we find out who or what is in there," Joe said.

"But, señor," Rosalyn objected, "my husband's men are there."

"Ma'am, don't look like there's anything there but some lizards and horny toads. I just want to make sure we don't find the Mescalero waiting to lift our hair. There ain't many places out here we could go, but this is one of them. If we know that, it's for sure those Apaches do too."

"Of course, I see your point."

"We'll wait a few minutes. If Chupta doesn't show, I'll ride down there myself and have a look."

"Would you like some company?" James asked.

"No, what I need to do, it just might be best to do alone."

James pulled at the brim of his hat, tipping it to him. "We will leave this to your discretion then."

"That would be best. When I get down there and look around, if I think it's safe for y'all to ride down, I'll wave my handkerchief from the wall down there. You give me time to look around and be watching."

"All right, I'll be watching."

Joe dismounted and lifted the stirrup on his saddle. He tightened his cinch. It had been a long ride, and with the little water they'd had, the horse he rode had grown thinner since the last time he'd checked it. If he had to bolt out of there quick like, he didn't want any sudden movement to unhorse him.

A short time later he mounted and rode down the slope toward the fort. The night sky and its stars stretched from horizon to horizon like a sprinkle of diamonds scattered out on black velvet, some of which had fallen off the table. The blackness of the mountains to the east reminded him of just how close the Mescalero were. *Zac was right*, he thought. *It was a fool thing to do to ride off through this country on somebody else's errand. Julian has gotten himself into scrapes before, mostly cause of his own greed and hatred. He got himself into this one. He should have been left to get himself out.*

There was a stillness in the air, as if the creatures of the night were deliberately staying away. The look of the place chilled his bones, even in the still, warm air. He watched as several birds flew off from the backside of the fort. They hadn't been spooked by him. It must have been something or someone else moving among them. Reaching down, he slipped the thong off the hammer of his Colt. If somebody was to jump him, he wanted to get it out in a hurry.

The bastion stood at the corner of the wall, dark and silent. The rocks that rounded themselves into the thing reached a height of some twenty feet. Slots for cannon dotted the upper story and stared down at him like the eyes of a blind giant. It would be a good place for them to hold up if they had to. They could build a fire that might be easily concealed in the story below and have a spot to fight it out.

He rode through the gate. A large, rocky parade field stretched out in front of him, and on either side of it were the empty quarters of the men who had been there years before. The barracks were low buildings with wooden porches. Long windows and doors stared at him with empty expressions, and wooden pillars held up the edges of flat rooftops. He rode past the shriveled remains of uncared for trees in the front of the buildings.

By all accounts the fort had only been permanently abandoned four years earlier, and from the looks of the place it wouldn't take long for the desert to take it back. There had been a battle near here during the war, Joe remembered that much. It was one of the few fought this far west, and it pressed anyone's mind to figure out why anybody bothered. Joe reckoned that was the way war was. Men fought and died for no reason at all. It never seemed so at the time for the men doing the dying, but the reason became completely lost to anyone's mind when a war was over.

A large rocky structure stood at the end of the parade field and behind it a row of buildings. No doubt these places were the headquarters building, the hospital, and the sutler's store. They faced him as he rode, their windows opened with only darkness inside. He'd have to take a look-see in every one of the buildings surrounding the parade field. This would be a perfect site for an ambush. A group of men could remain in the darkness of the buildings and have them in the light of the sky when they rode in. Joe pulled up and stepped out of the saddle.

Withdrawing his Colt from its nest, he moved toward the first of the low buildings to his right. He tied the horse to the remains of a tree and stepped inside. There was complete darkness in the hall, only the light from the stars shining through the open windows. He walked into the first of the rooms. It must have been an enlisted men's barracks. The large room had a potbellied stove in the center and the remains of what had been rough-cut bunks scattered around.

The second room had overturned tables and chairs, obviously an eating place. The kitchen would be out back. Seldom did anyone trust the cooking fires enough to have the kitchen connected to any of the main buildings. Cooks were forgetful at times, and in a structure with connected buildings, a little bit of carelessness could go a long way. That was the way it was, combined with the fact that many cookfires were kept going throughout the night.

The second and third buildings on the right side of the field were like the first. These were soldier's quarters with a place to sleep and a few scattered tables for eating and card playing.

As he stepped across the last of the parade field, Joe's eyes were drawn to the rocky building. There was no wood here and no windows. An artificial mountain of stone, it stood in command of the center of the fort. More than likely, it had been the powder magazine. There had been cannon here, that was apparent, and they would have needed a place to store the black powder, a place where fire could not put them all in jeopardy. That would be the place.

Stepping onto the walkway that fronted the row of buildings behind the power magazine, he pushed open the first door. The night air and soft light filtered into the large room. Empty shelves dotted the walls and a large wooden bar cut the room by a third. This would be the sutler's store. Even out here men needed a few of the luxuries a store could provide; a fresh plug of tobacco, books and magazines, and an occasional drink. For this lonely place in the desert, the store and its bar would be the only place a man could go.

He heard something scurry in the corner of the room and jerked his head around. A rat skittered past the light from the door and ran outside. Joe smiled. Not even that rat could find anything to eat in here, not anymore. He walked outside, following the rat.

Each building was the same, empty and dark, yet he couldn't shake the notion that something wasn't quite right here. The señora had said her husband's men would be here waiting for them, but there was no sign of them. There was also the feeling of a presence, eyes that were watching him. It gave him the sensation of what he liked to call "chicken skin" rolling up his arms.

He stepped out of what appeared to be the fort's hospital and looked down the parade field. There stood his horse in the distance, motionless, tied to the old tree where he'd left it. Looking across at the magazine, he decided that would be his next stop. He walked toward it, inspecting the outside. There were no doors to the building and no windows. It would be blacker than Egypt inside.

Stepping around it, he looked it over. The wall curled around the entrance, allowing men to run in and out without opening a door, and the entryway was wide, wide enough for a wagon or men with wheelbarrows. He stepped inside and, fishing in his pocket, found a match. There would be no way for light to escape this place. Using his thumbnail, he struck the match.

The bright flare of the sulfur glared in his eyes, and he blinked to get accustomed to the sudden light. Holding it out in front of him, he stepped inside. The place was large. Sandy floors were flanked by clay and rock ledges. Adobe bricks mixed with straw formed a second tier of ledge work. He held the flame up and looked over the adobe and wooden ceiling. This would be a good place for a night fire if they had to have one. As long as they kept it small with dry wood, the smoke wouldn't bother them and no light would escape.

Turning to go back outside, he was suddenly struck and pinned to the wall. "No fire!" a man's voice said, blowing out the match. It was Chupta.

Joe breathed a sigh of relief. "I was wondering where you were."

Chupta held his hand up to his lips. "Someone else here." He dropped Joe's hand.

"Where?" Joe asked.

Chupta swung his head around and pointed with his chin. "Out there, they out there."

"I saw some birds take off when I rode in. I figured there might be somebody here, but I thought it was the Mexican soldiers."

"No soldiers here. They all gone."

"You see sign of them?"

"Chupta see sign, but they not here for two, three days now."

Joe scratched the back of his head. "That's strange. What made them go?"

Chupta shook his head.

"Should I signal those other folks to come down?"

Chupta nodded. "Signal quiet. Mescalero out there. It be better if everyone comes in here."

"All right, I'll do that. I figure to put them in that round part of the wall with the windows on top."

"Tell them, no fire."

"That I'll do."

Joe left Chupta standing in the entrance of the magazine and walked back over the parade ground. Finding an adobe stairway that led to the top of the wall, he climbed it. When he had climbed it, he looked out over the flat rocky land that led to the hill beyond. The ground was still and quiet. He could see the party on the rise of the next hill. There was no mistaking them. It had been wrong to leave them there. If he could see them clearly, so could anyone else. He pulled out his handkerchief and waved it over his head.

They started down the hill, toward the fort in single file, a slow caravan of tired people. They were soon to be disappointed, he knew that. They were expecting supplies, fresh hot food, and protection. Here they would only find danger. Minutes later they rode into the dark and deserted fort.

"Strip your saddles and leave them lie," Joe said. "We'll be holding up here for a spell." He pointed toward the open door of the bastion. "We'll all be in there. There'll be no fire though, not even a match."

"What's wrong, señor?" Rosalyn asked. "Have you found my husband's men?"

"No, ma'am, we ain't. Chupta's here, though. He says your husband's men haven't been here for several days now."

"I can't believe it."

"I'm sorry, ma'am, but I'm afraid that's right."

Joe looked at the group. "I'm afraid we're eating cold tonight. You'd best fish around for whatever you've got. I don't know how long we'll be able to stay."

"Señor," Rosalyn interrupted, "we can't leave without my husband's men."

"What seems to be the problem?" James asked. The rest of the people gathered around Joe to hear the report.

"This place isn't safe. It's the one spot those Mescalero would figure us to go, and if they're not here already, they're on their way. The señora's men aren't around and haven't been here for days. They've either been killed or scared off, I figure. Now, with what little time we've got, we can't afford to be here for long. The longer we stay, the more time we give those Apaches to catch up to us with a force strong enough to finish us off. Safest thing for us to do is keep moving."

"We can't leave without my husband's men," Rosalyn protested. "They wouldn't have just left us here to die, not with me and my daughter."

"Ma'am, whatever they did, I'm sure they figured they had no choice. They had no choice and we don't either. If we stay here, we're gonna be dead."

"We will die going south without help," Gaucho said.

"That may be, but staying here makes that maybe a certainty."

CHAPTER 15

THE DAYS HAD PASSED SLOWLY in the ever-shrinking cell under the mission. Julian had taken to scooting the chair over by the high window and peering out into the courtyard. There was very little to see, only an occasional donkey with its back laden, following behind passersby. What he was most interested in, though, was the evening cart filled with hooded men. Tonight they had come in late, and Julian got to his feet every so often to take another look.

He watched with anticipation as the gate slowly opened. There was the covered cart that he had seen so many times before. It was being drawn by two rather haggard-looking horses. The beasts clomped along slowly, showing the wear of a long day, and the wagon seemed to buckle with each movement of the harness, swaying back and forth, the stays beneath the canvas quivering with each bounce.

It pulled up outside the side doors and one by one the men slowly climbed down. Each one moved like an old man, dropping a leg and feeling for firm ground, then gingerly getting his weight under him before stepping outside the wagon. The men generally arrived before sunset, but not today. It was unusual. The night was dark now. Torches were lit on the side of the church, and their blaze lit up the dirty, chalk-colored robes the men wore. Ropes were tied around their waists, giving form to their otherwise nondescript features. Their faces were covered by the hoods that made up the top of the robes.

The driver had gotten down, and Julian could hear him turn the heavy key in the door that led below. Those men lived beneath the church the same as he did. He had never seen them walking around, only getting in the cart by morning and back off by sunset. One by one they slowly shuffled toward the door. They seemed to be prisoners, like him, but without guns or guards to herd them along. It was almost as if they were being held prisoner by something else, some force that he could neither see nor understand.

Then it happened, something unexpected. As one man lowered himself to the ground, the canvas on the wagon brushed his hood aside. What Julian saw was perplexing. The man's face looked like it had been eaten away, as if by night some animal was taking his fill of nibbles at what human flesh might be found. The sight sent shivers up his spine. He stumbled back off of his chair, his heart pounding.

Walking back to his small table, he took a seat in the remaining chair and laid his head down. His head and his heart thumped a steady rhythm of blood into his brain. There were more secrets in this place than the treasure he had locked away in his mind, terrible and dark secrets.

He had seen quiet whispers spoken before, watched men's eyes as they shared a common knowledge. The pictures flooded back into his mind at the thought of them. Some of the veil of darkness was being lifted. He had been told it would only be a matter of time that what he saw or thought about would trigger the locked memories in his brain, and now it was happening. He saw pictures of men in uniforms, spangled uniforms with plumes of feathers on their hats. These were strange sights for him to recall, but across the room in his mind's eye, he could see the emperor of Mexico.

The man was short and slight with a well-kept beard. His eyes danced as he stood beside his officers. Julian could hear the words, but only slightly, and what he heard was in a strange tongue. It was a remembered scene he could make no sense of except for the secrecy that surrounded it. Perhaps he had been trusted to be there for that reason only, because he couldn't understand what was being said. He only knew what was being done. An escape plan was being prepared for the emperor, an escape plan that only he and the few others in the room were privy to. Somewhere in his mind he could make out only a few of the words: "Gold, flour, America, Galveston, France." He heard the words repeated but couldn't remember the rest of the gibberish that surrounded them.

He moved his head back and forth on his arm, resting it finally on the table. There must be more to think about, something that would make sense of it all. The shrouds that covered the faces of the men in the wagon outside were kin to the one that covered his mind. All was dark inside.

He heard the key turn to the hallway outside his door. It was just as it had been before. Every evening when the hooded men came back from their day, his evening meal was delivered. Tonight it was late. They had been late. He listened and soon heard the familiar dragging sound that meant Sister Mary was on her way. She was with the guards and the food tonight. He hoped the food would taste better.

He sat up as the guard unlocked his cell. The nun ambled in over the stones, caring a wooden tray. "Gracias," she said to the guard. The man locked the door behind her and sauntered away and out of sight.

"I have brought you something special tonight," she said. "I bring you some chicken."

The notion brought him to full attention in his chair.

"May I sit with you for a while?"

"Surely," he said. It was then that he realized that he hadn't bothered to replace the other chair from under the window. She noticed it right away.

"I see you have been spying on the people outside."

"I only hanker for the feel of some sunlight on my skin, Sister, that's all."

"This is dangerous, you know. If you are seen, you will be punished. I am afraid for your own protection we will have to place your table and chair outside until you need it."

Julian shook his head. "Sister, that's not right. A man needs to feel the light. It makes a body hang on when he's not looking at evening all the time. This place gets damp and stays dark."

"You are seeing things you shouldn't see, señor, things that could put you in danger."

She put the tray down.

"I don't rightly see how I could get into more trouble here than I'm already in."

"Trust me, señor, you could. It is my duty to watch out for you and to keep you safe from harm."

"Keep me safe from seeing things, you mean."

"What have you seen, señor?"

"Nothing—just flowers, peddlers, and sunshine."

She pulled the chair over to the table and sat down. Reaching over, she removed the lid on the dish. There before him was something that looked akin to chicken. Pieces of meat were scrambled with parts of the gizzard and heart. A stewed yam sat in the midst of the mixed meat and alongside it a piece of stale bread. "I hope you like it," she said. "I made the cook save you some of the meat."

He picked up his fork and stabbed a piece of the meat. "Oh, I'm going to like it just fine. Just you look on and see."

She watched him spade the food into his mouth and chew. There was very little warmth to it but an overabundance of black pepper. It made very little difference to him. He didn't expect to find the same vittles that graced the general's table, but was all too glad to see something that might be deemed as edible.

"And how does your mind go?" she asked.

"I got a few strange pictures in it this evening, like no place I've ever been and nothing I've ever seen."

"This is good. These are places you have been and things you have seen. Tell me more."

"I was in a room where men talked strangely."

"Talked about what?"

"I couldn't make out much, but I think I remember the words flour and gold."

"This is good." A broad smile creased her face. "The emperor carted away his gold in barrels of flour, we know that. You are thinking about the right things, now you must tell me more."

"I can't remember anymore just yet. That was all that came to my mind."

"Did the men say where they were taking the flour and gold?"

"Sister, I can't find their words in me. Most of it was strange and foreign. Even if I had been listening to them in the next room five minutes ago, I more than likely wouldn't be able to tell you any of it."

"You are making progress. Sometimes these things happen, and the slightest break in the dam that is keeping your mind shut may rip it open. When that happens, it will all come falling to you, just like it happened this evening."

"I hope so."

"I hope so too, señor. The sooner you can remember, the sooner you can be free."

"You don't think that man has the first notion of letting me live, do you?"

"Why, of course. General Escobar is a man of his word. I have known him since I was a girl. His family and my family were very good friends."

Julian shook his head. "Somehow I just can't place you with that man. It just doesn't fall out right."

"Well, it's true. Had it not been for this leg of mine and my change of heart, we might have been married. It was always to be so."

"Married? To him?"

"Yes, but I was a child, and I thought of childish things. Now my mind is on the important things. I want justice and mercy."

Julian speared the yam and bit off a piece. "It ain't often a body sees both of those. Most folks that think on mercy never mull over justice, and the folks that ponder justice never quite seem to get around to mercy."

"It is only in the cross that these two things come together."

"That may be so, but they rarely get coupled by the followers of the cross. I've heard some folks say that the last real Christian was nailed to a tree."

"I think you remember more than you are saying, Señor Cobb. You can think of words that to any other man in your condition would have little or no meaning."

"How do you figure that happens?"

"You aren't telling me the truth."

Joe walked around the dark room, nudging each sleeper. "It's getting on toward dawn. We best be moving along."

James sat up straight. "Haven't you slept?" he asked.

"No, Chupta and me watched. I'll do my sleeping in the saddle, I reckon."

"That won't do, not at all. We need you fresh, not some stuffed raggedy doll sitting in the saddle."

"I reckon it'll have to do. Fact is, I ain't slept and we gotta go. I want to be out a far piece over that desert before the sun climbs up too high."

Rosalyn stirred herself, pushing the hair back from her face. "Do you purpose to follow the river or go through the desert?"

"I reckon we best go due south over the desert. We'll go to the river first and give the horses and us a good drink, then we'll say good-bye to wetness for a spell."

Dom, one of Rosalyn's caballeros, sat up and was pulling on his boots. "Señor, the Jornada del Muerto is very dangerous. Even the men who do make it through never come out the way they went in."

"I've heard. Been through a desert or two in my time, and I know a little about how it can be."

"Why do we do this then?" he asked.

"I'm afraid we stirred up a hornet's nest when we whipped into them Mescalero. We need as much distance between us and them as possible, and if we follow the meanderings of that river, it'll take us out of the way and slow us down considerable."

Dom forced a smile. "You think good, señor, but my feet and my head don't like the way you think. I like the shade."

"The grave's mighty shady for a very long time," Joe replied. "Now, I have us a fire going over in the magazine, and there's coffee on. You want to go on down there, and we'll make us some breakfast and drink our fill of that black stuff. We'll be getting water at the river, so we might as well use as much of it as we can stomach right now and then some."

"Sí, señor," said Dom. Gaucho grunted.

Baptiste, another of the Mexican cowboys, was a wiry man with a build like a boy. Dark circles surrounded his eyes and several of his front teeth were missing. To see him at a distance, one would count him as a youngster, but when he came closer and smiled, it was apparent he was a man used to hard living. Throughout the trip, Joe hadn't heard more than two words from him. Now he rolled out of his bedroll and jumped to his feet. "Coffee is good now," he said.

The sound of his voice startled the others in the room. It was slight and shrill, but it was also apparent that he was trying hard to force it lower.

Joe blinked. "Well, why don't you take Quell over there and get you some." Quell had a tired expression on his face that marked his constant demeanor. His black hair fell like straw over his eyes. It was a wonder he could see at all, but he constantly brushed it back and made the best of it. He kicked at his boots to jam them onto his feet and waddled in the direction Baptiste had set.

Palmira straightened her dress and then began to comb her hair with long strokes, the polished comb flashing in the moonlight. James watched her.

Ellie and Oscar had rolled their blankets up and tied them with piggin string. They cinched it down tight. One thing Joe always admired about the folks from Scandinavia was the way they tended to the little details. They were thorough, leaving nothing out of place and everything in readiness.

Palmira and Rosalyn stooped out of the door, followed quickly by Ellie and Oscar.

Joe smirked at James and motioned toward the door. "After you, big brother. This is a fine mess we've gotten ourselves into."

James ducked down and went out, followed by Joe. "I suppose Zac always was the smartest one of the bunch," he said.

They began their walk in the direction of the magazine. "Maybe it's just been the hard knocks that's educated him a mite. I think he plans on things not being quite the way they're presented to be. He listens to the trouble people think they're going to find and doubles it to start with."

James laughed. "That's such a different way to think. Being an educator, I try to have my students cut their trouble down to what is true and leave out the ideas of fear and the nonsensical thinking that keeps them from life. I find when I do that, most of the things we are terrorized by turn out to be nothing, nothing at all."

"That's the difference between the classroom and real life. Out here you find out that there are things to fear, some that you've never seen or even heard of. In the West the collection of a man's troubles runs long and deep. We don't care when the streetcar runs. We're just more concerned that it doesn't run over us."

"I suppose you're right. Few men where I come from know of such things." His head swiveled around. "Speaking of that, where's our Indian friend?"

"Chupta?"

"Yes, Chupta."

"He's around. I think he works best when nobody knows where he is, not even us."

When they had gathered in the magazine, Ellie busied herself with pouring the coffee. "You better make sure Joe here gets plenty," James said, "he's had no sleep."

Ellie poured Joe a steaming cup full, looking up into his eyes as she poured. "Some men seem to want to do for others," she said. She sat the pot down and started to slice the cured bacon. The pan popped and bubbled when she laid the strips in it, sending a pleasant aroma into the room. "What we have here won't last us," she said, "but I figured we'd have no better time to eat it than now." She looked at Joe. "It will keep our strength up."

"You got that right," Joe said. "A man makes a mistake by scrimping in the desert, especially when it comes to water."

"Why is that?" Oscar asked.

"You do with little and your brain fogs up considerable from the lack of it," Joe said. "A man can go loco and do all the wrong things out there—and sometimes with half a canteen. Believe me, when you're in need, the thing you need most is your wits about you."

"Do you suppose that holds true with sleep, little brother?" James asked the question and smiled.

"All right, you made your point. But missing sleep also might keep you from getting a knife in the back. I've traveled through Indian country a time or two and always made it a point to sleep uncomfortable. I don't want to get into too deep of a sleep. I'll save that for my featherbed at home."

"The bacon will be ready in just a bit," Ellie said.

Palmira passed around hard tack. The flattened cakes were hard enough to break rocks with, but they carried nourishment in them. Then, fishing into the rawhide bag, she pulled out dried apples.

As they sat to eat, Chupta walked through the opening in the adobe and stone walls. He stood watching them.

"You better come over here and have your fill of some of this grub," Joe said.

Chupta nodded. Walking over to the fire, he picked up some bacon from the bubbling grease, bouncing it in his hands to cool it off. "When you done," he said, "you better come with me. I find Mexican soldiers."

Rosalyn jumped to her feet. "My husband's men, are they here?"

Chupta nodded as he bit into the bacon. "They here."

The woman raced to the door and stood impatiently. "I must go speak with them."

Chupta stuffed some of the dried apples into his mouth. "Men dead," he said.

"Dead!" Palmira shrieked. "Where?"

Chupta motioned with his head over his shoulder. "They in old corral behind soldier house. Me saw sign last night, find now."

The group sat in stone-cold silence. For a group of any size to die would mean bigger trouble than imagined. Joe cut the silence with a question to Rosalyn. "Do you know how many men your husband was sending?"

"No, I don't. I know he didn't want to send a full company for fear of accidentally meeting a group of American soldiers. Plus he knew we had some men with us."

"He must have a lot of confidence in you, ma'am," Joe replied. "I know I wouldn't send my wife and daughter through this area with less then a full army in the field. 'Course, I'm a cautious man by nature."

"I'm sure he had the best of intentions," James quickly added. "He does know this area, I assume."

Rosalyn stared off into the darkness through the opening. Palmira got to her feet. "Yes, my father knows this place well. It used to belong to my family."

"You see anything else out there?" Joe asked.

"Chupta see sign. Mescalero."

"How old?"

"After rain. It new."

They finished their meal in silence. Joe kicked the coals around with his boot. "We better go see to what Chupta found."

They quietly filed out the door, each one fearful of what they might see and dreading the knowledge of a nearby enemy who might have done such a thing. Circling around the headquarters building, they came to the old pole corrals. The stables were inside the adobe walls and the corrals stretched out from them, their gates broken down and lying in the sand and dust. Chupta hurried to the spot he had found beside the wall. Standing over it, he signaled.

The first rays of the sun were painting the sky to the east with the dull gray of predawn. The group gathered around the shallow grave and saw the body of a man in uniform. He was scalped.

"You know this man?" Joe asked.

"Yes," Rosalyn answered. "Lieutenant Sanchez. He was to command the force my husband sent."

"You find more graves?" Joe asked.

Chupta nodded. "There is more over there." Chupta pointed to the wall. "Me only dig this one up."

Joe brushed off the sand from the man. "That's odd."

"What's that?" James asked.

"There appear to be no wounds on this man."

The Mexican cowboys bent over to give it a better inspection. Baptiste crossed himself, and Dom gave off a low whistle. "You right," he said.

Gaucho bent over the body and, taking a closer look, walked away murmuring to himself.

"There's something else very strange," Joe said. He knelt over the body and gave it a long look. "This man's been scalped like the Apache did it, but that couldn't be."

"Why not?" Ellie asked.

"Apache not bury dead enemy," Chupta responded.

CHAPTER 16

+ + + + + + +

ZAC AND PABLO RODE through the night. Occasionally the boy would drift asleep on the front of Zac's saddle. That was fine with Zac. It made him feel right at home. The boy was younger than his own boy, Skip, but having a child close to him made him feel like a father again, not just some no-account gunman. The steady movement of the dun had a lulling effect, combining the rocking motion with the plodding sound of the horse's hooves. It was close to morning when Zac spotted the river. The cottonwoods and scrub oak dotted the banks of the stream, forming a barrier to an otherwise endless view of the horizon. Over an hour before they got there, Zac could see the trees and knew where the river lay.

Winding the dun through the cholla cactus, Zac sat upright and stretched as far as he dared to see down the bank of the river. He watched for any sign of movement—a wise precaution, given the hour. Deer, along with the predators that fed on them, came out to drink in the coolness of the predawn hours. Of course the men they were trailing were still ahead of them. Zac had only guessed they would go due west before they hit the river. If they had, they would be close. If they'd done the same as Zac and turned more to the southwest, they might be as much as six hours ahead of them.

They meandered toward the stand of trees. The oaks stood out in the darkness, their black outlines scrawled against the still starry sky. The branches twisted and folded themselves toward the east. Trees loved the morning sun and bent themselves to get it. The light of the afternoon was a killer for both vegetation and men. This place would offer some shade. It was why travelers often chose to follow the river into Mexico. In the desert, shade and water were not only luxuries, they were a matter of life and death.

Reaching the trees, Zac bent low to miss the branches and started the dun down to the water. The Rio Grande shimmered in the moonlight, oozing its way south. At times, this river could easily have the texture of the Mississippi, too thick to drink and too thin to plow. But it was no matter. The water was cool, and it could be made drinkable.

The grade down to the water steepened, and Pablo roused himself out of his sleep. "Where are we?" he asked.

"This is the Rio Grande, button. We'll pull up and give the dun a drink and maybe take a bath."

"A bath? In the dark?"

"Why sure. I couldn't think of a better time, unless some cougar comes along and mistakes us for a couple of pale mule deer. We have a hard ride through the sun today and starting out just a little cleaner will make us go farther without feeling it. The salt that comes off your body has a way of caking on your clothes. We'll wash the last few days off and just make room for some more. 'Sides, I been carrying you in front of me all night, and you're startin' to stink to the high heavens. The way you smell, you couldn't sneak up on a polecat."

The boy shook his head. "I ain't never had no bath in the dark. How can a body see where the dirt is?"

"Take my word for it. There ain't a place on that body of yours where the dirt isn't. You can scrub yourself down, and I'll wash out your clothes."

"What am I gonna wear?"

"You'll wear your wet clothes, when I'm done with them."

"Wet clothes?"

"You bet. It'll feel plenty cold at first, but in a few hours you'll be thankful for it. We ought to hit that old fort long about noontime, and if our luck holds out, we'll still be a bit damp to the touch."

Zac pulled up beside the stream and stepped down. He started stripping the saddle from the horse. "We'll give the dun here a good washing. I'm sure he'll be plenty thankful for that. You leave the moccasins here, then wade in and toss your clothes back onto the bank."

Pablo slipped the leather shoes off of his feet and placed his toes in the water. "It's cold," he said. "It looks dirty, too. How can we get clean in that?"

Zac chuckled. "That's another good reason to take our baths here before the sun comes up. If you were to see it, you'd more than likely shy away from it."

The boy waded in deeper. Removing his shirt and then his trousers, he threw them onto the muddy shoreline.

Zac picked up the boy's clothes and, laying them on top of the horse, walked the animal slowly into the stream. In no time at all, he had given the horse and Pablo's clothes a good scrubbing. He laid them across the back of the wet horse and took his own clothes off. Rubbing them vigorously, he squeezed them out and laid them on the back of the horse as well. Then he took his own bath. After a good scrubbing he felt like a new man. The water did feel grimy, but there was a noticeable change in the scent of both him and the clothes.

The sun was peeking up over the horizon, sending a trickle of pink color on the tops of the cactus and glancing off the rocks. The leaves of the oaks along the river gave off a hint of shine with the new day. After they dressed and ate, Zac saddled the dun and they crossed the river. He'd decided to use the west bank that paralleled the river. It would keep them at least partially out of sight, and it was the side of the river that the fort was built on, as he recalled.

They had ridden more than two hours, and the heat of the day was building when Zac pulled up on the reins.

"What's wrong?" Pablo asked.

"I just spotted something we ought to check—hang on, button." With that, Zac kicked the dun's sides, sending the animal down the bank of the river and into the stream. Pablo hung on to the horse's neck, and they swam to the other side. Pulling themselves out of the water, Zac stepped down from the saddle. He walked over to where several rocks lay in a circle and bent down.

"What you looking at?"

"This is where they cooked their breakfast. From the looks of things and the feel of the coals, I'd say it was about three or four hours ago." Zac circled the ground around the old fire pit.

"How do you know it was them?"

"Same prints as we saw back at the mesa last night. One of the men has a slash across the sole of his left boot. Obviously, he went to a boot repair man that did things in a hurry."

Zac swung himself back onto the dun and started them off. "They're ahead of us, but not by much. When we catch them will depend on how determined they are to find and keep up with that other bunch. For some reason it looks to me like they're bound and determined to do just that and after being sent away—it makes a man wonder."

They spotted the fort a few hours later. It could be seen for a long ways off. During the war, General Henry Hopkins Sibley had tried to take the Rio Grande Valley for the Confederacy. No one really knew why. He'd fought the bloodiest battle of the southwest nearby, and while he'd won it, the troops that were stationed at Fort Craig refused to leave the confines of the structure. Sibley had lost most of his supplies, and in this kind of land, that was akin to losing a battle no matter what the outcome of the shooting was.

Now the place was just lonely looking, standing all by itself in the parched sun. It commanded a vast area and could never be approached by day without the riders being seen for quite some time. Zac pulled up the dun and looked the place over. "Doesn't appear to be anyone there, but you can never tell, not from here."

"Are we going in?"

"We got one of two choices. We can sit here and watch a mite, or just ride in like we own the place. Personally, that would be my druthers."

The boy looked at him incredulously.

"Well, those men don't know us."

Pablo gulped.

"Do they know you?"

The boy thought for a moment and then shook his head.

"You set yourself out on this adventure of yours to be a hunter of men, didn't you?"

"Sí."

"Then if you're about to do that, you better get one thing right and get it good. Never let a man into your head. If you look at a man like you want to kill him, it makes his trigger finger itchy without you moving a muscle. He'll see you coming before you've a mind to. But if you smile and say something different on the outside . . . you put him to sleep, make him think you're no harm at all. With some men, the men you want to kill, that works best. 'Course there's others, the rascal that's just looking for trouble. With those, it's best to do just the opposite. With them, if they see any weakness at all, they'll prod you and back you into a corner. Being nice to a fool can get a man killed. A man's got to know who he's up against."

Pablo nodded.

"So, if they're down in that fort, you be my little boy and smile. You understand that? Smile and grin, even if it kills you. Do I make myself understood?"

Zac got a blank stare.

"You hear me?" He repeated the question.

"Sí, señor, I hear."

"Good."

Zac kicked the sides of the dun, sending them across the old trail and toward the broken gates of Fort Craig. They rode slowly and deliberately, plodding one step at a time as if they had all day. A short time later, they trotted into the broken adobe walls of the old fort. There, across the courtyard, three horses were tied. The men were there all right, but where?

Zac moved the dun up to the other horses and got down, pulling Pablo down after him. "Hello," he yelled out.

From the area of the sutler's store, a man walked out and leaned against the rail holding up the roof. He nodded at Zac. The man was a tall blonde with large ears. His eyes sparkled as if there was a laugh inside his head. "We're over here," he said.

Zac spoke softly to Pablo. "Just stay close to me and follow my lead." With that, he walked over in the direction of the tall man. "Howdy," he said. "We didn't figure to find anybody in here."

Two other men, one with a black beard and another with an angry scar, walked out from the building and stood side by side.

"Name's Zachary Taylor." Zac would often just use his first and middle name when meeting strangers. He was getting to be just a little too well known for his own liking.

"What you doing out in a place like this?" The man with the beard was whittling down a piece of wood. He asked the question without seeming interested.

"My son and me are going down to Mexico to see his mother. I just figured to go through here to show him the old fort."

"See you were a Johnny Reb," the bearded man stated.

"That's right."

"Name's Torrie, this here's Web, and over there you got Yuma. Ain't never had much use for Johnny Rebs before."

Zac ignored the insult and smiled. "We're pleased to meet you, gentlemen. We were a mite concerned about who would be here, though, hoping it to be a white man."

"That is a curiosity," Torrie said. "There ain't too many white men that ride through here, especially with their young'uns." He stared at Pablo, as if trying to place him. "The boy looks like a Mex, too. You ain't no Mex."

Zac put his hand on Pablo's head. "That's his momma you see in him. Guess we're just in a hurry to get home. I got a hankerin' to see her, and I figured to cut some time in the saddle thisaway."

"Them Mescalero might have something to say about that," Web said.

"Not if they don't see us," Zac responded.

Yuma chuckled.

"That ain't very likely." Torrie smirked. "Them folks see everything out here."

Zac took off his hat and wiped his forehead. "I suppose we'll have to travel by dark then. We'll just look about, and I'll show the boy 'round the fort here. Long about dark we'll head off."

"Okay by us." Torrie waved the whittled stick around the empty fort. "There's plenty to hold a boy's interest hereby. You just take your time. We stopped off to chow down some grub. We might just wait out the sunshine ourselves."

Zac put his hat back on. "That'd be fine by us. The company would do us some good." He looked down at Pablo. "Come on, button, let's have us a look-see."

Taking the dun by the reins, Zac led him and the boy to the far side of the compound. The horse was a special animal to look on, and in spite of how friendly the men appeared to be, he wasn't about to leave the dun tied up near the men's animals. Out here, a man on foot was a dead man, and leaving folks like that with such a temptation was more than lunacy.

They tied him up outside the bastion on the far wall beside the gates they'd ridden through and stepped inside. The place was cramped and peculiar, the round walls having no corners. Two windows let the light stream in, and on the far wall, four long rifle slots gleamed with intruding midday sun.

"Why didn't you shoot them?" Pablo asked.

Zac looked down at him. "Son, them folks are the seedy variety. I might be a shootist, but I ain't no gunslinger. Chances are they'd have gotten off one or two shots, and you were standing right beside me."

"That don't make no nevermind to me."

"Maybe not. Your life may be a throwaway to you, but it's pretty special to me."

Sitting down, Zac passed the bag of jerky to the boy. They had a bite of lunch—not enough to fill them, but just enough to stave off the hunger. They took their time eating. Zac wanted to give the men out there plenty of time to decide how to play their hand. Once they'd done that, he'd be able to see it in their eyes. If they knew what they were going to do, he'd have a much better idea of his own best move. Getting up, he dusted himself off. "We better go see to them men," he said.

The boy clinched his teeth. "Sí."

They stepped out of the dark rocky blockhouse and into the bright sun. The sun overhead was blazing down on them, sending an overpowering glare into their eyes from the surface of the rocks. The dun was tied up outside, just where they'd left him. They looked out over the rocky square and stopped in their tracks. The three horses were gone.

Dom was a proud man, too proud to see a lady walk while he was riding. He'd given Ellie his horse, and now he stumbled forward. His balding head and ample waist showed that walking was something he was not cut out for—maybe for a short while, but not for hours in the desert.

James trotted his horse back to him. "I think you should ride for a while," he said.

"I walk," Dom said.

"You've been walking, now you should ride."

Dom looked up at Oscar in the distance. The old gringo was still walking and had been since they had left the fort in the darkness of the early morning. James watched the Mexican's eyes. He could tell that this was an arrogant man, perhaps too arrogant to admit when he was done in. "I walk," he said.

"There's no need to be foolish." James circled the walking man with his horse. "Every man has his limits. It's the wise man who knows what his are. Why don't you ride my horse for a while."

It was plain to see the idea of accepting the charity of an American didn't sit well with the man. He gritted his teeth. "I will walk," he said.

James shrugged his shoulders. "All right, suit yourself. Keep an eye out for Joe, though. He's behind us. I suppose he just can't get over the idea that someone may be following us. Why he insists on riding away from the main party here, I'll never know."

"Your brother knows what he is doing," Dom said. "He is a good man."

"Perhaps so, but there would seem to be greater safety in numbers."

Dom looked up at him and frowned.

"Of course," James went on, "I suppose he's simply thinking about all of our safety and not just his own."

"Sí."

"I'd just feel better if I could see him, what with the Indians out there."

Dom motioned toward the group up ahead. "You go see to the women, señor. I am fine."

James trotted his horse on ahead. He looked back at the man, who still seemed to be laboring on his feet, and shook his head.

They had left the grassy sand some time ago and now it was nothing but rock and cacti. The mountains in the distance held the promise of cool shade. Their peaks rose above the scorching heat of the sandy rocks.

It was easy to imagine a cool place there, while on the playa it was only a man's imagination that kept him going, one step and one foot at a time. He rode up to Palmira.

"Your man back there won't take my horse."

"Why should he? Do you think yourself a better man than he?"

"No, I just figured it might be my time to walk. I don't look on these things as trying to prove anything."

Palmira looked back at the struggling Dom. "He is a man, señor. I think he sees what he does every day as proving that."

James shook his head. "There must be something about your people that I am not aware of, señorita. This thing about manhood strikes me as odd. So does this constant need to show everyone on the outside what you are on the inside."

Palmira wiped her forehead. "Dom is a poor man, but he is a man. He earns what it takes to feed his family. The doing of that is enough for him. When that is all you are, I think you take great pride in being all the man you can be."

"Well, I for one will never doubt him. I can see why you chose him to come with you."

Palmira swung her head around, looking over the rocks and boulders that were scattered over the desert floor. "I do not like this place."

"It seems peaceful enough," James said. "Of course, I could do without this heat."

"It is too peaceful. I have not seen a bird on the wing for over an hour now. Something is not right."

James held his hand to the sun and looked up. "Now that you mention it, I haven't either. Of course, if I had the choice and the wings, I might choose to not be flying here today either."

"The birds are flying today," she said. "They just are not flying here."

"And you see that as some sort of bad omen?"

"Something or someone has sent them away. They see movement they do not like."

James smiled. "Probably us, and I can't say as I like it either. You know, this little journey of ours hasn't quite lived up to our expectations."

"Do you think you should have gone home like your brother?"

"No, I didn't say that. I'm hoping to find my brother Julian. If he's in as serious trouble as they say, he may need me."

"Is that the only reason you're glad you've come?"

James smiled. "No, it isn't. You know that."

"Do I?"

"Now, here you are, appealing to my ego again." James smiled.

"And you are such a strange man to me, James. When one sees and hears you speak, it is easy to discount you as simply a man who has studied life, having never lived it. But the more I see of you, the more I know that is not true."

The group wound its way through a crop of large boulders. Even there, with the sun overhead, there was no shade, only the glare of the sunlight glistening off the surface of hot stones. A rattlesnake up ahead gave out a series of buzzing rattles. Gaucho and Baptiste were on it in a matter of moments, pinning it to the ground and lopping off its head. They held it up.

"I think they plan on including that in our lunch," Palmira said.

"Part of the bounty of the desert, I'm sure." James turned around. Moving through the rocks, they had lost sight of Dom. "I better go back and try to find your man," he said.

"No need," Palmira responded. She pointed up ahead to Gaucho. "He is stopping us to rest."

"And to eat his snake, I suppose."

"Oh yes," she laughed, "I'm certain of that."

The group milled about a clearing in the rocks while Baptiste started a fire. In a matter of moments, the huge diamondback had been skinned and was turning on a sharpened stick over the flames. James made his way to the front of the group and watched the suddenly grinning cowboys. There was something about a small victory over the desert that brought a sweet reward to the hardship. James held up his hand and looked into the sun. It was a small victory indeed.

As they finished the remainder of the snake and some of the dried fruit and pemmican they were carrying, they heard the sound of a horse. Standing up, they saw Joe rounding the rocks. He was riding fast, not trotting or walking. It sent a feeling of panic into them.

Joe brought the horse to a stop, and James ran forward, taking his reins. "Did you pass Dom back there?"

"I did. He's dead. Mescalero."

CHAPTER 17

+ + + + + + +

PANICKED, THE GROUP SCURRIED for their horses. Joe circled around them and held up his hand. "All right now, calm down. This ain't gonna do us no good."

"We go, señor," Gaucho said. "We go quick."

"There's no need to go storming off. The Mescalero killed Dom back there, but they're not here in force, at least not yet."

"How do you know that?" Rosalyn asked.

"Because we're still breathing. If they had sizable numbers, they would have already hit us and hit us hard. I figure them to be a small party out looking for us. The Mescalero probably have several of those scout parties out, only this group found us. They'll send a rider back to the main village, and meanwhile the rest of the scout party will trail us and try to take us out one by one."

"By jiggers, let's stand our ground," Oscar said.

"We won't do that," Joe said. "When they do get here we won't have near enough strength to put up a good fight. By that time we'd have little or no water. No, we'll move on. I just don't want people doing something foolish. You've got to stay together. We can't have people walking for too long at a time, either. You keep circulating the horses. Anybody seen Chupta?"

"No, señor," Baptiste said. He pointed in the direction of the rocks to the south. "He go off that way, and he not come back."

"What if something's happened to him?" Ellie asked.

"I wouldn't worry about that," Joe said. "That man can take care of himself. He's probably safer alone that he would be with us."

"Maybe that would be true for all of us, señor," Rosalyn interjected. "Perhaps we should divide up and make a run for it. We're only three days away from our home."

"We do that and they'll hunt us down like quail," Joe said. "They wouldn't even have to wait for a larger group. That small bunch could do it. Don't think they couldn't find you, and don't think they couldn't come on faster than you could run. Water isn't a problem for these people. This is their land."

James stepped forward. Removing his hat and sweeping it to his stomach, he forced a smile. "Well, speaking for myself, I'd be perfectly willing to give it back this very minute." James had always been known for his gallows humor. When people were in the greatest time of confusion, it always seemed to be the time for him to turn a phrase or make a joke.

"If we could find them before they found us, maybe we could do just that. Until then," Joe went on, "I'd suggest we put some distance between us and them and stay together. Try to keep in the open as much as possible." He held his hand up to the sun. "I know that's going to be hard to do in this sun, but we'll just have to."

"The Apache is in the shade," Gaucho said, "and we are in the sun."

"It is their land," Joe said. "They know the water, and they know the shade."

Joe trotted his horse south. "Follow me. We'll keep close together and give them an idea of how far and how fast we're moving."

Palmira turned to James. "Now why would we do that?" she asked.

"I'm certain I don't know, my dear, but whatever Joe's reason is, I'm confident it's a very good one."

"You seem to be a very trusting man when it comes to another man's wisdom."

"It depends on the man. You may have grown up with men who were headstrong and willing to twist you to whatever direction they wanted you to go in, but that's never been my experience, certainly not in my youth."

She threw her head back. "Most men I've seen are the same. They have their ideas, and you must fit into them. A woman who is smart will turn his ideas." She smiled. "My mother says that a man is the head of the house, and a woman is the neck. The neck turns the head."

James chuckled. "From what I've seen of both you and your mother, I'd say you've both turned a few heads in your day, and yours, my dear, has barely started."

"Every woman wants a man who she knows will go in the right direction, a man she can trust."

"Perhaps what you mean to say is that she wants a man who she knows will do as she suggests."

"My father is not that way," she said. "He's ambitious, and he knows his own mind."

James studied the beautiful woman riding up ahead. Rosalyn was strong. Anybody could see that plainly. She rode her horse with her shoulders held high and carried herself with pride. No matter what the dirt might do to others, there was a beauty to her that showed through. "I think, dear girl, that your mother is just as ambitious as that father of yours. There are things she wants and very little she will not do to get them."

"How can you say that? You don't know her."

"You're quite right. I'll be fair. I've known women like her. Before the war, the South was full of women who were the wives of wealthy planters. They shopped in Paris and gave glittering parties. When you talked to them, it was obvious they always knew the right things to say to just the right people." He chuckled. "The only problem was those same women might say just the opposite to a different set of right people."

"What does that have to do with my mother?"

"Your mother is a strong woman. Those women were strong too. They knew what they wanted, and their husband's success was simply a means of getting them there. Their men were simply powerful tools in their hands. It was a convenient thing that these men had their minds absorbed with business. I heard them complain a thousand times about how much those men of theirs pored over their books, but deep down those same women were happy they did."

"And you think my mother is a woman like that?"

"I think the señora is a powerful lady. She's had to be. She's married to a strong, ambitious man. If she's to survive and not just become a decoration on his wall, she has to have a heavy hand. She knows what she wants and how to get it. She brought you here with her, didn't she?"

"Yes, I told you that."

"Well, somehow I think men and women feel more secure as equals. For a man and a woman who love each other, there is trust and friendship."

"I'm not sure I've ever viewed marriage as a friendship," she said. "I've always seen it as more than that."

"There is nothing deeper than friendship. My wife and I were best friends. We always looked after the other's best interest without regard as to how it would affect ourselves."

Palmira rode with her head straight ahead, deep in thought. "I suppose I've never seen that before," she said. "I would like to believe it's true."

"It's true. When a man and a woman marry for love, they tell each other that their own happiness is centered solely in the well-being of their partner. That happens frequently in a marriage ceremony—unfortunately all too infrequently in marriage."

Together, en masse, they moved south. The horses had some staying power yet, having drunk their fill that morning, and everyone was determined to make the best use of them. James gave up his horse to Ellie and kept close to her as they moved along the desert floor. It was hardest on him and Oscar as they kept up the pace, occasionally grabbing on to one of the animal's tails in an uphill climb.

It was almost humorous to watch the group. Every head seemed to move from side to side, and in the distance each and every lizard and roadrunner was viewed long and hard as a potential enemy. They steered clear of the rocks, choosing the open desert instead.

"Are you all right?" Ellie asked James.

"A walk in the park," he said.

"I feel bad about taking your horse."

"Then put that thought out of your head. I was raised to hardship. I've only recently grown more accustomed to comfort. And a gentleman would never allow a lady to walk. My mother would have me horsewhipped."

"I see you've made a friend on this trip." Ellie nodded her head back in Palmira's direction.

"Yes, I suppose I have. She's a very sweet girl. She also appears to have been kept in a cage for quite some time, kept like livestock to be used at her family's pleasure."

"She appears to be more than a girl, if you ask me."

James turned his eyes in Palmira's direction and then back to Ellie. "Yes, I suppose she is, at that."

"And her mother seems to be such a hard lady, very hard and very manipulative. And you know what they say?"

"I think Señora Escobar has had a difficult life for a woman of such beauty. I get the impression that these women are just toys or tools to be used by the general."

"They say that if you want to know what a woman will become, you should look at her mother."

James ignored the comment. He was happy to have Ellie thinking about something else, anything else other than the shadowy trackers who were following them. "Your own mother must have been an exceptional woman," he said. "She seems to have turned out a fine daughter."

Ellie dropped her chin. "Thank you for being so nice. I shouldn't have said those things. I suppose I've spent so much time on the road with my father that I wouldn't know what to do with a man's attention. When I get a little bit, I'm afraid the jealousy hidden inside comes to the surface."

James patted her hand on the reins of his horse. "I'm flattered you would be jealous on my account, Ellie. I think you're a beautiful woman, both inside and out."

In late afternoon, they saw Chupta in the distance. Joe rode out to meet him. The group continued to move south as the two men talked. Having finished his report and heard about Dom, Chupta rode back with Joe to meet with the group. They pulled up in front of them.

Joe pointed in the distance. "You see those rocks out there?"

"Yes," Rosalyn said.

"That's where we're heading. Whoever is following us will be drawn into that after us."

"We gonna stand and fight, boy?" Oscar asked.

"Not exactly," Joe said. "But we are going to try and take care of the group that's following us."

"Now how you reckon to do that?"

"When we go through the first group of rocks, Chupta will fall off and James here can ride his horse. In the second group I'm gonna drop off. They may not have counted us and they won't know how many come out of that second batch of boulders, but the rest of you keep right on riding south. We'll catch up to you when we're done."

"And what if you don't catch up to us, señor?" Palmira asked.

"Then we'll be dead, and you'd best keep moving south, only faster."

About an hour later, they neared the first group of large boulders. James ran ahead on foot and put his hand on Joe's horse. "Are you sure you know what you're doing, little brother?"

"If I knew what I was doing, I'd be back in Texas with Karen right now. No, I'm not sure this will work. All I know is we've got to carry the fight to those people back there. We can't have them hovering over us all the way to Mexico. If we allow that, we won't make it. Besides, this will give them something to think about. Even if we don't get any of them, it'll slow them down considerable."

James patted his leg. "Then I'll leave it to your best judgment, you and the Indian there."

Joe started to speak, but James raised his hand to stop him. "Chupta. I'll leave it to you and Chupta. The man has a name. I know that."

"And he's a good man, too. No matter what happens, we'll give a good account of ourselves."

"I'm sure you will."

Riding into the first of the boulder stands, Chupta slipped off his horse and held the reins for James. James took them and climbed on. "Thank you, Chupta. You take care of that baby brother of mine and take care of yourself too." With that, he caught up with the group and tried his best to blend in and not look back. He saw one or two of the group start to look around and warned them. "Don't look back," he said. "We don't want to give anybody watching us the idea that anything's changed."

Shortly after they had cleared the first set of rocks, they came to the second. Joe pulled rein on his horse and stepped out of the saddle. Taking out his rifle from the boot, he left the horse and ran in the direction of the first group of rocks. Crouching down, he spotted Chupta. The scout had lowered himself to the ground and, finding a wash between the rocks, was hurrying to catch up. Joe watched carefully. If Chupta could make it to where he was, they would wait there. Chupta ran low to the ground, bobbing and weaving as he ran up the wash. Getting close to where Joe stood, Chupta caught Joe's eye and waited.

Joe looked over the ground carefully and signaled him to come ahead. In one bold scramble, Chupta ran for the rocky cover. He hit the rocky pass and swung around Joe, breathing hard.

"You okay?" Joe asked.

"They come, they come now. Me see them."

"How many?" Joe asked.

"Me see three."

The two of them backed away from the entrance. There was no assurance the Mescalero would ride through the rocks. It was a chance they were taking, their only chance. If the Apache stopped long enough to see the departing group at a distance, they might feel safe enough to ride on. Now all Joe and Chupta could hope for was that the group to the south of them stayed in sight long enough for their pursuers to see them. It wouldn't take long, and it had to happen now.

Joe and Chupta backed away from the entrance and tried their best to blend into the rocks. They soon saw the first Indian rider. The man neared the exit of the first set of rocks and moved his horse up for cover. Edging forward, he looked out over the playa. He must have seen the group traveling south, because Chupta and Joe saw him signal to the men behind him. They watched the men leave the stand of boulders and head toward them.

Joe backed away, pulling Chupta's sleeve. "We got to find us a spot, maybe even a couple of places. If we could get them in a cross fire, one of us in front and the other behind them, we could finish them."

Chupta looked up over the rocks and spotted a likely place. It was a rounded large rock that looked to be big enough to support a man. He pointed up. "Me go up there." Looking off to the other side of the passage, he pointed to another group of rocks along the ground. "You go to those rocks. Wait for me to shoot first."

Joe nodded. "It's good," he said.

Chupta caught his arm. "Take care, leave no tracks." Pointing to the side of the rocks, he traced a path for Joe. "Go over rocks. Get to place near and walk across soft."

Joe nodded. He moved gingerly over the rocks closest to the large rocks shadowing the passage. Some were sharp and others were rounded and flat. Skipping over them, he worked to get into position. Moments later, he came to the narrow place between the rocks.

He stepped lightly over the packed sand, taking care to leave little that would indicate his presence. It wasn't too hard to do. The group that had just gone through had left a collection of prints, and his would blend in nicely. Hunkering down behind the rocks Chupta had pointed out, he jacked a round into the chamber and waited.

His heart beat fast. An ambush had never been his idea of a fight, but this was a matter of survival. If they could cut down their pursuers, it might give them enough time to outrun the rest. They'd have to ride all night, but disposing of the bodies and making good time might confuse the Mescalero long enough. At least he hoped so.

He heard the sound of the horses, and his heart beat faster. Chupta would get off the first shot from above, and Joe had to jump up and take quick aim. The men would be working on returning fire, and he'd have to stand in the face of it and deliver. His shot from behind them would send them into confusion, though. Surprise would be on their side.

The one thing he had to make sure of was that each man would die. If even one rode out from between them, it wouldn't take long for him to find the main body of Apache and come back. They'd make up the distance with fresh horses, and before the next day was out, the group would be in the same mess they were in today, only with a much larger force going up against them. They'd be determined, too. Their land had been trespassed on and members of their group killed. He shuddered to think of what they might do, given half the chance. His hand began to sweat as he held the Winchester.

The first explosion of rifle fire jerked him to attention. Standing up, he laid the rifle on the rocks and sighted down the barrel. What he saw surprised him. There were not three Indians following them, but four. One had fallen from Chupta's shot and quickly he sighted down on a man returning the fire from above. Joe squeezed the trigger, sending a hot round directly into the man's side and knocking him from his horse. The other two swung their horses around and screamed. Joe aimed deliberately at a second as the man fired hurriedly in his direction.

The man kicked his horse toward Joe and continued to fire his rifle from the hip. Bits of rock flew near where Joe stood. Charging Joe, the Indian fired wildly. Each explosion sent a shower of broken rock that peppered him. Stilling his heart, Joe knew he had to make this shot count. Speed wasn't the issue here, deliberation was. He jacked another round into the chamber and calmly looked down to where the sight flashed in his eyes. Squaring the bead into the man's chest, he followed the bouncing horse. Gently, he squeezed off his shot.

The man flew off his horse as if he were a child being kicked by a mule. Joe watched as the fourth man swung his horse around and sent a swift kick into its sides. It bolted toward the north entrance of the pass.

Leaving his position, Joe ran as fast as he could to try to cut the man off.

Chupta had gotten down off his perch and was catching one of the Indian ponies to ride after the fleeing attacker. Joe got down on one knee and took careful aim at the fleeing man. He fired. The shot missed. He watched Chupta race by him and lifted his rear sight. This had to be a good shot. He'd wait until the man hit some flat ground. Waiting, he watched Chupta race after the man. Bracing his elbow on his knee, he took a slow and deliberate breath. He let the air out of his mouth and took his aim through the two sights. Easing back, he nudged the trigger and the Winchester bucked in his hands. He watched the Indian fall.

Chupta rode up to the man and, after inspecting him, rode off to gather in his horse. Moments later, he returned to the rocks, leading the horse with the man on its back.

Joe got to his feet and began to gather in the other three horses. The Indian ponies seemed surprisingly calm in the face of fire. They had obviously been trained to stand by their fallen riders.

Sweat was pouring off his head, and his heart continued to race as Chupta rode up to the rocks. Chupta slid down from his pony. "You do good," he said. "Brother right. He say you a good man, and you are."

"I'm whole lots better with the long gun than the short one on my hip when it comes to hitting where I aim."

Chupta smiled. "You good shot."

It took them some time to find a place to store the bodies. They covered them with rocks. It wouldn't pay to leave a trace of the scout band for the Mescalero to run across. Joe wanted as much doubt in the pursuers' minds as possible. Mounting up, they strung a lead rope for the two horses each of them would have in tow. Now no one would have to walk.

They trotted their horses south, directly in the path the group had taken. It was good to mix their trail with the others. They wanted to catch up to them quickly, but what they didn't want to do was to make their tracks distinguishable from the rest of the group, and running horses tended to dig deeper. Still any pursuers, given time, would be able to tell the difference.

It was a good hour later when they caught sight of the group up ahead. James and the bunch had lost no time in putting distance between them, and that was good. Turning around in his saddle, James spotted them and called the group to a halt. A short time later, Joe and Chupta caught up.

Chupta slid off the Indian pony and smiled at James as he took the reins of his own animal. "Your brother good shot."

"Well, sure. We all know that."

"We've got to keep moving," Joe said. "I'd feel a whole lot better if we put as much distance between us and whoever might be coming along as we can tonight. We have some fresh horses here and several bags of water for them. If it was up to me, I wouldn't get off my horse until we hit Mexico."

Swinging their horses around, they watched as Oscar slid onto the back of one of the Indian ponies. His grin was wide as he kicked the sides of the animal. Joe signaled the group on ahead. Once again, he was determined to ride at the rear and make his frequent visits to their back trail. He rode for a spell with James and Ellie.

"What you did back there took courage," James said.

"Desperation is more like it," Joe replied. "This whole trip has been a mixture of pride, foolishness, and desperation."

PART 2

+ + +

THE HACIENDA

CHAPTER 18

+ + + + + + +

AFTER THE LONG NIGHT spent in the saddle without sleep and two days of hard riding, they trotted over the last hill that led to Escobar land. Rosalyn and Palmira were excited. Proudly, Rosalyn pointed out the countryside. It was beautiful, an oasis in the middle of northern Mexico. Vast grasslands rolled over the tops of green hills. The mountains in the distance were brown but, unlike what they had seen in the desert of New Mexico, this land, the place of the tumbling valleys and hills, seemed well watered and cool.

Rosalyn sat in her saddle and breathed deeply. "This is my land, señores. It is beautiful, no?"

"It is very beautiful," James said.

"How far to your house?" Joe asked.

"We will be there tonight."

James looked at the sun. It had barely been up for three hours. "This is your land, and it will take us the rest of the day to get to your house?"

"Sí, señor. For the last six days we have been riding through the lands my ancestors owned. My great-grandfather was governor of New Mexico. He lived in the governor's palace in Santa Fe. He owned most of the Rio Grande Valley and farmed it."

"Sounds like you have quite the family tree," James said.

"Sí, we are proud of our family history. It gives us a place to stand in the earth."

"And what do you folks think of all this?" James directed his question to Ellie and Oscar. They sat on their horses and looked out over the green hillside. Cattle were grazing and they appeared to be fat.

"As long as these people have themselves a bathtub, I'm going to be one happy man." Oscar rubbed the front of his shirt. Sweat had dried a salty film on the front and across the back of what had once been a white shirt. He felt sticky and his skin itched.

"I think we'd all feel better with a bath," Ellie quipped.

"You will be quite comfortable," Rosalyn assured them. "You will be our guests. My husband will have a fiesta, and you will be able to sample what we grow here."

Oscar rubbed the stubble on his chin. "Ma'am, I could use some hot food, and I think I could sleep for a week."

Ellie reached over and patted his shoulder. "We all could, Papa."

He looked at her. "We come outta this thing, girl, but I done lost us everything, everything we had in the world. A man who can't provide ain't good for much."

"Papa, every closed door is the key to another. We'll do fine."

They spurred their horses down the hill, scattering the cattle as they rode. Somehow, the woman seemed to ride more proudly with each stride of the animal. This was her land and her cattle, and the vision of it filled her mind. James had his eyes fixed on her. This lady was a woman of mystery to him. She had quite a proud history, and James wondered what lengths she would go to in order to recapture it. The idea of one measuring themselves by their family's history had never occurred to him. It was a strange notion.

Rosalyn jerked on her reins and turned her horse quickly. She spoke to Joe in a fearful voice. "Quick, señor, we must hide." Her horse stamped from side to side as she continued to jerk and pull on the reins.

Joe could see a line of men topping the crest of the hill in the distance, men in uniform.

"We must go—now, señor." With that, she pulled Palmira after her, and the two women galloped back into the draw from where they had come, followed by Gaucho, Baptiste, and Quell.

James turned to the others. "Guess we'd better go too," he said.

Joe nodded. "Guess we had."

The group of Americans followed Rosalyn and her band down the hill. They rode hard. It seemed the women and the Mexican cowboys might never stop and that the devil himself was hot on their heels. Once again they scattered the cattle, sending them scurrying and kicking from side to side, out of sorts with being moved from the grass they were feeding on. Joe watched as the woman whipped her horse's withers with the reins. Not content with a simple run, she was doing her best to put as much distance as possible between those men and her.

Soon, they were out of sight among the cottonwoods in the small valley. Joe drew rein beside Rosalyn, his horse breathing hard. "What seems to be the problem? I thought this was your land."

"The Rurales!" she said.

"The Rurales are the mounted police, aren't they? What would be the problem in that?" Joe asked.

"They belong to President Diaz. They are his private army, and they hate my husband and my family."

The idea was a strange one. James and Joe exchanged puzzled glances.

"That seems mighty odd," Joe said. "A man as powerful as your husband appears to be wouldn't want to cross swords with the president, I would think. Might be an unhealthy thing."

"Unless he wanted to be the president himself," James added.

Rosalyn spit on the ground in a display of temper. "Diaz is a pig. He cares nothing about the culture and history of my country. His Rurales ride the land as if it is theirs and think little of harassing me or the men who work here. They are Diaz's army. They do not belong to my country."

It was the very first time either Joe or James had seen the woman lose her composure. In times gone by, even when she wanted to do differently, she had always maintained her poise. Whatever was going on inside her head, she practiced never showing it. And now there was genuine anger. It may have been because she was near home and felt more relaxed—or perhaps she had decided she no longer needed them and didn't have to pretend any longer. Whatever the reason, the volcano underneath had erupted.

"Diaz or not," Joe said, "those men are Mexican police. They belong to your army."

Rosalyn rose in the saddle on the balls of her feet. "They are not my army."

"You called the man we found back at the fort Lieutenant Sanchez," Joe said. "Sounds like to me this husband of yours has an army of his own. That just might make any president a bit nervous."

Palmira kicked her horse closer. "My father is a powerful man. He would make any man who tries to claim what is not his angry."

"Well, it's not many folks who keep their own army," Joe said.

"My husband has been a general. He has many loyal followers who admire him. This man Diaz has followed the reforms of Juarez. They have taken the land and wealth of the church and the people who built this great nation and are giving it to the undeserving."

"And I suppose it's your husband who knows who the truly deserving are." Joe smirked.

Joe's words hit her like a thunderbolt. She reared back in her saddle as though he had struck her. "I don't think I like your attitude, señor.

These are matters you know nothing about and a nation that does not belong to you."

"The lady has a point there, Joe," James said. "I think we should mind our own business."

Joe turned aside and trotted his horse away from the two women, followed by James. In a low tone, he muttered, "That woman's a devil, either that or her husband is and she's right alongside him."

James looked over at the two women. Their stares chilled him as well. "You could be right, but they're the ones with the whip hand now. We're on their land, and we've got some innocent people here depending on our good sense to get them out, to say nothing about Julian."

Joe's eyebrows arched and his forehead furrowed. It was a look of stubborn determination and James had seen it before. "That don't make them right."

"They don't have to be right. They can be wrong all they want after we're out of here with Julian."

"And what do you reckon we should do about the Ralfsruds?" Joe asked. "We've dragged them here. Didn't have much choice. But I don't rightly want them in the way when things begin to pop."

"There must be a town nearby. We'll eat, sleep, take our baths, and then try to get them on a stage back to Santa Fe. Meanwhile, we just have to behave ourselves and stay out of these people's politics."

"You're right," Joe agreed. "We've got fish to fry in our own bucket."

"Yes, we do, and it's obvious you hit a sore spot with the lady back there. We're going to need their help, though, if we expect to get Julian out of here. I think he's in a bigger mess than even he can imagine."

Joe nodded.

"Now for all our sakes, I'd suggest you just swallow that Cobb pride of yours and go back and apologize to the lady. I know I'm the one with words, but this time mine won't do. It has to come from you, and the look on your face has to reflect the words coming out of your mouth."

"I ain't sure I can do that."

"I'm not either, but you're going to have to try."

Zac and Pablo rode slowly into the sleepy village of Hermosa. It was close to evening, and a number of the women were carrying unsold goods home from the market. Zac watched several of them pass, fruit baskets half full. One carried a large, round, flat basket of tortillas. He signaled her over.

"How much, señorita?"

The woman looked down at the basket and then back up at the hungry man and boy. Picking up four of the flat flour cakes, she handed them up to the hungry riders and waved their money away.

"Gracias," Zac said, tipping his hat.

Zac gave two of the bread servings to the boy and both of them nibbled on the tasty treat as they rode down the street. Music played from the cantina, and inside they could hear laughter. He had a mind to find a stable. The dun had taken more than his share of punishment since they'd left Santa Fe. Oats would be a strange reward, but it was well deserved.

The days for the both of them had been hard. They had lost the three men in the fort, their tracks mixing with those of Joe's group and then suddenly disappearing. That had been hard for the boy. It seemed to be the only thing he had on his mind, and no amount of explaining could shoo away his disappointment. Whatever the boy had on his mind, it involved the death of those three men.

Redondo and his band of Mescalero had seen Zac and Pablo on their ride south. In spite of how the man obviously felt about them, he reluctantly gave them passage. Nani and his word of honor was important to those people, and Zac well knew it. Honor was a word that was often lost on the white man, but for the Indian, who had so little materially, it was everything.

For the last day and a half he had asked every Mexican traveler they had come across about the Escobars. All had directed them to this place. Wherever Joe and James were, it must be near the village of Hermosa.

Small houses dotted the hillside. Candles were lit, shining through the open windows. The houses must have been quite a sight at night, like hundreds of beady eyes looking down through the darkness at the village below.

A pack of stray dogs roamed the street. The dogs were of every color and description, panting and probing at the doors and then stirring the refuse that had been tossed out onto the street.

At the end of town, Zac spotted a large building with double doors. That would be the stable. He headed off in that direction. "You speak the Spanish pretty good, don't you, button?"

"Sí, it is my talk," Pablo replied.

"Good, then when we get to the stables there, you bargain us a spot for the dun. I'm gonna want some oats for him, but I'll feed him myself. You can tell the man we're gonna bed down with the horse too. I don't come into any strange place and leave the thing that brought me with people I don't know. You tell him that, and tell it straight."

"Sí, señor."

Riding up to the entrance, Zac stepped out of the saddle and helped Pablo down.

"Now, you go and find the man inside and tell him what I told you, comprende?"

Pablo nodded and ran inside.

Zac turned around and looked the town over. It wasn't much to talk about. Smoke curled lazily out of a number of stovepipes. A few of the places had brick chimneys, but they were rare and far between. There were no wooden sidewalks, just the dust of the street lapping up next to every door. It must have made for quite a mess during the rainy season.

He watched as a covered wagon rolled up the street. The thing was full, and it seemed out of place. It rocked back and forth as the two tired horses pulled it. The man in the driver's seat wore some kind of uniform, his jacket open and a dirty white shirt peeking through. His hat sat beside him and his grease-streaked hair curled over a balding forehead. He'd evidently been well fed, and his belly hung over a large belt with a gleaming brass buckle. The man eyed Zac as he passed, a curious, long look.

Pablo came back out of the stables, followed by the man who ran the place. The man wore a bright blue shirt, a shirt that he was obviously proud of, and mud-caked trousers that had one time been brown. It struck Zac as amusing at first glance. It was a clean shirt, but everything else about him was very dirty. It looked to be something he had hung up for special occasions and just pulled down when the notion took hold of him. He followed Pablo with a smile, holding both hands clinched in front of him.

"The man he say it is two bits to stable the horse, four bits if you give him oats, and a dollar if we sleep with him."

"Tell him that's fine by me."

Pablo turned and told him it was a deal.

"He wants the money now, señor."

"I understand. I don't blame him one iota." With that, Zac reached into his pocket and produced the money. He handed it to the man, who bowed repeatedly, smiling.

"Let's us see to the dun first," Zac said. "Then we'll go and see about some comida and grano de café. I think hot beans and coffee would go over with my belly pretty well about now, don't you?"

"Sí, señor, it sounds pretty fine to me."

They walked the dun into the stables, and Zac went to one of the last stalls and opened the door. "I'll strip the saddle, and you can find us some fresh hay to sleep on. I'd rather roll around on that than whatever else is in here."

They made the necessary preparations. Zac took off the saddle and bridle and worked at rubbing the dun down with a brush. Finding a bucket of oats, he scattered some of the sweet mixture into a trough. The dun seemed pleased, and Zac knew he deserved to be.

When they had finished, Zac picked up his beaded bag containing the Sharps rifle. Putting it under his arm, he closed the stall door. "I suppose that will keep him for a while. He'll have us for company tonight, so we want him in a good mood. I think he's grown used to us by now."

They had started out of the stables when something caught Zac's eye and froze him in his tracks—the sight of the same horses they had seen at the fort. It was either those same three horses or three that looked too similar to be coincidental. "Hold up one second, button."

He opened the stall door of one of the animals, a black with a blaze down his muzzle. Zac walked over to him and picked up one of his feet. He put it down and looked at another. Finishing with the horse, he moved to the animal in the next stall. Again he repeated the procedure. Satisfied, he walked out and closed the door behind him.

"What is it, señor?"

Zac pointed out the three horses. "You recognize them?"

The boy looked the horses over carefully. Zac could see the recognition cross his face. "It's them."

"It's them all right. One of them had a shoe with a star on the bottom of it. I saw it in the tracks at the fort. Those fellas seem plenty determined to follow that other group, and I'd say we've come to the right place."

Pablo continued to stare at the horses. "They are here, in this place."

Stooping down in front of the boy, Zac put his hands on the boy's arms, looking him right in the eye. "All right, fair is fair. I've got to know what I'm up against here. You know me well enough to tell me the truth."

The boy hung his head in silence.

"I won't think any the less of you if you tell me the truth, but I've got to know. I'm putting my life on the line here and yours too."

When the boy looked up, his eyes were filled with tears. He shook as he spoke. "Those men kill my momma, my papa, and my sister. They kill them, and they scalp them. When they rode off, they see me coming in from the field. They just laughed and waved."

He began to cry softly, and Zac pulled him closer, wrapping his arms around the boy. "That's all right, son, you need to cry."

"I had to bury them myself." He continued with a series of jerky sobs. "I bury them, and I take my papa's gun. I swear on their graves that I will kill those men, or I will be with my family in heaven."

Zac held him back, looking into his swollen and teary eyes. "Son, I can understand your anger. You need to know this, though, revenge is never an easy food to swallow. It burns going down and it kills you when you've eaten it. Only God is the judge, and His judgment is swift and sure. It may not come in our time, and we may never see it, but it will come. My brother, who is here somewhere, never learned that lesson—and he's a grown-up man. I don't want you growing up with that bitterness in your soul. You're too good a boy for that."

"They are here, in this place."

"And we may find them. But if we do, I don't want you tipping our hand, you understand? You don't let your face show what your mind is thinking. Will you try to do that for me?"

"You will let them go, like you did at the fort."

"We will just pick our best time. Now I told you we'd find them again, and we did, didn't we?"

The boy nodded.

"Then you've got to trust me. I don't want any gunplay in this town. We'd be in a heap of trouble, and they'd be scattered to the four winds. Do I make myself clear?"

"Sí."

The men's saddles were hung on top of the stall doors, and Zac walked over and opened one of the saddlebags. Reaching in, he pulled out a fistful of dried scalps. Keeping his back to the boy, he stuffed them back in the saddlebags. Taking the big Sharps out of the leather bag, he walked back and slung the bag on top of his saddle.

"Okay, boy, let's go eat. You remember what I said now."

The two of them started down the dark street toward the noisy cantina. The dogs had had their fill of what was to be found in the trash and had moved on. Zac broke open the Sharps and, finding a round in his pocket, slipped it in. Jerking it up, he slammed it shut with a well-oiled, crisp sound.

They got to the broken, dirty batwing doors, and Zac put his hand on them. "All right," he said, "we're just here to eat."

Pushing open the doors, the two of them stepped into the smoke-filled room and made their way over to an empty table. Several used glasses were scattered on the table, and righting them, Zac pushed them away. The place had a distinctive odor to it, like stale beer, mixed with tobacco smoke and the sweat of hundreds of men. It wasn't near full, maybe only twenty or so patrons, but that didn't change the smell.

The bartender spotted the pair and, shrugging his shoulders, walked around the bar in their direction. Zac watched him. The large man had jet black straight hair and large lips the size of orange slices.

"Tell the man we want beans and rice if he's got them," Zac said. "And have him bring us two glasses of buttermilk and some cornbread on the side."

"Buttermilk?"

"Yes, nobody can spoil that. It's spoiled already."

When the man had taken their order, Zac watched the boy glance around the room. Looking to the far side, he froze.

"Well, hey . . ." Zac recognized the voice, even from a distance. "Looky what we got here."

The burly man with the black beard pulled his scar-faced friend along with him, and the two of them walked over to Zac and Pablo's table. "Well, we meet again," the man said. "And the injuns ain't scalped you."

"Where's your other friend?" Zac asked.

"Oh, Web is back there playin' cards. Yuma and me is huntin' us up some women." Reaching over, he pinched Pablo's cheek. "I see you brung yer young'un, too."

CHAPTER 19

ZAC WATCHED PABLO GRIMACE. The man's touch obviously made his skin crawl. "Just you back off there," Zac said.

Torrie released Pablo's cheek. "Why sure. I didn't mean no harm to the boy."

"They sure is touchy folks for being pilgrims," Yuma drawled.

"Guess they don't recognize their betters when they see them," Torrie chuckled. "We didn't know you was headed down this way or we'd of had you ride with us."

"We choose our own company," Zac said.

"They'ze feisty pilgrims, too," Yuma grunted.

Torrie backed away, eyeing the two of them. "Now, how you figure them two belong together? The gent here appears to have some sand and savvy, but this kid of his seems pure green and raw. Plus the fact, they don't look at all like each other."

"Ain't we seen this here kid before?" Yuma asked.

Zac wasn't about to let them ponder over that. "The boy's mother is Mexican, and he looks like her. All Mex kids look alike, don't you know that?"

Yuma continued to study the boy closely. "I ain't so sure," he said. "I ain't never seen you before, but that kid's face seems to fit somewheres."

"You might be right," Torrie said. "Where you two say yer from?"

"We didn't say."

"Well, you come from up north 'cause you were riding this way."

"I'm from Taos," Zac lied, pushing back the guilt that immediately pointed its finger, "but the boy here stays with his mother down here when he's not with me."

Torrie gave out a low, guttural chuckle. "See here, Yuma, we got us a good family man. He runs off and fathers children down in Mexico, but he don't forget them none. Now where you s'pose we'd be if'n we kept track of all the imps we sired? We'd keep ourselves plumb busy just trying to find them all."

Yuma laughed. "Lovin' a woman don't mean lovin' her brats."

"I suppose that's just one of the differences between you and me," Zac said. "I take care of my business, all my business."

"He's a softhearted man too," Torrie sneered.

"Probably a sodbuster," Yuma said. "He's got his huntin' gun here with him."

Torrie's eyes were immediately drawn to the checkered grips on Zac's rifle. That it was a Sharps was plain to see, but it was unlike any they had ever seen before. The grips and stock were handmade, and the length of the barrel was several inches longer than most.

He reached out for it, and Zac grabbed his wrist. "You just keep your hands to yourself," Zac said.

"I told you he was touchy," Yuma said.

"I am about my firearms," Zac responded.

"He ain't no sodbuster," Torrie said. "The man's from Taos. He's a woodsman sort, maybe one of the last there is. Yes sir, the last of a dying breed. And this here popgun of his goes out fer them critters at a good long distance, I'd wager. How far can you hit something with that Sharps cannon of yours?"

Zac looked down at the rifle on the table. "It's a Creedmore, and I special load it. I've been known to take down an animal at five hundred yards or better."

"Whew . . . eee! Five hundred yards! That's a fair piece." He backed off and nudged the scar-faced Yuma, motioning toward Zac. "You see them steely eyes? Them's the eyes of a distance shooter. Is that right, fella, you a mountain man?"

"I do what I can to get by."

"Well, that's what we do. We do whatever we can to get by, ain't that right, Yuma?"

"We might could use a feller like this and a gun like his," Yuma offered. "It just might be needful for what we got to do."

"Now it might at that. So how's about it there, Mr. Mountain Man? You wanna join up and earn some serious money in gold?"

"And what is it you do?" Zac asked.

Torrie smiled at Yuma. "What is it we do? What do you figure we should tell him about our business down here?"

"That all depends," Yuma said.

Torrie looked down at the big rifle again. "I s'pose it does. But from the looks of this here feller and this Creedmore thing he's a packing, it might be interesting."

Yuma's mind was working on it.

"What do we do?" Torrie asked the question simply to give himself a moment to think.

"You are murderers." Pablo said the words without a second thought, and there was anger in his voice. The three men looked shocked.

Zac put his hand on the boy's and patted it to calm him down.

Torrie smiled. "Fer a quiet like kid, he sure can get a bit mouthy now and then, can't he?"

"Yeah," Yuma snarled, "he sure can." The man studied the boy's face, reflecting on it.

"Let's just put it this way, we're bounty men. We bring in men who have a price tag on their heads."

"And scalps," Pablo added angrily.

The boy's words stung them. They stood up straight. What they did as a sideline had its worth, but it was something they didn't want spread around too much, unless it was to a buyer. Neither of the men seemed sure if the word had been used for emphasis by a know-nothing kid or because these two strangers really knew something.

"Scalps too," Torrie went on. "There's a good price for injun scalps in Santa Fe."

The bartender brought over Zac's and Pablo's food—bowls of red rice and beans and two glasses of buttermilk along with some cornbread. He sat it down on their table and clanked down two thick plates along with spoons. Zac pulled out a dollar and pushed it across the table at him.

When the man left, Torrie continued his proposition. "If you're any kind of shot at all with that there thing—and I'll wager you are—I could promise you a hundred dollars in gold for just one pull of the trigger. Now how does that sound to you? That kind of money could get lots of beans and rice for that Mex woman of yours, you being the responsible sort and all."

"Who is this man you want me to kill?" Zac asked.

"A picky sort, ain't he?" Yuma said.

"Why shore," Torrie responded. "And he gets right to the point—I like that in a man. You wouldn't spect some feller that takes care of his woman and all to go to shootin' just anybody, now would you?"

Yuma shook his head.

"No siree, our man here is the real moral sort, he is. He wouldn't just kill any old feller." The man spoke in a slow and low tone, the kind that got to traveling up your backbone and made you feel as though you should wash when he was finished. "You ever killed a man before?" Torrie asked.

"I served in the war," Zac responded.

"That's right, that gray hat of yours."

"He's a Johnny Reb," Yuma sneered.

"Well, ya see, he is a moral killer. He don't fight fer nothin' that ain't right. The man's got hisself some scruples." He stroked his hand through his black beard. "Then you squeezed the trigger on many a man you didn't know and got yerself kicked in the teeth for your trouble. This would be lots different and a whole lots easier."

"Who is this man?"

"He's a no-account prisoner. He's gonna talk about something, and there's folks who want him down before he does."

"And he's close by. I wouldn't have to go far?" Zac asked.

"He's close."

Yuma chuckled under his breath. "Real close."

"Why, you could come out with us to do the job after breakfast when we'ze ready and be back to that woman of yours by lunchtime. Now ain't that real easy?"

"Things are never as easy as they seem."

"This one is. I get word to the right folks and they'll stop for water when they're moving him. They'll stand the feller up at just the spot where we want him, and with that thing there, all ya got to do is drop yer bead on him and spend yer hundred dollars."

"How do I know you got a hundred dollars?"

Torrie crossed his arms. "You seem the honest sort. I tell ya what. You say yes to this here deal and we'll give you the hundred dollars on the spot. Then you can just give it to that woman to spend and ride off with us when we're ready. Sound fair enough?"

"Well, why don't you let me ponder this. We're gonna eat our food now, and if you're here tomorrow I can let you know then."

"All right, fine. We'll be here. You just think it over. The man's a prisoner and a bad sort from what I hear. He won't be facing you, and he won't be shootin' at you none. It's just that with that big gun of yours, you can reach out and get him, and we won't even have to come that close."

Zac picked up his spoon and stared at the men.

Torrie raised his hands apologetically. "All right, we can see you're gonna be busy. You just think on the matter and let us know. You'd make our job a whole lots easier, and we'd make you a whole lots richer."

"I'll think on it."

The two men walked away, slinking back to the dark side of the bar from where they'd come. Zac could see them talking as they walked. It was obvious they'd be paying him only a small amount of what they'd been given, and with the Creedmore he carried, he'd be the only one needed to do the work. He watched Yuma take one last look at Pablo. The man obviously had some remnant of a memory in his head, and like a lot of men, he'd push on it until it came to him. Zac picked up the cornbread and crumbled it into his buttermilk. Pablo watched him.

"Why you do that?" he asked.

"I like cornbread in my buttermilk."

"No, why you make deal with those men?"

"I told you, button, I don't want to get into a shooting war with those men. Not just yet. Besides, I've made no deal with them."

"But you talked."

"I talked about thinking."

Pablo put his hand on Zac's arm. "You not going to do it, are you?"

Zac put down his spoon and looked directly into the boy's eyes. "Do you know who those men plan on killing?"

"No."

"My brother. They want me to murder my own brother."

The thought shocked Pablo. His mouth dropped open.

"You're not going to do that, are you?"

"Of course not. But if I don't play along with them, they're just going to find some other way to get it done. Now would you just leave them be if you knew it was your brother they were hired to kill?"

Pablo thought the matter over. "No."

"Well, I ain't gonna do that either."

"I would kill them right here." Pablo scooted closer to Zac in his chair. "Why don't we kill them here? You could give me back my pistol, and I'd help. Then you wouldn't have to worry about your brother."

Zac stirred the cornbread into his buttermilk. "That's the difference between you and me, button. I got a curious mind. Your mind is just thinking about one thing. Revenge does that to a body. It takes away everything from a man's mind except the doing of it, and you've got yourself a good mind, too good to waste. I'd like to find out for sure just who these men are working for. I've got an idea, but I don't know for sure. You see, son, when you kill a snake, you want to cut off the head."

It was dark when the group rode into the hacienda, and the horses were played out. The house itself was enormous, with ornate windows of stained glass and two doors that swung open to a veranda. A fountain bubbled up from the center of the veranda and trickled over polished rocks. They had ridden through a series of walls and gates, the first and the last guarded by armed men. Rosalyn had called out to them, and as if she had spoken a word of magic, the gates had swung open.

The courtyard in front of the house was paved with red brick, and the sound of the horses' hooves echoed between the house and the inner walls. The place was built like a fort, with turrets at each corner and a shooting platform on the walls. Most men wouldn't want to turn their home into a battleground, but should it become necessary, it was obvious General Escobar was ready.

They pulled the horses up outside what appeared to be a combination carriage house and stable. An old man in white peasant attire and black polished boots ran out.

"Señora, you are here. We are so glad to see you."

All of them gingerly got down from their saddles. It felt good to be on firm ground after so many days on the quarterdeck of a horse.

"Is the general home?" she asked.

"No, ma'am. The general and Major Hess are gone. They say they be back later."

"See to los caballos," she said.

"Sí," the man said, bowing low.

The hacienda was like another world to the travelers. Flowering vines blossomed on the sides of the big orange house, climbing all the way to the second story, leaving a trail of brilliant beauty, red and purple.

The large doors opened before they got to them. A young, beautiful woman pulled them ajar and, stepping outside, smiled and bowed repeatedly. "It is so good to have you home, señora." She bowed again. "We have missed you and the señorita."

The group stepped inside. The front hallway was studded with coatracks and iron hatstands, obviously used for large gatherings. Moving through it, they came to the great room. It was sunken, with walkways and carpeted polished floors circling it. Large sections of red leather couches and chairs surrounded the middle of the room, with several settings of chairs on the corners for more intimate conversation. Black polished tables with gleaming lamps on them dotted the floor, giving a soft feeling to the place. But a person's eyes were immediately drawn to the very center of the room. An open circular fireplace blazed with a massive brass round awning over it. The awning tapered as it rose in midair and finally exited through the ceiling overhead. It was breathtaking.

Rosalyn turned to the group. "Usted está en su casa; make yourself at home."

Every head was turned up to the brass awning. The gleam of the roaring fire, along with the twinkling lights, glinted off its polished surface. The group stepped forward, their heads craned upward toward the dark wood ceiling and the huge support beams that held the house in place.

Rosalyn clapped her hands together, and the young woman who had been at the door scrambled to get in front of her. She bowed.

"All of us will need baths, very hot baths," Rosalyn said. "They will also need clean clothes to wear."

"Sí, señora."

"Prepare rooms and bring us some drinks in here. We will wait here until our baths are ready."

"Sí, señora." With that the woman quickly moved away.

"This is quite the place." As usual, James was the first to speak. Everyone's gaze had gone to the second story. A balcony circled around the room and two large staircases wound themselves up to it.

"I am glad you like it," she said. "Your rooms are up there. I think you will find them warm and comfortable."

"I'm sure of it," James said.

Chupta seemed about as out of place as a man could be. He took care not to lift his eyes to the room, keeping his lips tightly sealed.

Ellie and Oscar had gone down to the area around the roaring fire. Ellie faced it and held up her hands, and Oscar busied himself with feeling the leather of the furniture. He pushed it with his fingers, watching the subtle spring of the oiled leather bounce back at his touch. Backing away, he admired the large rugs. They were a powder blue with ornate Indian designs. Looking back, he expressed his admiration. "These are fine rugs, señora. Who makes them?"

"They are Zapotec," she said. "They are made by Indian peasants." Almost under her breath, she went on, "The tribe of one of our illustrious presidents."

Joe heard the tone of the words, and in spite of his previous run-in with the woman, he couldn't resist a further inquiry. "You had an Indian president?"

"Yes, Benito Juarez. It was the beginning of the end for our nation."

"Now, why is that? We have lots of Indian tribes in the United States, and I think I could find chiefs in any one of them who might be able to do a better job than some of the men we've had serve as president."

Chupta's ears perked up.

James grinned. "We got one now that seems no better than the

Apache. He steals from you, scalps you, and then tries to make you feel good about it." Looking down at the rugs, he added, "The only thing is, I don't think he could create the first thing of real beauty."

Joe put his hand on Chupta's arm. "I've learned to trust this man. He goes where he's supposed to, does what he says he's going to do, and doesn't care who gets the credit."

"Well this one, señor, began to steal from the church. So great was our indebtedness and so deep his passion to give away our wealth that he had to turn to the house of God to take what was left."

"And I suppose you would like to right that wrong," Joe added.

"Yes, señor, and my husband will do that."

James took off his hat and scratched his head. The dust had been caked in it for many days now, and it was beginning to infuriate him. "There's many a man who has tried to change history, señora," he said, "and most have just wound up as footnotes in it."

"That may be true in your country, but my own is filled with little people and a few men with big dreams. My husband is one of those men."

Joe stepped away to admire the fire. Turning his back to it, he warmed his hands. "I'd be willing to wager that that type of man needs to have a woman behind him with more than dreams."

Rosalyn lifted her chin. "Perhaps you are right."

The servant girl raced back into the room. "The rooms and the baths are ready." She curtsied.

Rosalyn looked at Chupta. "Your scout can stay in my servant quarters."

"Then that's where I'll be," Joe said. "Like I told you in Santa Fe, if this man doesn't go, then I don't either. If we hadn't had him with us, none of us would be here now."

Rosalyn clamped her jaw tight. There was anger boiling in her, and Joe could see it. "Very well then, he can sleep in your room. I'll have the servants bring a cot."

"Chupta sleep on floor, need only blanket."

"Palmira, why don't you show our guests to their rooms, and then you and I can get ready for dinner." Turning to face the group, Rosalyn held her hand toward the upstairs area behind the overlooking balconies. "My daughter will take you to your rooms now. We will have dinner in two hours. Perhaps my husband will be home by then."

They nodded and followed the young woman up the sweeping staircase. Rosalyn watched from below, and as Joe turned to look, it seemed that she hadn't taken her eyes off him. Maybe she hadn't believed his apology. It was for certain, though, that she didn't trust his politics.

Palmira opened the door to the first of several rooms. She nodded to Ellie. "This is your room. Your father will be next door."

"Thank you," Ellie said.

Having deposited the Ralfsruds, she walked to the end of the hall and opened the door to the corner room. "And this is yours, gentlemen. My mother would want you to have it."

The four of them stepped into the massive room. A fire glowed in the stone fireplace next to the wall; around it were scattered several overstuffed chairs and a table with liquor decanters and glasses. Several paces away from the blazing fire, French doors opened up to an outside balcony. The doors' brass handles and cut glass gleamed and twinkled with the light from the fire and the overhead lamp. Two ornate, hand-carved beds flanked them, one on each wall. Giant bearskins lay on both beds, the teeth of the slain behemoths shining in a perpetual snarl at the foot of each bed.

"I hope you like your room, gentlemen. We save it for special guests."

Chupta walked over to the fire. Both Cobb brothers stood at the entrance, their mouths slightly ajar. Joe clamped his shut. "I think it'll do."

"It'll do?" James marched into the room and turned in its center. "I'm not sure Versailles would do any better than this, señorita."

Palmira went into and came out of the bathroom. "Your baths are drawn in there. The help seems to have brought up a second tub for you to use, so I suppose you will have to fight over the marble one." She smiled. "But we'll leave you to work it out."

Moving quickly to the beds, she pointed to the clothes laid out, two black suits along with white shirts and gold cuff links. "These things may fit—if not, we have others of various sizes hung in the closet. I think you'll find everything in order. We even have numerous boots in all sizes for you to look over. We do dress for dinner here at the hacienda."

"I can see that," Joe said.

She looked at Chupta. "I'll have other clothes brought up for you."

"We appreciate that," Joe said.

"Fine then." She moved to the door. "We want to make your stay as pleasant as possible." With that, she closed the door behind her.

James turned circles in the middle of the room, looking over the set of expensive paintings on the wall. "This is quite a palace," he said.

Chupta had moved to the balcony and opened the doors. He looked out and then motioned Joe over.

Joe gave the view a long look. "Not exactly a palace, brother of mine," Joe said. He pointed across the courtyard. There, opposite them, was the corner turret. Inside stood a guard with a rifle crossed in his arms and a cigarette glowing in his teeth. "A prison, more likely."

CHAPTER 20

JULIAN PACED IN HIS CELL, as he'd been doing all day. His mind tumbled, filled with sights, sounds, and names. Over and over he worked on recalling his life. Staring up at the bars in the window he could no longer reach made him think of the prison he'd been in during the last years of the war. It was much different, though. That prison had been dark, made out of logs, and it was stuck into the neck of Lake Michigan. The cold, howling winds of winter had sent constant chills through the men. Many had died of pneumonia, chills, and fever ravaging their bodies. At least the fever brought some relief from the bitter cold outside. Ice would form on the inside of the logs, and the men's breath would steam in the bitter cold of their cells. It had been a hell on earth and a cold one, at that.

He racked his brain for some memory of life other than the hard times and the few boyhood experiences he could conjure up. He must have had a life somewhere. Obviously, these people thought he did. The remembrance of the meeting in the emperor's office in Mexico City had been a start, but how he'd gotten to the place and what had happened after that was a blank.

There was no longer furniture in his cell. The table and chairs sat outside in the hallway. He could see them through the bars. They were simple things, but right now they reminded him that once he had been a human being. There had been a time when he wasn't an animal in a cage. The cot in the corner was something anyone might put down for a dog, and the critters that made their home in it made his sleeping difficult. The last few nights, he'd resorted to the bare, cold floor to get relief.

Reaching over, he pulled up the old, thin horse blanket. He shook it vigorously and then, taking it in his hands, began to swing it, pounding it against the wall. Walking over to the far wall, he laid it down beneath the high window and carefully spread it out. Tonight he'd use the blanket. It might keep him from the chills that seemed to run through him in the wee hours. Sitting down on it, he looked up at the window. The daily sound of the cart and the strange men that were unloaded from it daily at least helped pass the time. From this spot he would be able to hear them. They said little, only a murmur or two as they got out of the wagon, but at least it was the sound of another human.

"Ahhhh . . . eeeeeee." He screeched at the open window above him. "I am here!" he yelled. There were times like this when he felt as though he was losing his mind, times when even the sound of his own voice was a blessed relief. Sitting down on the blanket, he began to pray. "Our Father, who art in heaven, hallowed be thy name, Thy kingdom come, Thy will be done, on earth as it is in heaven. Give us this day," he paused, "our daily bread!" He yelled out the words for emphasis, as if God had not heard him and might pay no attention even if He did. "And forgive us our debts as we forgive our debtors. Lead us not into temptation but deliver us from evil. For thine is the kingdom and the power and the glory, forever. Amen."

The notion of being forgiven struck him as strange. He didn't know the sum of what he had done but figured it to be plenty. Thinking back, he remembered the story his mother had read about the generous landlord. It had been somewhere in the Gospels. The man hired laborers to work his land and paid those who had come to work last the same as those who'd worked all day. Naturally, the workers he'd hired earlier were plenty mad, even though they worked for what they'd bargained for. But he figured the folks who'd barely broken a sweat were plenty grateful. The man's generosity surprised them. *Maybe that was me*, Julian thought. He'd never done too much in the way of pleasing God, but maybe, just maybe, this was the last hour.

He looked up at the paint-peeled ceiling and spoke to it as if it were the face of God himself. It seemed like a funny thing to do, but the sound of his own voice was like music to his ears. "Lord, I don't deserve a thing, and I haven't worked a lick for you. Of that I'm sure. I don't exactly know what I've done, but I know I haven't done that. Forgive me of my sins, whatever they are. I'm trusting you. I just ain't got nowheres else to go."

The words rang in his ears. It made him feel clean inside, even in his dirty prison cell. It also made the face of his mother come back to him, just slightly. But it was her voice he remembered most, and it spoke his name. "Julian, Jesus will help you, if you only ask Him." Well, he'd done that. After that, he didn't know much else to do.

He heard the big key turn in the outer door, and the sound made his muscles tense. He'd sit just where he was. If it was his food, he'd finally get to use a chair. He hoped it was.

The sister was coming down the hall. She normally brought his spirits up, but today he wasn't sure anything would work.

The guard came to the door, followed by Sister Mary. She held the tray as the guard unlocked his cell door. Stepping back, she allowed the man to place first the chairs and then the table into the center of the room. She nodded to the guard, and he backed away and turned the key in the lock.

"I have food for you." She set the tray down.

Julian kept his seat on the floor.

"Come and eat it."

He bowed his head, resting it facedown on his knees. There was a determination in him to spill his feelings to her in a strong way. But he didn't want to hurt her; she'd been his only friend.

"What is wrong, señor?"

"The name's Julian. I answer to Julian. That's my name." He knew that was short, but right now he wanted to be treated like a person. He wanted furniture, and he wanted exercise outside the walls of this cell.

She walked over toward him. He didn't look up.

"Then what is wrong, Julian? You must come and eat. It will keep your strength up."

He looked at her. "I am not an animal. I am a man." He shook his shirt vigorously with his right hand. "I have nothing but these rags to wear. I have nothing to sit on and nothing to think on."

"Perhaps this will help you to remember. A man's mind must have thoughts, and if yours are free to roam, perhaps it will return to familiar places and people you have known."

"Even if I did remember, I wouldn't give anybody who'd treated me this way the satisfaction. It's making me crazier than the bedbugs in my cot over yonder. I got to have something to do." He waved his hand at the room. "Just seeing this place day after day is shaking out my brain. I need someone to at least take me for a walk, anything to get me out of here. This place is inhuman."

"Your spirit seems to be returning. This is good."

"But my mind is going."

"Do you want me to leave?"

Julian stared at her. There was at least a practiced kindness to her face. He wasn't sure of the sincerity of it, though. He hadn't been sure of that since she'd had the chairs and table taken out. "No, I don't want you to leave."

"Then you come over here. Sit down and eat."

He got to his feet and made his way to the table. Pulling out a chair, he sat down. Sister Mary took the seat in front of him. She lifted the napkin that covered his dish, a subtle smile crossing her face. There on his plate were several tortillas. There was also a small brick of cheese, and it wasn't moldy. It was a bright yellow, like a square piece of the sun. Several large portions of beef sat at the center of the plate. A bright yellow squash had been mashed up. It cornered the yellow cheese, forming a plate of brown, white, and brilliant yellow. It reminded him of the sun, the thing he missed so much.

His eyes had been transfixed on the plate. What little he had been getting was generally unpresentable, but then from time to time, Sister Mary brought something like this. He could never figure out why or why it wasn't more often. "What's the reason for this?" he asked.

"You asked the general for better food."

"That was God only knows how long ago."

"Well, perhaps his orders are just filtering down to the people in the kitchen."

Julian picked up the meat with his fingers and tore it apart. They never gave him a knife, no matter how dull. Most of the time he hadn't needed any. There had been few meats served to him, and then only scraps. He lifted a tortilla and, clamping it around the meat, broke off some cheese and stuffed it alongside the meat. Then he bit into it, chewing vigorously.

"I see you are pleased."

"Mmm," he nodded with his mouth full. "I am."

"Good, good. Perhaps we have some other surprises for you soon. How is your memory?"

"I'm starting to recall a few things. I remembered my mother's voice, and I said the Lord's prayer."

"The Lord's prayer? This is wonderful. Perhaps you will find other things coming back to your mind as well."

"Seems to me to be happening mighty slow. Thoughts appear to creep into my head and then run out the back door."

"Maybe it will take a more powerful stimulus to bring back your memory." Reaching into her haversack, she produced the familiar bottle of brandy and a glass.

Julian smiled. "Well, I don't know about that. Most of the time people use that to forget, not recollect."

"Oh no, I wasn't referring to the brandy. This is just to celebrate."

"Celebrate?"

"Yes, celebrate the return of your memory. I believe we will see some results and see them soon."

"And what makes you so confident, Sister?" He picked up his spoon and filled it with the squash.

"You remembered your mother's voice and the prayer of our Lord. From my reading on others who have had memory losses like yours, I believe yours will return in a flood of thoughts. Perhaps at first only a trickle, but then like the opening of the mighty waters. Sometimes it takes a special event to cause this to happen."

"Well, I can think of a few special events I'd love to see go on right about now."

"Such as?"

"My inauguration as President of the United States or my wedding night would be a good start."

She laughed.

"I think we do have something that will surprise you and someone who may help you recall your thoughts."

He looked at her. The simplicity of her face could be deceiving. It was a plain and simple face that once had been quite beautiful. Her rough life had taken its toll on her, though—the sun, the wind, and the hardships. The wrinkles that formed small crow's-feet around her eyes gave no hint of emotion, and her eyes were like the beautiful eyes of a doll—they shone, but showed little.

"You know, many of the victims of this malady have their memory restored in a very short time by their families," she went on. "Of course most accidents like yours occur to people near their home, and when surrounded by loved ones, they soon have their lives back and their minds clear."

"Mine wasn't an accident, and I'm nowhere near home."

"This is true—and it is why we have brought your home to you."

Julian looked puzzled by the idea. "How is a thing like that possible?"

"You are most fortunate, señor. We already knew your name. In some strange sense you were near your home in my country. You have lived here. People know you."

"And you've told me what you know."

"Yes, but we couldn't put your life together, the life you had before you came to Mexico to fight for the emperor, but now we can. We can do this and so can you."

He blinked at her. She sounded so mysterious and yet so confident, all at the same time. It did give him some hope, but nothing he'd want to display. He picked up the cheese and bit into it.

"Wouldn't you like to know how?"

"Yes, I would."

"We have brought two of your brothers here to Mexico, James and Joe."

Initially, the names meant nothing to him. They were just names he recognized as Judeo-Christian ones, but he associated no faces with them. "Those names don't mean anything to me, I'm afraid. Should they?"

"Perhaps, perhaps not. It may take you meeting them and the three of you talking before you can begin to put your life back into the right place."

"When do we do that?"

"The general is working out the details even now. We need the information in your head, and the general has been kind enough to extend his pardon and amnesty to you in exchange for the knowledge you have. In addition to that he is giving you quite a large sum of money."

"How do I really know I can trust this general?"

She patted his hand. "Señor Julian, you can trust him in the same way you can trust me."

The new clothes felt strange on their freshly washed skin, and the razor had pulled smoothly through the stubble on their faces and necks. James seemed right at home, however. He patted a palmful of bay rum on his cheeks and dabbed it onto his smooth throat. Straightening his black string tie under the starched collar, he turned his head from side to side. "Not bad, if I do say so myself."

"Saying so yourself has never bothered you none, as I recall," Joe said.

James backed away from the mirror and extended his hands, palms up. It was as if he were beholding a painting by a famous Italian artist. "Well, I have eyes."

"I have eyes, too, and there's some things about all this that I don't like, not in the least."

James shook his head. "Joseph, some men see the opportunity in every difficulty. Others see only the difficulty in every opportunity. You are one of the latter. It may serve you well when faced with the desert and Indians, but at a dinner party it's a bore."

Joe ran a brush through his hair. "All I see is this whole picture, and I can't say as I care for it. It's their trip. It's their home. These are their clothes, and we're going down to their table. If you ask me, that puts us in the same spot as a Thanksgiving goose in Momma's pot."

"You are such a worrier. I just find it amazing that we came out of the same womb."

"To me, it's a comfort. God don't make no cookie-cutter people."

Chupta had cleaned himself up and sported the new clean clothes that the servants had brought up for him. Joe had protested initially. They were the white pants and shirt of a servant, but Chupta liked them. He insisted on wearing them, fearing the feel of a suit. He tucked the white bloused pants into his knee-high moccasins and combed his hair straight back. He had found a clean handkerchief to tie it with. He was clean, but he was all Apache.

Joe rummaged through the closet and came out with a striped vest belonging to one of the suits on the rack. He held it out to Chupta. "Here, why don't you put this on? You stay like you are and those folks down there will have you filling their glasses."

Chupta took the vest and slipped it on. It was silk and like nothing he'd ever felt before. It shone and glistened under the lamp. He beamed, giving off a rare smile.

Joe strapped on his gunbelt. "All right, I suppose we better go get ourselves served up."

"Is that necessary?" James asked, pointing at Joe's revolver.

"A body doesn't know what's necessary or not until the time comes."

Listening, Chupta picked up his own gunbelt and strapped it on.

"Well, my revolver is staying right here."

"Suit yourself," Joe said. "We best get down there. More than likely, they're already fixing our stuffing." He smiled.

Moving out onto the balcony, they looked down at the great room below. Several soldiers stood near the fire. One was a tall blonde with a carefully trimmed beard. Joe turned back to James. "Sure you don't wanna change your mind about that pistol?"

James shook his head.

They came down the stairs, and right away the men below spotted them, watching them closely. As they reached the bottom, the blond officer walked toward them and held out his hand. "Good evening, gentlemen. I am Major Manfried Hess."

"Pleased to meet you, Major." James shook his hand.

Joe nodded in the man's direction.

"Your other friends are already in the dining room, and I believe our meal is near completion," the major said. "If you will follow me."

"Lead on, Major," James said.

Moving out of the great room, the party passed through a hallway that flanked the veranda. They could see the beautiful garden through the glass doors and windows on that side of the house. The greenery was full leafed and in bloom, giving off neither a hint of the desert nor of the hot climate. There was a mystical quality to it.

Walking into the dining room, they could see the people milling about the oak sideboards and pouring drinks while they waited for dinner. Ellie and her father held their glasses, and Oscar smiled at them. Rosalyn leaned over and whispered in a man's ear. The man wore a dark dress uniform with shoulder boards and ribbons. He was large, with a balding head and a massive mustache. He regarded them with piercing black eyes.

"I believe that is our host," James said.

"I reckon so."

The man moved in their direction. Pushing his mustache aside with the back of his hand, he forced a smile and extended his hand. "Good evening, gentlemen. I am General Escobar. You don't know how happy I am to see you, and I want to thank you personally for bringing my wife and daughter home safely. They have already told me so much about your trip and what bold and intelligent men you both are."

James shook his hand. "Thank you, General. I am James Cobb, and this is my brother Joe."

Joe stepped forward and politely shook the man's hand. Turning back, he motioned toward Chupta. "I'm Joe Cobb, and this man back here was largely responsible for us getting here. He's a White Mountain Apache named Chupta."

Joe stood back and watched the man's reaction. The general nodded at Chupta and said nothing.

Joe went on, "In fact, if it hadn't been for Chupta here, we'd all be dead. A man's got to know his way around out there, and very few folks do, don't you think, General?"

"You may be right," Escobar said.

"I am right," Joe said.

"You have a beautiful home here, General," James said. It was obvious James wanted to do his best to ease the tension Joe seemed so bent on creating.

"Gracias," the general said. "It has been built slowly and well. I suppose you gentlemen will want to see the rest of the house."

"That would be delightful," James said.

"And you will want to see your brother."

"Yes, we will," Joe said.

"He has been in great trouble here in my country, serving as he did with the Austrian dictator. I have done my best to give him protection, but the people still clamor for revenge."

"I'm sure you've been quite the host for old Julian." Joe grinned.

CHAPTER 21

+ + + + + + +

THE NEXT MORNING CAME EARLY for Joe and even earlier for Chupta. Both men paced the room like tigers in a cage. It was James who found getting up to be such a chore. He tossed in his big bed and made noises like a bear being forced out of early hibernation. "What are you two doing?" he asked.

"We've done it all," Joe snapped. "The sun's been up and whatever we're going to do, we better get at it."

James sat up in bed. "You all that anxious to see Julian?"

"I'm all that anxious to get home. The quicker we take care of our business here, the sooner I can get my behind back to Texas and Karen."

James threw back his covers. "All right, I can see that." He blinked at the men. They stood in the room in the same clothes they'd come in with the night before, only now they were clean and freshly starched. "Where'd you get those?" he asked.

"People 'round here get right down to business," Joe said. "They were right outside our room this morning in the neatest little pile you ever saw. Yours are over in the chair yonder. Now I'd suggest you get in them, and we'll get outta here."

James pushed his feet onto the carpeted floor and rubbed his face. "Well, I will have to shave. This clean face I found last night is something I discovered I'd been missing."

"Fine, just do what ya gotta do. Chupta here's going pure crazy."

James looked over to see the Apache out on the balcony, tugging at the vine as if to explore some way of climbing down. James stood up and stretched. "I'm not sure it's Chupta we need to worry about. You're the one with ants in his britches."

With that James sauntered into the bathroom and opened his razor. A short time later he was tugging on his boots over fresh-washed jeans. "Are we going to tell Ellie and her father about sending them to Santa Fe on the stage?" he asked.

"Well, I don't plan on telling them. I know how much store you set in lighting up the faces of single ladies. I'll let you tell her. Maybe she'll be mighty grateful. I'm just a little too married to have womenfolk grateful at me."

James grinned. "You are so understanding, dear brother."

The three of them headed downstairs together and entered the massive dining room. The places had been set and a large assortment of breads, fruit, bacon, ham, and eggs was arranged on the sideboard. They began to fill their plates. Moments later the Ralfsruds joined them.

"You folks sleep well?" James asked.

"Like a king." Oscar smiled. "A king what is broke."

"A king never needs money," James laughed, "only his good name."

"Well, that I got, and while it may serve me well here, it ain't worth spit where I come from."

"Joe and I discussed that before we turned in last night," James said. "We know you folks are in a tight spot. I have some money set aside and plan on putting you both on the stage for Santa Fe at the nearest town. We'll stake you a little besides that."

The man's face turned red. "I can't have you two do that. I wouldn't know how to begin to pay you back."

"We think you're worth the risk," Joe said. "You know goods, and that counts for a lot in most any place. You can go to Santa Fe and start something there. You just stay put for a while—the customers will find you."

Oscar continued to shake his head. "I've never owed a man in my life."

Ellie put her arms around him. "Papa, you know we have that little nest egg in the bank in Denver. We could have them wire it to a bank in Santa Fe, and you could start a business with it."

"We wuz saving that. I wuz saving that for you, girl. You've earned it, all of it. It's yours."

"Yes and I'm investing it in you, Papa."

"Well, it won't do you much good here in Mexico," James said. "And it's a long, hot walk back to Santa Fe. So we won't have any more talk about it. We're advancing your stage fare, and we'll send you on your way. You'd do the same for us if the shoe was on the other foot."

"Just take it as part of the grace of God, Papa. I know that's hard for you. It always has been."

He mumbled and patted her hand.

They filled their plates, and cups of coffee steamed in their hands. Ellie motioned over to James, and he slipped over to her side. "I saw a beautiful garden outside. Would you care to take breakfast with me out there?"

James bowed his head slightly. "Now I am embarrassed," he said.

"Why is that?"

"I'm embarrassed that I didn't think of it first."

She smiled. "Men never think of these things first. They just believe they do."

He laughed. "I suppose you're right there. Women always seem to have a mind for things of beauty, and even if the idea doesn't begin in their own heads, they usually are the inspiration for it." He nodded toward the French doors. "It would seem appropriate for me to follow you."

She smiled and walked through the doors, followed by James. "This unfortunately may surprise you, James, but there are many times when the best ideas do begin in a woman's head."

The veranda was a beautiful place, more beautiful by morning than it had been the evening before. Bees and hummingbirds darted among the flowers, and the blooming vines that covered that side of the house towered above them and spread their blossoms. The fountain in the middle bubbled with sparkling water. Ellie soon found a bench large enough to accommodate them and sat down.

James took his seat beside her and the two of them started to nibble on their food. "This place is beautiful, isn't it?" he asked.

"Yes, it turns my heart to God," Ellie said.

James sipped his coffee.

Ellie lifted her eyes to the blue sky above and the morning sunlight that bathed the plants. "This world's a room so small within my Master's house, and the open sky up there is but a small part of His yard."

"It does make a man feel small, doesn't it?"

"Yes it does. But I think a man is very large when he reflects the goodness of God, and you and your brother did that this morning with my father."

"Nothing we have belongs to us," James said. "It's all on loan for us to use wisely, and we feel it's a wise use of what resources we have." He sipped his coffee. "This whole world is a wonder, but none of it more wonderful than the people in it. You and your father are both good people, very good people. And I believe I'm here sitting next to the most beautiful thing in the garden."

"You know, James, I've never been close to a man before, not real close. I've been with my father for fourteen years now, and we've been traveling."

"That is a great loss to many a man, I'm sure."

"Perhaps, but I feel like I've been saving myself for only one man."

James looked at her. She was a pretty woman—not beautiful like Palmira, but pretty in a plain sense. Her hair was fixed in a loose bun with curls falling softly down the side of her face. Her eyes were steady in their gaze. It was apparent from the way she looked at him that she had nothing to hide, and it was this purity of spirit that allowed her to see into his heart. "Do you find yourself wondering about people?" James asked.

"Yes, I often do," she said. "My father says it's a gift."

"I thought as much. Do you watch them and then try to imagine what they're thinking, where they come from, what it is that they want most in life?"

"Yes, I do. I've always thought it was because of our work. We'd stop and begin to sell things, and I would see someone and think about what might interest them. My father says I'm a natural at selling."

"You have a direct way about you, Ellie. There's no pretense, no attempt to hide. And you seem to have a genuine love for people. I'm like that in some ways, but people see that as my love of poetry and verse."

"There is a softness to you, James."

"Thank you. I take that as a high compliment. I was just thinking, though, as I looked at you, that there's a purity in you. I remember a verse of Scripture that my mother would quote to us children when she tried to teach us matters of the heart. It says, 'Blessed are the pure in heart, for they shall see God.' Then she'd go on to tell us that the purity of our hearts would allow us to see into people as well. Without the twistedness of self-interest, she'd say that someone could clearly see other people. I find that in you, Ellie. You've spent so much time serving your father and others that you've had so little for yourself."

"I wish that were totally true. My father wants to hang on to me, but I've told him this next stop is my last. As long as he has me, he will never get over losing my mother."

"And you think that is selfish on your part?"

"Yes, very."

James munched on a piece of bacon and mulled the matter over. "I don't see it that way. I think you're thinking about him there too, just as you always have. I find you truly a remarkable woman."

She smiled. "Something tells me you've found many remarkable women in your life. Is there any room in your life for such a woman?" she asked.

He stopped his eating and put down the plate. "Any room in my life? Why would you ask that? Of course there is." He could see her thinking about an answer, seemingly for the longest time. It was almost as if there was a thought in her head—one she'd rather not say.

Hesitating, she began, "Well, you're a widower, and I've seen it in my father. There is nothing so perfect in life as a dead wife—nothing so pure, nothing so lovely, nothing so intelligent, and nothing that will ever satisfy a man in the same way. They make the perfect mate, dead wives do, because they can always be holy and lovely at the same time. You need never let them into your real world again. They can comfortably continue as some gossamer fantasy that need never step out of the picture frame, need never be anything more than an illusion. And a figment of one's imagination is so very cozy, James. That way any real woman will never quite live up to it. They may get close enough to remind you of the feelings you once had, but never so close as to threaten the fantasy."

James was stunned. He sat listening to the thoughts rattle around in his mind, and he was purely shaken. "Are you speaking of your father, or are you referring to me?"

She put down her cup and leaned toward him. "James, I'm talking about you. The same might be said of my father, but it most definitely is true of you." She smiled and chuckled slightly. "I'm sorry I spoiled your picture-book idea of women. You seem to enjoy keeping us in the image-only category. To keep us at a distance is to keep us safe. I mean, James, you're too much of a gentleman to allow us to become too close. It would prick your conscience to break someone's heart, at least break it enough for you to see."

"I have women friends that I am close to."

"Of that, I'm quite certain," she said. "Of course, they don't get close enough to make any changes in you or inconvenience your life in any way. You just seem to have the best of all possible worlds, James, sad though it is."

James sat back. "I'm stupefied. I don't think I've ever had anyone talk to me in this manner, let alone a woman."

"Don't you think we're smart enough to recognize the truth when we see it?"

"Of course you are, I just didn't realize—"

She cut him off, "That I was intelligent enough."

"No, that's not what I meant to say. I . . . I didn't mean that at all. I don't know what I meant to say." He shook his head, then looked up at her as if studying her for the first time. "I just don't think I've ever seen those things you say you see in me." He looked her directly in her eyes. "How did you?"

"You talked to me so easily and so flirtatiously, and then there was Palmira. She's a very beautiful woman. Anyone can see that. You always seemed just as at ease in your conversations with her and just as interested in her too. Then it occurred to me. It wasn't that you couldn't make up your mind. It was that you already had made up your mind some time ago. And you were just content with bringing the feelings into your life every now and then while you stayed at ease with your memories. That's why you seem interested in many women, but never too interested in just one."

James sat and watched her, soaking in her words. "Where did you come from? How did you get this way?"

"From living with and loving my father." She picked up her cup of coffee and held it to her lips to sip it. Almost as an afterthought, she breathed the words over the lip of the cup, "And from loving you, James Cobb."

"There you both are. I've been looking for you." It was Palmira. "Especially for you, James." The young woman wore a full bright yellow skirt along with a ruffled and strikingly white top. She had a yellow rose in her hair that seemed to match perfectly. It was beautiful, breathtaking to any eye. "I wanted to show you around the grounds," she went on.

"I . . . I . . . I was just talking to Ellie here." He spoke the words haltingly, his face white as a sheet of paper.

"That can wait, I'm sure." She looked at Ellie. "Don't you think so?"

Ellie sipped her coffee without an answer.

"No, I'm afraid it can't," James responded.

Just then they heard the sound of more footsteps on the bricks. It was Joe following behind the hip-booted Major Hess. "You see," Hess said, "they are here."

"Let's go, James," Joe said. "The major here is going to take us to the church where they've got Julian."

James turned to Ellie. "We must finish this."

She smiled at him. "James, I'd love to see you finish almost anything that involves a woman."

Julian was surprised by the sound of the key in the door, and even more astonished when it was the sound of several men, their heels clicking over the stone floor.

Several guards opened the door. One held a stack of clean clothes in his hand. "You are to come with us, señor. You will have a baño, a bath."

"A bath?" Julian got to his feet. "Why are you giving me a bath?"

"Because you stink, señor."

Julian lifted his shirt and smelled it. "Well, I been stinkin' for quite a while. Why go and bathe me now?"

"Do not ask questions, señor. Just come with us."

Julian shuffled through the underground tunnels. They were going to a place he had never been to before. He had hoped the men would take him into the sunshine. He'd have gladly given up his privacy for even a few minutes in the sun. However, it was evidently not to be.

The torches burned in the dark hallway, and at the very top of the wall, a series of small grated windows let in the dim light. He passed a kitchen area where the stove was still warm. The tables were filled with what seemed to have been the ingredients of his own breakfast that morning. That much surprised him.

Next he passed by a series of what appeared to be underground apartments. The rooms were sparsely furnished—two cots, a table, two chairs, and a candlestick. One difference between these rooms and his were the bars in his. The other was the fact that these rooms each had a religious painting hanging on the wall and a cross. Perhaps they were the rooms of the priests of the mission, but there seemed to be so many of them.

Rounding a corner, they came to a large room with several tubs of water sitting in it along with lye soap and rough towels. The guard pushed him toward one of the tubs. "Wash yourself," he yelled, "and put on these clothes."

"Why now?" Julian asked.

"You have visitors today."

A short time later, the men clanged the doors on his cell shut. They had replaced his bedbug-ridden mat with a cot and a new mattress. They also arranged the table and chairs back into his cell. His cell had taken on a new look, but it was for show, and he knew it.

He paced the floor in his remade cell, smelling fresh and looking over the clothes he was being allowed to wear. The boots were not new, but they did fit. The jeans seemed to have little wear, a bit faded but washed and clean. The blue denim shirt he wore was frayed around the collar, but washed and starched. They had used a pin to set his sleeve just below the stump on his left elbow. He'd been shaved by one of the guards, and his face had taken on a new appearance, still needing some sun but clean and smelling of shaving cream. He felt like a new man.

He heard the key in the outside door once again. A group was making their way down the hall, and he could hear the familiar drag of Sister Mary Perizza's foot. He faced the cell doors to greet them.

Two men and the sister stood at the door, flanked by several of the guards. One of the guards turned the key and stepped back as the nun and the two men entered his cell. Julian straightened the eye patch over his left eye and regarded them stoically.

"Do you recognize your brothers?" Sister Mary asked.

"No," Julian replied.

The men looked at the fresh bandage on his head. "I'm your brother James," the first one said, extending his hand.

Julian reached out and shook it.

"And I'm Joe." The man looked somber, much more dour than the first man, but he held out his hand for a shake. Julian complied.

"Why don't you men sit down on the bed there," Sister Mary said. "We can pull up the chairs and talk."

"You look well, Julian," James said.

"I do now."

James looked around the cell. "I suppose it isn't much here, but you appear to be well taken care of."

Julian and Sister Mary exchanged glances.

"We've met this General Escobar who has you here," Joe said. "The man says you've lost your memory. He says we might be able to help you get it back."

"We certainly hope so," Sister Mary interjected.

Joe caught sight of the small bars in the window, high above on the wall. "Frankly, I just want to get you out of here. Getting that memory of yours back or not doesn't concern me much. There's a lot of what you've done that I'd just as soon you'd forget about, if you ask me."

"I'd sure like to see some sunshine," Julian said.

"Perhaps we can arrange that," the sister said. She got up and, going back to the barred hallway, talked to the guards. They nodded in agreement. Turning around, she smiled. "We're all going to take a walk. The guards will go with us, but I think you'll find certain parts of the mission, the garden, perhaps, to be most pleasing."

"Fine," Joe said. "Let's get him out of here so we can talk."

Minutes later, the group was strolling in the bright sunshine, taking in the sights of the vegetable and flower garden. The sun was overhead, and the heat beat down on them. Julian lifted his head, watching the path of the sun as if it might be his last chance to see it.

"The general says you know the whereabouts of something he wants to find," James said. "He says if you can remember he will let you go a free man, a free man and a rich man."

Julian stopped in his tracks. "I tell you what. Even if I did know, I wouldn't tell him. He's tried to line me up and shoot me before. This time he'd have to use real bullets."

The four of them spent the remainder of the morning talking about home. At times Julian seemed to know nothing about the memories they were trying to bring up, but then at other times his face would brighten and he'd talk about events, even before James and Joe could bring them up. Near lunchtime, the guards walked up and announced it was time for their visit to end.

James hugged Julian, who stood there like a stone. "Don't you worry, Julian," he said. "We'll work on getting you out of here."

"Don't make no deals," Julian said. "I ain't telling that man a thing."

With that, the guards led him away.

Sister Mary Perizza looked at the somber Joe. "I can see you weren't too happy over your visit."

"Very little of what that man ever does makes me happy," Joe responded.

"You would like to see him out of here, though, wouldn't you?"

Joe studied her. It was obvious she had something in mind behind those eyes of hers, something she was reluctant to say outright.

James looked at her, suddenly curious. "What do you have in mind, Sister?"

"I'd like both of you to meet me here tonight," she said. "Bring an extra horse."

CHAPTER 22

+ + + + + + +

WHEN MAJOR HESS BROUGHT the two men back to the hacienda, he took their horses. "I vill see to your animals," he said. "I hope you had a good visit with your brother and that he vill cooperate."

"Yes," James said. "It was good to see him, if only for the morning."

Joe walked off without giving an answer to the officer. Reaching the big doors, he turned and walked into the gardens. He stood, staring at the high walls around the house. The place gave him an uncomfortable feeling. The guards on the walls and gates looked them over as if they all knew something they weren't talking about. Joe had worn his revolver when they left that morning, but he still felt trapped. Maybe it was just being here that gave him an uncomfortable feeling.

James caught up with him. "You seemed pretty quiet back there."

"Why should I tell that man what I think?" Joe said. "Besides, Julian ain't going to cooperate, not with that general or with anybody else."

"His mind was coming around at the end, you could see that, couldn't you?"

Joe and James had spent a good deal of time with Julian, mostly talking about things dealing with their boyhood in Georgia. Thoughts had started reentering his head—they could all see that, including Sister Mary. However, whenever the conversation turned to his wound and how he got into the position he was in right now, he would clam up and say little or nothing. It was as if the memories were returning and he was keeping all of them close to his vest.

"I could see that," Joe said, "but they're his thoughts. They don't belong to anybody else. A man can stick you into a prison and he's got your body, but that don't mean he's got your mind and your soul."

"I'm not sure our brother's mind and soul would be coveted by anyone."

"I'm not so sure they couldn't," Joe said. "There appeared to be a softness to him that I can't remember seeing before."

"That was just that cell speaking."

"Maybe, maybe not." Joe watched the wall behind James as a guard walked it and then stood there, watching them. "Maybe it's just this place that I don't like. I feel like there's eyes all over us everywhere we are. It gives me the shivers, and I'll feel whole lots better when we've cleared out of here." Joe continued to stare at the wall.

James turned around and saw the guard. "I see what you mean," he said.

"It's like that all the time. The man in that tower was staring into our room all night—made a fella wary to even get undressed."

"And why do you suppose that nun wants to meet with us tomorrow night?" James turned around and asked.

"I'm not sure, but she seemed pretty serious about us saying nothing to no one about it."

"Do you think she wants to bust him out?" James asked.

Joe shook his head. "A nun? Now why would she get involved with a thing like that? That seems pretty strange to me. The woman's religious, and this thing is about politics and a man we both know is a killer, even if he is our brother."

"Well, it sounds like to me that things are going to move fast here," James said. "I think if we're going to see the Ralfsruds off to Santa Fe, we'd better take them to town this afternoon. We don't want them here if things get rough."

"You're right. Maybe that would help me too. Right now I think I'd enjoy a ride without an escort shadowing us. I'd just as soon get to a bar and sit down to watch somebody else for a change."

James laughed. "That sounds good to me. I'll go see if I can find them, and we'll take them into town."

James wound his way through the garden, passing the spot where Ellie had opened up his soul. The thought stirred him. Few people had ever questioned him after he'd completed his doctoral dissertation. Even then, there had been no queries about his soul, only his mind. He wondered, *Could she be right? Have I been more at home with the world of my memories than in the real world with a real woman?*

He made his way down the hall and into the great room. The place had a hollow, soulless quality to it—he could feel that. Reaching the bottom of the stairs, he bounded up them two at a time. He knocked on Ellie's door.

"Come in," she said.

James walked in. Ellie was seated on a sofa in the oversized bedroom, reading a book. She put it down and smiled.

The room had a softer quality to it with wallpaper that had scenes of red birds flying through fields of yellow flowers. The fireplace contained burnt logs. Perhaps the Ralfsruds had also enjoyed a fire the night before.

"Did you have a nice visit with your brother?" she asked.

"Yes we did, but something's come up. We need to get you into town and get tickets to Santa Fe for you today."

"Today? Why so soon? I was just beginning to enjoy this place, although I'm sure Papa is anxious to leave. He sees himself as a burden."

"Yes, I can see your father thinking just that. Something may break here, and I wouldn't want you and your father in the cross fire."

"Are you sure this has nothing to do with what we talked about this morning?"

"No, nothing to do with that. You'll need some traveling clothes and a little bit of food, I imagine."

Ellie stood up. "I'm very sorry I was so abrasive with you at breakfast. That isn't at all like me. And I know it was partially because I know our time is short here. I'm somewhat used to that. I've been traveling for so long and never taken the time to develop a relationship with someone slowly, let alone a man who appeals to me."

"And I appeal to you that much?"

"Of course you do. Do you think I would waste my time telling you the truth if I didn't have any feelings for you? I'm not the kind of woman to open her mind up to just any man."

James shook his head. "And your feelings, I must say, took me totally by surprise. There I was with you telling me what you did and then me having to go and see my brother . . . I've thought of little else all day."

"I'm sorry, James. These are emotions I've never felt for any man before. I've never been able to, moving about and all. Of course, you've been carefully cultivating them for days. I think you do that to women and just aren't aware of it. I may have made a terrible mistake in feeling the way I do. I don't normally express myself so boldly."

"You certainly did today. I'd hate to see what you might do with a man who cheated you in business."

She laughed. "If I ever found a man who could cheat me, I'd want to thank him for the education. Papa is so sharp in business. He does what he does to make sure he never has neighbors, not to avoid being a success with a store. Often what men choose to do in life has nothing to do with the job itself."

"I like my position. I enjoy teaching at the college."

"I'm sure you do. Think about all those young pliable minds you must impress and with no one to question you."

James chuckled. "You are an amazing woman. I'm going to say something here that I'm certain I will live to regret, but I will say it anyway. I find you my equal in every respect, and in this area of knowing people, you are my definitive superior. I am simply unarmed by you."

"True humility can deliver you from any dilemma, James."

She walked over to the bed where her clean traveling clothes had been left and, turning them over, caressed the pretty white dress that lay on top of the pile.

James stepped closer to her. "You did open your heart to me, Ellie, and while it took me by surprise, it wasn't unpleasant."

"It wasn't?"

"No. Few people have ever talked to me in that way before. It draws me close to you."

She stepped toward him. "How close, James?"

"We do have to go, however, and as soon as possible."

"I suppose this will be convenient for you."

"How is that?"

"Let's face it, I got too personal with you this morning, much too personal. I stepped out of the dollhouse you had me locked in."

James smiled. "Yes you did, but that will have to wait for another time."

"Another time? Maybe I don't want to wait for another time."

"My dear, if you remain here, you may be in danger."

"And you care about me being in danger?"

"Let me just have out and say it, Ellie. I find myself falling in love with you, everything about you. You are gentle and yet can be honest and insightful like no woman I've ever known. You are appealing both to my eye and to my heart. There, now, I've said it. I've thought seriously about it all morning, and now it's out. I've never been the kind of man who thinks silently and then delivers a final edict on anything, but that is where my mind is going, and I know you know it."

She stepped closer to him. "James, I am good for you. I'm not sure anyone's ever told you the truth about who you are in quite some time, and I love you. I've told you that."

"Ellie, you do frighten me. You frighten and fascinate me at the same time. You make my mind go back to a snake charmer I saw in India. He played the flute as the snake danced in front of him. You could see no fear in the man's eyes, even though there was good reason. He simply played the flute, and all of us were enticed by the spectacle as much as the music. I'm afraid, however, I'm not very good with the flute."

Ellie laughed. "You need to read more geography, James, and less poetry."

"How is that?"

"In the books I've read that talk about the snake charmers of India and their dancing cobras, there's one little fact you've overlooked."

"What would that be?"

"They sew the mouths of the snakes shut. They force-feed them and stitch their mouths. When the serpents die, they simply find another to dance in front of them. There is no danger to the man, only death for the snake." She put down her book. "Perhaps there is more similarity there than you care to realize."

James reached out and took her in his arms. "I think you've said enough." Bending down, he gently kissed her. "Now, there. I still want you ready to go in the next few minutes."

She was surprised and slightly flustered. "I don't know what to say."

"Good, then that will be a first for you today," he laughed. "But I want you ready to go. I'll go and find your father and have your horses saddled."

As he moved to the door, she caught his sleeve. "James, I'll get ready, but I don't want to leave you."

"We'll take you and your father to the stage, and you can both talk the matter over. I want to see you safe, and that has everything to do with you not being with me."

"Perhaps, but I've been safe long enough. Now, my only interest is in being alive and with you."

Hours later, Zac and Pablo had finished lunch and were walking back to the stables. The town had taken on a fresh, lively quality to it during the morning. Street vendors stood on the sides of the street, and at one end wagons were busy setting up shop to hawk their wares. One old man banged on pots to attract the attention of women to his hardware. Zac had stopped and bought Pablo some striped candy. The boy's eyes danced as he poked the end of it in his eager mouth. Suddenly, they spotted the three men swaggering toward them.

The man called Torrie gave off a big grin through his beard. He nudged the other two, and they picked up their pace in Zac's direction.

"Hold on to your candy, boy," Zac said.

"Better still, you ought to keep it in your mouth. Just trust me."

"Did you have a chance to think about our deal?" Torrie asked.

"Yes, I did."

"Well?"

"I'll take the job, but I have to know more about it."

"Why, sure." He turned back to the other two men. "How 'bout that, boys, we got us a shootist. Gonna make our job lots easier."

Yuma continued to stare at Pablo, working hard to place him.

Torrie looked down at the boy. "So, how's the little feller today? You gettin' him his milk on time along with that candy?"

"He's doin' fine and looking forward to us getting our business done so he can get back home. I told him to keep that candy in his mouth. You fellers look like the sort to take a boy's candy."

Web laughed. "See there, Torrie, this man's got us placed."

"Yeah," Yuma said, "and I wish I could place that kid."

Zac put his hand on Pablo's shoulder and pulled him closer. "I said I'd take the job. I just need to know more of the particulars."

"Good," Torrie said. Reaching into his pocket, he pulled out a leather bag that jingled. He loosened the drawstring on it and poured five Double Eagle twenty-dollar gold coins into the palm of Zac's hand. "There ya be, friend."

"Now tell me where this man is exactly and when you plan on doing this."

Torrie swung his head around to make sure no one could overhear. "He's close by."

"You gonna tell 'em?" Web asked.

"Yes, Web, I am."

"You ain't even showed me yet," Web said. "How come yer tellin' him?"

"I ain't showed you 'cause you don't need to know just yet. 'Sides, with this feller, you might not even have to know, not now, not ever."

"Then you can tell both of us at the same time," Zac said.

"Close by here there's an old mission. Right now, it's a leper colony. This feller's being held in a dungeon under the old church. It's pretty carefully guarded, and I don't reckon as to how we could get ourselves in there, least not any easy way. My man in there tells me, though, that they plan on movin' that feller, maybe even tomorrow. I got myself a spot fixed in the draw that's about ten miles north of the mission."

He pointed toward a road that led west out of town. "That would be about five miles north of here. You follow that road, and it'd take you right to the spot. There's a creek runs through there. My man's in charge of the detail. He says when they get to the creek that he'll take the men out to water the horses and stand the feller up outside the wagon. I wuz planning on makin' some kind of noise, maybe even some shootin' west of the wagon, and having Yuma here ride up and kill the man, but with you there, it wouldn't be necessary."

"How far is the shot?"

Torrie stroked his beard. "I'm figuring about three hundred yards."

"That should be easy," Zac said. "If you three stay west of the place where the wagon stops, you can keep the guards busy while I shoot."

"Why don't you let me go with him?" Yuma asked. "I could show him his spot."

"I'll pick my own spot," Zac shot back. "Besides, I work best alone. Havin' somebody lookin' over my shoulder makes me nervous."

Zac suddenly turned his eyes up the road. Riding into town from the south were Joe, James, and Chupta. They had a man and a woman with them.

Yuma saw them too. He nudged Torrie and pointed. "Look who's comin' down the road."

They all peered down the street to see the group riding forward. Yuma slunk back, but gazed around Web. When they turned around, Zac and Pablo were gone.

Joe looked down the street and saw the three men staring at them. A moment before they'd been talking to a man and a boy, but now they stood alone in the street, watching them. "Look at what we got waitin' for us," Joe said.

James looked up. "Is that who I think it is?"

"You bet," Joe said. "Those people are like a sickness you can't seem to shake. Just when you think you're over it and can get your appetite back, they come poking into your life again."

Ellie and Oscar spotted them. "It's those evil men," Ellie said.

"The very ones," James responded. He looked over at Joe. "I don't plan on leaving Ellie here with those men lurking around."

"James, I'm not sure you plan on leaving Ellie anyway."

They rode past the three men.

Torrie tipped his hat to Ellie and grinned. "Pleased to see you folks again—especially you, ma'am."

Without saying a word, the five of them continued their ride to the end of the street. They rode their horses down to the hitching rail in front of the stage stop and, stepping down, tied the animals up to the rail.

Ellie looked at Joe. "You just need to buy one ticket for Papa. I'm coming with you."

"Now, Ellie, girl," Oscar said, "you're just getting in these gentlemen's way."

"Papa, we've talked about this. We agreed the next stop was my last, and this is the next stop. You go on to Santa Fe and get settled, and we will catch up to you."

"How am I gonna get myself settled without you?"

Ellie put her hand on his shoulder and looked into his blue eyes. "Papa, this is important to me. I don't want to disappoint you, but I should be allowed to have a life of my own. You promised me that much."

Oscar nodded silently, a tear forming in his eye.

Joe gave her a hard look. "Miss, this is going to be a difficult trip with lots of hard riding. I don't know if we're going to be followed, but there's plenty of people hereabouts who want to stop us."

"Mr. Cobb, I've been through some hard riding for the last fourteen years, and I wouldn't call what I've already gone through with you a Sunday afternoon jaunt. I can take whatever comes, and I have a mind of my own."

Joe looked at James and Oscar. "Your father and I will go in and see to the stage. James, why don't you try and talk some sense into Ellie here while we're gone."

James nodded and the two men walked up the stairs and into the office.

Turning to Chupta, he looked a bit embarrassed. "The lady and I are just going to take a walk."

Chupta nodded.

They started walking and James dropped his hand to his side, picking up hers. "I want you to reconsider this, Ellie. There is no need for you to do this. I'll do what I have to do and come to Santa Fe when it's over. We can catch up then."

"James, a man and a woman get to know each other by living life together, not living it alone and then reporting on it in some rose garden. I know it may sound romantic to you to do something like that, but to me it just sounds lonely."

"Joe is right. We don't know what may happen on this trip. We're not even sure of what will happen tonight. What if we're killed trying to get my brother out of here?"

"Then I'll be right there with the man I love."

"But you're so young. You're not even sure of what love is."

"Exactly, and that is why I want to find out. I have no illusion of you showing me a good time or coddling me like some child. Don't even let that thought enter your head or I'll scratch your eyes out. I will not be patronized, and I will not be babied."

"What if I don't want you to come with us?"

"It would depend on your reason." They stopped and she looked at him. "Now don't lie to me, James. Don't continue creating this illusion of yours just to feel romantic at the moment. Tell me the truth. Do you have honest feelings for me?"

"Ellie, I am a people person. I am surrounded by people all day, every day. But inside, I'm a lonely man. I didn't realize how lonely I was until you told me the truth this morning. Now, for the first time in my life, I stand with someone who truly knows me and loves me just the same. I will never be the same, not ever."

He bowed his head slightly, staring at the top of his boots, then lifted it to look directly into her eyes. "In many ways this is new ground for me, like nothing I've ever felt before. It frightens me."

"Then just tell me good-bye, James. I'll go with my father, and you'll never see me again."

"No, I do not want that. I don't want you to accompany us either. I just don't want to put you in any danger, but I don't want to lose you either, Ellie. I love you."

She lifted herself on the balls of her feet and kissed him. It was a soft and sweet kiss, filled with warmth. Settling back down on her feet, she smiled at him. "Then it's settled."

"So you'll go with your father, and I'll come to Santa Fe?"

"No, I'm going with you."

Neither one of them observed the small boy talking to Chupta. Both were lost in the moment.

CHAPTER 23

+ + + + + + +

ZAC WAITED AS PABLO TALKED to Chupta and then watched as the boy led the scout over to the alleyway. Coming around the corner, the look of surprise on the Apache's face was instant. "That's right," Zac said, "it's me."

"You follow us?"

"Yes. I've been behind you since Santa Fe. I wanted to tell you, but I couldn't. I was afraid that some look by one of those brothers of mine, especially James, might give me away."

"Why you follow?"

"I just didn't trust that government agent in Santa Fe. I figured to watch and see who he might send to do his dirty work, and now I think I know."

"Those men out there."

"Yes, but there might be others."

"They scalp hunters."

"I know." Zac put his hand on Pablo's head. "They killed the boy's folks and sister and took their scalps too, so they aren't too particular about the source of their hair or their money, I reckon."

"I see scalps," Chupta said. "Some not Indian."

"So why are you in town?" Zac asked.

"We come get stage ticket for two white people, but woman, she don't go. She go with your brother James."

Zac bowed his head for a moment, studying the ground and raking the toe of his boot over it. "Yes, I'm afraid James has been quite the lady's man."

"This seem serious. I think she catch him. She want to go with us."

"You're not taking her, are you?"

Chupta shrugged.

"Have they seen Julian?"

"They see Julian. He at church. They think church woman help them take him out of jail tonight."

"Church woman? A nun?"

"That what they say."

"Listen, those men out there have somebody working with them inside that jail. I don't think it's a nun, though." He shook his head. "Somehow I find that hard to imagine. They plan on killing Julian, though, when they move him. They've hired me to do the killing."

Chupta seemed puzzled.

"Don't say anything to those brothers of mine just yet. I'll keep following you. The boy and I will watch that place tonight. If you do manage to get him out, I'll be right behind you, so don't go to shooting strangers you can't see clearly in the dark. You understand? Especially ones traveling with small boys."

Chupta nodded. "You better tell brother Joe. He watch back trail real good. He is good man, just like you say."

"I'm glad, and I'm glad for their sakes that you're along with them. It makes me sleep a lot easier."

"Chupta glad you here and follow."

Zac put his hand on Chupta's shoulder. "Thank you, friend. I'll be behind you at least for a while yet. I'm always better when I work alone." He looked down into Pablo's face. "Of course, now I have some help."

Zac watched as Chupta walked back to his spot in front of the stage depot. It wasn't long before Joe and the older man came out. They talked for some time with James and the woman, and then she said her good-byes to the old man. Zac studied the scene. It told him all he needed to know. He watched as his brothers rode out of town, along with Chupta and the woman.

"I suppose we better see if we can find those employers of ours. They'll be missing us, and we wouldn't want them hiring somebody else, now, would we?"

Pablo reluctantly shook his head.

"Besides, we've got their money."

A short time later, Zac and Pablo were walking the streets of Hermosa. They stopped at one of the carts, and Zac forked over money for some dried fruit. He moved down the line of merchants, making careful purchases of everything from flour to coffee to jerky. It would be enough to carry them as far as they needed to go.

They walked the length of the street, turning into the cantina. Zac held the doors until he spotted a free table. Taking his seat, he signaled for the bartender. This was a different man from the one they had seen the night before—a tall, spindly man with a long mustache that he seemed terribly proud of. The man smiled at them and curled it with his fingers. Zac signaled him over.

Rounding the end of the bar, he walked up to Zac's table. "What can I serve you, señor?" He noticed Pablo. "We don't have much for children."

The music stopped as the piano player in the corner sipped a beer.

"Do you have something hot to eat?" Zac asked.

"We have some stew. The lady who's married to the owner fixed it this morning."

"She a good cook?"

Looking around, the man pretended to spit. "Pheww. She's the worst cook there is, señor, and she washes clothes even worse than she cooks. She does make a stew that you can eat, though, but you should be glad you were not here yesterday. She cooked green chilies that could have killed my horse."

"Well, let's be glad it's today, then. Why don't you bring us two bowls of that stew and two glasses of buttermilk."

"You don't want whiskey?"

Zac shook his head. "No, I've seen liquor served in places like this. What yesterday's green chilies couldn't kill, most of that stuff would."

The man turned and reported the order to the back room. Zac pushed himself away from the table. "Places like this are a necessity for men who do what I do, but I wouldn't choose to spend my time in one if I didn't have to. More men have been killed by bad liquor than bullets."

"Why do men drink it, señor?"

"Because the life they live is sometimes not worth the living. They drink to forget, and some drink to remember. Personally, I think it's better for a man if he just lives the life he has right now. He should work hard and keep his own head about him."

"Sí, señor. I think that is good too."

Zac reached over and mussed up Pablo's long black hair. "Good, then maybe we're learning something after all."

Pablo and Zac had nearly finished their barely edible stew when the three bounty hunters walked in. The men spotted them right away and sauntered over to their table. "You're a sight to see," Torrie said. "We were feared we'd lost you and our money to boot."

"No, I'm right here, just like I said I'd be."

"Good. I think that job is gonna be tomorrow. Should be passing by that spot in the morning, so you'll have to be ready."

"I'll be there."

"You ought to get yerself a clean shot."

"One thing you never told me," Zac said. "I always like to know just who it is I'm really working for. Now, just who is it that's paying you?"

Torrie and Yuma seemed surprised by the question. Torrie cleared his throat. "We don't give that out."

"You'd be plenty surprised," Web chimed in, "plenty surprised."

"Well, surprise me then."

"I don't know," Torrie said. "I think this whole thing is some sort of secret."

"What could be so secret that you'd find somebody off the street to do it?"

"We've worked for this here feller before," Torrie went on. "He's a real important type, wears a white shirt, suit and tie."

"That don't cut no mustard with me," Zac said.

"Well, I just don't know if he'd take too kindly to me giving out his name like that."

Zac reached into his pocket and took out the five twenty-dollar gold pieces. He laid them on the table and pushed them toward the man. "Then I reckon you'll have to do this yourself. I don't plan on being the only man here who doesn't know who I'm really working for."

Torrie pulled up a chair and sat down. He pushed the coins back in Zac's direction. Leaning down, he lowered his voice. "Okay, here it is. This man's a government man. That's partly why we can do whatever it is we want. This feller has us a guarantee that we ain't gonna get ourselves arrested for anything."

Looking up at the other two men, he smiled. "I guess we just know too much."

"Well, you don't know me," Zac said. "I work for people I know."

"Come on," Yuma said. "We can do this just like we planned before we met this guy."

Torrie batted his hand away. "No, I like this idea of a long distance shot, less messy thataway." He hunkered forward. "Man's name is Michael Delemarian, and he works for the Secret Service outta Santa Fe. How 'bout that, the United States Secret Service? Now, don't that beat all?"

"You the only people he's got working on this here thing?"

"Well, fact is we ain't too sure 'bout that ourselves. The man's a real careful sort. He says he always likes to have things done. He always seems to have some sort of ace in the hole when he wants something done." Torrie looked back at Yuma and Wes. "Fact is, we kinda figured at first it was you. You appear to be the kind Delemarian would choose."

"I'm not." Zac picked up the coins and put them back in his pocket. "I suppose you told me all you know, and that's good enough for me."

Yuma had continued staring at Pablo. He bent over the table. "I swear I seen this kid before. You an orphan boy?"

Sister Mary was waiting for them outside the mission walls and next to the creek, just as she'd promised. They thought they might have some difficulty in slipping away, but after explaining how much they wanted to see the night sky on horseback, the general roared his approval. That was all they needed. It seemed Palmira and Rosalyn were right—whatever the man wanted, he got. It wasn't until they got to the stables that they asked for the extra horse. A short time later, they rode up to the nun under the trees and stepped down from their horses.

"Why is the young woman here?" Sister Mary asked. "This was not part of our agreement."

"You try and talk her out of it," Joe said. "We did our best today, but she's a woman in love."

"But there is danger here, much danger."

Ellie wrapped her arm around James. "If there is danger, then I wouldn't want to be anywhere else."

They could see that the thought of Ellie going along had put second thoughts into Sister Mary's head. She was finding this a difficult adjustment. "When I made this plan with you, it was with the understanding that it would be just the two of you and your scout. There was no talk of a woman."

"That was then," Ellie said, "and this is now."

"I don't know. This is wrong."

"Should we wait?" James asked.

"No, there is a plan to move your brother tomorrow, and I fear what will happen to him should they carry it out."

"Then we best go ahead with whatever you got in mind," Joe said. "Ellie or no."

"Very well." She reached into a burlap bag she was carrying. "I will have to take James with me." With that, she pulled out the black habit of a nun and held it up. "Here, put this on."

"Why me?" James asked.

"Because, señor, you are the one with the smooth face. Very few of my sisters have mustaches."

James stepped into the baggy black garment, and Sister Mary buttoned it up for him and arranged his headgear."

"It seems to suit you," Joe snickered.

"Yeah, I thought about becoming a man of the cloth a time or two, but never a woman of the cloth."

"You follow me closely and with your head down," she said. "We will go in the door I always go through, and I will explain to the guard why I have brought another sister with me. Say nothing. Allow me to do all the talking."

She looked back at the others. "Stay here with the horses. There is to be no shooting. If you were to kill someone after what I have done, my conscience would be scarred forever. I do this to save a life, not to take others."

Joe nodded. "We understand, sister, and we appreciate what you're doing here. You've been kind to us and much kinder to Julian than he deserves."

"It is my mission," she said.

She moved out of the shadows under the trees, followed closely by James. They walked right through the gates and up to the door that led to the prison below. She spoke some brief instructions to the guard in Spanish, and he turned the key and led them to the cells below. Getting to Julian's cell door, the man turned the key and stepped back.

"Gracias," she said to the man. Locking the door, he went back out the entrance.

Julian seemed surprised to see her. He rolled off his bunk and stuffed his feet into his boots.

She looked around and held her hand up to her lips. "You must be quiet, señor."

James pulled back his headgear. "It's me!" he said.

"What are you doing here and in that?"

"We have come to make your escape," Sister Mary whispered. To both of their amazed looks, she unbuttoned and pulled off the habit.

"What the blazes are you doing?" Julian asked.

She handed it to him. "Here, put this on."

Julian took the black garment and stepped into it. He found it hard to take his eyes off her, however. She stood in the room in a white flimsy shift with her bare legs showing from her knees to the floor.

"I just never thought of you that way," he mumbled.

"Thank God," she said. "Few men ever have. No one really knows what we wear under our vestments, and I hope few ever find out."

Turning him around, she buttoned up the garment and arranged his headgear. "You will leave out the other door. Go down the hall to your right, to the place you were given your bath today. There is a door leading to the outside from there. That way, you will not have to pass by the guard. If anyone speaks to either of you, hold your finger up to your mouth. They will think you have taken a vow of silence and let you pass."

They moved to the cell door, and reaching into the pocket on Julian's robe, she produced a key. "I have a spare key to your cell." She handed it to Julian.

Reaching through the bars, he unlocked the cell door. "Will you be all right?" he asked. "That general is going to be plenty mad when he finds this out, and I wouldn't want anything happening to you."

"Do not worry about me, señor. Worry about yourself and your own soul. I will tell them that you overpowered me and left me here. Who can doubt that? Now you go. Go quickly."

Julian pocketed the key and both brothers headed down the long, dark corridor. Several candles flickered on the walls, showing the way. Up ahead light streamed out the apartments Julian had seen earlier in the day. They slowed their pace and walked by the open doors.

What they passed inside the rooms shocked them. The men seated at the tables were barely recognizable as men. Some had noses and cheeks that had been eaten away, and others only had stubs that once had been fingers and hands. One man cast a glance at Julian that froze his heart. The man's eye's stared out from his withered face and locked onto Julian's gaze. It was more than surprise and fear that raced through Julian's mind. It was the totally unfamiliar feeling of human pity. These men were far greater prisoners than he had ever thought himself to be. They were locked away in hopeless bodies, unable to ever make contact with other human beings.

In a brutal way, Julian felt he was looking at his own soul. They had been with him down here in more ways than one. They were trapped inside who they were and who they would forever be. Only death would free them. His mind raced back to the prayer he had angrily uttered that morning. Could he be free?

Moving past the apartments, Julian pushed the door to the washing room open. He stared momentarily at the tubs, one of which he had bathed in. Glancing to the side of the room, he noticed the towels neatly hung in their places. Between them was the door.

Racing over to it, Julian turned the knob, and they both stepped out into the dark courtyard. The night was still, except for the chirping of the crickets, a sound that quickly ended as they walked toward the gate. A breeze blew on their faces as they reverently bowed their heads and continued onward.

Several guards noticed them as they passed, but both of them kept their heads down and kept walking. It was a short time later, in the darkness outside the mission, when James pointed to the trees. "The horses are under those trees, over there by the creek."

They both ran toward the spot, stripping off their habits as they went. Joe and Chupta greeted them with the reins of the animals.

"You got some clothes that might fit me?" Julian asked.

"I think so," Joe said. "But why? We got to get."

"Where are they?" He began pulling off his shirt.

"Look, we ain't got time for you to change now. Those things you're wearing look fine to me."

"Get those other clothes."

Joe walked back to his horse and untied a bag. Reaching in, he produced a pair of jeans and a yellow-and-blue printed shirt.

Julian had already completely stripped and waded into the creek. He went under and came up, scrubbing himself all over.

"I thought you had yourself a bath this morning," Joe said. "Why take another one now?"

James nodded back at the mission. "Lepers," he said. "That place back there is full of lepers."

Getting out of the creek, Julian proceeded to put on his new clothes. "And it was their water I bathed in this morning," he said. "I might deserve a lot of things for what I done, but that ain't one of them."

Squashing his wet feet into his boots, he took the reins of his horse. "You have an extra pistol?" he asked.

"I thought you might want that," Joe said. "Yes, I carry a second with me." With that, he reached into his saddlebag and brought out a short barrel Colt .45. Julian stuck it into his pants.

When Sister Mary Perizza heard the footsteps in the hall, she picked up the blanket and wrapped it around herself. Moving to the door of the cell, she waited patiently. It was the sound she expected, but by the noise being made, she could tell right away that this was more than the guard or even the general himself.

Escobar led the group into the prison hall. Stopping in front of the nun, he unlocked the door and stepped in. He smiled. "Sister Mary, I would never expect to see you this way, undressed and in a man's bedroom."

"Stop it, that's enough," she snapped.

"I take it everything is going according to plan. They suspect nothing?"

"No, they have no suspicions. I have seen to that. The earliest they would think about you beginning a search would be tomorrow morning."

"And you are certain this will work?"

"Yes, it is the only way. Just as I told you, the American would sooner die than tell you what he knows. His memory is returning to him, however, and with his brothers, he will lead you to the place."

She marched out into the crowded hallway. Allowing the general to follow, she slammed the cell door behind him. Her eyes narrowed and her face hardened as she lifted her chin. "You are prepared?" she asked.

"Very," he replied. "Major Hess and I have ten good men and enough supplies with our pack mules to last us several weeks. We are taking Utant with us. He is our best tracker. They will not lose us. Of that you can be sure."

"Just make certain they don't know you are following them. The man is wary, and at least one of his brothers is a man of great caution."

CHAPTER 24

ZAC AND PABLO HAD LEFT Hermosa before dark. Zac always believed in getting prepared and taking the lay of the land while there was daylight. The three bounty hunters had agreed, even though they chose to stay behind for another night of drinking. He had found the spot overlooking the creek and had stripped off the saddles and hobbled the horses.

One thing he made sure of before he left the stables was to get Pablo his own horse. The animal was a bay mare that appeared to be ten years old or better. She was bowed at the back, with knees that seemed to knock when she walked. She wouldn't set any speed records, Zac was sure of that, but the animal looked dependable and sure of foot. That was really all Pablo needed. He'd also bought a third horse for Julian, a much more spirited black gelding with good lines.

When night crept over the area, Zac spread the blankets out, and he and Pablo took a last look at the stars before trying to get some sleep. If the men were right, they would be up for hours before the wagon carrying Julian passed.

The bluff they were on overlooked the valley and the creek that wound through it. The stream meandered near the mission and flowed down between two sets of tabletop hills. Zac supposed in the rainy season it covered the entire place with a thin runoff that kept the grass green. Right below where they were bedded down, it cut across the floor of the valley and made its way west around the bluff that faced them.

It would be a good clean shot from where Zac sat, and already in his head he'd made plans about what to do. He'd send Pablo down with the two horses while he kept the heads of the guards down. The three men already had plans to draw them away from the wagon, and Zac would just make sure the mercenaries got the surprise of their lives along with the guards.

He lay down on his back and crossed his feet. Looking over, he saw the boy in the exact same posture, as if trying to do his best to copy Zac in every detail. "You going to sleep?" he asked.

"I try, but the stars are too pretty."

"They are at that. Makes a man wonder about the trouble it took to put them there."

"It is no trouble for God, señor," Pablo said.

"I suppose we spend a lot of time worrying about how big the job is instead of just admiring how pretty it is."

"Sí."

"I think that's the way we were put together, though. Details seem to crowd our heads, and if a man's careful, he pays attention to the details."

"Will we eat before your brother comes?"

"Yes, way before. You hungry?"

"A little bit maybe."

Reaching over, Zac picked up a bag and tossed it to the boy. "I got us some sweet bread down in the town. You might as well eat some of it now. It's gonna be hard in a day or so, but it's still soft now."

Zac watched the boy rummage through the bag before he came up with one of the smooth, sugar-dusted rolls. The boy ripped it open with his teeth and began to chew. Zac smiled as he watched him. There had been an improvement in the boy's looks since they'd done a little shopping in the square earlier today. Now he wore brogans that almost fit his feet and brown trousers that lapped around his ankles along with a green shirt that might serve him as a night shirt when it wasn't crammed into the new breeches. At the time he figured maybe having a new set of clothes that made the boy look civilized might go at least some distance at putting Yuma's mind to rest in trying to place him. This way the boy might pass as belonging to him.

"This is good," Pablo said. He handed a leftover piece to Zac.

Zac took it and began to chew. "Yep, it is good. I figured from the size of the woman who sold it to me that she knew her way around the kitchen and what an oven was all about."

Pablo laughed. "Sí, she knows plenty good."

Zac watched the horses stir. The dun picked up his head and then flipped his ears forward, followed by the black and then the bay mare. He'd learned a long time ago that a horse was the best way to pick up anything that wasn't quite right. They were always the first to hear if something was out of place.

Zac flipped over on his belly, followed by Pablo. Both of them stretched their gaze into the blackness below. Moments later, they heard the sound of horses moving along the edge of the creek. Quietly and one at a time, they watched a string of horses and riders come out of the darkness. The horses were trotting and every now and then they would break into a slow canter. Whoever it was wasn't content with just taking a ride. These people rode with determination.

Zac counted five riders in all, three men leading a woman and followed by a fourth man. He could tell the fourth rider was most probably a woman by the blond hair that hung down from her hat and the slight way she was built.

Try as he could, he couldn't make out their faces, but he began to study them. The harder he looked at them, the more unsettled he became. The first rider was an Indian with long black hair and a white shirt. He wore a vest and moccasins that came up to his knees. It looked like Chupta.

With that notion, he edged forward and looked more intently at the rest. Yes, it appeared to be his brothers. He'd seen James, Joe, Chupta, and the woman in town that day. Looking closer, he figured the fourth man might be Julian.

"Who are they?" Pablo asked.

"They look to be my brothers," Zac whispered, "and the Apache and the woman you saw them with today."

"Why are they here now?"

"I don't know, unless they got word of that move and hatched some plan to get Julian out. Whatever they thought of, it must have worked."

"You gonna call to them?" Pablo asked.

Zac thought the matter over. "No, we'll just follow them a ways. They seem to know where they're going, and I don't spect they'll lose me."

Reaching over, Zac picked up his boots and pulled them on. He stood up and buckled on his holster. "I suppose we ought to saddle up," he said.

"Do we take the third horse and saddle?"

"Yes, we paid for him. Might as well take him. Besides, before we're through, you might wind up riding the black there."

"I ride."

Zac looked at him. "I've seen you ride with me. I just want to make sure you can handle the animal before I put you up on the black. Horses are finicky, like some people I know. Some of them have to be around you and figure you mean business with them before they trust you with your hand on the reins." Zac put his hand on the boy's shoulder. "You're a lot like that, you know."

"I am?"

"Yes, a few days ago you wouldn't have thought about following those people down there. You'd be worried about one thing—settling the score with those three men. And you wouldn't have trusted me to do it in my own time."

Zac could see the notion taking hold of the boy, like a creeping snake crawling up his pants leg. "What about those three men, señor?"

"They'll be behind us, coming on strong. The man they're after won't show up, and the man they paid to kill him will be long gone. Do you really think they'll just walk off?"

Pablo thought the matter over. "No, I don't think so."

"Me neither. I figure they'll show up in the morning, and it'll take them a while to figure out what's happened. By then we'll have a six-hour start on them, but they'll be coming on. You just have to keep watching our back trail. Do you think you can do that?"

"Sí, señor."

Zac picked up the blanket and flung it onto the back of the dun. Hoisting up his well-worn saddle, he dropped it onto the horse's back and cinched it down. He watched Pablo repeat the same procedure with the bay mare and then talked him through it with the black.

"Before we head out, I reckon we ought to give you something a mite more substantial for that belly of yours. I bought some fresh fruit I thought we'd eat the first day here. Maybe we should get at it now. It ain't gonna keep for long."

They sat down and began to eat the fresh peaches and pears Zac had bought in the square. The sweet taste brightened the boy's eyes, and Zac watched Pablo's tongue dart over his lips to try to get all the leftover juice before starting another piece.

The peach juice trickled into Zac's mustache. It was sticky and reminded him of home. Peaches would always take him back home. In a way it was the small things that brought the memories back. He could never see a blackberry bush without thinking of the times his grandmother and mother had taken them all out to pick. They'd pick the berries, and Grandmother would tell them stories from the Bible. To pick berries with Grandmother was like being one of the disciples in biblical times. She'd stoop over low for a berry and talk about Jesus.

His mother would occasionally scold them for eating the berries before they got them home, but not Grandmother. She'd laugh and remind all of them about the Bible's notion of muzzling the ox that stomped the grain. It seemed payment for work should be right off according to the Bible, and the oxen that mashed the grain along with the boys that picked the berries were examples in the old woman's mind of just how practical and wonderful the teachings of Scripture were supposed to be. The words in that book were more than long-ago promises. They had right now living in them too. Zac had always remembered that.

For days afterward, the kitchen would be steaming with the aroma of fresh jelly and sticky, thick jam. Every pot and every jar was filled to overflowing and the sweet-smelling perfume of the purple pots flavored their clothes for months. The mind was a funny thing and a peach was more than a peach—it was a summer day in Georgia.

It took them some time before they'd finished half of the fruit Zac had bought for the morning. He stood up and wiped his jeans with what remained on his hands after the licking he'd given his fingers. Running his tongue over his black mustache, Zac took in the last taste of the peach and the last of that long-ago summer.

It was then that they heard the second group of riders. Zac held his hand up to make sure Pablo said nothing. Taking the reins of the horses, he backed them up from the brow of the bluff. He moved forward cautiously and, stooping down, began to count the men below. They were a much larger group and following the same path that his brothers had taken. Pablo took his place beside him.

"I count twelve," Zac said. "No, thirteen. That's a fair size bunch, and they've got three pack animals too."

Pablo nodded.

Hours later, Chupta rode back to the group. The sky was blooming with the dawn. Looking like a piece of tin left in the fire, it glowed and rippled with color. The long grass had disappeared with the departing stream, and now the sage was dotting the brown earth around them. Behind them, patches of green and oak dotted with juniper pockmarked the smooth, brown, balding hills.

Chupta's eyes were fixed on the sky to the south of them, however. Joe turned around to look. A large flight of birds had taken off and were winding their way west, followed by another smaller group of birds on the opposite side of the distant valley.

"You figure we're being followed?" Joe asked.

Chupta nodded.

"We're being followed, all right," Julian said. "They're looking for me already." The man sat awkwardly in his new clothes. Normally, anything Joe might provide for Julian would fit with nary a wrinkle, but these hung loose. The time spent in the mission prison had been hard on him, that was plain to see. His skin was white like parchment, and the veins on his head and neck stood out like blue and red spider webs. He would brown easily, given time. He'd always been dark-skinned, and his green eye showed itself well against his normally bronzed face. It would take some time for that color to return, though. Meanwhile, he'd look odd to anyone who'd ever known him.

"Large group," Chupta said, still staring at the two flights of birds.

"Why would you say that?" James asked, obviously curious.

Chupta pointed to the birds. "Birds come from both sides of canyon. Few might cause one group to fly, but it take many to make both go."

James stared and nodded. He was getting an education.

"Small creek, running water up ahead," Chupta said.

"All right," Joe said. "Julian, you better take the lead. You know where we're going. You take us upstream or down, whichever way you choose."

They rode off with Julian in the lead. It was a calculated risk for Joe to even bring up the idea that Julian might have a notion of where he was taking them. Julian still hadn't talked much about his memory returning, and Joe didn't want to press the issue of how much of it had. He also wasn't sure that even if Julian did remember something about the emperor's gold that he'd ever tell them, and he hadn't stopped to think about whether or not he'd even want to know. Julian's business always dealt in blood, and it was money Joe wanted no part of.

They rode for some distance to the creek. It was a sandy-bottom stream that appeared to be seasonal. Now it had water running in it and was moving swiftly toward the Rio Grande in the east. Julian hit the water and turned his horse upstream in a westerly direction. He cantered the horse in the middle of the surging water, sending splashes to both sides of the bank. They all followed.

Losing their tracks in the creek would give them some time. The people trailing them would have to stop and split up to cover both sides of the creek in either direction. They'd be looking for a spot where the creek played out and the best place for that would be heading upstream right where they were going. That wouldn't make a lot of sense if Julian just had losing these people in mind. He had to have another reason.

As soon as the trackers spotted the place where they'd left the stream, they'd regroup and be on their trail once again. The process would take time, however, and it would give them the chance to put more territory between them, territory and time.

Joe was following close behind Julian, and Chupta had doubled back to be the last in line. Joe knew he would watch for any telltale sign they might leave. He'd come to know and be grateful for the way Chupta thought. Looking back, he saw the man step off his horse midstream and squat down in the water. One of the horses had kicked over a rock, and Chupta returned it to its place. Moving water made its mark on rocks and a rock of a different color would tell a good tracker just where in the stream they had turned. Joe shouted at Julian up ahead. "Slow down. Take it in a walk. We don't want to leave any signs."

Julian caught on right away and slowed his horse down to a walk. He ambled forward, carefully stepping the horse around the smooth rocks that littered the bottom. Turning back to Ellie and James, Joe repeated his instructions and added, "We won't have to do this long, just long enough to make them split up when they come to the place we went in."

The water looked cool and clear, obvious runoff from the mountains to the south. Small fish darted between the horses, and the sun glinted down on the water like fiery glass on the end of a glass blower's pipe. The banks of the creek had small stubs of oak and grass that appeared to be wading in the stream.

In a matter of minutes, the terrain put them out of sight from where they'd stepped into the creek. The creek cut its path between several small hills, making a gentle climb at first and then a steeper one as the water came tumbling over rocks. Julian climbed out of his saddle and, leading his horse, began to wade up the watery grade. Joe quickly followed suit and motioned for James and Ellie to do likewise. He looked at Julian up ahead. "How long you figure it will take them to mind the fact we know we're being followed?" Joe asked.

"If they got half a brain they know it already," Julian shot back. "They might just figure on us being careful, but the longer they have to look and the madder they get, the more they'll figure on us knowing."

"Well, I'm all for making them as ornery as possible."

They walked the horses for an hour or better, taking care not to disturb anything they might move over or around. It was tough going in the cold water and their toes were becoming numb. The horses picked their way over the rocks. The sun was higher now and its rays warmed their backs. Winding their way around a bend in the stream, they came to a low, rocky shelf that ran down to the water's edge. The creek had cut underneath it and the sharp rock reached out for their ankles. Julian stopped.

"Take those people up that rock," he said. "Just wait for me up there. Make sure they walk the horses, though. I'll head upstream a ways and turn a few rocks over. Might make them think we didn't leave the creek here when they ride up this direction."

Joe nodded and signaled for James and Ellie to follow him. The three of them climbed the hill, then sat waiting for Julian and Chupta.

Julian turned a few rocks and broke off a branch upstream. He led his horse back downstream to Chupta and, taking the Apache's horse, led both of them up the rocky ledge. The Apache crouched down in the creek, carefully inspecting the spot where they'd left it. Stepping onto the slope, he walked the area carefully, scanning it with his eyes for any sign of their passing. The watermarks and soaked footprints were plain enough to see, but an hour or so of sunlight would cure that. Minutes later, he joined them.

The area that stretched below them was a series of rocky canyons, dotted with spruce and juniper. They could see pine trees up higher, and in the distance the mountains were covered in greenery. If they were careful, it would take them some time to negotiate the downhill walk—and they would be very careful. The rocky shelf they stood on was more than a hundred yards of sheer stone. They would leave no sign there, but anyone thinking about where a party would disappear to would normally think of that place. It wouldn't take their trackers long to ride the area over and discover some clues.

Julian pointed below them. "We'll head down there, and when we get to the bottom, ride back east. That way we won't be in sight when they come near this place. We'll have to walk the horses downhill, but when we do hit the bottom and ride east, we'll travel fast."

They started down the hill. It was important to get out of sight as soon as possible, and the longer they stayed on the hillside below them, the greater the chances were that the people following them might ride up and see them. That might undo a lot of the work they'd just put in, a risk they didn't want to take.

They led the horses down into a steep incline. Stones gave way, and branches of small deadfalls seemed to reach out for them. None of them had a great deal of practice at being a mountain goat, but it was a skill they felt called upon to use right at the moment.

Ellie slipped and James quickly grabbed her arm. "You okay?"

She nodded. "I'm fine. I'll make it."

"Just don't turn an ankle." He smiled. "I wouldn't want one of those pretty things puffed up out of shape."

"You just don't want to carry me."

"I wouldn't be so sure about that. Carrying you is a thought that has some appeal, but not down this hillside."

Chupta lagged behind and kept a close watch on the bluffs above. If they were to be discovered, nobody wanted it to happen so quickly or cheaply. It took them over an hour to reach the bottom of the draw, and the scrapes on their arms gave evidence to the fact that it hadn't been an easy task. They rounded the hill, putting the top of the bluff finally out of sight.

"We should rest up here a few minutes," Julian said. "Then we'll ride."

Ellie turned to James. "I hate the thought of people following us. Are we going to have to put up with this much longer?"

Joe overheard the question. "Sorry, but I'm afraid so. They'll be on our tails for as long as we're in the territory. They have too much to lose to give up—they won't just turn around and go home."

"But we've done all those things, walking the horses and being very careful. How can they find us?"

"No one just disappears. They'll ride wide circles, and they're going to cut our trail somewhere. Rain might help, but then it would just help for a little bit. You can just about double the time we've spent laying down a hidden trail and figure to set those people back by that much. Of course, there's no guarantee of that."

"That's not much time," she said.

"No, it isn't. I'm afraid we won't be spending a lot of time eating and sleeping. Every minute we're sitting still gives them more time to catch up."

"Only thing is," Julian said, "they don't much want to catch up. They just want to follow us until we get to where I'm going. They don't want you. They want me."

The thought stunned Ellie for a moment. He was right. They were all putting themselves in great danger for a common criminal, and everybody knew it.

James watched her expression. He put his hand on Julian's shoulder. "What they want, they can't have."

Julian stared at him, the glint in his green eye searching James's face. "I was just thinking that it might be better if I just let you folks go your own way. They wouldn't know I'd left, and you could just ride on to Santa Fe."

Joe and Chupta listened to the notion and exchanged glances.

PART 3

+ + +

THE GREEN BLACK GOLD

CHAPTER 25

+ + + + + + +

ESCOBAR AND HIS GROUP MADE their way slowly down the valley. The Cobb brothers were riding harder than they were, but that was all according to his plan. Escobar had to make sure they felt at least some measure of safety; without it, the man might not head for the gold. Escobar had always doubted the story of Julian's memory loss, but the firing squad had changed all that. No man would face death with the ability to forestall it and then still refuse. It convinced him that Mary had been right all along. It also made him angry. He never liked to admit it when he was wrong, and while he hadn't said so, both Mary and he knew he'd been wrong.

The nun was still the same frustrating woman he'd known since boyhood. Even then, she had filled her head with books and what she called the higher matters of thinking. She also loved to exercise control. It had been the thing that had been her downfall. The horse she had ridden on the day her leg had been crushed was a spirited stallion everyone told her not to ride. Not to be denied, she'd taken the animal through its paces, a test of wills. When she fell to the ground after the animal had refused a jump, her leg had been shattered.

It had been quite a blow to her family to have a daughter with a crippled leg, but it just made Mary work all the harder. Her time in bed rehabilitating was long and drawn out, but he'd never seen her cry. It was as if she accepted her fate, cruel though it was. She left the bed early, and the first thing she did was get a rifle and shoot the stallion. There was a hardness to her, a brittle spirit that still lived inside of her no matter what her dress and no matter how many prayers she said. He often wondered if the woman really served God or fought with God in her quest to get Him to serve her.

The lecture she had given him in front of his men about not following the Cobb brothers too close grated on him. He'd bit his tongue then and cursed her under his breath. At one time he had loved her, but now he simply admired her. Mary was untouchable, and she liked it just that way.

Utant rode back to them as they neared the end of the valley. The man seemed bent on something, and Escobar didn't like the look on his face. Utant was Apache, born of a Mexican mother. He'd been raised with the Chiricahuas, and since coming back to Mexico to escape the American slavery of the reservation, he had served Escobar well. Taller than most Apaches, Utant had long black hair that shined in the sunlight. He was well muscled and had an angular jaw and thin face. The flat, broad nose that most Indians had was missing from Utant. Instead, there was the beaklike nose of a hawk and two eyes that would penetrate a man at first glance, the eyes of a hunter.

Escobar watched him ride up. Utant had on a shirt the color of an old tortilla dotted with blue fleur-de-lis. Around his arms he had tied two red bandanas that matched the color of the one around his head. The handkerchiefs around his arms held his sleeves up and gave them a puffy look. Today he wore a breechcloth and moccasins that rose up above his knees. They were heavily leathered on the bottom with padded soles that appeared to have been folded back and forth underneath and then stitched with elk gut.

Major Hess rode at the general's side, and the sight of the scout galloping back so fast got his attention. Utant reached them, bringing his horse to a sliding stop. He pointed behind him. "Creek ahead. They ride into it and tracks disappear."

"Do you think they know they are being followed?" Hess asked.

Escobar thought on the matter and then shook his head. "No. How could they? It would be much too early for them to think about that." Even as he said it, he knew that he wouldn't have admitted it even if he had thought it was true. He wouldn't admit that Mary had thought of a possibility that he himself couldn't see. Quickly he added, "I think they are just being cautious."

"Let us hope they do not become too cautious," Hess said.

"We have a good tracker. Utant will find them."

Hess turned back to the group and signaled them to ride faster. The men spurred their horses to a lope in the direction of the stream Utant had told them about. In a matter of minutes they rode up to the place the Cobb party had seemingly disappeared.

Utant walked his horse into the stream and, bending down, carefully scrutinized the rocks under the stream. He turned around. "I go downstream. If they go out, they will want much water."

"What if they rode upstream?" Hess asked.

"Major," Escobar said, "you take four men and ride upstream. Scatter yourselves on both sides of the water and look for signs. I'll go with Utant down the creek. If we see anything, we will send a man back for you."

Hess saluted.

"Major," Escobar stopped him. "Make sure you look the north side of the stream over very carefully. That is the way they will be going."

Hess nodded and, taking four men, fanned out through the area, one man in the water and the others scattered on both sides of the creek.

It had been a simple thing to say, Escobar knew that. The major knew full well which direction the group was going. Rosalyn had told him many times that his tendency to over explain and treat others as though they were idiots made the men grumble. It was a lesson he'd have to learn, and she was determined to teach him. All of his life he'd been subjected to being groomed by the women in his world. First there had been his mother and now there was Rosalyn and Sister Mary Perizza. At times it seemed to him that they had more at stake in his being president of Mexico than he did.

He rode downstream with Utant and the other six men. Both he and the scout were sure that was the direction the group had gone. There would be more water there, and the hills above them made the creek more narrow and more difficult to negotiate upstream. He knew Hess and the men with him were not the best of trackers, but after all, if there was nothing to see there would be nothing to track.

Over an hour later, he was growing weary. A number of times Utant had gotten off his horse to explore possible signs. Each time had brought a disgusted look to the man's face. It was like they had disappeared from the face of the earth, or perhaps had been so patient and so careful that they had ridden down the creek much farther than seemed possible. The going would be much slower in the water, but perhaps he'd underestimated them. It could be that these Cobb men were the most careful men he'd ever known.

"You don't think they rode upstream, do you?"

Utant stood upright and looked at him. "Maybe," he said. "This too far to go, and me not see any sign in the water."

Escobar knew enough not to ask him what sign he'd be looking for in the water. He himself had no idea, but to ask the question would be to betray his ignorance, and ignorance or the appearance of it was something he could never afford to show.

Suddenly, from upstream, they heard the sound of shouting. One of Hess's men was riding toward them in full gallop and waving an arm.

"Perhaps the major has found something."

The man stopped and saluted. Even though they were dressed in civilian clothes for the sake of any Americans they would see, some habits were hard to break. "They have gone up the water," the man said. "We found a broken branch."

Utant swung himself onto his saddle, and Escobar turned the men around. They began a gallop that skirted the stream on the northern side. It took them some time, but before long they had Hess and his men in view. Traversing a rocky shelf, they finally reached the major. It was a landmark that immediately drew Utant's attention, and as Escobar and his men rode on, Utant got off his horse to look it over.

"What have you found, Major Hess?" Escobar asked.

Hess walked over to the edge of the stream and, bending over, picked up a small tree. It had been snapped back, and recently. It gave every appearance of having been broken by a horse that had passed that part of the stream much too close to the bank.

Escobar pointed to the men and barked orders, "You two, take the other side. The rest of you stay here on the north. Scatter yourselves and ride slowly."

They moved ahead. Escobar looked back for Utant. The man had left his horse on the cusp of a rocky shelf close to the stream and was walking over it. He watched as the scout neared the edge of the bluff and then disappeared from view over it. Turning back to the men in front of him, he continued to give out orders.

"Watch closely. Let nothing escape your view. Anything you find may be important." As he turned his attention to the bluffs overhead, a sudden concern shot through him. This might be a good place for an ambush. What better way to get rid of one's followers than to kill them?

Minutes later Utant rode up to him. "They back there," he said. Pointing back to the rocky slope, he explained. "Men go out of water over rock. I go down hill and find sign. Men and horses go down there."

Escobar was startled. It had taken them far longer to keep track of these people than he had imagined it would. That was all right, though. He wanted them to feel safe from pursuers, just not so far ahead that they would be lost. He looked at Utant and beamed. That would not be possible. He should have known that. This man was far too good a tracker to allow that to happen.

Julian was out in front of the group, riding hard. They were trying to put as much distance as possible between themselves and their pursuers, and just at this moment speed seemed to be their best recourse.

James rode next to Ellie. Neither one of them had spent a great deal of time in the saddle, and riding next to her to offer assistance was, for him, absurd. Nonetheless, he did. She was in some respects a hard-bitten woman. Perhaps the years of knocking about the West with her father had made her not only knowledgeable about people but wary of taking help from them as well.

Being near her engaged his mind, though. Ellie was a woman of strength, and this ability was measured in far more than her physical attributes. She had strength of character and one of the best minds he had ever run across. It invigorated him just talking to her. In the college there were only a few women, and Ellie was every bit as alive and powerful mentally as they were.

He watched her as she rode, trying her best to maintain control. This was a woman of character and conviction. That was obvious. She could be anything she wanted to be; he wasn't one to limit anyone's potential—even a woman's. Perhaps thinking of her being the mother of his children was selfish on his part. The public world had come to be seen as the only important proving ground for an individual's worth, but in the long run James knew that attitude would lead to disaster.

For the mind to flow freely, there had to be a moral restraint and a spiritual nature of absolute right and wrong to guide it. In the American South of his boyhood, women had managed the minds and souls of the children. Childrearing was the important spade work in providing the backbone for the country's thought life and soul, and it had always rested in feminine hands. If women were not present in the same degree in the raising of future generations, who then would take charge of the molding of a child's mind and soul? The schools? Never. The public institutions? He had never seen one he would trust with the raising of his daughter.

When he looked at Ellie, he saw more than a woman who appealed to him. He felt what she did to him on a personal level, however. She had penetrated his soul. She was able to place her finger on the most private part of his heart and yet treat it tenderly. He'd been drawn to her because she seemed to know him and love him all the same, and it was a quality he could trust when it came to raising children. Closeness that did not sacrifice the brain and the soul was an appealing thing. Being attracted to someone was a process of the mind, not merely the eye.

He knew Ellie could be just as capable in any court of law or public forum as any man he'd ever known. However, he wanted to keep a large part of her energy in his home, directed at his daughter and the children they would have. The major contribution he would have to the next generation would be his children and he knew it.

Just looking at Julian and Joe brought that point back home to him. The children of the Cobb home had been a mixed blessing at best. Joe was the steady sort, the kind to keep things going in the right direction. Zac had been the bold avenger. Armed with a great sense of right and wrong, he had often seen his role in the world as being the knight on his charger. It was Julian who had been the one to show them all what could go wrong if a man allowed bitterness and hatred to consume him. James knew he was the poet and philosopher. It was his task to rock the cradle of a man's thoughts and dreams. Behind it all had been their mother and father, but principally their mother. There had been something about not only the stories she told but the way she lived her life that showed what right and wrong would look like in human flesh. That was the task he wanted for Ellie.

Rounding a bend, James watched Julian pull his horse up. The man was taking a long look at the gap in the hills below them. He and Ellie rode up to him, followed by Joe and Chupta. There below was another creek flowing down the hill and under a bridge. There was evidently a road over the creek going north and south.

Julian pointed it out. "We'll get in the creek close to the bridge and see if there's a spot we can circle up to get on the road. There's bound to be plenty of tracks on the road down there, and we just might lose them for a bit."

Joe shrugged his shoulders. "A blind man could tell which way we're going. Why don't we just cut out the nonsense and ride. We can find us a spot to trade horses and just keep going. No sense wasting our time with trying to hide."

Julian looked at Ellie and James. "What do you two think? Are you up to some hard riding?"

James spoke up. He had no desire to put Ellie on the spot. She'd chosen to come on this ride and would more than likely go over her limit to prove she could keep up. "I know I am just a college professor. I've never been a cowboy, and I've never been accustomed to spending the whole day in the saddle. If you ask me, we've been doing a lot of hard riding for the last couple of hours. I'm not certain my rump has either the fortitude or the substance to go all night and then all day as well."

He could tell by the way Ellie looked at him that she was grateful he'd been the one to say what she was thinking. It made him feel closer to her just being able to read her thoughts.

"Silver City's not too far away," Julian said. "About an hour or more. That's where that road down yonder leads. If we can make it there, we can trade horses. The tracks in town will go a long way to making us disappear. We just have to give ourselves plenty of time to get there, get fixed up with mounts and supplies, and get gone before whoever that is back there catches up to us."

"Sounds good to me," James said. He trotted his horse up next to Ellie. "You all right? You think you can make it that far?" Aware of Joe's opposition to Ellie's coming along, he added, "She's been doing really well. She rides much better than I do."

"I can speak for myself," she said.

James blinked his eyes. She obviously wanted no part in being babied—not by him, not by anybody. "Of course you can," he said.

"Fine then, let me do that." Turning back to Joe, she took off her hat and ran her fingers through her hair. "I can stay on the back of this animal as long as he continues to run. I've bounced on a wagon seat for twelve hours at a time and I can take this leather chair I'm sitting on now."

James stood up in his stirrups and rubbed the rear of his jeans. "Consider it me, then, I was trying to defend. An hour more would be of little concern, considering how I'm numb already."

"All right then," Joe said. "If Julian here's right, we won't have long before we can all climb out of the saddle." He looked down at the gap and the creek flowing under the bridge. "Chupta can go first. We'll go under the bridge, and if he can find us a spot, we'll turn up onto the road."

They rode off with Chupta in the lead. Winding down the hill, the horses picked their way over the loose rock scattered over the surface of the hard-packed, red dirt. Small ponderosa pine trees squeezed up through the rocks and twisted toward the light.

At the base of the hill, the creek curved into view. It cut a swath in the red clay, with steep banks on both sides. Chupta picked his way down the bank and into the water.

They made their way under the bridge and watched as Chupta turned his horse and circled up to some grassy ground. He pointed down at the bank on the side of the stream. "Step horses over bank," he said. It was apparent he didn't want to leave the plain sign of horses climbing up the soft clay.

One by one, each of them stepped their horses up the bank. Chupta had dismounted. He stood beside the stream as he watched them go by.

For some time, they walked the horses over the soft grass beside the road. Chupta got back on his horse and rode back into the stream. Taking it downstream to a steep bank made of soft clay on the south side of the creek, he climbed the horse up the bank. Turning around, he ran his horse up and down the embankment repeatedly, creating a clear trail that appeared at first glance to be a group of horses. Picking his way back into the creek, he rode to the place where the group had departed. He stepped the horse up the bank and, getting down off his saddle, took the time to rearrange the rocks that had been disturbed. In a short time he closed with the group as they walked beside the road. Finding a spot of hard earth, the group stepped onto the road.

The road was hard packed. The sun had baked it dry, and it would be easy to mix their tracks with the wagon ruts and hoofprints of the last days and weeks. This was one of those roads where a man had to pick his ruts well. Once a wagon got into one of them, it would more than likely stay there all the way into town.

Julian kicked the sides of his horse, sending it forward at a gallop. The others soon followed suit. Time would be important to them now. It was hard to tell just how much time they had gained by what they'd laid down in the way of a false trail, and it might just backfire on them. If the men behind them had any idea they'd been spotted, they might just throw caution to the wind and come on hard.

Just under an hour later, they reached the vicinity of the first mine. Silver City was a boomtown, and the mines that dotted the hills around it employed a large number of men. One of the shifts had just ended, and the roads were beginning to be clogged with men on foot. The miners, caked with dirt from their heads to their feet, all watched as they rode by.

It would be no problem to get into town and find what they needed. There would be other things to be concerned about, though. The prices would be steep. Real wealth was made in a town like this—not by what came out of the ground, but by the money that spent such a short amount of time in the pockets of the miners. They'd also have to pick a time to leave. It would do them little good to mix their tracks in town only to have someone watch them leave and pass that information on to their trackers. It made every eye that saw them a potentially lethal enemy.

Julian slowed his horse to a walk. There was no need in attracting attention. They strung themselves out in a line, and then Julian called them to a halt. He turned around. "Silver City's up ahead. I think we'd be better to split up. Five people riding into town together might just cause folks to pay attention."

"Good idea," Joe said.

"Ellie and I will go in together," James said.

"Fine." Joe smiled. "Wouldn't have it any other way. The three of us will go to the livery and trade for some horses. You two go to the general store and get supplies. When you finish there, you can go to the livery and make your own trade. That way we won't be showing ourselves all at once."

"Fine," James said. "I'm sure with Ellie here, we'll be less likely to forget the essentials we'll need for the trip."

"That's just what I was thinking," Joe said. "When you get done with your horse trading, you can meet us at the post office." He turned to Julian. "They do have a post office here, don't they?"

Julian nodded. "They do."

"One thing, though," Joe went on, "just make sure that when you get to the livery, you don't trade for the horses Chupta and I are riding."

CHAPTER 26

+ + + + + + +

SILVER CITY WAS NOT AN EASY place to forget. The shift of men that had just gotten off filled the town. One might think that after an entire night of working, a miner would be ready to drop his weary body into a bed somewhere, but few ever did. The honky-tonks were blasting every type of cattywampus music known to man and a few that hadn't yet been invented. The cacophonous noise poured out the doors and around the painted windows, slamming each passerby with the dissonant discord of harsh, belching sound. Ellie held her hands up to her ears, but nothing seemed to help.

The main street in the town had become a canyon with a river at the bottom. Something, perhaps overbuilding, had prompted a cave-in of enormous proportions, sending the former street into the depths of the river, only to be washed away. Now, the steep streets were crowded with people, each jostling to squeeze themselves past one another on their way to another blaring pit of destruction.

James and Ellie walked their horses slowly. People crossed and darted in front of them, some shouting and others staring. How a newcomer could be recognized was anybody's guess. The crowd seemed to have a life of its own, pushing and stirring itself, and then surging ahead.

Finding a break at one of the intersections, James swung his horse around the corner, followed by Ellie. They almost ran a man down as he attempted to dart in front of them. The man was wicked in appearance, with a long shock of white hair and a peg leg, and he wore the dirty uniform of a seaman. His azure blue eyes blazed at them. "Watch where yer going!" the man shouted. "You coulda kilt me."

"Excuse me, sir," James shouted. "How might I find the general store?"

The man leaned on his crutch and pointed down a relatively quiet side street, shaking his finger as he did. "It's over yonder ways. Tell 'em Capt'n Sam sent ye."

James tipped his hat. "That I will, sir, and I am sorry."

They both trotted their horses up to a false-fronted store that had a simple advertisement emblazoned across the top of the door, "Cheap things."

Ellie looked the place over from the outside. "That sounds appropriate," she grunted.

The tops of the two windows were snarled with the depiction of painted horses on parade, and the clear bottom of each pane of glass proudly displayed trousers and brightly colored shirts along with a mixture of mining tools and lamps. There on the window next to the door was the symbol of proud ownership written in bold box letters, "Horace Simple, proprietor."

James climbed down from his horse and then helped Ellie, tying the animals up to the hitching rail.

"Is this the only place we can find?" Ellie asked.

"Do you really want to go looking around this town for another store?"

"No, I suppose not." With that, she opened the flimsy door. The bell above the door sounded as it opened but got no notice. Several people were poking through tables and trays of piled-together clothing. What once might have been neat stacks of shirts and trousers had become a hodgepodge of disarrayed clutter. Barrels of fruit were tipped toward the customer's eyes, and boxes of every shape and description littered the floor. The shelves bore some semblance of order, but even they were stuffed with mismatched articles pouring out of their bins and threatening each shopper or shopkeeper with an avalanche of precariously piled items. Ellie shook her head in disgust.

James smiled, trying to make the best of it. "I suppose the fella stays in business."

"Yes. What my father could do with a place like this, though, would not be believed."

"Perhaps Silver City would be a good location for him. Maybe we should send him a telegram."

The sound of the cash register turned both of their heads. On the front counter a man had piled an array of boots and various clothing, along with a sack of tobacco and several bottles of whiskey.

"Just the bare necessities of life." James grinned.

They walked past several bins of apples and a bold sign proclaiming the price, "5 cents." Ellie gasped. "You could buy these for a penny anywhere, and look at them." She held up several apples. One was shriveled, and the others had bruises and the beginnings of dry rot. Putting them back, she wiped her hands on her blouse. To her it seemed the shirt she had worn on the road was cleaner than the fruit.

The man behind the counter noticed them and waddled in their direction. He was a large man with a double chin and a neck with flab that made him look like a turkey fattened for the kill. His skin was a bleached white, which made his otherwise featureless face look like a pan of dough ready to go into the oven. Two small black eyes peered over his cheeks. "Can I help you folks?" he asked.

"Are you Mr. Simple?" James inquired.

"That'd be me."

"Capt'n Sam sent us," James said.

The man blew out a breath, rattling his oversized lips as he did so. "That coot! I thought he might be dead."

"Well, I tried to kill him with my horse, but I can assure you I left him very much alive."

"Just saw the old buzzard in here a week or so ago, but folks can die real quick 'round here."

"I'm certain of that," James said.

"We just need a few supplies," Ellie added.

"And what would that be?"

"To start with," she said, "we'd like two pounds of flour and a pound of coffee. We will also need two pounds of bacon, but only if it's fresh and has been salted. Then you could give us some jerky—beef preferably."

The man looked at her and then at James. "Is you folks newlyweds?"

James smiled and slipped his arm around Ellie. "Now, why would you ask that?"

"Oh, no reason." The man waved his paw at them. "Just figured you might be, is all."

James was amused at the observation, and his curiosity was piqued. "You must have a reason."

Mr. Simple smiled at them, showing a set of white teeth behind his oversized lips. "Well, you're a man and a woman in here. We don't get many menfolks coming in here for foodstuffs with a woman and her doing the talkin'. Plus, you got yer arm 'round her, and it's been my experience that newlywed folks can't seem to keep their hands off each other."

Ellie flushed with embarrassment, but James just smiled all the more. "I suppose you spotted us right away," he said.

"Yep, I did, and you folks just look like yer in love." He turned back and yelled at the woman working the other end of the counter. "Elvira, come meet these here folks. They is honeymooners come to town."

The woman was scrawny, in contrast to her husband. With sharp features and a pointed nose that rested between her brown eyes, she gave off a grin that displayed a gold tooth. Skirting the counter, she extended her hand to Ellie, pumping it wildly. "Howdy, sure am glad to meet you. I didn't catch the name."

"Cobb," James broke into the conversation. "Mr. and Mrs. James Cobb."

"Well, it sure is a pleasure." The woman continued shaking Ellie's hand. "It's always a dee-light meeting up with married folks, ain't it, Horace? We get so very few of them in town, just mostly miners and what they like to call 'soiled doves.' But we're happy to know you. We hope you're staying on. You are, aren't you?"

"We just might, at that," James said.

"Well, good, good." The woman nodded and finally released Ellie. Turning back, she saw the customer she'd left at the end of the counter. "Now you take good care of these folks, Horace."

The man grinned as he watched his wife scoot back to the customer. "A good woman is a hard thing to find," he said.

James nodded and squeezed Ellie's waist a little tighter. "Yes, and once you find one, a man would be a fool to let her go."

Horace nodded. "Now, will there be anything else? We have some fresh eggs in."

"That will be fine," Ellie said. "But we're camping just yet. So if you could put them up in a jar, they would be safer."

The man scratched his head. "I reckon we could do that. It'll cost you extra for the jar, though."

"We need a bag of sugar too, and a small one of salt. I would like some apples, but I noticed the ones you have out here are old."

"I do have some new ones in the back. They were brought in yesterday. We just have been so busy I ain't had time to put them out yet."

"Your prices on these apples are outrageous," Ellie said. "I could buy apples in Santa Fe for a penny each and have an extra thrown in for a baker's dozen."

"Well, ma'am, we ain't in Santa Fe, now is we? The new ones I got in the back I charge a dime for."

Ellie stiffened. "That is unbelievable."

"There ain't that many apple trees hereabouts. Folks is plantin' them, but they take a good while to grow."

"That's all right, Ellie. We don't need apples."

"James, fresh fruit keeps people healthy."

"Looky here," Horace interjected. "Seein' you folks is new in town and in love too, I won't have you going off without something sweet for your tummy. I'll let you have the new ones out back for the same price as the ones up here. A man can't be more fair than that, now can he?"

They finished shopping and paying for their supplies, and Horace loaded them into two gunnysacks. James grabbed hold of the bags and asked, "Is there a livery stable here that's reliable, preferably one that trades horses?"

The man grinned. "Funny you should ask. I own one my ownself. It's the Circle S, and it's right down the street. Your horses tied up out there?"

James nodded. "They are right out front."

"Fine, let me just take a look at them." With that, the man lifted the hinged counter top and ducked under it. The three of them walked out to the street where he patted James and Ellie's horses down and looked them over. "You folks appear to have come quite a ways today. I'd say these here animals are plumb tuckered out."

"We did have a hard ride," James admitted.

"Tell you what I'm gonna do. You take these animals down to the Circle S and tell Lefty to swap 'em up even for the calico and that gray. They're nice animals and the gray won't be giving the little lady here a bit of trouble. I had 'em both shod just yesterday with my own brand of shoe. Now how's that sound to you?"

"Seems fair," James said.

"Good, then you just go on down there and do it. I best get back to the store. I don't like to leave Elvira all alone in there for very long." Swinging around, he clomped back up the stairs and into the building.

They found the post office a short time later. The place was a new brick building and proudly displayed the flag flying from a wooden pole. Joe was strapping down an extra blanket he'd bought behind his saddle, and Julian sat on a rock nearby whittling on a piece of wood. As usual, Chupta was on watch. He stood near the busy street and craned his neck at the crowd.

It was midafternoon, and while the crush of the miners getting off of work had died down, the street was still a busy place. On the other side of the pit a man played a hand organ while a monkey danced on the end of a leather leash. The amazing thing was that people could distinguish the music coming out of the hand organ from the rest of the noise surging from the bars around it. The small furry beast was drawing quite a crowd, and that was fine with Joe. He watched the crowd gather and tied the last of the cinches. "Glad that feller over there showed up. It ought to give us lots less attention. I see you found us some grub."

"Yes we did," James said.

"Prices here are outrageous," Ellie added. "I do believe the richest people in town are the shopkeepers."

"And you got some horses too, I see." Joe opened the mouth of the calico and looked at the animal's teeth. "This one appears to be about eight years old." He patted the legs of the horse and ran his hand over its rump. Moving over to the gray, he repeated the same procedure. "This one's ten years or better. I hope you got some money for the ones you were riding."

"No, we made a straight trade," James said.

"Then you got took."

James held up the bags of food. "I'm afraid after I tell you what we paid for our supplies then, you will say we really got hornswoggled."

Julian got to his feet and put his knife away. "That's the way of these type of places," he said. "Everything's scarce, and there's too many people."

Joe turned his eyes to the busy street. "I suppose that's part of the price we have to pay, but frankly I sure do like the sight of so much traffic. I ain't sure the best tracker in the world could trail a company of cavalry through all this."

Joe looked over at Julian. "I don't think you're going to have to worry about lighting out on your own."

"It don't seem so," Julian said. "We best head out, though. We still have a couple of hours or better of riding time, and then we can stop for the night."

"Stop?" Ellie asked the question with some doubt, mixed with hope.

"We might as well," Joe said. "Ain't nobody gonna find us in all this mess, and it'll be close to dark, I reckon, before they show themselves in town here. We'd better straggle out, though. Julian and Chupta can go first, then you two. I'll follow along a little later."

James looked up and nudged Ellie. He nodded at the man hobbling up the cobblestones. It was Capt'n Sam. The man held his head down, making sure the crutch that supported the peg leg made contact with the stones. Suddenly looking up, he spotted them. "You people again. Glad you ain't on the back of no horse."

"We are too," James said.

"You get yerselves over to the store I told you about?"

"Yes we did, and we told them you'd sent us."

"Good, good."

"They thought you were dead."

"Well, I ain't. I'se too mean to die just yet. Got to sweeten' up a mite before folks'll sing songs over me." He held up an envelope. "I does write though. I guess a body's got to have a few folks he knows somewhere in the world." He tipped his hand to his face and continued stumping up the walkway.

"You know that man?" Joe asked.

"That is Captain Sam," James replied. "The man showed us where to find the store we bought our supplies in after we almost ran him down."

Joe watched the old man hobble through the door of the post office.

"How about that?" James remarked to Ellie. "I suppose we killed two birds with one stone, and we have Captain Sam to thank for it."

"It seems we have Captain Sam to thank for our wedding as well."

James smiled. "Ellie, I'm sorry. I didn't mean to embarrass you. I suppose I just couldn't resist that. I haven't called a woman Mrs. Cobb in five years now. It sounded good."

Joe's head jerked around, and Julian dropped the stick he'd been carving on. "You told somebody your name here?" Julian asked.

James looked at him with a blank stare. "Yes, the shopkeepers."

"Why'd you go and do a fool thing like that?"

"Because they asked me. I've never made a habit of lying, and I've never been on the run before." He mumbled to himself and shook his head. "But I should have known better."

Escobar and the civilian-clothed troops arrived in town several hours later. Silver City was erupting in full swing, with the night yet young. For the Mexican soldiers, the place was a wonder. Their heads turned from side to side as they rode, taking in every blazing light and listening to the uproar.

Up the street a drunk exploded in shouted song. He raised his six-gun and fired into the air, sending repeated stabs of flame into the darkness. The soldiers were taken off guard, several reaching for their revolvers, but Hess calmed them down. "Be at ease, men," he said. "It's only a drunk."

In a matter of moments, several peace officers had the man under control. They clubbed him and proceeded to drag him off to jail. The men watched, but Escobar and Hess were worried. Their group was much too large not to attract attention, and the last notice they needed was from an American lawman.

Hess turned several of the men aside and together they separated from the main body and rode around the corner. Escobar signaled for three of the men to cross to the other side.

Moments later all seemed peaceful once again, if anyone could call it peaceful. The saloons were full of not only the strange mixture of music but the loud buzz of men talking and laughing. The place was a sight to behold, like another world in another time.

Their horses were tired and so were they, but this was a spectacle too good to pass up, and the men couldn't take their eyes off it. Mexicans had never been popular north of the border, Escobar knew that. Finding a hotel that would allow them to sleep might be a problem. He signaled Hess.

"Yes, General?"

"Major, you will need to find us a room for the night. We can go no farther. Find one for me and one for you. You are a German and should have no trouble. When you have done this, bring me back the key. Then you must take the men out of town to make camp. Make certain none of them come back into this place tonight." He stared at the troops. "Look at them."

Hess turned around and looked the men over. They were talking to one another and pointing out the various saloons, their faces animated. "Yes sir, I see your point."

"These gringos here have no love for us, and I want no trouble. We will need every man we have."

Hess started to salute, but Escobar stopped him. "Not here, Major. Not now."

Awkwardly, Hess dropped his hand back to his side. "Yes, sir. I am sorry. Old habits are very hard to change."

"Well, see that you break that one until we get home."

"Yes, sir."

"Now, why don't you see to our rooms. There is a hotel over there, and right now my back could use a bed, any bed."

With that, the major swung his horse around and trotted to the Cosmopolitan Hotel. It was three stories high, the largest structure in town. The windows high up were only partially lit, and Escobar took hope that that meant there were vacancies. Perhaps the people who filled the streets were all local, or just maybe they were so consumed with the notion of drunkenness they hadn't bothered to take a room for the night. He signaled the men to dismount, and they climbed off their horses.

When Hess returned from the hotel a short time later, he had two room keys, one for himself and one for the general. "Yours is on the second floor, General, room 212. The man says the room will be empty except for you. There is only one bed."

This came as good news. Many of the hotels piled men into rooms like cordwood, making any privacy impossible and sleep itself a scarce item. Escobar took the key and nodded.

"I will take the men north of town and find a place for us to camp," Hess said. He looked over at the men. "It will not be an American hotel, but at least they can make a fire and have hot food. We have enough supplies, and we can buy the fresh meat we need tomorrow."

"Good," Escobar said. "Tomorrow we ask questions. If we can discover the direction they rode off in, Utant can find their trail."

Two riders watched from behind the group of soldiers in the darkness. They had halted their horses some distance away and were sitting on their horses in the shadows. Zac and Pablo would wait to see what the Mexicans planned to do.

CHAPTER 27

UTANT RODE OUT OF TOWN with Hess and the rest of the men following him. Hess would go back to the white man's hotel, but for now he wanted to watch the weary group get settled for the night. Utant could tell that a number of the men resented the fact that their officers would be sleeping in warm rooms and beds tonight, while they would be on the ground. Several had already grumbled about seeing the alluring saloons and wishing for a taste of whiskey, knowing they wouldn't have a chance to enjoy it. Utant would have to find a place for them to camp or perhaps a number of locations where the men could spread out. Twelve men together attracted too much attention and might cause a passerby to report them to the local police.

The ground north of town was hilly, with undergrowth and green pine trees forming a dense woods. Silver City sat on the edge of mountainous terrain. It wouldn't take much to spread the men out so that they wouldn't be noticeable from the road, and yet they could still keep close enough to one another for protection.

Hess would make sure all the details were taken care of; Utant knew that much about him. The man was always a soldier, and strategy and tactics seemed to be his specialty. This job they were on, though, was not one for soldiers. Escobar had made a mistake in bringing them. Deep down he suspected the man had dragged these men along for his own protection, not to try and keep track of this man Julian Cobb. If he wanted to do that, he could have sent Utant alone or with one or two others from his band. They could have tracked the man and found out where he was going much easier without this crowd along for the ride. Then they would have killed Mr. Cobb and sent back for wagons and men. It was a simple plan and one Utant had suggested, but suggested only once. He never made it a practice of arguing with a man who already had his mind made up. He gave his opinion once, and after that, it was up to his superiors to make a decision. Whatever had been in Escobar's head, Utant was sure it had nothing to do with common sense.

Escobar had been good to him in one way, though—the man had given him and his people protection. The Mexican army wanted to hunt down and kill all Apache, and living on Escobar's land gave them the chance to be as they had always been.

The Americans had planted them on the San Carlos reservation. It was a place of nothingness—there was little water and very little game. San Carlos was a dry, tortured place nobody wanted, and the Americans were using it to store Indians of all description. Traditional enemies with different cultures were mixed together there. In the eyes of the white American, an Indian was an Indian, there was no difference. The food was spoiled and given to them as an evil stepfather giving poison to a bad child. To live there was death for a man inside his spirit, a breathless life where a man died one little piece at a time.

Utant was a man without a country. He had a family, and he had a band of close followers, however, and that was enough. He would serve Escobar well, and he would do what he had always done and what his father and grandfather had done before him. He would hunt and he would kill.

As the band of men rode on into the canyon, the noise from the town died down. There would be no escaping the town's pull on them, however, and none of them wanted to. Tantalizingly close, it reminded each man about what they could do with the promised reward from Escobar. It would be a small fraction of the gold they would recover, but for each of them it would be a king's ransom.

The lights of Silver City shone brightly below them, twinkling like moonlight on a small lake. The road they had taken north of town was a well-traveled one. It headed into the Mogollon Mountains, with steep canyon walls on either side. It was one of the places they might hope to find the tracks of the people they were looking for, if they had continued north.

Hess rode up front next to Utant. "Ve must start finding a place. I do not want the men too far out of town only to discover those people have gone another way."

Utant nodded. "We camp in small groups—two, three men at a place. Not want people to see big group."

"Good thinking," Hess said. "I vill start dividing the men into pairs. There is a creek over there. It vill provide water for the horses and for cooking."

Beginning with the men in the front of the column, Hess began to portion them out over the treed ground. "Paco and Morales, you take this place. Get water and picket your horses near the creek." The men nodded and dropped off of their saddles.

The group continued to meander up the dark canyon. The sound of the running water mixed itself with the faint noise from the town below. Trees cast dark spirelike shapes into the darkness, each of them blotting out the stars and the dim light of the moon. It was a far cry from the desert they were used to riding through, and the elevation sent a slight chill through the air. It made Hess shiver and he thought of his warm but noisy bed waiting below.

One group at a time split off as Hess instructed them. They held the pack animals until they had dispatched the third group of men, Hess instructing them to divide the supplies for the night and to make sure they started a fire. He wanted to be certain that even though they'd been denied the opportunity of the revelry of Silver City, they would at least have some hot food and drink to comfort them. It was a small thing, but morale was important.

When the last of the troops had been assigned to their locations, Hess sat on his horse beside Utant and watched the men make camp. "Ve vill try to get an early start," he said. "Ve must make inquiries in town and see if anyone has seen those people and has any idea of vere they might be going."

Utant nodded his head slightly and pointed up the hill. "I go up there. I do better alone."

"However you choose, just make sure the men are up by sunrise. I vant them to have eaten and ready to ride at the first light."

Swinging his horse around, Hess started back down the canyon. The men were already making preparations. In the trees, a number of the men had picketed their horses over by the stream and others had started fires. The glow of the small cookfires made the trees sparkle. The men and their campsites dotted this entire stretch of dark canyon.

Each group he passed rose to give their greetings. It was plain to see they were unhappy with being left out in the open, but the fires would cheer them.

As he got to the first two men he had positioned, Paco and Morales got to their feet. The men had already gotten their fire into a blazing circle. They stood warming their hands next to it. "You be back in the morning?" Morales asked.

The man was someone Hess thought well of as a fighter but had very little respect for as a soldier. He was too hot-headed and much too aggressive. These were things that fit well in the heat of battle, but in the preparation for battle they might undo any advantage. The man was lean and angry looking. His dark hair fell into his face, highlighting two black, lifeless eyes—the eyes of a killer. Hess had seen the look before. It had no conscience, and neither did Morales. Twice, Morales had been dismissed from the regular army for insubordination and rape. His lean look showed him to be a hungry man, but not for food.

"Yes, I vill be back in the morning, early in the morning. Ve have much to do in town to try and discover the direction those people went. I expect you two men to be ready."

"Oh, we will be ready, Major. Won't we, Paco?"

Hess knew at once it had been a mistake to put these two together. Paco was much too agreeable and eager to please. He also had a deep admiration for Morales, almost a hero worship.

The man bobbed his head at Morales eagerly. "Sí, we will be ready."

"You see, Major," Morales grinned, "you have nothing to worry about here. You can ride back to that warm bed of yours down there and sleep like a baby."

Hess didn't much care for the way the man agreed with him. There was a cutting tone to the words and a toothy grin that peeked out from the man's oversized mustache. It betrayed a man who was thinking of something else, something more than an overnight sleep in the woods.

"See that you two stay in camp tonight," Hess said. "I don't vant you vandering away for any reason."

Morales shrugged his shoulders, feigning an innocent look. "Now, Major, where are we to go? We have a nice camp here, and our bedrolls are already spread out for us. I have meat on the fire, and we are heating up some coffee. You don't worry about us. We will be fine."

Hess was unconvinced. Morales was the type of man who would look you right in the eye with the evidence standing before you and he would work very hard at persuading you of your own blindness.

"Do as I say," Hess shot back. "That town down there is a dangerous place, very dangerous for a Mexican. You two go down there and there is more you vill find than bad whiskey. I can assure you of that. Our enemies may even be waiting there, and there is nothing they would like better than killing us one or two at a time."

Morales flagged his hands, waving off the notion. "We are very tired, Major. I think Paco and I will be asleep before you are."

"See that you are." With that Hess spurred his horse out of the men's small camp. He wound his way down the hill, stopping at the bottom to look back one more time. From where he was, he could see the scattered collection of the men's cooking fires. Hess was proud of Utant's plan. A rider passing by might think it odd that so many men had chosen to camp in such close proximity, but none would mistake them as being together. Besides, who else would be riding this way in the dark?

Zac and Pablo crouched in the trees up the hill from where the man on horseback sat looking at the campfires dotting the hillside. The two had indeed followed them up the canyon. They watched as the men separated themselves into separate camps in the dark woods, and they silently looked on as the major turned his horse and trotted back down to the noisy streets below.

"What we do now, señor?" Pablo asked.

"We wait. We wait for those men to settle down and get to sleep."

"Then what we do?"

Zac put his hand on the boy's shoulder. "We're gonna do us a little injun trick. You might learn a thing or two before the night's over. Before we're finished here, those men will all be walking."

It didn't take long, however, before Zac and Pablo were surprised by what they saw. The two men in the nearest camp had saddled their horses and were riding out alone. They rode in hushed whispers as they made their way through the brush. Reining their horses back and forth around the trees, it became obvious they had no intention of staying on the mountain that night. They were going to Silver City.

"What now?" Pablo asked.

"Nothing, we just wait. We'll see to those two later. It might be best if we try to get a little sleep, though. I'll wake you up."

It was more than two hours before Zac stirred again. He'd gotten a little sleep, but not too much. In times like this he liked to use an old trick he'd learned during the war. It let him sleep but not for very long. Curling up with his left arm underneath him, he slept on it. The arm would soon grow numb and he would wake up. If there was any noise, any noise at all, the uncomfortableness of the position would allow him to wake even sooner, and the feeling in his right hand would still be there. He could still draw a weapon and use it quickly if he had to.

He rubbed the arm and massaged the fingers on his left hand. Soon the feeling returned. Reaching over, he roused Pablo.

The boy rolled over, murmuring, "What is it?"

"It's time for us to do our work." Zac got up and, moving to the dun, reached into the saddlebags and pulled out his moccasins. Wrenching his boots off, he dropped them and donned the soft leather shoes.

"You walk better in those?" Pablo asked.

"They're a little quieter. A man can feel a branch under his foot before he puts his weight down. With boots a body might snap one at just the wrong time."

Looking up the dark canyon, they could both see that the fires had died down to coals, and some had gone out entirely. The idea of breaking the large group up into smaller ones had been a smart one if a man wasn't expecting trouble and didn't want to arouse suspicion. It did have one problem, though—with smaller groups like that, it wouldn't be practical for one person to guard only two horses all night. These people hadn't been expecting any overnight callers, and now they were going to get an education.

Zac pointed to the far side of the canyon. "We'll go over the creek and along that hill over there. When we get to the first campsite, we move down. You ready?"

"Sí, señor, I am ready."

"Good boy."

Zac and Pablo kept low, skirting the brush along the side of the trail. They could hear the fast-moving water beyond. Stepping over the dirt and the clearing beside the trail, they came to the creek. It bubbled past them, reflecting the light of the moon on the rocks, fallen trees, and snags. It wasn't much of a stream as creeks go, but it would be enough to muffle any sound they might make by mistake, and it would keep the horses occupied. Zac found a spot with a log crossing it and picked his way over the wet downfall. Turning back, he waited for Pablo.

The two of them moved up the side of the hill. The trees and snags of the brush pulled against their clothing and made the going slow. Inching upward, Zac took it one step at a time, turning occasionally to pull Pablo up after him. Several boulders stood above them, and Zac wedged his feet in between them. The cracks in the rocks made for good footing and got him on top in a matter of minutes. Pablo had less trouble than he did. The boy scooted up the breaks in the rock, feeling his way as he climbed.

They moved along the side of the steep canyon. Zac kept his eyes trained on the dying fires below. Occasionally, he could make out the shapes of horses as they fed at the edge of the stream. Everything seemed quiet, perhaps too quiet.

When they neared the first campsite, Zac pulled Pablo aside. "Okay, we're going down here." He pointed out a spot with a gradual decent, broken up by tall ponderosa pines. "We follow that way and it'll take us somewhat above the horses, but it looks to be the easiest way to get down. Take it from me, getting down can be much harder than getting up."

The two of them started down the hill. The slope they were traveling over had at some time been an avalanche of rock and debris; loose rocks were scattered about, and Zac stepped on and over them carefully. Moments later, they were once again on the canyon floor next to the creek. Off to their right, more than a hundred yards away, two horses grazed. "Those will be our first ones," Zac said, pointing them out in the distance. "You wait here for a bit until I get up next to them."

"Can I come to?"

"I don't want you too close to me."

The boy bobbed his head in approval.

Zac moved quietly through the tall grass. He stopped to look, peering into the darkness.

Suddenly, from behind, a man tumbled over him, knocking him to the ground. Zac scrambled to his feet just as the man rammed him with a vicious head butt, which knocked the wind out of him. The man drew a knife and jumped on Zac's chest. He could see the man was an Indian. He struggled and tried to get his breath as the man grabbed his hair and leaned into him. It was then he heard a loud crack. The man's eyes flashed, then closed. The Indian fell on top of him, and Zac quickly pushed him off.

Pablo stood there, a large rock clutched in both his hands. The boy looked frightened and started to shake. Zac got to his feet and took him in his arms. "That's fine," Zac said. "You did good."

Pablo pointed behind him. "I saw him watching you. I didn't know what to do. I couldn't yell."

"You did just fine, son, just fine."

"Is he dead?" Pablo asked.

Zac reached down and felt the man's neck. Looking back up at the boy, he shook his head. "No, son, just out cold."

Zac looked down at the horses. They were still grazing peacefully.

"I don't gotta take his scalp, do I?" Pablo asked.

"No, we'll just leave him be. He ought to have a headache he'll remember tomorrow, but we'll just leave it at that. We best go get those horses, though."

Keeping close to the stream, Zac and Pablo moved down the canyon to a spot near the horses. Looking across the trail, he could see the still and silent forms of two men sleeping in their blankets. One of them was snoring loudly. Zac stood up and walked calmly to the feeding animals, his knife drawn. Cutting the ropes off the picket line the horses were tied to, he turned and signaled to Pablo. The boy scampered forward, and Zac handed him the ropes.

"You just hang on to these," he said. "We'll move along the creek and gather them up as we go."

They moved down the creek, gathering in the horses as they did. It didn't take them long to get the eight horses. Zac held the lead ropes on five of the animals and Pablo hung on to three. They exchanged broad smiles. "Now, let's go on down the canyon a ways. I'll go back for the pack animals when we let these go."

Zac quickly retrieved the pack animals. He'd managed to load the gear on two of them. One load of supplies had obviously been scattered among the men to use that night, but the loss of this load alone would delay them for a day or better, and they would have to find other horses as well.

Zac mounted the dun, and Pablo climbed aboard the old mare. The horses they'd gathered were feeding below, and Zac pointed them out. "We'll drive those animals south of town and get them running. I don't spect they'll be seen by those fellers back there, though."

Pablo pointed at one of the horses. "Can I have that one?"

"No, we're not horse thieves. No matter what you saw tonight, this isn't something we're doing for ourselves."

It took them more than an hour to get the animals out to the open range south of town. Pablo enjoyed herding the horses. It became a game to him. Zac watched as the boy pulled the reins on the mare, weaving back and forth behind the horses to keep them going in the right way.

Zac pulled out his revolver. "Okay, pardner, let's send these critters a flying." With that, he fired several shots into the air. The horses were startled. They rattled off to the open desert south of town, first in a group and then separating into twos and threes and disappearing in the darkness.

"That ought to do it," Zac said, dropping the gun back into his holster. "Now, why don't we go find hay for these mounts of ours. I'll get you bedded down, too, and then do some looking around."

A short while later, they trotted their horses up to the Circle S stables. The place had a light on in the barn and one in a small office off to the side. Zac got down and pounded on the barn door.

The weathered door opened, revealing a man holding a lamp up. He was an older man in red long johns with his feet hastily stuffed into his boots. His bushy salt-and-pepper beard and a pair of eyebrows that looked to be mats of gray were the only hair on the man's head. He stooped over, holding his back. "Name's Lefty. Can I hep ye?"

"Just need a place to lay down for the night and a stall for our horses."

"That's what we do. Cost you a buck a piece and two for them animals of yours."

"That's fine," Zac said, leading the three horses in. They still had the black he'd bought for Julian and the extra saddle. "I might be interested in selling one of these two." Zac pointed over to Pablo's horse and the black.

"Well then, we just might be interested in buying. We do that, ya know. We can trade fer yer horses too. Had me a trade just this afternoon." He pointed out two horses in the first stall.

Zac walked over to them. He thought he recognized one of the animals, a blood bay with a blaze down his face and three white stockings. It looked like the horse he'd seen in Hermosa standing next to James. "You traded for them?"

"That's right, mighty fine trade it was, too."

"Man say what his name was?"

The old man tugged on his beard, his eyes rolling up. "I believe his name was Cobb. Newlywed feller with a mighty fine-looking woman too."

CHAPTER 28

+ + + + + + +

ZAC WALKED DOWN THE STREET, occasionally pushing open a door to one of the bars and looking inside. He had two things on his mind, both of them difficult to deal with. The first was trying to determine the whereabouts of his brothers. Finding someone who could actually remember seeing them would be hard enough, but finding someone who might know which direction they rode off in would be an even greater task.

He could always deadhead a guess, but it might be wrong. If the stories about the treasure were to be believed, they wouldn't have gone west from here. Maximilian was trying to escape out of Galveston, Texas, and he would have wanted to stay in the United States for as short a time as possible. That left only north and east, and north seemed to be the best guess. Directly east of here was a land that was almost impossible to cross, and it was directly through the territory belonging to the Mescalero. That would be a foolish thing to do, even for an armed column of soldiers. During the Civil War that same group of Indians had massacred an entire company of Confederate cavalry. No, it would have to be north. The emperor would have gone north through here and then east once he'd cleared Apache land. Of course, that way was directly in the path of the men he had taken the horses from tonight.

He could only suppose that Escobar had figured that out as well. Whatever else the man was, he wasn't ignorant. He and Pablo would have a day on them though, a day at least. Maybe he could catch up with his brothers and let them know just what was behind them.

As he passed the hitching rails alongside the boardwalks, he looked over each horse and saddle. There would be no assurance the men who rode the horses would be inside the saloons they were tied out in front of, but it would at least be an indicator of some kind. Most men didn't like to leave their horses too far afield from where they landed. With all the bad liquor, many of them might not be able to walk very far.

On the second block he spotted the two horses he'd been looking for, the ones the Mexicans had ridden out of the canyon. They had saddles that appeared to be army issue and saddlebags. Tucked into each boot was a military-style carbine.

Using the big Sharps, he pushed open the batwing doors of the Silver Spittoon Saloon. He peered inside. At least his other question was answered. The two men were there. They stood next to the bar with glasses in hand, hunched over a half-empty bottle. Stepping inside, he allowed the two doors to rock shut behind him, then he walked over and slid in next to them, laying the big gun on the bar. He caught the bartender's attention. "I'd like a buttermilk," he said.

The man did a double take. "Buttermilk?"

"That's right," Zac said. "If you don't have that, I'll have a goat's milk."

The bartender shook his head, muttering to himself. "I'll see what they got in the back."

The Silver Spittoon was full to overflowing. Men mixed with the women who obviously worked there. In the front of the place a balding man banged away at a well-worn piano. Beside him sat a number of brass instruments, including a trombone and a trumpet. Those members of the band were obviously missing, and Zac was thankful at least for that. It was often the blessing of less that he appreciated most.

The wallpaper that took up space on three out of the four walls was a dirty red with textured raised designs. It made the place look smaller and closed-in. The woodwork was simple, as were the stairs and banisters that wound their way to the cribs of the women upstairs. Low-hanging lamps with brass shades cast shadows on the walls. The lampshades had cut-out designs in them and small beams of light poured out, giving the illusion of stars that danced on the shadowy walls.

Smoke filled the place, taking away Zac's appetite. The grayness clung to the dirt-streaked wallpaper, coating the interior of the building with a haze. Zac pulled out his briar pipe. The thing smoked cool and the smell was pleasing. At least it would allow him to fight off the aroma of the paper cigarettes and cigars.

The bartender brought back a tall glass of white liquid and sat it down in front of him. "Goat's milk. We don't have no buttermilk."

"I'd like a small shot of brandy, too," Zac said. The man seemed a bit startled, but the look of surprise soon broke into a smile.

"That makes the second thing you want of something we ain't got much call for." He shot his index finger into the air. "But that one I got."

Moments later he poured Zac a small shot of brandy. "That'll be two dollars, mister."

Zac paid. He watched the two men beside him drink their whiskey. They hadn't said much, preferring to keep their thoughts to themselves. Zac imagined being Mexicans in a boom-town saloon filled with drunks made them feel a bit shy.

Zac sipped on the goat's milk. It was warm but appeared to be fresh. He was at least thankful for that. Some places had so little call for milk that what they had on hand was the leftovers from last month's milking; most of it was rancid and sour.

Zac took out a small cloth from his pocket and soaked it in the brandy. Wedging a corner of it into the stem of the pipe, he reached over and took a match stick from a glass full of them that sat nearby. Using the match, he pushed the brandy-soaked cloth down the stem of the pipe and into the bowl. Clean pipes always smoked sweeter.

He noticed the two Mexicans watching him. It was what he'd hoped for by taking out his pipe. Many times it took odd behavior to start a conversation, and if he hadn't been the one to start it, most of the time he could get folks to answer seemingly innocent questions. He opened the leather bag of tobacco he carried and, picking up the remainder of the brandy, poured it in, stirring the damp tobacco with his finger.

"What you doing?" The taller of the two men asked the question. The man had a large mustache and a set of steady eyes, even if they were glossed over with whiskey.

"Just flavoring some smoking tobacco," he said.

"And what is that thing?" The man pointed to his pipe.

"This, my man, is an English briar pipe." Zac held it up. "It smokes cool and flavorful."

"Let me see."

"And who might you gentlemen be?" Zac asked.

"I am Morales," the mustached man proclaimed proudly, "and he is Paco."

"Always like to know the folks who handle my things."

Morales swung around and, putting his elbows on the table, stuck out a hand.

Zac dropped the pipe into the outstretched paw. The man held it up, looking it over carefully. "I ain't never seen this kind of thing before."

Zac smiled and took it back. Opening up the pouch, he stuffed the bowl of the pipe with his freshly sweetened mixture. Taking another match from the glass, he struck it and puffed a small flame on the top of the bowl. The man could hardly take his eyes off the process.

"How long you two gents in town?" Zac asked as the pipe caught life.

"We go tomorrow."

"Is that so? Where to?" Zac could tell the question had caught them off guard. It was a simple one and a natural thing to ask, but neither one of them wanted to answer it.

Morales shook his fingers in the air, in the general direction of north. "We go north."

"That's pretty country up that way, from what I hear. You got some family up there?" Each question he asked seemed to catch both of them off guard. Zac could tell that the questions were starting to irritate Morales especially.

"No," the man said, "we ain't got no family."

"Well, I have plenty of family." Zac grinned. "Cobb's the name and I got me kin everywhere."

Both men choked on their drinks, their heads bobbing forward. "Cobb? You say Cobb?"

"That's right. You heard of my family before?"

Zac watched the two men as their eyes danced back and forth between them. It was amusing to try and read their minds. He could see the notion of danger in their thinking along with an idea of being a hero. Morales forced a sneer onto his lips. "We heard about your family. They say you are all cowards."

Zac laughed. He wasn't about to let the man provoke him that easily, but he was enjoying the nervousness he saw in both of their faces. "I'd say you were right about many of them. I s'pose they just love staying alive, no matter what it takes."

The man leaned closer to him. "Maybe you a coward too."

"Let's just say I'm careful."

"You not just careful"—Morales leaned closer, the stench of his breath scalding Zac's sensibilities—"you a coward."

Zac drew a deep breath and blew the sweet-smelling tobacco smoke across the man's face.

Morales dropped his hand to his holstered six-gun. Had there been only one man in front of him, Zac would have grabbed for the man's hand, but with two he had to take one out of action immediately, and he did. Reaching across his waist, Zac came up with the Greener knife. He sliced up with the blade, raking it across the Morales' hand as it came out of the holster. The revolver spilled to the floor, and the man howled, clutching his hand and doubling over.

Quickly, Zac came up with his knee, slamming it into the man's forehead. It was a violent, crushing blow, and the force of it sent him sprawling backward into Paco, who stumbled along the front of the bar.

Zac dropped the knife back into its sheath and, reaching for the big rifle, pulled the hammer back. Stepping over the now-prone Morales, he pushed the barrel into Paco's midsection. "All right, my friend, just take that six-gun out and slide it along the floor."

The man lifted it from his holster with two fingers and dropped it to the floor. Zac kicked it and sent it sliding over the sawdust-covered hardwood. The Silver Spittoon had grown suddenly silent as every eye watched them.

Zac nudged the man with the big gun. "Now, you just take that friend of yours to a doctor and stop up that bleeding of his."

Paco nodded.

"I may see you two down the trail, and next time I won't be so kind. You make sure that friend of yours understands that. 'Course, if I was you, I'd head on back to Old Mexico. Nobody's gonna take too kindly to you getting yourselves all beat up and cut on."

Stepping around the silent onlookers, Zac made his way to the door. He took one last look at the two men. Morales was still on the floor, stunned and bleeding. Paco was stretched across the bar, both arms spread out. He hadn't moved a muscle. His eyes looked as big as two brown plumbs.

Zac stepped out of the saloon. The doors swung behind him with a rhythmic sound. He once again spotted the two horses. Walking over to them, he took out the Greener and cut the reins. He then took off his hat and slapped their backsides, sending them bolting into and down the dark street. *Now they're all on foot,* he thought.

"Well, looky who we got us here!"

Zac swung around and saw the last thing he wanted to see. Torrie, Yuma, and Web had ridden into town. They stood on the dark boardwalk not ten feet from him.

A number of miles to the north, through the canyons and creeks that formed that part of the Mogollon Mountains, a tiny fire blazed next to a lake. The small body of water was placid and smooth; marsh grasses swayed as the movement of the breeze lapped the waters onto the shore. The fir and tall pine trees gave cover for the fire, and the people huddled around it to keep warm. The elevation was only slightly above two thousand feet, but suddenly it felt much colder.

Chupta had ridden back to the other side of the lake. He wanted to keep watch over the pass for anyone ambitious enough to be riding up it at night. The odds of that were slim, however. Even if someone had seen them leave, trailing them in the dark would be difficult. But Chupta had never been one to take chances. There really was only one way to go if a man decided to travel north, and that was up this pass and to the place the group was camped in.

Joe got up from the fire and walked to the edge of the lake. Soon he was joined by Julian. "I figure them two might want to have some time to themselves," Julian said.

Joe continued to stare over the lake.

"It won't take those people long to come after us," Julian went on.

"I know, hardly any time at all. All they gotta do is think." He turned around to look Julian in the eye. "That memory of yours coming back?"

"Some of it is. At times it takes the seeing of a place to recollect it, and I do remember this here lake."

"Well, that's something. Do you recall what you've been like, the things that you've done?"

Julian had his arm across his chest, holding the stump of his left arm. "The chill on nights like this brings back the feeling in the hand I ain't got. It's a funny thing that way. Sometimes a man can think all he has to do is reach out and grab something, and he can use a hand and an arm that ain't there no more. Right now I'd believe I could just hold out that left hand of mine"—he stuck out his right hand and wiggled his fingers—"and I could just see it. My eyes tell me different, though."

Joe continued his silent stare, seemingly right through his brother.

"Yes, I can recall those things. I don't like to think about them anymore. It didn't used to bother me, but now it does. There are times that I'm riding along and I see things—pictures that flash into my head. I suppose the only comfort I can take is in thinking about them as part of another man—his life, not mine."

"The problem is, they are your life. Zac wouldn't lift a finger to help you. He'd rather hunt you down and lock you up or see you hang."

"Why did you bother? You ought to be back at that ranch of yours in Texas with your wife."

"I really don't know. If I think about you as a man I have one set of thoughts that come into my head, but when I recall the way you used to be, I get another."

"Maybe you're doing the same thing as me," Julian said. "Maybe you're holding out a hand that ain't there anymore."

"Maybe so. Then again maybe I'm just remembering what Pa and Mama use to say about us Cobbs needing to stick together to make a go of things. Or perhaps I just couldn't abide the idea of some government agent having you killed. I don't really know."

Julian grabbed the stump on his left arm once again and walked to the edge of the lake. "Do you really think a man can ever change?" he asked. "I mean really change once his way has been set?"

"The Bible says a man can. That's all I really have to go by on that score. I can't really say as I've seen that much of it, men changing and all. I know some preachers that set store by it, but I figure it's their job to give folks hope. It ain't exactly in my line of work."

"Then you don't think it can happen?"

"I didn't say that. I just haven't seen much of it. I reckon a man could if he wanted to bad enough."

Julian turned his back to the water and looked straight at Joe. "Well, I want to bad enough. I figure it's got to take more, though, than just the wanting of a thing." He held his head up, looking at the stars. "I figure God has to do a miracle for a man to be different. He made that sky up there, and ofttimes I think we see Him as just stopping with the big things and leaving the smallness of what goes on inside people for them to reckon with, but that ain't right. I think He pays careful attention to what's inside a man, not just the mountains he rides through."

"You've changed a bit already."

"Maybe I have."

"But I still wouldn't trust you as far as I could pitch you."

Julian grinned. "No reason you should."

"A man might change, but old habits die hard," Joe said.

"I guess a feller has to take care of old habits by making himself some new ones."

"I s'pose," Joe spoke the words and made a careful study of his brother. He could never remember many conversations with the man, even when they were boys. Each event in Julian's life seemed to be spoken to and acted on but never contemplated.

"You know, from what I can remember of my life I've always just had one thing in mind, and that was whatever seemed right for Julian Cobb. Even when I fought the Yankees, I didn't much do it for the cause. I mostly did it cause I hated them fellers." Julian scratched his chin. "And for the pure mean cussedness of the matter, I reckon."

Julian's face had always been hard, like a piece of flint one would chip off the surface of a boulder; sharp, rigid, full of fire and spark. The black patch over his left eye gave him the appearance of a scrapper, and that he was. Joe knew full well that Julian should have been killed many times over, and there were few who really knew the man who didn't think it would have been a good idea. But there had to have been a purpose in him living. It was just no one had figured it out just yet or wanted to even try.

"Maybe the first new habit I ought to think on is doing something for other folks and not just for myself."

"Maybe," Joe replied. Joe had been listening to his brother, but his head spun as he did. Julian had never been much for talking and had never told another soul what was on his heart. Most people figured it was because he didn't have one. But here, now, the things he was saying made Joe almost think his brother might be changing, almost.

"You know, if those people do catch up with us," Julian said, "some of you might just get killed."

"There's always that chance."

Julian shook his head. "I don't think you being along with me is such a good idea. They don't want you. You were the man's guests, and from what you told me, he owes you plenty for getting his wife and daughter home safe. Now, if you find yourself in the way of his getting to me, you just might wind up dead for your troubles. I'd sure hate to see you leave a widow and orphan in Texas."

"I would too. I was wondering, though—what do you plan on doing if you find all that gold?"

"I'm not sure of that. It doesn't belong to me." He grinned. "Now, that's a new thought. But I'm not even sure if I can find it. The man I was with said the answers were in the T-shaped door."

"The T-shaped door?"

"Yes, that's all he said."

"And you think you know where that T-shaped door is?"

Julian looked off to the mountains. They were dark against the sky, and the moon hung low over them. The treeline on the hills nearby stood out in front of the moon like the fur on the back of an angry dog. The beauty was enough to distract any man, but Joe didn't know if that was the problem or if Julian just didn't want to say what he knew. Overhead, several bats swooped low.

Joe watched the man, obviously deep in thought. Most men made snap decisions and a few, like James, thought best when the words were already hanging in the air. Julian, however, had never been that way. Now, Julian's thoughts seemed to be clawing their way out of his mind like hundreds of small spiders crawling out of a paper bag—first one, then another, then the entire angry bunch.

"I'm not sure where that door is, not even entirely sure of what the man meant by it, but it'll come to me."

"I suppose we ought to get back to those other two," Joe said. "That brother of ours has already found his treasure, I think."

"I suppose he has."

The two of them walked slowly back to the fire pit. Their small cooking fire had burned down to glowing coals. James and Ellie had already spread their blankets on the ground, and James had laid his coat on top of the young woman.

"You two finished with all your talking?" James asked.

"For now we have," Joe said.

"And do you know where we're going tomorrow?"

Joe looked at Julian.

Julian took the toe of his boot and stirred the coals. "I think you best put this out," he said. "No sense in telling everybody where we are."

CHAPTER 29

+ + + + + + +

ZAC STOOD ON THE BOARDWALK outside the Silver Spittoon and lifted the big gun, laying it across his arms. "Glad to see you, gents," he said. "Been waiting for you."

"You been waiting for us?" Yuma asked. "We showed up and you weren't there."

" 'Course not. That feller you wanted me to shoot rode by us with some other men in the middle of the night. We followed them here, and I've been asking questions about where they might have gone to." Zac took a couple of steps forward. "I gotta say, you got yourself a bargain. You paid me to just shoot him, and I've spent two days and a night tracking that man and haven't caught up with him yet."

Yuma pressed forward, but Torrie swept his arm up, holding the man back. "We paid you to be with us," Torrie said, "not go riding off on your own. Now how is we gonna know where you are?"

"You didn't want to lose those people, did you? Besides, if I'd waited for you, there's no telling where they'd be right now. Their trail could have gone plumb cold." Zac patted his coat pocket. "I got your money here. You wanna be shuck of me, all you got to do is say it."

"We don't need him," Yuma growled.

"Maybe we do, maybe we don't," Torrie barked.

"Well, you just say the word. I'll give you your gold back and you can just go on your way and do whatever you want in following those people. Frankly, a hundred dollars is a fair price for what you asked me to do, but it don't buy two, three days of my time along with it."

"Man's got a point there," Web said.

" 'Course," Zac went on, "whoever else that government man hired might just get to that feller first, and then where would you be?"

Zac could tell the idea of a second player in the game struck them with a sense of foreboding. Sometimes doubt did that to a person. It could scare an otherwise cocky man into refusing to move. "Two hundred dollars more might satisfy me," Zac said.

He threw out the figure, knowing they would refuse. There was something about the audacity of it, though, that made his story sound all the more convincing.

"Two hundred dollars?" Yuma screeched. "You got a lot of nerve."

Torrie narrowed his eyes. "Sounds like to me yer trying to weasel out of our deal, either that or run off with our money."

"I'm not trying to do either one," Zac said. "I'm just trying to be fair with you, and I expect you to be the same with me. I reckon I'm just trying to sweeten the deal we made. Fair is fair."

"I don't trust him," Yuma said, "don't trust him one little bit."

"That's fine with me," Zac said. He pulled the five gold coins out of his pocket and bounced them in the palm of his left hand. They made a rattling sound, clear and sharp in the night air.

"Where's that kid of yours?" Yuma asked.

"He's sleeping, right where I ought to be about now. Why do you ask?"

"Oh, no reason," Yuma said.

Zac didn't care for the look in the man's eyes. He was like a snake ready to strike, with a knowing, passive, drawing-down-on-a-target look in his eyes. Right now, though, the man fixed his gaze on Zac's eyes and then shifted it to the Sharps he carried on his arm. There would be no way the man could draw his revolver before Zac leveled the big gun and sent him into eternity. Zac knew that whatever it was the man had in mind, he wouldn't do anything about it, not just yet.

"Well, here"—Zac handed back the money to Torrie—"I can tell thinking on this is causing you some pain. I'll be here in the morning, and you can tell me what you pondered on then. If you decide to pay me more I'll go with you. If you don't, you got your money, and I'll just be on my way."

With that, Zac turned on his heels and walked swiftly away. He'd given them enough to think about to know they'd be hesitant to make a move. Still, he didn't like it. He didn't like the fact that these men were becoming his shadows, and he especially didn't care for Yuma's continued interest in Pablo. That could be dangerous. If a man worked too hard at a notion, the thoughts generally would come back to him. He had known right away that the less time both him and the boy spent around those three men, the healthier it would be for them.

Getting back to the barn, he opened the first stall and shook Pablo awake. "Let's go, pardner. We got to be moving."

The boy rolled over, rubbing his eyes. "Where we going?"

"We're going to the spot we just came from, that canyon. We'll bed down near the mouth of it and wait for those fellers to clear out come morning."

Slowly, the boy got to his feet. He was still numb from too little sleep, and Zac knew what sleep he and the boy had had was interrupted and fitful. "Why are we going?"

"I just ran into those three bounty hunters, and I didn't much like the look in that feller Yuma's eyes when he asked about you. How well did he see you after they killed your parents?"

The boy scratched at his hair. "He saw me pretty good all right, rode right past me when I was walking home."

"I reckon they'd all had their bloodlust satisfied for the day or they'd have killed you too," Zac said. "You were lucky, boy. Those three kill and it never crosses their minds, the right or wrongness of the thing. Some people are like that, and in my line of work it's my misfortune to meet up with them all the time."

Zac threw his blanket and saddle on the dun.

"Can I ride the black?" Pablo asked.

"I think I got something that might fit your pistol better. You go wake up that feller in the office. Tell him we're leaving and that we want to make a trade."

Zac continued saddling the dun. He was pulling the cinches tight when the old man waddled out of his office, rubbing the sleep from his eyes. "Land sakes, with you two, a body can't get himself no sleep a'tall."

"Sorry about that, but we're heading out now."

"You're going? It's the middle of the night and you done paid for the whole thing."

"That's right, we have. I will make you a deal, though—the kid's horse and the black along with the saddle he came in with for that bay gelding over there." Zac pointed across the barn to an attractive horse with a white blaze down his face.

"That there's a fine animal, a good riding horse."

"That may be, but I want something the boy can handle and something that will go all day too. That one looks like he can fit the bill. Now, don't quibble with me. I'm giving you the better end of the deal, and you know it. The black there has the looks of a fine bloodline and he's a stallion with fire, to boot. You won't get a better deal in a month."

"No, I reckon I won't."

"One more thing," Zac said, "I'll take forty dollars in cash along with it."

"Forty dollars!"

"That's right, forty dollars in gold. You didn't jump fast enough at my first offer, and if you don't move your behind now, you won't like my next one in the least."

"All right, all right." The man held up both hands plaintively. "Just you hang on. I'll go get my cash box."

Zac pointed to Pablo's saddle and blanket on the top of the stall. "You better get your blanket and saddle and put them on that bay horse. We want to be out of here soon as that feller gets back."

Minutes later, the old man came back with the forty dollars. He dropped the coins in Zac's hand and shook his head. "You made yerself a fine deal."

"No, you did."

"I put shoes on that animal you're taking, along with them horses I traded for yesterday." He held up a horseshoe to show Zac what he was getting. "It's a nice piece of work. I do myself proud with the smithing."

Zac turned the shoe over in his hand. Underneath, it had a distinctive mark etched into the metal, an S encompassed by a circle. "Those horses you traded had these shoes on them?"

"Yes, they did—brand new, too."

Suddenly, something caught Zac's eye. The front door to the barn was slowly being opened, the end of a rifle poking through it. He pulled the old man aside and whispered, "I did see some robbers tonight, just lay low."

The man's eyes widened, and he stepped inside the stall next to him.

Zac quickly dived across the barn in Pablo's direction. Rolling over behind a standing bale of hay, Zac reached for Pablo. Catching the boy's pants legs, Zac wrenched him to the ground.

The door opened a crack. Zac caught the startled eyes of the old man on the opposite side of the barn. Zac held his hand up to his mouth and pointed at the door. Quietly, he settled his back into the bale.

The door continued to open. "Hey there." It was Web's voice. "We need to talk some more. Saw ya come in here."

From where Zac now sat, he could see directly to the back door of the barn, a sliding door on rollers and a track that led to the corral area. Zac watched it move aside, ever so slightly. The men were obviously planning on coming at him from both directions, but Web was trying to get his attention from the front door. Zac wouldn't disappoint him. He called out, "Sure, I'm in here. Come on in."

Web pushed the front door open and stepped inside the dimly lit barn. "Where are you?"

"Right here," Zac said, "over by the horses." He said the words casually, hoping to draw both men into the open.

With that, the back door slid open and Yuma stepped in, his gun drawn.

Zac sat where he was and leveled the big rifle. "You looking for me?" he asked.

Yuma spotted him and snapped off a shot. Zac had the Sharps already lowered and pointed it at Yuma before the man ever saw him. He squeezed off the back trigger and a thunderous explosion erupted from the end of the big gun. The shot caught the wiry man full on, the force picking him up off his feet and launching him into the darkness outside. Laying down the Sharps, Zac drew his Colt.

When Web saw the shot and its effect on Yuma, it sent him into a sudden scrambling panic. He crouched down behind a barrel of water in the front of the barn and called out in a shaky, high voice. "He got Yuma. He's in here someplace."

Only silence followed the warning. Zac imagined Torrie would take time now to figure his next move. He heard the creaking of the pulley outside the barn that led to the loft above their heads. That would be where the man was going. They still had getting him into a cross fire in mind.

"I see you figured out who the boy was," Zac shouted out.

"Yeah, Yuma finally placed him," Web shouted. "And then we sure 'nuff thought about who you must be. Don't know that yet, but it's fer durn sure you ain't that boy's pappy."

"You boys would be plenty surprised to find out just who I am."

"Who's that?"

"I'm the man I'll wager that Delemarian fella warned you about. The name's Zac Cobb. That's my brother you hired me to kill."

Zac leaned around the bale of hay and caught sight of Web. The man fired a shot at him. It sent the dull thud of a round into the hay, and Zac jerked his head back. Reaching over, he picked up the Sharps and broke it open. Taking one of his special loads from a loop in his belt, he dropped it into place, then snapped the rifle shut.

The barrel of water that Web crouched behind was little more than ten yards away. It was close enough for a well-placed pistol shot, and Zac had every confidence the man might just get off a good one if he gave him half a chance. He also knew the man had little or no understanding of the power he held in his hand. Looking up, he heard the pulley continue its creaking noise. He had to move quickly.

"You best throw out that gun of yours and step out from there," Zac yelled.

"Why should I? You ain't goin' nowheres."

In spite of how brave the man tried to sound, Zac could read the caution in his voice. Obviously Delemarian had told them all about the man they were supposed to kill and his kin too. Someone like that agent wouldn't have left out any of the details. And no matter what kind of bravado the man tried to spit out, Zac could tell he was as nervous as a duck in the desert.

"You don't think that little water barrel's gonna give you cover, do you?" Zac asked.

"Sure," Web said, " I got myself plenty of cover. Why don't you just come on out and have a look-see?"

Web had a single-action Colt, the same kind Zac carried. He could get off one shot, but for a second, he'd have to thumb the hammer back. The man blasted another round into the edge of the hay Zac was behind. The next shot would be fatal for Web, but Zac knew he'd have to move fast. Torrie was getting into the loft—the sound of the pulley had stopped.

Reaching out, Zac gathered a handful of loose hay. He took off his hat, stuffing it full of the matting. "Well, I'll just have to do that. You watch yourself now."

"Oh, I surely will."

Zac got up on the balls of his feet behind the hay. This would have to be it. Positioning the hat and straw on the tip of the big gun's barrel, he held it out from the other end of the bale. On cue, Web sent another blast in his direction. Zac jumped to his feet. Leveling the big gun, he sent a blast directly into the water. The barrel seemed to explode. Wooden stays collapsed, and water flew in all directions. Zac drew his revolver and started firing at the reeling man, slamming him time and again into the barn door. He watched the tall man hit the door, then slide to the floor.

The horses spooked, kicking at the sides of their stalls. Reaching out for the door of the gelding's stall, Zac swung it open. He raced into it, pushing the big bay horse aside and grabbing Pablo by the belt. He lifted the youngster off the ground and ran to the other side, where the old man still cowered, quivering. He dropped Pablo to the ground. "Just wait here," he said. "Don't move."

Pushing open the gate on the revolver, Zac extracted the spent cartridges, four of them. He slipped five .45 rounds out from his belt and dropped them in one at a time. He never carried a cartridge under the hammer, but this time he just might need six.

He looked over at Pablo. The boy was quaking with fear, his eyes shining like diamonds. Zac knew the feeling. He'd known it for years. It never changed for a man who had any sense, and he hoped it never would. Fear either served to freeze a man solid or sharpen his senses to a fine razor's edge, and right now, Zac knew he could use all the edge he could get.

Backing into the open area of the barn, Zac kept his head cocked at the loft. This was a man he'd have to deal with. Torrie wouldn't turn around and go home. "You up there, Torrie?" Zac called out. "You're the only one left, you know."

Leaning down through the opening in the loft, the man began to fire his six-gun. One shot after the other hit the ground. Zac danced aside, and when he looked up, the man was gone.

The opening to the loft was small, narrow, and very dark. A man might be able to stand up there and see the light from the stable below, but when a man looked up, all he could see was the darkness of the open space up above. Zac knew he couldn't afford to show himself or at least not well. The man could just stand up in the darkness and shoot without any worry about being shot himself.

Close by, he saw the big Sharps Creedmore. He could make big holes in the floor of the loft with that thing. Maybe it was worth a try. Lifting the revolver, he began to snap off shots into the dark opening—first one, then two, then three. He scrambled for the big gun and, picking it up, began to roll along the surface of the barn floor.

Torrie started returning fire. Slug after slug found their way into the floor.

Rolling to the side, Zac scooted over and out of the line of fire. He broke open the big gun and dropped a load into the breech. Snapping it shut, he raised it and unleashed a load of fury. The roar was like the belching of a dragon up from a bottomless pit. The force of the explosion once again filled the barn with smoke and showered the floor with fragments of wood. It left a gaping, smoldering hole near the opening in the loft. He knew if nothing else, the ferocity of the blast would frighten the man to death. Having a gun like he had was the kind of edge Zac knew he needed. In his line of work he always seemed to be outmanned, but he was determined never to be outgunned.

He broke open the rifle once again, dropping in another oversized cartridge. The noise of the weapon as it opened and closed was unmistakable—a crisp, metallic sound of doom. Raising it to his shoulder, he picked another spot and squeezed off the trigger. The gun roared.

This time it was far too much for Torrie to take. Screaming at the top of his lungs, the man slid down the ladder, revolver in hand, firing as he came.

Zac pulled out his Colt and fired back. The first shot hit the man. Cocking the hammer, Zac fired again. The second shot sent him falling to the floor. There was no movement when he hit it, only the escape of his last breath.

Walking over, Zac turned the man over with the toe of his boot. He was lifeless, his eyes wide in death.

Moments later, the old man and Pablo emerged from their hiding place. Pablo shook, a mixture of hatred and fear lingering in the boy's eyes.

Zac motioned to the men on the floor. "These men are carrying gold on them. I know we've done some damage here," he said, "but I reckon it'll more than cover it. Come to think of it, it might be enough for you to buy the place."

The noise on the main street still sounded out its mixture of metallic wailing, but Zac knew it wouldn't take long for the curious to form a crowd. They'd wait until they were sure the shooting was over, and then they'd fill up the place.

"Get your horse, son, we got some riding to do."

The stillness of the early morning hour around the lake made Joe's eyes pop wide open. Something was wrong, and he knew it. He threw back his blankets and hurriedly pulled on his boots. Crouching next to his bedroll, he first felt for, then strapped on his gun belt.

The quiet calm was broken up by the sound of fluttering wings. Two large Canadian geese swooped down, landing on the nearby lake. Joe watched them. The beauty of the birds was unmistakable, even in the dim moonlight. Tucking their wings behind them, the big majestic birds began a gentle glide.

Joe got to his feet. There was something that was not right. He could feel it run up and down his skin. Adjusting his eyes to the darkness, he counted the bedrolls. It was then that he knew. Julian was gone.

He scampered over and shook James. "Wake up! Wake up, big brother. Julian's gone!"

The man rolled over, muttering. Getting up any time before the sun was well up had never been an activity suited to James.

"What?" he asked. "What did you say?"

"I said, Julian's gone."

By this time, Ellie was fully awake. She sat up straight. "Maybe he's just looking for breakfast."

"Breakfast!" James yapped, "It's the middle of the night."

"No it's not, but it is a couple of hours before the sun comes up. I'd suggest we get a fire going and make us some breakfast. I want to be saddled up and looking for his tracks when morning hits us."

"Why would he leave?" Ellie asked.

James got to his feet. "That's our brother," he said. "I suppose you and Zac have been right about him all along. The man doesn't think of anybody but himself."

"I'm not so sure. Last night we were talking, and I think he's trying to put us out of harm's way. Somehow he figures Escobar would go light on us if he wasn't around."

James pulled on his boots. "Now, isn't that amazing? You thinking the best about him and me thinking the worst."

"It doesn't much matter which one of us is right. We still need to find him. The state his mind is in, he could go wandering around in circles."

"It's foolish to think Escobar would go easy on us," James said. "The man isn't going to allow anyone who knows what he's talking about to live. Killing us would be an easy thing for him."

"It sure would."

CHAPTER 30

THE NEXT MORNING, HESS rode out in the direction of the canyon. The sun was not up yet. The first rays of dawn were only peeking over the eastern hills. He desperately wanted to be at the campsites before they were ready to leave. The idea of not sleeping with his men in the field was a repugnant one to him, and he already knew that many of them viewed the matter the same way. He had seen their eyes and heard their whispers. Now, if he could be there before some of them even awakened, he would feel he'd taken the moral high road once again. His Prussian pride prevented him from doing anything short of that. An officer must be looked up to, especially a German officer.

The trees stretched out from the canyon, bowing down with leaves that looked heavy. The scattering of pine among them grew closer and closer together higher up, until finally they choked out any light. Where he rode, the ground was soft. His horse's hooves sunk slightly into the turf as it trotted over the moist dirt. The tall grass that grew there was wet, coating the legs of the animal and leaving a shine that glistened on his boots in the early light.

Hess brushed back his large blond mustache. He had waxed it this morning, and even though he wore modest civilian clothing—a dark pair of dungarees and a tan shirt with buckskin vest—he looked very military. A man could see it just by looking at him, the way he sat his horse and the manner in which he held his shoulders back with head erect.

He saw movement through the trees, men on foot. Drawing the reins on his horse, he sat and took a long look. There were a number of them, and they were all walking toward him. It took several moments more before he recognized the first two, Paco and Morales. Morales had his hand bandaged and behind him were the others, all on foot.

The group emerged from the trees, and behind them was a lone rider. Utant caught sight of Hess and, kicking his horse, rode toward him, looking straight ahead. Utant seemed more sober than usual.

Putting his spurs to the horse, Hess galloped forward to meet Utant in the front of the column. "What happened?" Hess asked.

"Two men come last night and steal horses."

"Indians?" Hess was used to assuming that horse thieves would be Indians.

"No, they white men. I fight with one of them and almost take his scalp." Utant touched the back of his head gingerly. "Another man hit Utant in back of head with rock."

Hess looked over at Morales. "What happened to you?"

The man looked sheepish. He hung his head. "I cut myself."

"Wonderful," Hess said. "I leave you people for one night and you see what happens to you. You should have kept the horses together and posted a guard. The general will be very angry. This will cost us a day, at least. Did they take the supplies?"

Utant nodded.

Hess gave out a series of loud curses, the roar of which would have scorched the trees. He turned his horse in circles, too upset to sit still. Utant stood and watched him rage, his hands on the reins.

When Hess calmed down, he backed his horse up, staring at the men. Turning to Utant, he spoke in a slow and deliberate tone, his voice dropping to a lower pitch. "I should have forced the general to listen to you. We would have been better off if I'd gone with you and just a few of your people. These men are useless."

Morales cleared his throat and stepped up to Hess. He couldn't have picked a worse time, but the man always had a knack for that. "The men have to have something to eat, Major. They are hungry."

Several men moved back and shuddered at the words. They had a great deal of fear when it came to this foreign officer. He was not Mexican and was unpredictable. They found most of his moods unreadable, except for his flashes of anger.

The words had the opposite effect, however—not what Morales and the rest of the men expected. Dejected, Hess sat on his horse, his mind racing but the rest of him stone-cold still. It was frightening. None of them knew what he would do or say next. He turned his horse, putting his back to them, and stared back down the hill to the town below.

Without saying a word, Hess began the slow ride to town, thinking of just what he would say to explain the situation to Escobar and knowing how the general would react. The men followed on foot. There wasn't much talking and there wasn't a one of them who didn't feel foolish.

As they made their way out of the mouth of the canyon, Zac and Pablo slipped in behind them and headed north. There was simply no way any of the men could have known that not more than a stone's throw away from them was the man responsible for their embarrassment.

Later that morning, Hess and Escobar were sorting over a list of supplies at the store. The shopkeeper, Horace Simple, had jotted it down as he listened to both of them talk and they were double-checking his notations. The supplies they would need wouldn't be as extensive as what they had lost, but they should be adequate. They would buy more ammunition and enough food and cooking necessities to last for over a week, but not knowing how long it might take to find the trail made things a bit more tricky. They knew the party was at least a day ahead of them, but they still had little idea in which direction to go.

The bell over the door jingled, and a white-haired man with a crutch limped in. Simple looked up and smiled at the man. "Capt'n Sam, good to see you. Will you be looking for some more chawin' tobacco?"

"That's right, I sure will, along with some whiskey and turnip greens too."

"Turnip greens?"

"Shore. Man my age is got to keep a watch on his innards, ya know." He patted his stomach and rubbed it in a circular motion. "Might want me some sugar cookies to go with them turnip greens too."

Simple shook his head. "Captain, the diet you got, it's a wonder you ain't dead yet. Yesterday I told that nice newlywed couple, the Cobbs, that we all figured you were done for."

Both Hess and Escobar jerked up their heads at the mention of the Cobb name.

"The wife and I appreciate you sending them two our way. They seemed like such nice folks and we hear they might plan on staying."

"Excuse me," Escobar spoke up. "Did you say their name was Cobb?"

"Why, sure," Simple said, "a James Cobb and his wife. They was in here yesterday buying some supplies like you folks. Not nearly as much, though."

"Did this man have a brother with him?" Escobar asked.

"No," Simple said. "Them folks was on their honeymoon. Now what man goes on his honeymoon with a brother along with him?"

Captain Sam listened. He scratched his chin and then spoke up, "I did see them later on, over by the post office. Looked like to me they'd met up with some other folks. Didn't rightly meet them other people, though. Couldn't say what their names were."

Hess asked, "Did one of the men have only one eye and one arm? He wears an eye patch over the left eye."

"I believe one of 'em did." The old seaman became more animated.

"Seemed to me to be a mean-lookin' type too, not at all like that couple. Had his left arm gone, right about the elbow."

By this time both Hess and Escobar were smiling. Just running into this man in the store was almost worth their supplies being stolen. Escobar almost found it hard to ask the next question. An answer would be too good to believe possible. "You didn't see which way they went, did you?"

The old man turned around in the store, trying to figure out the direction. He shifted his feet and then turned around once more. It was obvious he wanted to stand in what his mind told him was the same position as the post office. He grinned. "I been to sea all my life, and never once have I ever been at a loss to tell one direction from the other, but on land I get myself in some troubles." He looked over at Simple. "Now, just how do you go to figuring a thing like that?"

Simple shrugged. "Ain't no way of telling. I suppose a man just gets too used to what he sees all the time."

"I know it." The old man slapped his thigh and laughed. "But it beats all, now don't it? With just the horizon in front of me, I can never get lost, but with all them buildings and trees, I gets myself turned around all the blame time."

Just then, the thought came to him. He pointed off in a direction. "Which way is that, Horace?"

"North," Simple said. "That's north."

"Well, then that'd be the way they rode off in. They didn't go all at once, though, and I thought that a mite strange. The injun and that one arm feller had already rid off when I come out from mailin' my letter, and the rest of them just tacked up after them. Maybe they weren't together at all, but that's the way they went, all right."

Julian rode with his shoulders hunched forward and his chin up. It was hardly the bearing of a man on parade, but rather the appearance of someone who had every muscle ready and every sense alert. There was a ramrod look to the man as he scanned the horizon with his one eye. Since the war, he'd found that having only one eye had its advantages. In a gunfight he was able to screen out everything and everyone but the object or person he was shooting at. It gave him a deliberation that was unnerving. But there had been times when he had missed something while he rode. Distances were never kind to him, and things others saw might just slip past him if he wasn't careful. So he stayed erect and swiveled his head, keeping his gaze moving. He was deep in thought. With each bend in the pass, it was as if there was something more that came to mind, something else he was seeing in a new way.

The last ride he'd taken in this area was with Jumpy, and this was the place the man talked about during their last meeting. Jumpy Suthers had ridden with him into Mexico after the war, and both of them found work in the emperor's private guard. The Republican revolutionaries made it hard for the Austrian prince to trust his Mexican bodyguards. Americans seemed to be a convenient alternative, and former Rebel soldiers were readily available. The woods were seemingly full of men in gray who were bitter and could no longer abide living in America. Julian prided himself in being un-Reconstructed. He'd never taken a loyalty oath, and he never would.

On top of that, there was some measure of trustworthiness with the Southerners. It wasn't that they couldn't be bought. The thing that made them so attractive to Maximilian was their disinterest in Mexican politics altogether and the fact that when these men were bought, they generally stayed bought.

Maximilian ruled Mexico at Napoleon's pleasure, and it was the French military who kept him in power. The one thing the man had managed to accomplish was the binding together of all the opposition, however. That had never happened before. Given the fact that Maximilian actually cared about the peasants and wanted to do the right thing, he had continued the reforms that so irritated the wealthy landholders. That turned out to be the wrong thing to do. Without even hardly trying, he'd lumped all the political factions into one pile, putting all of them in opposition to him.

Julian thought the lesson was obvious—never try to do the right thing. Always pick a wrong side and give it all you've got. He knew that kind of thinking was corrupt and went against everything he'd ever been taught, and right now he knew he'd walk away from doing that again, but, at the time, it made sense. It also seemed to confirm the cynical view he'd taken on the world back then and the lack of real truth he felt existed in the first place. It was a bad way for a man to live his life.

Jumpy was a laugher. A man had to be when he thought the world was upside down to begin with. Julian could still remember the man chuckling over the lessons on life Mexican politics had taught them. Politics would be the thing that finally killed him. Jumpy had been on that last trip with the emperor's gold and jewels. Jumpy knew exactly what had gone wrong. When Julian met up with him, Jumpy told him very little, just enough to get him interested. He was going to tell him more, but Escobar's men had found them and just at the wrong time.

Julian came up over the pass just after dawn. Pine trees dotted the slope in front of him, and the sandstone bluffs he was heading toward seemed to glow right below him. They were a burnt tangerine color, contrasting sharply with the green trees. In the distance the Mogollon Mountains rolled off of each other's backs, like sand dunes plastered with greenery. Beyond them was the valley and then the Malpais.

Julian started winding down the face of the hills. Pine trees brushed him as he went by, and the juniper pulled at his breeches. The Gila River was below, cutting its way through the hills and winding south to Silver City. Up here it wasn't much of a river, as those things go. It joined up with two more branches and the creeks that seeped down off the mountains, becoming something a man might call a river.

An hour later, Julian rode down the rocky face and spotted the river. The loose stones his horse kicked tumbled down the flat sheet of sandstone below. They rattled, sending a shower of loose dirt and pebbles echoing into the valley. The river flowed through the valley and the silt it carried flattened out, forming two large banks on either side, a nice piece of farmland the old Indians in the area used well. Trees grew along either side of the slow-poking water, and boulders provided islands in the fertile topsoil.

Between two trees on the side of the river, he saw a lean-to. The structure had been well laid out, two cut poles forming the frame and tied chest high to a pair of young pines. A pillow of pine boughs were laced together on top and in front of the makeshift shelter. A small fire circle had been laid, and it was black with the leavings of the last fire. Julian thought he detected a small puff of rising smoke from it. There wasn't enough to show sign of a man in the camp, but just enough to show that breakfast had been cooked there earlier.

Julian drew rein to look it over. The lean-to appeared empty, but behind it a thicket of trees might just shelter anything. It couldn't be a large group, though—one or two men at best. The small shelter wouldn't hold more than that, and he couldn't see any sign of a second structure. He kicked his horse in the sides and once again the animal made its descent.

In a matter of minutes he was alongside the stream. He pulled up and got down, dropping his reins to allow the animal to drink. It was then he saw the man stepping out from the trees. The stranger wore a battered black hat and a white sheepskin vest over a pale blue shirt and denim jeans. His face was craggy and pockmarked with the black stubble of a beard that coated it like soot from a kerosene lamp.

He looked to be a hunter. The Winchester he carried had a strap that ran from a steel loop on the stock to the barrel of the gun. It lay casually across his arms like a baby carried by its mother. Julian also saw that he carried a pearl-handled Colt tied down at his side. It wasn't exactly the sidearm of a hunter.

"Howdy," the stranger said. "Come a huntin'?"

"Figured on it," Julian replied. "You found anything?"

"A little bit, but there ain't much around. I did see a couple of white-tails early this morning, drinking down by the stream."

Julian surveyed the camp carefully. There was no game hanging up and no racks that had been erected for drying.

"The name is Frank Gordon," the man said.

"Pleased to meet you," Julian replied. He had no intention of returning the favor by giving the man his own name, and Julian suspected the man would never ask. Most things out here in the West were private to a man, and if a body didn't volunteer information, it was best to never ask. "Looks like you got yourself a nice camp here. I was up there at the lake last night."

"That would be Lake Roberts," the man said. "Pretty place, peaceful."

Julian made no attempt to come closer to the man, and Gordon seemed to be content not to approach him either. It was plain to see they were sizing each other up. His two dark brown eyes fixed on one spot, Julian's eye. The man never seemed to blink.

"I s'pose I'll be riding on," Julian said. "Appears to me you got this place pretty well staked out."

"Things do seem to be looking up here," Gordon said. "You come on back if you manage to find something. We'll have coffee."

"I'll do that."

"Well, you have a good ride."

"Been riding for a while. I think I'll go on foot a ways and stretch my legs."

Walking around the horse to the left side of the animal, Julian kept his mount between himself and Gordon. Getting up on the horse and simply riding off would provide too good a target, and something inside told him that was exactly what the man was waiting for. Picking up the reins, he walked off, making sure the horse served as his cover. It seemed like a strange thing to do, but it would let the man know that he had no intention of presenting himself as a target. A man always avoided trouble by showing that he wasn't an easy mark—the West was full of the graves of easy marks.

He hadn't gone more than a quarter a mile before he moved over to the trees. What he didn't want was the man following him and waiting for a chance at a clean shot. He'd walk the same treeline the man was in and take a few turns at stopping to listen.

Several times, he brought the horse to a stop and once he even doubled back. He waited longer than it might take for any but the most careful man to make his presence known. He could tell, though, just by looking at the man, that whoever this Gordon was, he was careful.

He led the horse through the trees, weaving his way in and out of them. They made themselves plenty of noise while they were moving, but then Julian would abruptly stop and give a careful listen. There was no sound, just the lapping of the river on the bank near him. Of course, the silence told him something too. The animals that might make the natural sounds of the forest were lying low for some reason. It might be just him, and then again, it might be Gordon.

Several miles down the river, he came to the place he'd been looking for. Scrub oak dotted the stream, and across it was a pointed bluff. It rose high above the valley and overlooked the river below. It pointed from the side of a hill, like the bow of a huge rocky ship. It seemed to be suspended in time, out of place on the land and abandoned to the ghostly valley. To the side of the pointed rock, two large pines had crossed themselves. They bent down in opposite directions, the victims of some long-ago avalanche. This was the place, the place he remembered, the place Jumpy had talked about. Now he had to find the T-shaped door.

Swinging himself onto the back of the horse, he kicked the animal sharply and thundered toward the river. He kept himself low in the saddle and swung the horse from side to side, still careful not to make himself an easy target. If Gordon had indeed followed him and was close by, he'd have to be a very good shot, and he'd have to make his first one count.

Hitting the river, the horse scattered the water in all directions. He'd picked a good spot to cross. The bank was flat here and the sandy river bottom spread out, making it shallow. It wouldn't take him long to get across, and there would be no swimming.

In a matter of moments, he hit the other side. The horse pounded up the wet sand, storming up the gradual bank and making for the trees. Once in them, Julian pulled rein and stepped to the ground.

Winding his way around the bluff, he caught sight of a trail. It was well worn and recently used. That bothered him a mite. It had been made by the Indians who lived in these cliffs. They had farmed the fertile valley and made their way from their fields to perches high on the cliffs. He'd seen it once before. It would be no trouble to find it again.

The small cut in the rocks gave way to the narrow trail. Overhead, a number of boulders provided natural lookouts. Several stands of rocks almost looked as if they had been erected, one at the head of the trail and two more on either side. These were breast works. They would give good cover for a band of men wishing not to be disturbed. This place had been a natural defense for the Indian. No enemy could come in undiscovered, and if they found themselves here, they would be made to pay.

Slowly, he climbed the trail, inching his way up the steep rocky incline. Off to the right, he could see it. The sides of the great rocky ship sloped down the gap in wavelike ripples. They were smooth, carved out by the wind and an ancient raging river. In tumbling mounds of elegant stone, they gave off the look of frozen liquid mushrooms. Underneath the stony cascade, dark rooms peeked out. These caves had been partially filled. Fitted flat stones and makeshift mortar formed the outline of a forgotten city, a ghost town of days long gone by.

It was a sight to behold, and Julian felt like an intruder. This was not his house. It belonged to another, a people he would never know or understand.

He took two more steps and behind him he heard the distinctive cock of a pistol.

CHAPTER 31

JULIAN FROZE IN HIS TRACKS. The sound of a pistol cocking carried great authority where he was concerned, and since his only hand was holding the reins of his horse, there wasn't much left for him to do but stand still.

"Jes' stay right where you is, mister." The voice was craggy. At least it wasn't the resonant baritone he'd heard from Frank Gordon. "Put yer other hand up. I can see ye got a holt of yer horse."

"I'm afraid I don't have another hand. I lost it and an eye at Gettysburg."

"Then you jes' stay where you is. I'll have myself a look-see."

"All right, pardner, I ain't moving a muscle."

The man giggled. "That's good. I ain't had me a buryin' in a coon's age. I mighta forgot the words."

Julian heard the man's boots scuffing the ground as he moved to get a better view. He obviously had been in the rocks beside the trail. Julian held out the stump of his right arm.

"I reckon you is right. You was in that big hullabaloo. Seems like you lost it, sure 'nuff."

"You mind if I turn around?" Julian asked. "I don't fancy being shot by somebody I can't see."

"That's fine. You just do that, but do yer turnin' real slow and easy like. I see you make any sudden twitchin' an' I is gonna blow yer head clean off. You read me there, feller?"

"I do."

With that, Julian began to turn around. He did so deliberately, continuing to hold the reins of the horse. His heart raced. There was no reason to believe this place would be abandoned, even though he had hoped it would be. It would make doing what he needed to do much more difficult.

He turned around, and what he saw almost turned his stomach. The man was old and stooped over. His shoulder-length hair was white and flying in all directions. What didn't point at the sky hung down in the old fellow's eyes. There was no wind, but from the looks of the man's hair, you would have sworn he was standing in the midst of a full-force gale. His red long johns stuck out of battered gray pantlegs. The red flannel top had holes the size of half dollars scattered in more than a dozen places, and his pants were stuffed into knee-high boots with straps on the side. The boots were torn and the soles were coming off.

"I don't mean you no harm," Julian said.

"So you say."

The man's white beard rolled off his face and down to his belly. His cheeks were a bright red, and his blue eyes shone like polished sapphires. They were blank, lost; as lost as the man they belonged to.

"I didn't know anybody was living up here."

"I'ma livin' here. You got yerself old Amos. That's the only name I goes by. Ain't been too proud of the other one, so I left it behind me many a year ago. And who might you be?"

"My name's Julian Cobb."

"You a hunted man? Ain't many folks that thinks to come up here, 'cept folks what is hunted."

Julian nodded. "I reckon I'm being hunted down in Mexico. Maybe some of them fellas are looking for me, and I suppose there might be some others."

The man brandished a large Colt Dragoon. It fired black powder and was designed to knock a man off his horse without worrying about him ever getting up again. Julian nodded toward it with his chin. "You mind putting that thing down, mister? It kinda makes me nervous standing here."

"Well, it should. This thing is for making you dead, not for making you nervous."

"Well, mister, if you intend to kill me, you best go ahead; otherwise, I'd sure appreciate you lowering that thing. Your hand looks a might shaky to me, and what might be a twitch to you could be pure deadly to me."

"I ain't no 'mister.' Like I done told you, I be jes' old Amos. Man calls you mister is gonna steal somethin' that don't belong to him. He's just lookin' for a way to get on yer good side till you let yer guard down." He nodded at Julian's gun belt. "You jes' drop them reins and pull that shooter out with two fingers. Drop it on the ground and kick it over my way some. Don't you go to giving me more reason to get shaky."

Julian did just that, easing his revolver out and lowering it to the ground. He reached his boot over and kicked the gun in the man's direction.

"Fine, fine. You be doin' that and we're gonna get ourselves along jes' fine till I figures out jes' what to do with ye."

"I hadn't planned on staying."

"Well, if you don't answer any of my questions the way I like or make any unexplained jumps, I'ma gonna rare back on this here trigger. You can bet yer bottom dollar then that yer gonna be here a real long time. Fact is, yer gonna be a permanent part of this here place. Am I making myself heard in yer ears?"

Julian nodded. "You are."

"Fine, fine. Now you jes' turn yerself 'round there and get to climbing up to them spook houses. You and me have got ourselves a bit of jawin' to do."

Julian slipped his hand on the horse's reins and, turning his back to the old man, started his climb up the hill. The gap in the rocks rose high, circling the small wooded space below with a creek running through it. In parts, the going was steep; in other places, it was as if stairs had been cut from the rocks. They proceeded gradually up and toward the yawning blackness of the cut-out houses on the face of the wall. Each of his steps echoed, followed by the sound of the old man's shuffle.

As they rounded the end of the valley, the caves seemed to disappear. They were flat against the opposite wall and the lower entrance was covered by oak. Above the high branches were the uppermost apartments of the cliff dwellings and a series of ladders that led up to them. This would be about as safe a spot as a man could find to hide from the law; evidently Amos had found it the ideal place to hide from life. How he lived here was anybody's guess. Obviously, though, the thing that bothered the old man most was the presence of an intruder, and right now that was Julian. He would have to find a way to make the man feel comfortable—and that might very well be an impossible task.

The ground on the other side, next to the cave town, started to flatten out, forming a wide walkway with a few scattered stands of brush to offer concealment. Julian figured it might be the result of hard work done by the people who'd lived there. Perhaps they'd spent a great deal of time carving out a level place for their babies to play, a place that was close enough for the mothers to keep an eye on them while working on their handicrafts.

The flat area leading up to the caves was about ten yards wide and some sixty yards long. Over the side, the slope tumbled down an outcropping of sandstone, coming to rest in the wooded creek bottom below.

The place was built for defense; that was plain to see.

The overhanging cliffs were blackened. They seemed to ripple with a smooth exterior; on closer examination, however, the surface proved to be rough to the touch. The caves began with a series of smaller openings along the pathway, an area obviously used for storage and play. Julian peered in as he walked by. Three round stone formations were sunk into the middle of the largest of the initial caves. These were most likely carved to hold large, round storage jars. Maybe they held water in case of a siege, or perhaps they stored food during the worst of the winter months.

The dwellings themselves were two stories high and adjoined the entrance of the largest of the caves like spokes on a wheel. Blackened roof beams the Indians called vigas, made from burnt juniper, stuck out from the roof of the middle and upper layers. The wood was scorched to make it harder and prevent it from warping.

A ladder stood at the bottom. It led to the middle level, where a series of stone stairs rose to the upper houses. In the middle there was a main entrance, a T-shaped door. Julian stopped and looked at it. It was the thing Jumpy had reminded him about. That's where the map was buried, somewhere in the stones surrounding the door.

"Ya ain't never seen one of them things afore, have ya?" Amos asked.

"No, can't say as I have."

The man laughed. "It takes some rattling of a man's head to think some things out 'round here. Near as I can figure, them folks used to carry things through that there door up there, or maybe they jest used the ledges on it to put some of their heathen idols in order to scare off the evil spirits."

"Maybe so," Julian said.

"My own self, I figure this here pistol works best at warding off ghosts. I heard myself plenty of spooky sounds 'round here, but it's the kind with two legs that I'm ready for. I was ready fer you, weren't I?"

"I'd say you were."

"Now you jes' strip off yer saddle and leave that horse be. First, though, you shuck out that saddle gun of yourn."

Julian slowly pulled out the Winchester. Turning back to the old man, he tossed it in his direction. Amos caught it.

"That's real fine. You're behavin' yerself right proper fer a seedy feller with one eye and one arm."

"I got nothing to hide," Julian said. "Like I said, I mean you no harm. Never even knew anybody was up here."

Julian was a bit worried by the man, though. He might just get nervous and shoot him no matter what he said. It was for sure the man was slowing him down. He had Joe and James coming on, and the Apache would be able to track him with little or no trouble. Then there was also Escobar and the men with him. It was only a matter of time before they came riding up. He'd have to find some way to get out of here with the map, and quickly.

"I seen scalawags like you afore," Amos said. "They jes' go to huntin' trouble. They poke themselves around where they don't belong and steal a man's claim too quick to talk about."

All at once, the thought came to Julian. Amos wasn't just a hermit, he was a prospector. He might even have found a strike somewhere back in the hills. That was why he was so overprotective. Most men living alone welcomed company, but it was plain to see Amos didn't. Perhaps if he told the man the truth, he'd realize he had nothing to fear from him. A man sitting on buried treasure would have no need to jump another man's claim.

Amos set the rifle down and motioned toward the ladder. "Now, just you climb up that thing and stay there. I'm gonna fix me a fire and get some vittles a goin'. Don't need you pokin' 'round down here whilst I do."

It seemed as though the man was going to keep him, at least for a while. That bothered Julian. He began to have second thoughts about telling him the truth. If he told him the truth, would he be likely to kill him and claim the treasure for himself? This man didn't know what he'd be up against and had no idea of the danger from the people who were on Julian's trail, but the temptation might be too much for any man to handle. "Do you have coffee?" Julian asked.

"Nah, ain't had me no coffee in many a month."

"I have some in my saddlebags. If you want to fix it, all I ask is for a cup or two."

The old man cocked his head to the side and grinned, flashing a smile with a number of missing teeth. "Fer a man that's taken to getting himself kilt one little piece at a time, you sure is a trustin' soul with yer outfit."

"I s'pose that's the way I am. I treat a man fairly and expect the same from him."

"Humph," the man grunted. "I'd say you was a fool, then."

"A man can afford to be a fool when another man's got a gun on him."

"You got yerself a point there. Now, get on up that ladder."

Julian mounted the ladder and took it one rung at a time. Climbing out onto the ledge that led to the upstairs room, he walked a few paces and stepped into the one with the T-shaped door.

Down below, he heard the sound of the ladder. Poking his head out, he watched Amos take it down. Now he was stuck. He might be able to jump or climb down, but doing it would make a lot of noise, and his horse was out by the old man.

He backed into the dimly lit room. The roof of the place was missing and the cave itself stared down at him, blackened by the fires of the Indians or by those of hunters and prospectors who had used it since. It would make a nice location for a nighttime fire. The warmth would be there, and from where the apartment sat, back in the cave, no one would see it.

The walls came up over a man's chest. They had been plastered with a claylike mixture, probably brought up from the river. Directly across from him was what appeared to be a stone keep. It was square in shape, and the roof of the place was built to the ceiling of the cave. One dark window looked at him, with another facing the light. He suspected the window closest to him had been a door or crawl space. Small stones beneath it gave the semblance of stairs.

Julian hoisted himself over the room's wall and lowered himself to the catwalk outside. Tiptoeing over to the square room, he climbed up the rocky stairs and peeked inside. The place was surprisingly small. Stones had been carefully fitted into place, and vigas that had once formed the roof of the story below were long since gone. Only the ends of the beams stuck out from the stones.

He looked down. Filling the bottom of the room beneath him were what appeared to be dried, miniature corncobs. If the place had stored winter food, this would be the leftovers. He imagined the Indians had used the plain around the river to grow their crops, and the matter of transporting them here would have been easy. They had had themselves a good life, plenty of food and water, along with the protection from their enemies a spot like this afforded them. It was amazing to think of what might have forced them to move. Maybe, just maybe, the old corncobs were the evidence of the last good crop those people ever pulled out of the ground. The lack of food makes many a man do what wouldn't seem possible.

Julian wedged himself in. This place would make a good spot for a last stand if it came to that. The old man might be hesitant to stick his gun in there if Julian was waiting on the other side. He slid back out, feeling for the top stone. As he pulled his head out, a shot was fired. The lead pasted the wall next to him, and the blast echoed down the canyon.

Julian dropped to the floor of the catwalk, hugging the stones.

"You get yerself outta there. I never told you to go maverickin' 'round this place."

Julian lay still. Picking up his head, he shouted down below. "You never told me not to. You should have. I ain't planning on being shot."

"I weren't trying to shoot you. If'n I had been, you'd be dead. You just stand up and get outta there. Go back to where you got yerself put."

Julian slowly got to his feet. He stared at the man, who was still looking down the barrel of the big pistol. Walking back, he stooped under the T-shaped door. This Amos fella didn't appear to be the forgiving sort. Julian would remember that. The room was bare, and he tried to imagine what it would have been like with rugs, utensils, and the necessities of life during the days of the Indian.

In the middle of the room a square hole had been dug in the floor, surrounded by stones. Called a kiva, it was the place for the fire, perhaps for these people's religious ceremonies.

He looked back at the door. The top of the door was layered with tongue-and-groove wood. The two ledges on the sides were also lined with the wood, but where they ended, the rocky plaster took over. Jumpy had said the map was in the T-door.

Julian moved to the door and looked out. The old man had his back to him, laying dry wood on the small fire. Julian felt the sides of the doorway; the panels held good. Reaching up, he tugged at the piece that went over the top. It moved slightly at first, then gave way. *This has to be the place,* Julian thought.

Pulling it down, he felt with his hand between the wood and the mud-caked wall. There was nothing. The rest of the wood would not move, only this one spot. He pulled on it harder, and it finally gave way. Lowering the plank, he looked inside. Except for the dirt one would expect to find, there was nothing, no treasure map.

Pushing it back up into place, Julian began to feel down the sides of the walls. Every stone and brick seemed to be plastered into position. Everything was secure. Julian's heart sank.

Moments later, he heard the ladder moving. Looking out, he could see that Amos was on his way up, carrying two cups of the coffee wrapped in a cloth and climbing with only his left hand to stabilize him. When he reached the catwalk, he drew out his revolver and stepped inside. He sat one cup down and handed the other to Julian. "I tasted some of it down there, and it's blame good."

Julian took the cup and, sitting down, held it to his lips. He sipped it slowly as Amos looked him over. Moving over to the other side of the room, the old man seated himself on the ledge that ran next to the wall.

Immediately his eyes were drawn to the doorway. Julian watched him as he looked it over. There was something about people who had been in the same place for a long time. They noticed the slightest disruption to any of their familiar surroundings. Julian could see that there was a gap between the wooden plank and the mud-mortar top of the door, a gap his exploring had created. It was a small space. Nothing ever went back exactly the way it was.

"You been doin' yerself some diggin', I see."

"What are you talking about?" Julian asked.

"Don't lie to me. You been doin' fine so far, and now yer takin' to lying."

Julian fell silent. Amos got to his feet and walked to the doorway, staring at the small gap. He put his hand up and felt the piece that covered the top of the door. It shifted easily. "Now, just what you think yer lookin' fer up there?" he asked.

"There was nothing in there," Julian said.

"No, there weren't, but you was lookin' all the same, now, weren't ya?"

"I was just curious, is all."

Amos turned and looked directly at him. He shook his head, wagging his beard back and forth. "You was more than just curious. There was something you was looking for in there, now, weren't there?"

"All right," Julian said. "That's the reason I came up here in the first place, and why you don't have any cause to worry about me jumping any claim you may have. A friend of mine, Jumpy Suthers, told me about it, right before he was shot and killed. We were plannin' on coming back for it together."

"Jumpy Suthers." Amos leaned toward him. "You a friend of his?"

"We served together during the war, were in the same prison camp the last part of it, and we both worked for Maximilian down in Mexico. So we knew each other a while, and we trusted each other."

Amos straightened himself. "Was it a map you was lookin' for?"

Julian didn't respond. He looked ahead, his jaw clamped shut.

Amos pointed his pistol and shook it, motioning Julian to his feet. "Get up."

Julian put down the cup and slowly got to his feet.

Amos stepped back and pointed the pistol out the door. "Now you jes' move on out to that there catwalk and saunter down to that storehouse you was so interested in. We'll jest see who you really is."

Julian stepped out of the room and made his way down the rocky ledge. Beneath him, a circular set of stone stairs wandered down to the apartments below. If the old man cocked the revolver, Julian knew he'd have to jump somewhere. He was picking his spots. He stopped at the bottom of the step that led up to the storeroom.

"You remember Jumpy's mother's name?" Amos asked.

"Sure do. He never stopped talkin' about her. Her name was Delia, Delia Suthers from Tupelo, Mississippi."

Amos grinned. "Then, you just reach down and look under that rock yer standin' on. You'll find what you been lookin' fer."

Julian stepped off of the flat rock and pulled it aside. There in the dirt was a folded piece of crisp, parchment-colored paper. He picked it up and opened it. It was the map, the map of the Malpais showing where Maximilian's men had stored the treasure. The Malpais was a stretch of badlands in New Mexico that had so many twists and turns a man couldn't even find the hand on the end of his arm without a map. Julian shook it at Amos. "You knew about me looking for this all along, didn't you?"

Amos grinned and stuck the revolver down in his pants. "I figured you might be lookin' for that. I just didn't know Jumpy had sent you. I figured he'd come himself, but he said he had someone in mind he thought could help. I s'pose that was you."

"I reckon so. Fact is, though, Jumpy was killed and I wasn't." Julian folded the map and stuck it down in his shirt. "And what would you have done if I hadn't remembered Jumpy's mother's name?"

"I'da killed you dead on the spot."

Julian grinned. "That's what I like, an honest thief."

"Well, I might be a thief, but I'm a man of my word. Jumpy said he was gonna be back with a friend to help, and I know'd we was gonna need the help. There's gonna be lots of hard cases lookin' fer it. Two men ain't got much chance, and a man alone no chance at all."

Julian looked down at the supplies and the fire. "Well, if you're coming, we best get to it. There's a group of Mexicans chasing me, and any time we kill here just gives them more of a chance to find us."

"Well, why didn't you say so, boy?"

It took a short time for Amos to get his horse from the spot up the canyon where he had built a concealed corral. Julian packed the supplies, and they walked the animals back down the hill. Standing at the edge of the river, Julian said, "I did see a stranger in the canyon earlier today. He looked to be a drifter, with a gun."

Amos stepped in front of him and put his foot in the stirrup. "We best get us goin', then."

Suddenly, a shot rang out from across the river. Amos fell off his horse at Julian's feet, dead.

CHAPTER 32

+ + + + + + +

JULIAN DOVE FOR THE GROUND as several shots splattered the soft sand around him. The horses stampeded down the side of the river next to the cliffs. There was no chance to stop them and no way he could get the rifle from his saddle boot with his animal gone. Julian could tell that whoever was shooting at him was using a Winchester. He'd heard the sound of the rifle many times before. It was the same gun he used, the same gun now bearing down on him pell-mell along the riverbank.

He rolled over and over, trying hard to keep low. Dropping over a rise, he pressed his face into the ground. Several rounds from the rifle hit the sand close to him. The shots were coming from the trees on the other side of the river, and it was obvious he had been the target. Amos had stepped in front of him just as the first shot rang out.

Julian pulled out his Colt. From where he was, there was no chance of hitting the man—he couldn't even see him. He looked back. The trees were more than twenty yards away. He couldn't make it that far. From the way this man was already walking his shots in, Julian would be dead before he took two steps. Looking to his left, he could see a large oak. The tree stood on the bank of the river, its branches spreading out over the water.

Another shot hit the back of the bank, scattering sand in Julian's face. Suddenly the shooting stopped. Maybe he was reloading or just maybe going for position. Julian sprang for the bank to his left, and a shot rang out, nicking his boot. The red clay rocks were a mite higher here. It would give him a little more protection, but not much.

Two more shots pecked at the sandy clay over his head, then the shooting stopped. Julian knew he was definitely pinned down. The man had a bead on him and seemed determined to do whatever it took to finish him off. His attacker would go for position somewhere else along the tree line, somewhere he could get a good look at Julian's prone body lying behind the bank. It was only a matter of time.

Julian took a chance and snapped a peek across the river. He could see a flash of movement through the trees. It was lucky timing on his part and gave him a few seconds. Scrambling to his feet, he launched himself toward the base of the old oak tree. He ran a few yards before he heard the next shot. It pecked at his feet, and he dived once more for the shallow bank near the tree.

Several more shots pelted the ground around him as he crawled forward toward the tree. The rocks piled up around the base of the big tree would at least offer some solid protection. Another shot hit the ground near his face. Whoever this man was, he was good. The man was leading him, obviously hoping his bullet and Julian would arrive at the same spot at the same time.

Julian's mind went back to Frank Gordon. The man had looked like a hunter, a hunter of men. Julian was a wanted man in some places and an extremely wanted man in Mexico. It couldn't be one of Escobar's men, though. The Mexicans wanted him alive, and it was obvious this man, whoever he was, wanted him dead.

He inched himself forward, and then with a sudden burst of energy, he raced in a crawl for the base of the tree. Shots splattered all around him, kicking up sand over his clothes and face. Moments later, Julian reached the tree and swung himself around it. Now the man wouldn't be able to get off a good shot from where he was. He'd have to move to get a better line of fire, and Julian was sure that was just what he would do.

The shooting stopped, and Julian used the lull to push sand up on either side of the tree trunk. Taking out his knife, he began to dig. The sand and the clay flew from the blade as it ripped into the soft earth. He would make himself a trench. Somehow, some way, he had to get lower than the ground around him. He wanted this man to come closer—he wanted to face him.

Julian suspected the man was on the move, but where? He took his hat off and laid it beside him, near the bank. If the man was ready to shoot just now, that target would certainly draw his fire. There was nothing, only silence. Did the man suspect he was only playing possum? He carefully lifted his head to look at the treeline to his right. There was nothing there, no movement at all. Swinging his head around to where he had placed his hat, he ventured another peek. Again, he could see no movement in the trees.

He rolled over and lay with the back of his head near the roots of the old oak. His heart was beating faster. Where was the man? What was his plan now? He murmured a prayer, "Lord, I don't deserve no mercy, never did, don't now. Help me now, Jesus. I'm asking the best I know how."

He breathed a sigh of relief, sensing the man was gone, something or someone had driven him away. He gasped out a prayer of thanks.

No sooner had he croaked out the short prayer than he heard a strange clamor, the sound of hoofbeats coming hard. The racket was coming from downriver. He rolled over to the right side of the trench and ever so slowly lifted his head.

Looking down the river, he could see two men riding. It was James and Joe. The woman was following at a distance. She had Julian's and Amos's horses under tow. Reaching back, he picked up his hat and waved it. They spotted him and started crossing the stream.

Slowly, Julian got to his feet. He didn't trust the situation enough to step out from the oak, but what he did see made him feel mighty good.

Joe brought his horse to a sliding stop near the tree and jumped down, followed by James. "You all right?" Joe asked. "We were worried about you."

"Looks like you had a right to. Somebody's been trying his darndest to kill me."

"We heard the shooting," James said.

"Chupta took off for the trees," Joe said. "I reckon he's over there somewhere."

"Good thing he is." Julian sighed. "You might have rode right into the shooting if he hadn't flushed whoever that was out of there. I owe all of you my life. That man had me dead to rights."

"That close, huh?" James asked.

"Yes, that close." He pointed over to Amos's body. "The old fella over there stepped in front of the first shot or that would have been me lying there."

"Who is he?" James asked.

"Called himself Amos. He was living up there in some Indian cliff ruins waiting on the man who told me about this." Julian reached into his shirt and pulled out the map. "This is what Escobar is looking for. It will pay for his army and make him president of Mexico."

"Your memory is coming back," James said.

"In bits and pieces, it is. I can tell you one thing, if I hadn't remembered Jumpy Suthers' mother's name, I'd be a dead man right now." Julian pointed over to the body. "That old man would have killed me."

"Who is Jumpy Suthers?" James asked.

"I'll tell you later."

Ellie rode up with the two horses. "There you are," she said. "It *is* you."

"Just barely," Julian said.

They watched as Chupta rode out from the trees and across the river. He carried his rifle in his hands. Trotting up to them, he swung out of the saddle and jumped to the ground. "Man go," Chupta said.

"Did you catch sight of him?" Julian asked.

"Just little. Man have white sheep top."

"Gordon. I met him downriver this morning. Had a peculiar feeling about the man when I saw him. It was almost as if he'd been staked out there to wait for me."

"He come toward me. When he saw me, he go other way. He ride north," Chupta said.

"He must have been moving to my right to get a better position when he saw you. I'm just lucky you all came riding up when you did. If you'd had a longer breakfast, I'd be dead by now."

"You shouldn't have left when you did," Joe said.

"I figured I'd caused you enough trouble." He pointed to the body. "Folks around me seem to turn up dead."

Joe frowned. "You just won't be beholden to anybody, will you?"

Julian clamped his mouth shut and looked right at Joe.

"I just wonder if you're worried about us or just worried that you might have to thank us. Taking help from anybody's never agreed with you much."

"What do you want me to say?" Julian asked.

"Thank you might be a good place to start," James said.

"All right, thank you."

"If you men are quite finished with settling your boyhood battles," Ellie said, "I'd suggest we get that man buried and be on our way."

Julian cracked a slight smile. "The lady's got herself a point there. I'd say you picked yourself a right smart woman there, James."

"Yes, I did, at that."

"All right," Joe added, "we'll do that." He pointed at Julian. "Don't think Ellie here's pulled your bacon out of the fire just yet. I know you. If you'd been rescued by the cavalry, you'd find yourself a reason to fault the Yankees who did it."

The four men worked at digging a grave beside the river while Ellie sat down and read a letter James found in the man's pocket. It had been sent to him some six months earlier to a general-delivery address in Silver City. "Your Mr. Amos Pettigrew evidently has a daughter," Ellie said, "a daughter and a grandson."

"Then, you should hang on to that address," James said. "She might have something coming to her."

She watched as the men lowered Amos into the fresh grave and began to cover him up. "I think you're forgetting," Ellie said. "If I remember correctly, no one has anything coming from that map. Whatever is there belongs to Mexico, doesn't it?"

Julian stood silently at the foot of the grave. James and Joe watched him. He might have the most claim to what the map would lead them to, but that was strictly squatter's rights. "Does it belong to Mexico?" Joe asked. He studied Julian's face carefully.

Turning his head slowly, Julian gazed at him. It was a distant look, the kind a man might give when he wasn't so much looking at someone he was talking to as looking for a memory he might have shared with him. "I had a dream once with a man I rode with for years, then we were buried together. I've been in the ground under the dirt where a man can hear nothing but the voices of the dead.

"Jumpy and me rode together for years, and when I was shot along with him, I thought I was dead. I wasn't, though. It was just a dream of death." Pointing into his ear, Julian worked on making himself clear. "And I heard the voices, the sound of the dead I've known through my whole life—the dead at Gettysburg where I fell, the dead in the Shenandoah, the dead I've rode with in this desert, and the dead buried out back of our place in Georgia. I went under the dirt with that man and I listened to the voices. Fact is, though, I came out of the ground and he's still there. I still ain't sure what those voices were telling me to do, but when I know, you'll know."

Julian picked up the reins of his horse and, without getting on, walked directly into the river. He wanted to feel it all—the deep emotion and the slow-moving river as it rose to waist level. He pulled the reins as he stepped onto the opposite bank. The others mounted their horses and followed.

A few minutes later, Julian began walking through the trees and looking over the ground. It wasn't long before he stooped down and signaled for the others. They walked to him, fanning out behind him.

"This is where he fired from first," Julian said, picking up his hand and targeting with his finger across to where he and Amos had been standing. He looked down and pointed out several cigarette butts. "He sat here waiting real patient for us to come out, real patient."

Picking up one of a number of brass cartridges from the ground, he flipped it at Joe. "There's plenty more of these. Whoever this man Gordon is, he lays down a field of fire—and I can tell you from being on the receiving end, it's straight."

"We'll have to move careful like then," Joe said, "and we have to stay together."

It was close to noon when Zac and Pablo came to the head of the pass, the place where Julian had turned off to the lake the night before. He got down off the dun and walked to the area, inspecting the comings and goings of the tracks.

"They come through here?" Pablo asked.

"That they did." He pointed out a number of tracks. "The ones that go east are older and then they came back this way and up the valley. You can see the shoes with the Circle S on them."

The boy looked down and nodded.

Several hours later they came to the spot, a lean-to tucked amidst the trees. It had obviously been occupied not that long ago—the firepit still gave off a morsel of heat. The makeshift shelter stood between the trees, and Zac got down to inspect some tracks. Following them with his eyes, he could see that the group, including James and the woman, with their horses' distinctive shoe prints, had gone west along the river and returned this way. Then they had gone north. He mounted up, leading Pablo in the same direction.

From the north, a creek flowed south, joining the river with two small knolls knotting the juncture. Julian's group had gone between them. They had avoided the creek and the growth of timber and brush that choked its banks.

The sky was spotted with clouds, and a bright sun glanced off the leaves. Julian and his group had made their way here with great care. They seemed to be in a hurry. It was almost as if they were expecting trouble in front of them, not coming up from their rear. Zac and Pablo wouldn't be so careful. They would work at closing the gap between them; where the ground permitted it, Zac broke the horses into a gentle lope.

He knew the men ahead would watch their back trail. Either Joe or Chupta would circle their trail and make sure they were not being followed. Pablo would come in handy. Even at a distance anyone could see that this was a man and a boy, and that way Zac had little worry he'd be shot at by mistake. No matter who they figured might be following them, the boy would throw them off.

He kept the trail in front of him as they wound their way around the small stands of pine and began a gentle climb. In the distance, he could see a higher peak. There was a slight dusting of snow on it, and he knew the group would swing around it one way or the other.

"We gonna catch up to them before night?" Pablo asked.

"I figure we will. I don't want to get too close to them, though, just close enough to keep an eye out for them."

"Why not?"

"We'll do a sight better for them if we can catch us a glimpse of who might be following them. We throw our eggs in with their basket, and we'll be as blind as they are."

Pablo studied Zac. It was the kind of look someone would give to a long-necked creature at the zoo—admiration mixed with wonder. "How do you think of these things, señor?"

"Experience, I reckon."

"I hope to have some of this experience when I get to be a man."

"You've got something far more worthwhile than experience, something I wish I had."

The thought astonished the boy. Zac could see that by his wide-eyed look. He knew the boy saw himself as someone not fully alive, just the glimmer of what a man could become. The feeling was a familiar one. He'd had it himself when he was young. It was almost as if Pablo was waiting on life to begin—not dead, but not quite alive either.

"What could I have, señor, that you or anyone else could want?"

"Your innocence and that idealism you carry around. Most men lose that with the experience they get, and it's a shame. You see things fresh, and still think they can be what they ought to be. You're also knotheaded enough to believe that it ought to be you that puts those things right. That's why you followed those three men. I'd give anything if I could see life that way again. It's a luxury, being a child."

"You want to be a child?"

Zac smiled. "I suppose. But only if I could have my own brain. I would like to see the best like you do and still believe I could do anything I set my mind on. I'm a little wiser now, though, and with all that wisdom comes the sadness of knowing I can't always be who or what I want to be."

It was afternoon before they rode down from the treelined bluff. The creek they had spotted to the east of them wound down below them now, and on the other side of the creek they could see Julian's group as they twisted up the east side of the mountain. He pulled rein and stopped Pablo.

"Is that them?"

"It sure is. We can get off and rest the horses for a spell here. We don't want to go riding up on them. Now that we know which way they're going, we don't much need to. We'll find their camp before dark."

Zac suddenly spotted something else. Reaching into his saddlebags, he pulled out a pair of binoculars. Above the canyon Julian and his group were riding up, there was a lone rider. Zac looked carefully through the field glasses. The man might well be a lone hunter, or he might just be something else. The way the man rode parallel to the group worried him, though.

"We'll rest here for a spell," Zac said, "and then we'll go up that other way, over the canyon."

It was getting close to nightfall when Joe spotted a stand of trees in the canyon. He pointed them out to the group. "We'll stop there and cook by daylight. Chupta's up ahead, but he'll come back and find us when he's ready."

"Are you sure he can find us?" Ellie asked.

"That man could sniff us out anywhere," Joe said.

They found a clearing near the trees and stripped the saddles from the horses, hobbling them so they could graze. They gathered some dry wood and soon had a small fire going under the trees and the start of supper. The boughs and branches of the pines would filter any smoke, and as dry as the wood was, there wouldn't be much smoke to worry about, anyway. They figured they were at least a day ahead of Escobar's group, but whoever had been shooting at Julian must still be close.

Ellie soon had bread cooking in a pan. She chopped up some dried carrots and potatoes and dropped them into boiling water, then added the meat. A short time later they all sat down to enjoy the savory stew.

The men ate their food in silence—all except James. Silence, especially at mealtime, was something he never appreciated. "Ellie, you do well with what you have here." He smiled.

"I wouldn't be getting used to this," she said. "I have a much better head for business than I do for a stove."

Her remark got more than a few glances from Julian and Joe.

"Well, the world's best chefs seem to be men," James said. "In my day I've had meals at a number of the finer restaurants on the East Coast, and in all of them, I've never discovered a woman in the kitchen."

"How good the food is depends on how hungry the man is," Joe said. "Right now, I'd say this was plenty good."

The group all lifted their heads at the sound of the incoming horse. Chupta walked the horse into camp and got down. His eyes were fixed on the pot of bubbling stew, and Ellie rose to her feet and spooned a bowl full of it up for him. He took it and began to eat, standing up.

"You seem quiet," James said.

"We are watched," Chupta responded. "Do not look."

Joe and Julian shifted in their seats, their hands moving down to unhitch the thongs that held their revolvers in place.

"Where is he?" Julian asked.

"One man up the hill behind us," Chupta said. "He watches and he waits."

CHAPTER 33

"WHAT DO YOU GENTLEMEN PROPOSE to do about this watcher of ours?" Ellie asked. Ellie studied Julian and Joe as they exchanged glances. These Cobb brothers amazed her with their seeming ability to pass thoughts through the air without the benefit of words. That such a thing could be done was something she knew well, but she had only seen it among women. Women minded the details of people; the way they sat, the way they moved, and the subtle shifts in the tones of their voices. Men, on the other hand, seldom bothered. For a man to actually think about what might be in another person's mind required a high degree of inspiration. It was obvious these Cobb men were motivated, but after all, they were still men.

Men might know a lot about cows, but she hadn't found one yet that knew much about women. Often she had threatened her father with her notion of starting a class to help men. She would have begun the first lesson with two pictures, one of a cow and the other of woman. She imagined her lesson with a smile. Taking out a pointer, she would explain, "This is a cow, and this is a woman." It was a small wonder in Ellie's mind that women were treated as little more than breeding stock—after all, most men couldn't tell the difference between a lady and a heifer. And very few men took the trouble to know another man unless he was sitting across a poker table from him.

These Cobb brothers were different, though. At times they seemed affectionate, and at other times, they were more like long-lost enemies. She doubted that her question had stumped them, though. It just seemed to be important for each of them to lead and neither of them to be wrong.

"Why don't we go find out who it is?" James asked.

Ellie smiled. It was one of the things she loved about the man. He was simple and direct in matters he knew little about. There was no pretension, and being proved wrong would never be a devastating blow to his manhood.

"Well, we can't do a thing until it gets dark," Joe said.

"And what if the man up the hill doesn't feel that way?" Ellie asked. "He might just decide that he needs to do something before it gets dark."

Chupta continued to spoon down the stew. For Ellie, it was strange to watch these men discuss an intruder without lifting a head in the stranger's direction. She supposed it had something to do with keeping an adversary in the dark, so to speak. Why tell an opponent you knew he was watching?

"I suppose we should spread out," Julian said. "When it gets dark, I'll go up and find him. Till then, we should lie low, not give him a good target to aim at."

"Why should you go?" Joe asked.

"Because it's me he's trying to kill."

"I seem to recall a time when I was a boy coming home from school. The Braxton brothers always took a lot of joy in making my walk home purely miserable. You pretty much went your own way till one of them decided to wail on me. Then you were on them like a duck on a June bug. Well, that was me they were trying to beat on. Not you."

"There was two of them. This is something I need to do by myself."

"Well, right now it's all of us he's following. I'd say what happens here is all of our business."

"I don't see it that way," Julian snapped.

"Well, big brother, I don't rightly care how you see it. We'll go up there together."

Julian scratched the back of his head, a vigorous scratch that had nothing to do with an itch. Ellie could see the man was frustrated with having to tell his feelings. Like most men, he simply expected his reasoning to be appreciated without explaining the rationale for it.

"This may be too simple a question," Ellie said, "but why don't you go together?"

James put his hand on her arm. It was a simple and direct question, but it was obvious that Joe was pushing Julian, and when it came to Joe and Julian, it was like a brick wall being swamped by the incoming tide. Something always had to give. Between these two there always had to be a winner and a loser.

"I'm for that," Joe said. "We'll go up when it gets dark. We can split up and put the man between us."

Julian was becoming more irritated by the minute, as if his thoughts were a geyser waiting to explode boiling water to the surface. He didn't look at Joe when he spoke; instead he turned his attention to James and Ellie and talked of Joe in the third person, almost as if the man wasn't there. "This man has a wife and child. Whatever happens to me don't count for much and is my problem. The stranger up there is following me."

"Why don't you let me decide for myself?" Joe asked. "I ain't just your little brother anymore, and I've already come a long way to pull your fat out of the fire."

Julian put down his tin plate and walked to the edge of the circle. "Look," he said, "I've already done enough things in this life to make a hundred men die of shame and guilt. I'm trying to make things right now. If you go up there with me and get yourself killed, I don't want to have to explain to that wife of yours why you were here in the first place."

Joe got to his feet. "Enough of this nonsense talk. You're still thinking about your pride. When it gets dark, we're going to do the common-sense thing. You and Chupta will go 'round the north side of the canyon, and I'll go south. We'll circle around and come on him. The only thing you're going to have to explain is if you shoot me in the dark by mistake, so make sure of your target. You're right, though. Till it does get dark, we'd better split up. We want him thinking twice about coming down that hill and shooting into the camp."

James and Ellie poured cups of coffee for themselves and then moved away from the camp. They found a spot under some trees, and James held her cup while she sat down. Handing her the drinks, he walked back to pick up his rifle. He was going to be ready in case anything happened ahead of time.

"Those two brothers of yours are very odd."

James laughed. "We're all odd in our own ways, I suppose. It's what makes us unique. My brother Zac is perhaps the strangest of all—excluding Julian, of course."

"Of course."

"Zac's always passed his time by correcting all the wrongs in the world."

"A preacher, then."

"Not hardly. The man is an agent for Wells Fargo, sort of a bounty hunter, but with a badge."

"Why isn't he a lawman?"

"I've never asked him that. I suppose he sees the law as too restrictive. He might have to follow the rules."

"Rules and the Cobb brothers seem to be quite incompatible."

James laughed. "Yes, they are at that. Zac is a fierce and determined sort of man, single-minded to a fault. Now it seems he's in love, and that's opened up a side to him I don't think any of us has ever seen before."

Ellie put her hand on his. She looked into his eyes with a deep, almost penetrating gaze. "Love has a way of changing a person from the inside out. It's not like a new set of rules, it's a new way of seeing the old rules. It opens a man up to see beyond the book."

She watched as James turned and looked back at Julian and Joe. The men had taken up different posts on either side of the camp. "This is the first time I've known Julian to concern himself with someone else dying, though," James said. "It is a marked difference to what he's been in the past."

"He seems to be looking for forgiveness," Ellie said.

"Yes, but like most of us, he goes about it in the wrong way. If Julian's ever considered himself Christian, it's been by means of his birth. It's never been something he's clung to in a personal way."

"And now you think he does?"

"I can't be sure of that, but things are different for him; I can tell that. Maybe it was that prison."

"He's been in prison before. You said he was a prisoner during the war."

"Yes, but this is different. He's gone through a spell of forgetfulness, and in his case that's a good thing. The man has spent a lifetime doing things that any sane person would want to forget."

"Then perhaps that head wound was a blessing."

"I think it was. Of course, for men who try to turn over a new leaf, it takes more than forgetting—a man must understand the nature of forgiveness. You're never forgiven by just starting over and thinking you can undo all the wrongs with a whole new list of right things to do. To even attempt that kind of life is to admit you never were forgiven in the first place, just given a temporary reprieve."

"You seem like such a strange man, James. There's a light in your eyes that only comes from a clear conscience."

He smiled. "I'm a forgiven man, Ellie, and I bask in the glory of that forgiveness. Nothing I ever do can come close to paying for my shortcomings."

Ellie was growing not only in her affection for James but in a deep admiration for him as well. He was a contented man, and she was beginning to see why. It was a satisfaction that started in his spirit and made its way through a very capable mind. James didn't always understand his own motivations, especially when it came to relating to women, but there was an honesty there that made the man want to change when faced with the truth. "I think you're a wonderful man, James. Sometimes you're a mystery to me, but somehow I find that just as charming as the more obvious of your traits."

When the sun settled behind the Mogollon Mountains about an hour later, an eerie dampness crept through the valley, broken only by the sound of an evening whippoorwill. The small group gathered around what had once been their cookfire. Coals still glowed softly, winking out at them from the middle of the rocks.

"We'll let Chupta go on ahead on horseback," Joe said. "He'll circle the canyon and come up on top, just in case our friend up there decides not to stay put. Julian, you can move up the slope just north of us, and I'll circle around to the south. James—"

"No need to tell me," James interjected. "I will stay here with Ellie and guard our ashes. We wouldn't want that man down here and cooking supper on them, now, would we?"

Joe patted his arm. "You're just better suited for this. You've never been in much of a shooting fight, but if things come to blows, you come a running."

"That I will."

They watched Chupta move off in the direction of his horse. Picking up the reins, he walked the animal into the darkness.

"I still don't like this," Julian said. "This is my fight, and I ought to finish it."

"Cobbs stick together," Joe said. "I don't like it either, but can you imagine what Pa would say if we walked off and left one or the other of us to face something by himself?"

"I know just what he would say. He said it many times before. 'A man who ain't worth keeping company with is a man who ain't even worth being alone.' Seems to me those were the words."

"I'd say that head of yours is making a recovery. Yes, those were the words, all right. They were well said then, and they're well said now. You step real lightly up that hill now, and give me a chance to come up behind him. If he starts blasting away, I want to be right there, not down the trail somewhere."

Julian took the map out of his shirt and handed it to James. "You better keep track of this. Anything happens to me, I want you to have it. Who knows, you might be able to buy your own college."

Joe picked up his rifle and moved to the north. The darkness had settled into the valley, and by the time he had made his way past the few pines that were to their left, he had disappeared from their view.

Times like this always made Joe think of coon hunting back home.

Only hunting coons was a lot noisier and involved a lot more running. The dogs would run in front of them, and they would all follow the sound of the barking. When the animals began to bay and wail, they knew they had the masked critter up a tree. They'd all run to the spot with torches in hand, anxious to bring the rascal down. Now they were back to hunting together. The only difference was, this coon was heavily armed.

Joe moved silently and swiftly through the trees. He wasn't sure what the man's plan might be, if he was the same man who had killed Amos and tried to kill Julian. Since he hadn't tried to take them all by daylight, perhaps he was going to wait and make his play while they were all sleeping. If that was the case, he was in for a final and deadly surprise.

The valley lay wrapped in a low fog that had crept into the draw hand in hand with the darkness, slithering into the ditches and spilling out onto the grassy undergrowth. It seemed to pick up color from the cloudy moonlight, glowing with a dull, smoky shine. Joe watched it curl around the base of the trees and slide along the ground like a giant snake that had neither head nor tail. It settled onto the ground, enveloping itself around his feet.

He kicked his way through it, not exactly sure of where he was stepping. Climbing the rocky slope wouldn't be easy on a night like this, but Julian was careful. Joe could give the man that. He'd been in more than his share of fights and in far too many life-and-death struggles.

The man on top would have a horse, but the animal was probably backed away from the edge of the bluff. Horses could sense someone coming close. A man at night had only to watch their reactions. Joe's hope was that the fog might dampen the horse's natural instincts and that Julian would go slow.

The trees brushed Joe's face as he ducked under the branches. The gnarled branches grabbed at his clothes and rifle, tugging on him. The thought hit him sudden like—if the man Chupta had seen decided to do exactly what Joe was doing, he might run right into him. It would be a smart thing for the man to do, too. Coming down a hillside at night could be a precarious matter at best; a kicked rock, a stepped-on branch, a sudden hole would all be dead giveaways. The smart thing to do would be to walk around the hillside and down into the valley. If he did that, the man might be right in front of him, and Joe would never know it, not in this fog.

Reaching for his revolver, Joe lifted it out of the holster. He kept the hammer on an empty chamber so there would be no chance of an accidental discharge. Still, the weight of it in his hand was reassuring. It made him feel a little more ready in this fog.

He looked up the hill. It looked like tar, black and sticky through the misty night air. Rocks dotted the side of the bluff, shining in the faint moonlight and making Joe think of stairs leading up to a child's room. The fog hung low; the rim of the canyon would be clear. It had taken him some thirty of forty minutes to wander through the trees, and climbing up from this point would put him within reach of the top. He'd be careful. The sound of any misstep might travel over the valley, and he couldn't afford to announce his arrival.

He stepped up to the first of the rocks, sliding his boot on top of it. He would take this one careful step at a time. Balancing himself, he stepped over the blackness between the rocks and onto the next one he could see. Deliberately, he worked at climbing the slope.

Seeing a rock that was slightly beyond the comfortable stepping range, he jumped for it. He teetered for a moment, flailing his arms as he tried to keep his balance. Both weapons, one in each hand, helped him regain his balance. *There*, he thought, *I got it*.

To his left, he heard something scamper in the brush—a sudden burst of speed followed by a quieter rustling. Joe smiled, trying to comfort himself. He'd stirred some jackrabbit up, and more than likely both of their hearts were racing.

The rocks were larger, more than able to conceal a man. Joe stepped gingerly off the rock he was standing on and onto the black ground. The fog was below him and the dark sky above.

Pushing his feet forward, he inched his way up the hill. Suddenly, he stopped, his foot suspended just above the ground. Underneath him was a branch. Stepping down would send a sharp report, and nobody would mistake that for a rabbit. Carefully, he stepped over the stout twig. Each movement would have to be a cautious one, or it just might be his last.

He spotted a large boulder at the top of the bluff. That would be his objective. If he could just get there, he could stop and rest. Then he could gather his wits and travel north along the top of the ridge to the place where Julian was climbing. The valley below was silent. Whatever Julian and Chupta were doing, they were doing it well. None of them had been discovered yet.

He moved quietly up the hill. Several times his boots scuffed the rocks he stepped over, and each time Joe would stand still and listen. The sounds were slight, and hopefully only a man standing close by could have heard him. His heart beat faster. He hoped the stranger hadn't moved to a spot close to where he was now.

Once again spotting the big rock, he moved up closer to it. It was only a few yards away, a few more yards of relative silence. He took several more steps, feeling the rocky ground under his feet.

He tiptoed over a few scattered rocks, each time working to keep his balance. The big rock was just ahead, and Joe stepped off to the ground once again. Moving quietly, he reached the near side of the boulder. Stopping to take a breath, he stuck his Colt back in his holster and shook his fingers out. They were stiff from being wrapped around the pistol, that and the tension of the moment.

He started to move around the big rock when suddenly someone grabbed him. The man slung him to the ground and, pouncing on his chest, threw a hand up to Joe's mouth. Joe's heart pounded, and he blinked his eyes at a razor-sharp knife, then he looked into his attacker's face. It was Zac.

"You sounded like a freight train coming up that hill." He lifted his hand from Joe's mouth.

"What the blazes are you doing here?" Joe said in a raspy tone.

Zac got up and, extending his hand, helped his brother to his feet. "I been following you since Santa Fe."

"What?"

"That's right, since Santa Fe."

Joe dusted himself off and picked up his rifle. "You scared the tar out of me."

"Better somebody scare you than kill you. You best stick to those cow ponies of yours, 'cause you ain't gonna make no scout."

"Julian's probably coming up that ridge about now, and Chupta's coming down from the north."

"Well, if you're looking for that feller in a sheepskin vest, he lit out of here a while back. I guess he decided he didn't much care for the odds."

"It's the same man who tried to kill Julian earlier today."

"I figured as much."

"How'd you know that?"

"That government man that sent you on this wild-goose chase hired some men to kill that brother of ours. I took care of three of them back in Silver City, and I guess this other fella is a backup."

"He just wanted us to get Julian out of that jail to make him a better target?"

"That's about the size of it."

"Well, you better come on down to camp, and we can tell you the rest of what we know. Julian went and found that map."

"I don't want no part of that. I just want you and James safe at home. Besides, Julian and I don't cut well together. If I see him, either I'm gonna kill him or he's gonna kill me."

"He's changed a mite. He took a glancing shot to the head and lost his memory, but he's getting it back now."

"I don't care how much he's altered that head of his. He's left too many widows and too many orphans for me to listen to any change of heart he might have. He might have changed, but the law hasn't."

"You plan on taking him in?"

"I haven't thought through on that just yet. Right now, I'm more concerned with just getting you and James back on that train in Santa Fe."

"So you're not coming down to camp?"

"No, I figure I can do better trailing along behind you. Those Mexicans that were following you are a day off your trail now, and those other three aren't going to be bothering anybody from where they lay. If I'd been riding with you, we'd all be catching it about now."

Joe stared at him, taking the thought in. Zac had always been a careful thinker, and this type of thing was what he did best. It wasn't the time or the place to question his judgment.

"You can all sleep tonight," Zac said. "Chupta knows I'm behind you, but him and you are the only ones I want to know."

Joe nodded. He heard movement behind him and turned around. "That would be Julian," he said. When he turned back around, Zac was gone. There was nothing but darkness.

CHAPTER 34

FRANK GORDON HAD BEEN A HUNTER all of his life. He was big, as men go, over six-foot-four, and lean, built like a cat. The hard life of the saddle and the open country kept his weight down to slightly over two hundred pounds, and all of it muscle. The weather and sun had baked and creased his skin in his thirty-eight years. A hard-looking man with high cheekbones and a hooked nose, he showed every bit of his Sioux mother and Scottish father. He'd skinned buffalo with his father since he was eight years old and killed his first man at fifteen.

He rode his hammerhead strawberry roan with ease. The thing had become a part of him during the three years they had been together. Gordon didn't say much, and all of his real thinking went from his head to the roan's with barely a word spoken. It was the way he preferred his conversation. People had little or no interest for him, except as moving targets.

The lonely mountains of southwestern New Mexico were one of the places he loved best. There were very few people out and around here, and those few stayed to themselves. The nine thousand feet of Eagle Peak rose in the Tularosa Mountains to the east of him, and up ahead were the Dillon, Gallo, and Fox Mountains. Large stretches of ponderosa and pinon pine mixed with juniper trees blanketed the hills and valleys, with clear creeks running through them.

He had a general idea of where the group he was trailing was heading, and with that in mind, he'd do all he could to shadow them without coming too close. He'd made that mistake once before, and the stranger and the boy had ridden right up on him. The man with the boy had a lean, hard look to him, but he didn't appear to be traveling with the group Frank was interested in. Perhaps, Frank thought, he'd have an easier time of it if he killed them first or just maybe they would turn off somewhere down the trail. They'd gotten too close, though, and he hadn't been watching for them. He wouldn't make that mistake again.

He kicked slightly at the roan's sides, sending it down the side of the steep valley. Now he was going to do his best to keep out of sight and ride through the lowest part of the hill country to keep from skylining himself. He was a man who chose his targets; he didn't intend to become one. He wouldn't make as good of time this way, but the roan would make up for that. He'd wait until he was ready to strike.

The roan picked his way down the rocks and into the shade and shelter of a grove of enormous sycamores. The trees towered overhead, filtering in the sunlight and making the air cool to the touch. Frank pulled up the collar on his sheepskin vest. The soft wool was warm around his neck but allowed his hands and arms free movement.

Whitewater Creek ran down through the narrow gorge, and what space wasn't taken up by the wooded giants was flooded by the creek. The roan picked his way over the rocky creek bottom and around the boulders that sent the water on its slithering path. There would be no chance of losing anyone who might be following him, even in the water. There was simply only one way a man who rode into this canyon could go. If the man and his boy traveled this way, it had to be on purpose—and they would be riding right into a gap that held little or no escape. Frank knew that if he found a good line of fire, he could empty their saddles before they knew what hit them.

A rocky game trail rose from the creek bed, and he swung the roan up toward it. Leaning forward, the horse clattered over the rocks and climbed the steep incline. This was a path for sheep, but it would allow him to make better time and skirt the choking rocks and water below. It snaked its way across the side of the canyon; up ahead he could see the sky as it peeked into the mouth of the gorge.

The game trail would make a good target line. If he could get to the other side of the valley without being seen, Frank knew he could wait for his targets to come to him. The side of the canyon would make a good background for a shot, and there was simply no place else to go to hide. On his horse or off of it, a man would be in plain sight.

It was the way Frank thought. When other people saw a mountain or a valley, they might look for the beauty of the place or perhaps for mineral-bearing rocks, but not Frank. He looked for a site to get a clean shot, a location where a man might be vulnerable.

The roan picked up his pace along the rocky trail. It was as if the horse could see the opening of the valley as well as Frank could. The breath from the roan's nostrils boiled a smoky vapor, puffing into the clear morning air. The trail dropped, once again descending into the watery gorge. Frank started down it, leaning back and straightening his legs to brace himself from the jarring decline. It took him several minutes to reach the bottom of the trail, the place where it spilled out once again into the creek. It was there he stopped.

Twisting back in his saddle, he looked up over the high trail. Several sycamores stood between him and a clear view of the area he'd just ridden over. He didn't like the line of fire. The first shot would have to count, and even then he'd only get a moment to make it. A man might drop from his horse and be obstructed by the big trees. He'd move on to the end of the gorge and wait for a better view. If the man and the boy had followed him into the valley, Frank was going to make sure they never came out.

Turning back, he gently kicked the sides of the roan, sending him down the creek and splashing the water in all directions. He wound his way around the large rocks and ducked underneath several low-hanging trees. Several times he picked up the creekside trail and each time rode the roan up the inclines and back down to the watery creek bottom.

In a short time, he found himself at the opening of the valley. Stepping out of the saddle, he pulled the Winchester out of its boot. From here, he'd get a clear aim at anyone winding their way up the creek. It was perfect. They would be coming at him head on. He and the roan could rest, and then he'd take care of the meddlesome strangers who seemed to be following him. Turning around to look north, he spotted something that changed his mind.

The group he was shadowing was making their way through a gap in the hills. He stepped forward to take a better look. They were some distance away, and from where he stood in the trees they wouldn't be able to see him. But he could certainly see them. They were making good time and the one-armed man he'd been sent to kill was with them. He counted them as they rode past his view, three men and the woman. The Indian who rode with them was up ahead, as usual.

This would take some thought. If the man trailing him was as close as he'd been the night before, it wouldn't be long before he showed himself. Frank could kill him and the boy and be on his way without losing too much time. But if the man had stopped—and traveling with a child made that a probable thing—it might be some time before he showed himself, if at all.

It was a thing to ponder. Frank knew he was being paid to kill one man and one man only. He had no problem with killing anyone who stood in his way—man, woman, or child, it didn't really matter. He was anxious to get it done, though. He was being paid for the job, not the time it took to do it. The longer it took, the less money he had to show for his time. From this distance there was also a chance his shots would be heard, a good chance.

Walking back to the roan, he shoved the Winchester back into place. He'd go for what he came to do, and he'd hurry up and be quick about it. It was a group of five he was keeping watch over. The next thing he had to do was make it a group of four. He had to get the odds more in his favor.

It was early afternoon before Hess had the men equipped with new mounts. He had talked with Escobar before about going with a smaller group, and now something would have to be done. Four of the horses he'd found were older animals, and a fifth was green broke. At least half would find it difficult to keep up, or they would all have to slow their pace to accommodate them. This would have been intolerable even if they weren't more than a day behind.

The general had finished his lunch in the hotel and stepped out onto the walkway to inspect the men. He was proud of the fact that they had determined the direction the Cobb brothers were traveling in. To lose them now would be fatal. But Hess knew it was a misplaced smugness. With what they had in the way of horses, they might as well be four days behind Julian's group.

Hess could see that Escobar had managed to find a shine for his boots in the hotel—the black calf-length riding boots, polished and gleaming, seemed out of place stretched over the top of his tan civilian trousers. For a man who wanted to stay inconspicuous, he stood out. His bearing was that of more than a mere general, however. Hess could see the confidence of the man had already grown to presidential proportions.

The general stroked his large mustache and sneered at the major. "Are the men ready?"

Hess looked around for any unwanted ears. There were people passing by, and he had no intention of making anyone aware of who this group of men were or where they were from. Already, the sight of so many armed Mexican riders had lifted more than a few eyebrows. Anyone could tell just from looking at them that they were more than mere cowboys on the drift. "I need to talk to you a moment," Hess said. "Alone."

The notion irritated the general, that was plain to see. He frowned and arched his eyebrows. He then signaled Hess up onto the porch. "All right, all right, but we're wasting time. We have spent enough of our money and time in this place already."

Hess walked up the steps and, taking Escobar by the elbow, led him aside.

Escobar shook his arm from Hess's grip. "I don't see Utant," he said.

"No, sir, I sent him on ahead. He has his supplies and horse. There vas no need to keep him here."

"I don't want to get too far behind him."

"He is to vait for us near the end of the canyon. This vill give him time to decide which direction the man's group was traveling in when they left the place. It will also save us time and give him something to do."

"I like that in a man," Escobar said.

"General, we can only take half of these men."

Escobar's eyes blazed at the notion.

"Five of the horses ve have been able to secure are inadequate, and they vill slow us down greatly, I fear."

"Major, when I give a man a job to do, I expect him to do it well. You will have to find five others."

"Sir, the horses in this town that are for sale are few. Ve did the best ve could in just using the time ve had this morning. Ve might be able to find five more, but in order to do that ve'd have to go out to some of the surrounding ranches. It might take us the rest of the day to do that, and even then ve vould have to hunt for them. There vould be no guarantees."

Escobar narrowed his eyes. "Major, you have been against this plan from the start. Why are you opposing me this way?"

Hess lowered his eyes. "Yes, sir, I have thought this number too many men to manage on this long of a trip." He paused and thought before saying the next words. They might sting but still they had to be said to drive home his point. "Had ve fewer men last night and only one camp, the horses vould not have been stolen, and ve vould not be so far behind."

"Be careful, Major. You go too far."

Hess dropped his gaze to the sidewalk.

Escobar turned and walked down to the steps leading to the street. He looked over the men and their horses. He knew Hess well. Whatever the man thought, he wouldn't have breathed a word of it to the men. Pointing his finger to three of the largest men, he motioned them forward. "Choose the best of the horses," he said.

The men turned and moved down the string of mounts.

"Paco and Morales, I want you two men also. Find yourselves good horses."

Hess's head snapped up. These were two men he would never have chosen. He had played his hand, though. He dared not question Escobar's decision again, not today.

Morales looked up at him from the street, evidently reading the major's mind. The man grinned and then turned to find a better horse.

Escobar looked at the men. "Only five of you will be going on from here—the men I have selected. The rest of you will take the horses provided and return to the rancho. We will be sending for you and wagons when we have found what we are looking for."

The men reluctantly nodded in agreement.

In a short time, the riders had sorted themselves out. Hess, Escobar, and the five men rode out past the post office and toward the canyon to the north. It took them the rest of the day to travel through the canyon, and it was near nightfall when they came upon Utant in the middle of the trail.

Hess saw the man at a distance and spurred his horse toward him. Moments later, he drew rein and got down beside the scout. "Vat have you found?" he asked.

Escobar and the others rode up just as Utant was giving out his afternoon's findings. He pointed east. "Group stop by lake. Make camp. They ride out north. Some try to rub out tracks, but Utant find them down in pass. They go north."

"Very nice work," Hess said. "You have saved us some time." He could see the Apache was looking over the smaller group with a puzzled face. "The general decided the group was too large," he said. "We can do better with this size." He knew this technically wasn't a lie. Escobar had made the final decision, and supporting the general in front of Utant was an important thing to do, especially with the man sitting on his horse behind him.

"Smaller is better," Utant said.

"How far is it to the bottom of the canyon?" Hess asked.

Turning his back to the group, Utant motioned down the hilly terrain. "It two, three hours down to the valley. River flow there and meet with creek. We see it in the morning."

"In the morning?" Escobar asked. "What's the sense of having a smaller group if we don't make better time than that? Your man here says he already has the lay of the land, and we know the direction these people are traveling. Vamanos. We need to move right along."

Utant looked up at Escobar. "General, the way is steep, and we will be traveling in the dark."

The sun was still up, but it was late in the day. Before long, twilight would be on them. Utant knew full well that night came quickly in the mountains. There would be no horizon for the sun to linger over, and the steep grade up ahead would be difficult for both horse and rider in the dark.

Hess stepped back to talk to him. "General, I think Utant is nervous about the ride in the dark. It might be better if ve waited until the morning."

Leaning down from his saddle, Escobar glared into Hess's face. "Major, it was you who was so worried about the delay, remember? Now you want me to kill one or two hours of usable daylight just because you and the Apache here are worried about these men riding down a hill in the dark. If these are not the kind of men who can sit a horse in the dark, none of them should be on this trip."

Hess leaned forward. He didn't want what he was going to say to be overheard. "General, you are the man in command here, and ve will carry out your orders. My suggestions are only that—suggestions. As general, it is you who devises a strategy, but as one of your officers, it is my job to carry them out effectively. It is also my task to explain my best thinking to you. I think it's dangerous to travel through these mountains at night, and there is no place to make camp on the side of a hill."

Escobar leaned back in his saddle. "And that you have done, Major. The horses are fresh, and it's quite obvious the men enjoyed too much sleep last night. My decision is that we take advantage of what little light we have and move on."

"As you vish, General." With that, Hess walked back to his horse and swung his feet into the stirrups. He gave Utant a nod, sending the man forward.

About an hour later they came to the decline that led to the valley before them. The sky was a dark gray with streaks of clouds a dull pink. Hess figured they wouldn't get much farther while everything was black, and what little moonlight would be found would still be hours in coming. They would be traveling blind, as blind as a man could be, and over rocks and deep gullies that would require all of the men to keep their best watch over just where the animals were stepping.

Utant looked back at him. It was a plaintive look of disbelief, but Hess signaled him forward, and down the steep decline they rode.

In a short time, it was pitch black. The rocks made the horses slow down, and from time to time, several of them stumbled. Moving down a steep slope that was covered with brush, trees, and rock was a difficult task in the broad daylight, but at night it could be perilous.

It wasn't until Escobar's horse stumbled, however, that he called a halt. "Hold on here!" he yelled. "How much farther until we get to the floor of the valley?"

Utant circled his horse, walking it carefully. "It may be one or two hours," he said.

"I think we should walk the horses from here, General," Hess added.

Escobar let out a sigh. "One or two hours of walking these horses down this hill—I think not. We will ride farther. We will walk the horses when I give the command. Who knows, perhaps it will get better farther ahead."

Utant whispered an aside to Hess, "It not get better. It get worse."

"Ve will do as the general commands," Hess replied.

"Sí, señor." Utant started his horse back down the hill.

They hadn't gone more than a few minutes more when one of the men's horses stepped in a crack in the rocks. The animal spooked, sending both horse and rider tumbling down the rocky slope. Hess jumped off his horse and, scurrying over the rocks, reached the man's side. "Are you all right?"

"No me puedo parar—I cannot stand on my leg."

"Is he all right?" Escobar yelled.

"No, General, I think his leg is broken." Hess moved around the man and stepped lightly over the rocks to the horse below. The animal was lying on its side, pawing the ground slowly with his right front hoof. "The horse's leg is definitely broken," Hess shouted.

With that, Hess pulled out his revolver and, putting it to the animal's ear, fired a shot. The echo sounded over the rocks and into the canyon below.

Escobar had shuffled down the rocks to the fallen man. "Why are you shooting, Major? That shot of yours can be heard for miles."

"General, I couldn't leave that animal to suffer. Besides, the people ve are chasing are well beyond the hearing of any sound ve might make."

The general wrapped his arms around himself and walked off, muttering. Hess could see he was troubled, and for good reason. It wasn't just disappointment he was fighting, it was the possible loss of a dream. They were no closer to finding the man they were all seeking, and at this point it appeared that each decision the general made only served to further delay them. Hess had seen this happen before. It would do no good to rehearse the man's mistakes. He could only hope Escobar would be quicker to listen the next time.

It took them some time to cut stout enough branches to build a litter. They would have to leave the fallen man somewhere; it just couldn't be on the side of a mountain. The four remaining soldiers took turns carrying him, but the going was rough. Each boulder in their way was a major hurdle, and the spaces between the rocks might easily turn a man's ankle.

What Utant guessed would be one or two hours turned into three, but finally they reached the valley floor. The creek from the north flowed into the slow-moving river, and across it was a stand of pine trees.

Utant came back from exploring the opposite side of the river. "Shelter built over there," he said. "No one here."

"Good," Hess said. "Ve vill take the men across and start a fire. I do not think the flame vill alert anyone to us, and some hot food vill do the men good."

Escobar merely watched Hess give out orders, watched in silence.

In short order they had a fire blazing. Hess stood beside the fire, watching as several of the men tried to set the injured man's leg. Two of them held the man still while a third worked to set the leg. The man's screams rolled down the floor of the valley, bouncing off the cliffs and echoing back at them. It was a bloodcurdling sound that rang in the men's ears. Hess could see the enthusiasm drain out of each man. The desire for gold was fast losing its appeal.

A pot of warm stew soon bubbled on some rocks, and the men turned and watched it expectedly. It would give them some comfort, but Hess wondered if it would be enough. They were fast drifting from being a military unit to becoming a squad of cowardly thieves. Would they ever hear an order again and obey it without question? Certainly Paco and Morales could be counted on to go their own way, but now he wondered about the other two. He could count on Utant to stay loyal, but perhaps that was all.

Escobar rolled out of the lean-to they had found and walked up to Hess. Motioning for him to follow, he said, "Major, we have a hard and fast day ahead of us, possibly riding into tomorrow night."

"Yes, sir, we do."

"We cannot take the injured man with us."

Hess was silent, wondering what Escobar might have in mind. He had no intention of shooting the man as he had done the horse.

"You say that I am to listen to your suggestions. I am now listening."

CHAPTER 35

+ + + + + + +

THE NEXT THREE DAYS PASSED without incident. Chupta rode ahead and came back to report to the group several times a day. Joe seemed more confident now, and he moved the group at a quicker pace. With Zac as a rear screen and Escobar's men more than a day behind them, he could afford to be more relaxed about moving ahead and trying to put even greater distance between them and the group that was on their trail.

The land had flattened out now, stretching north to the Malpais and east to the Mesa Negra. For days, there had been no chance of a man coming up on them without being seen. Occasionally they would see a mesquite tree on the grassy plain, but mostly there was the wind. The strong, stiff breeze cut through them like a whetted knife. The sharp-honed edge of the easterly breeze stirred up massive clouds, dark and full of rain. This was the last place a man would want to be in a storm. There was no shelter and very little hint of a rise in the flowing grasslands. Up ahead, however, they could see the sandstone bluffs of the Cebolla. This would be the place where they would camp tonight, and the sanctuary would be welcome.

Ellie watched the men slip into the silence of the saddle. Each seemed ill content but rode on with barely a sound. Even James had quieted his normal discourse. He rode beside her for many a mile without a word. The bleak nature of the land seemed to turn all of them into living stone on horseback. She kicked her horse up next to James. "Are you cold?" she asked.

"Freezing. I'm just too tired for my teeth to chatter."

"What are you thinking about? You've barely said anything."

James turned his head from side to side, taking in the expanse of the land. "I was thinking about my daughter and how very small she is, and then thinking about this place and how enormous the West must be. One

I love more than life itself, and the other I'm growing to hate with every mile I sit on this animal."

She laughed. "I can understand that. Really I can. I have spent many years rolling over this land on my father's wagon. It's very beautiful, but it is large."

"Yes, large. Interesting thing, though, normally we measure our affection for a thing by its size. Myself, I'm learning to appreciate the small things, the people I can put my arms around."

"Why did you ever come on this trip?"

James looked up ahead at Joe and Julian. "I've been giving some thought to that. I was the most enthusiastic. In a small way, I suppose I was out to recapture something in my life."

"Recapture something?"

"Yes"—he looked up ahead at the hardened Julian—"the memory, the affection, and the decency of my brother up there. I've heard so many contemptible things about him in these last years, yet the only thing I could remember was the boy who helped me to read." He looked at her and smiled. "And you know my love for books."

"Yes, I do."

As they rode on she watched his face take on a remote look, as if a distant memory flashed across it. James always struck her as an exuberant man, someone who was quick to look on the bright side of any dim event, but the trip was obviously wearing on him. "What is there about men?" she asked. "They always take great delight in reliving things and trying to remake their past. Either that, or their minds seem always to be in a different place or time. Women tend to look ahead at what they might be, and men brood over what never was. I see that in your brother up there. He's still living in 1863, still fighting the battle of Gettysburg."

"You're right. This is the first I've seen him in many years. From what I've heard, he is still fighting the war. I suppose it becomes hard to let go when you carry around in your body the all too graphic reminders of what you've lost. I'm not normally that way. I suppose it's the lack of scenery that causes my mind to wander."

She looked at him, staring until she caught his eye. "And just what are you seeing now?"

He flashed his big smile at her. It was something she hadn't seen in days. "I'm seeing you, Ellie."

"That's right, and I'm right here beside you, beside you in this place."

"There, you see. You have a way of sharpening my senses to the truth without even trying hard. You're amazing, girl."

"Not amazing, James. I'm just a woman who happens to love you, that's all."

"And I find that the most amazing thing of all. I can feel close to you by thinking of you. Thoughts and words seem like such small things, and I tend to overuse them, which cheapens them all the more. In times like this, though, when I can think of you, I want to hold you in them, caress you in my heart."

"You make me feel warm, even in the cold wind."

They reached the edge of the Malpais in midafternoon. The sandstone bluffs that towered over them to the east had cut the wind to a bearable chill and the badlands presented a formidable object that defied passage. Ancient lava flows had backed up to the edge of the sandstone, and time had splintered them into black shards of uplifted sharp black stone. Small pines pushed their way up from the cracks in the rock, struggling to reach knee-high proportions. A horse trying to cross this expansive place would cut itself to pieces, and game lost on it would find it was a place of slow and agonizing death.

Ellie looked out on the Malpais, trying to see the end of the blackness. It seemed to stretch on forever, as far as the eye could see. In the distance beyond, she could see the tops of several sandstone peaks that evidently marked its westward boundary. Looking up at Julian riding in front, she lifted her voice so Julian could hear her. "Where are we going in this place?"

Julian swung his horse around and pointed to the sandstone peaks on the far horizon. "Over there," he shouted. "That's our first stop tomorrow night."

She muttered to James in an aside, "I was afraid of that."

"So was I. How a man can get from here to there boggles the imagination."

"Men are so resourceful," she said in a sarcastic tone, "when they want something bad enough."

James chuckled. It was good to hear him laugh, even under his breath. "If oceans and sea monsters couldn't stop men from trying to find a quicker way to a few spices, I'm not sure we could expect to find miles of broken lava that could prevent him from getting to a vast fortune."

A short time later, Joe called a halt to their day. A creek flowed down a canyon leading up to the sandstone bluffs, and a fragment of level ground had formed a pasture of sweet green grass. It was an inviting location and one that offered protection—to the south of them, there was a clear, unobstructed view of anyone who might be following them. Behind them the bluffs rose to the sky, and in front of them lay the impenetrable Malpais.

"We'll camp here for the night," Joe announced.

Quickly, the men prepared a fire. There was still a small amount of daylight left, and they seemed determined to get their cooking done and the fire out before the night descended upon them. Ellie was grateful that these men knew what they were doing. She was also thankful for Chupta, even though she seldom if ever saw him. She was glad he was making sure they wouldn't meet with any surprises in front of them.

The pasture was full of bright yellow flowers with a scattered peppering of purple blooms. They pushed themselves into the grass with each breeze, and the men had left the horses to graze while they ate. It was in many respects a flawless scene, one where any person could imagine they would be happy living forever—if they didn't mind being totally alone.

She watched as James ate his food while surveying the landscape. "Are you thinking what I'm thinking?" she asked.

"Quite possibly. I do find my thoughts running a parallel course to yours, my dear, and I suppose it's an experience that eventually I may become accustomed to." He looked at the pasture. "I was just thinking about what an ideal site this would be for a honeymoon cabin, along with what a perfectly horrible location it would be after the honeymoon."

"Those were my thoughts exactly. I know you, James. You are, after all, someone who likes being around people. It would be all right for you to give your attention to only one person for a while, but after that you'd grow restless. You'd grow restless in your need to influence people. You have very little desire to control things, but you have an enormous ambition to be in a position of leverage."

"Women are such wonderful students of men."

"Yes, especially the men they love."

It was a short time later when Chupta came riding into camp. Julian and Joe pulled him aside and, taking out the map, made their marching plans for the next day. They stood for a long time looking out over the Malpais, speaking in low tones while Chupta motioned with his hand in the direction of the faraway peaks.

"Are you sure you don't want to join them?" Ellie asked.

"And leave you, this beautiful place, and my hot food? Not on your life. You forget, those men are the controllers." He smiled. "I think I'd be better served by influencing you."

At that, Ellie threw back her head and laughed. "James, James, you've already accomplished that. You've made a lifelong impression on me. I hope you know that."

He reached over and patted her hand. "I hope so."

Seeing the meeting around the map break up, they watched as Chupta filled his plate and picked up a piece of bread. James lifted his hand and signaled for the man to join them. Chupta nodded.

"Please have a seat," James said. "We'd like to hear all about these badlands you've seen."

Chupta squatted down and crossed his legs. He soaked his bread in the stew and stuck it into his mouth.

"Now tell us," James went on, "is this place impassable?"

"There is trail up ahead," Chupta mumbled. "Indian use for long time. It save us from having to go 'round Malpais."

"Good, good, that's wonderful to hear. I'll bet you are looking forward to getting back home."

Chupta nodded. He motioned at Ellie. "Me have wife and children. They wait for me there in San Carlos."

"I've heard San Carlos is an awful place," Ellie said.

"My wife and children make it beautiful place," Chupta responded.

James and Ellie exchanged glances and smiled. This was a man they had spoken little to, but perhaps one of the few who understood their own feelings.

The quiet morning was disturbed by the sound of a distant shot. It was a ways off, but came booming across the face of the sandstone bluffs and rattling near where James had been sleeping. He sat up in his bedroll. "What was that?" he asked.

Joe and Julian sat by the fire while Ellie poured them coffee.

"Chupta's gone," Joe said. "He took off before the sun came up. I'd say he found us some fresh meat for supper. If it was more than that, we'd be hearing more shooting by now. Why don't you just climb out of that soft bed and get yourself some coffee and what's left of these pancakes. We're heading out directly."

James struggled to his feet and crammed them into his boots one at a time. He looked down at the saddle he'd been using for a pillow. He shook his head at the thing, barely wanting to face it, let alone sit on it all day. At this point, he was up for a good walk. Meandering over to the fire, he took the cup of hot coffee Ellie held out for him. "Thank you."

"It's my pleasure. I hope you slept well."

"Any opportunity I might have to be on firm ground relaxes me like few things I can think of." He looked over at his horse, still feeding on the grass. "That animal is an instrument of great torture. I think I shall rue the day we ever met."

"We're sure sorry we don't have any carriages for you," Julian said.

"I'm afraid that and those feet of yours are all we have to offer," Joe added.

James rubbed his backside and then looked down at his feet. "Right about now, I'd say it was a toss-up as to which gives me the greatest discomfort, my rump or my bunions."

"There's a few pictures on that wall over there that might take your mind off that rear end of yours," Julian said. "Indian drawings from some time back, I reckon."

James took the cup and, stepping over the small creek, made his way over to where Julian had pointed. The wall of the bluff was covered with strange faces and arms that bore a resemblance to pictures he had seen of totem poles.

"I know they're not books," Julian shouted, "but they're as close as you're going to come out here."

"I think they are beautiful, very strong and powerful. One wonders what purpose they might have served for the people who drew them."

"Just to tell folks they'd been here, I reckon," Julian said. "Few people want to go on unrecognized."

A short time later they had buried what had been their fire. Mounting their horses, they started down the narrows between the bluffs and the Malpais. The crisp morning air tingled their faces and the foreboding lava piles served to send another set of shivers down their backs. The black rocks stood in sheets, some with jagged edges pointing skyward and others lying in piles. To the casual observer, the place looked like the card room of giants. Decks of black cards had been shuffled and then haphazardly thrown to the floor, their edges piled over one another, giving no rhyme nor reason for where they lay. It was plain to see why this place was called badlands. Nothing could cross it, and nothing could live on it for long.

"I have seen lava beds before," James said, "but nothing like this."

"It is a wonder, isn't it?" asked Ellie.

"Yes, almost as if God himself in anger stomped down a colossal pile of thick black glass. How could anyone hope to cross this?"

"It seems our friend Chupta has found a place."

"The man is astonishing. Did you notice his eyes when we spoke last night? It was as if he knew our thoughts without benefit of words. I have the feeling that is the way he sees the land. He can read its mind and the secrets that lie hidden from the normal person."

"I think it takes study, James. You're that way with poetry and Shakespeare. I am quite certain you dazzle your students in the same way Chupta amazes us."

He smiled. "I do try. It's the exercise of my ego, you know. At times, however, some of the brightest students make me feel like I'm one of the raccoons back home running slightly ahead of the dogs. They push me to know more and make sure I can never relax in my ignorance."

Nearly an hour later, they turned a curve in the trail. Joe held up his hand and stared while the rest of the group stopped nearly in their tracks. In the distance was a tall man and a boy. A body lay on the ground, and three horses stood beside their riders.

"Is that who I think it is?" Julian asked.

"It is," Joe answered.

"I think I'd recognize that gray cavalry hat of his almost anywhere," Julian said. "What is he doing here?"

Joe looked over at Julian. "Let's hope he hasn't come looking for you."

"Who is it?" Ellie asked.

"That is my little brother Zac," James said.

"Who's that on the ground?" Julian asked.

Joe was silent. He touched his spurs to the sides of his horse and galloped forward.

"We had better see," James said.

The three of them pushed their horses into a run, moments later, pulling rein near where Zac and Pablo were standing.

Chupta's body lay in the middle of the trail, and it was plain to see that Zac was grim. His face was drawn and the corners of his mouth turned down at the edges of his black mustache. Chupta had been shot through the heart. He'd evidently died right where he fell.

Joe stepped up to Zac. "You know anything about this?"

Zac looked back at a stand of rocks in front of them. "The man that shot him did it from those rocks." He handed Joe a brass Winchester casing. "It only took one shot. He was waiting. I figure it was the same man who's been following you. Probably figured it might be best to take you down one at a time. We were following his trail but lost sight of him last night. Now I'm sorry we did."

Joe's eyes fell on Pablo. "And who might this be?"

"His name is Pablo. His folks were killed. I'm taking him to his aunt in Santa Fe."

"Pleased to meet you, Pablo," Joe said. "Sorry it couldn't have been in better times."

The boy nodded, blinking his eyes. He was obviously not used to adults treating him in such a respectful way.

"We got a grave to dig," Joe said. "I liked this man. He was every bit as good as you said he was. I'm sorry he got himself killed protecting this sorry operation."

"It was nobody's fault but the man who pulled the trigger," Zac said.

Using plates and knives, it took them a while to dig a respectable grave, but soon they were standing over it. The mound of dirt was piled and the men took off their hats.

"You know his wife and kids?" Joe asked.

"I know of them," Zac said. "Never met them. I had hoped to someday, and now I guess I will."

"Maybe you better say the words," Joe said. "You knew him best."

Zac lifted his eyes. "Lord, we give the body of our friend here back to the ground. He was a friend to the righteous and an enemy to the corrupt. We ask that you look on him with mercy"—he looked over at Julian, who had been silent—"and on the rest of us too."

There was a pause and Ellie stepped forward. "I'd like to lead us in a song, if I may."

Joe nodded.

Ellie lifted her voice and began to sing. "Rock of ages, cleft for me, let me hide myself in thee. Let the water and the blood . . ." The rest of the group joined her as best they could until the song was finished.

"The man that killed him may be close by," Zac said. "I'd suggest we move out and keep together."

"Do you know this pass Chupta told us about?" Joe asked. "The one through the Malpais?"

"It's just up ahead," Zac said, "around the next bend. I'm not sure if this tracker of yours is on that thing now or waiting for us farther on, but it might be a good bet to take it. There would be no cover for him there, at least no place he could put a horse."

"Why don't you let me go first?" Julian asked. "I'm the one he really wants."

Zac gave him a long, cold stare. "He'd be doing the people a favor, but I still wouldn't want to give him the satisfaction. No, I'll go." Turning to Ellie, he asked, "Ma'am, could you and James here ride with Pablo?"

"We would be happy to," Ellie said.

It wasn't long before they hit the westward trail leading through the Malpais. They could all see what Zac had meant when he said there would be no place for the man to put his horse. The broken trail was simply smaller shards of lava broken down into a passable walkway. The black, broken rock covered the ground all around it. It would take a great deal of trust not to think you would end up stuck somewhere only to have to turn around.

They rode all day before breaking out on the north side of the Malpais. There, for the first time, they found trees and grass. Zac signaled them ahead, and they started to pick up the pace, moving from a fast walk to an occasional lope. In the twilight of the day, they rode up to the peaks that had been far away when the day was young.

Juniper trees and cottonwoods were nestled in the shade of the towering cliffs. Like a fort in the desert, the rocks stood upright, rising over two hundred feet in the line of the dying sun. The walls of the rock were sheer, a pinkish orange in the ebbing day. Flat on top with parapets of smooth, rounded stone and level edges of carved boulders, it gave off the appearance of a massive castle from a child's storybook. One of the walls appeared to have stripes running down its side, dark streaks where water poured after a heavy rain.

Nestled in between the rocks was a meeting place of stone. The cliffs up above formed an overlapping series of sharp mushrooms, and the juncture of the rocks gave way to a bright waterfall. The thin line of cascading water dropped from rock to rock and then slid down the side of the concave stone face and into a waiting pond below. Circling the pond was a large stand of cattails. Their brown bulbs swayed on the end of bright green stalks, trailing into the pond.

It was a beautiful oasis on the edge of the ugliest land God had ever created, and it brought out a groan from Ellie. "This is truly wonderful," she said.

"It's called Inscription Rock by some folks," Zac said. "Others call it El Moro. I've been here a time or two. It's one of the few places you can get fresh water and a bath."

"A bath," Ellie sighed. "Imagine that."

"I never would have thought a place like this was possible," James added.

"You see," she said, "the West is full of places like this."

"That may be, but you have to ride quite a ways to get here." Almost as if the thought of his hard saddle suddenly struck him, James jumped off of his horse. He walked awkwardly around to help Ellie, shaking out his legs as he went.

Joe turned to Julian. "Where do we go from here?" he asked.

Taking out his map, Julian looked it over. "You're not going to like this," he said. "None of you are, I'm afraid. We go back into the Malpais, deep into the Malpais."

CHAPTER 36

+ + + + + + +

THE COOKFIRE WAS DYING OUT just after sunset, and the group stood around the smoldering coals, sharing the last of the soup Ellie had made. It made them feel warm inside. Zac had moved off to a spot under the juniper. He sat cleaning his guns while he watched the boy explore the pond.

Ellie stared long and hard at Zac. "That brother of yours seems quite distant," she said.

"He's always been that way," James said. "He does love Tennyson's poetry, however—I'll give him that much. He also has a way with music. He plays the violin."

"The violin and poetry? I could never imagine that. Things like the violin and poetry are warm to the thought, and he seems so cold."

James looked over at Zac. "Don't be fooled by him. There's a lot about that man that I don't think anybody knows. He has changed, though, since that woman in California came into his life."

"I just think he feels particularly disagreeable about what happened to Chupta," Joe said. "No matter what he says, he holds himself to blame. When a man feels guilty he keeps to himself. He's afraid that what he sees in other folks' eyes are the same accusations he's telling himself."

"No," Julian said, "I'm the one to blame, and he knows it."

"He hasn't said that to you," Ellie said.

"He ain't said nothing." Julian pulled his revolver out of his holster and, clamping it under his left stump, opened the gate on the cylinder. He checked his loads, making sure the empty chamber was placed under the hammer. Closing it, he stuck it back in the holster. "I reckon I'll take the first watch," he said. "You can figure out with our brother over there who ought to have the second."

Seeing Julian walking away, Zac got to his feet. "Where do you think you're going?" he asked.

"I'm taking the first watch. Figure you and Joe can decide who gets the rest."

"No, you're not." Zac stepped closer to him.

"How you figure that?"

Back at the campsite, Joe was watching the two brothers. He edged himself closer to the edge of the group to listen.

"You already left these folks one time before," Zac said. "I saw your tracks in that valley in the Mogollons. You light a shuck out of here looking for that gold of yours this time and somebody else is gonna get killed."

Julian's frown widened, and he stepped toward Zac. "You don't know me. What I did back there was because those people were coming after me, not them."

"I know you."

Julian took another step in Zac's direction. "The man you used to know is dead and gone," he said.

"Not by a long shot. I wouldn't trust you to guard a dead mule if you thought there was a profit in the carcass."

"Why don't you just have at me and get it over with? You blame me for that man's death back there. Go ahead and say it."

With lightning speed, Zac sent a roundhouse punch into Julian's jaw, spilling him to the ground.

Julian dropped his right hand to his holster.

"Go ahead," Zac said, "there's nothing I'd like better."

As Julian lay on the ground, Joe raced in their direction, followed by James.

"You're forgetting, little brother, speed with a six-gun has never been what you do best. You may have a good aim, but you don't get off a first shot."

"First shot or second, you're gonna be dead all the same. There'll be less widows and orphans out there if you're in the ground."

"And how 'bout that lady you plan on marrying? You think she's gonna take kindly to your memory, dying on account of revenge?"

Joe stepped in between the two. He reached over at Zac and pushed him back slightly. "That's enough for tonight. Just what the blazes do you think you're doing?"

James helped Julian to his feet. "He's just blaming me is all," Julian explained.

"That's enough for both of you," Joe said.

"You feel better landing that punch?" Julian asked.

"Not nearly good enough."

"We got ourselves enough to fret about without having you two going at it," Joe said.

"You got yourself a man you're protecting here that belongs on the hangman's gallows in three states."

"New Mexico ain't one of them," Joe said. "And, no matter what you may think, you're not the law."

"You've got a wife and child to go back to," Zac said. "You let him wander off with the horses and you just may not wake up again."

"I'm just carrying my load," Julian said, "same as the rest."

"I understand your concern," James interjected, "but Ellie and I are willing to trust him with our lives."

"And I'll trust him with mine," Joe added.

"All right, he can have the first watch, and I'll take the second, but that map stays here in camp."

Julian braced at the notion, shaking his head. "The man just wants the second watch so he won't sleep and he can keep an eye on me."

"It doesn't matter what his reasons are. Zac goes his own way, same as always. He's already taken on three men trying to kill you and slowed down the rest. That ought to be worth something."

Julian seemed stunned at the idea. "Three men trying to kill me?"

"That's right," Zac said. "They were hired by the government to make sure that gold stayed hidden. Fact is, they were willing to pay me a hundred dollars to make wolf meat out of you myself."

"Why didn't you take it? I know how much you enjoy your work."

"In spite of what you might think, I don't do my work for personal reasons."

Julian rubbed his sore chin. "You could have fooled me a minute ago."

"All right," Joe said. "You can have the first watch, Julian, and if it will make Zac here feel more at ease, you better give me the map."

The morning was tense, the memory of the night before still on everyone's mind. Ellie stirred pancake batter and watched as the men began their morning routine. Zac had kept the second watch of the night, but just as Julian suspected, he hadn't slept during Julian's guard duty. He was up early, however, gathering firewood. He laid a stack of the wood at Ellie's feet by the fire.

"Did the boy sleep well?" she asked.

"Yes, he did. I told him a story, and he was asleep halfway through."

"You like children, don't you?"

"I like them a lot. It's just too bad some of them grow up."

"You're speaking of your brother, I assume."

Stooping down next to the fire, he added some wood to it. "Ma'am, I make a living chasing men that were all children at one time. Something went wrong somewhere, something that made them think they were the most important thing there was. They don't have to account for themselves, until they account to me."

"It must be an awful burden for you to right other people's wrongs."

"That is something I don't have to do. I just have to protect Wells Fargo's money."

"It appears that you're trying to account for your brother."

Zac pushed back his hat. "I'm here, and James and Joe are here because of that man. Frankly, I don't think he's worth the trouble."

"Mr. Cobb, you and your brothers are here because you chose to be. Julian didn't send for you. You can blame him for many things, but the trouble with blaming is it always goes too far. It doesn't know when to stop. Shame is the deepest arrow that could ever penetrate a man's soul. A man feels it deeply and gives it out far too liberally."

Zac looked over at the still sleeping James. "Miss Ellie, I can understand now what that brother of mine sees in you. You do have a way of making a man look at things, don't you? I know what that's like. My Jenny back home does that to me, and I let her because I know she loves me."

"There's something about the truth coming from someone who loves you that makes all the difference, don't you think?"

"I tend to respect the truth, no matter where I hear it. It just goes down a mite easier when it's someone who cares. A knife and a scalpel both have sharp edges. The difference is the reason they've used and the hand that's on them."

She smiled. "Then, consider my words a scalpel."

After breakfast the group saddled their horses. There was something about the black lava fields that made even the early dawn seem brighter than usual. Its orange glow warmed the rocky face of the stone castle. They mounted and rode past it. Julian and Joe rode at the front of the group with Zac close behind.

It was easy to see why the place was called Inscription Rock. The pleasant location with trees, fresh water, and a bathing pond had been a stopover for many travelers down through the years. She could see many names etched into the sandstone, some dating back over a hundred years. Many of the names were Spanish with crosses.

"Are we going to take the horses over that?" she asked. "If we are, I don't think they're going to make it."

"No," Julian said. "You're right, the horses would never make it over the Malpais. We're looking for an entrance marked on the map. I'll know it when I see it."

Zac looked back at her. "Wolves have chased deer out on that thing. The deer always get themselves so cut up they never get out alive. It makes the wolves' job that much easier."

They rode next to the black wall of lava for at least two hours, Julian and Joe checking the map several times. The cliff rose at times to a height of fifty feet. It seemed like the side of a huge sleeping elephant, its rough, abrasive skin a dull black mixed with gray. Large black boulders the size of a house were mixed with pumpkin-sized clumps of the frozen stone. The brush was abundant, wiry, and full of thorns. Prickly pear cactus sat next to the black rock along with a scattered mixture of spindly dwarfed pine trees. It was an odd collection, something Ellie had never seen before.

Julian called the group to a halt in front of a lone oak tree. The tree stood out as a giant among pygmies, its trunk split in two by a lightning strike. Life still struggled in the tree and some of the branches had green leaves in spite of the wrath of the thunderbolt. "There is an opening here, somewhere," Julian said. "If this map is right, it ought to be behind this tree."

The group dismounted and fanned out close to the lava shelf. Several times they would see what seemed to be an opening in the rock, only to find that it was a dead end. Zac climbed up the shelf to get a better look. It was Ellie who spotted the ledge of quartz. The sparkling rock, a blazing splash of white embedded in the dark lava, drew her attention.

Pushing toward it, she stepped over a trunk of lava lying along the ground. She could see the shiny rock, but it was beyond her reach.

Moving to the side and around an edge of the curving lava shelf, she could see a patch of ground behind it. She advanced around the bend and there found what seemed to be a bridge of the same stone.

Backing up, she studied it. The ground was free of the lava flow, and the bridge appeared to be high enough for a horse to pass under it. It may have led to nothing, but Ellie was curious. Stepping forward, she ducked under the black overpass.

Surprisingly, she found herself in a narrow passageway. It seemed to end at about the distance of ten feet, but she walked forward to inspect it. Much to her surprise, another shelf cut down across the back wall. It stood some three feet from the wall. From where she had entered the narrow approach, there had been no way to see it. The edge of this new shelf blended perfectly into the wall behind it. She moved around it and down under another overhang.

Stepping out, what she saw shocked her. There in front of her was a lush island of green. Trees, pine and aspen, dotted the place. Grass covered a large area, and against the wall stood a small cabin. A small stream trickled down from the black rock behind the cabin and, meandering across the meadow, made its way out under a shelf of rock on the other side. There appeared to be several fruit trees, planted by what could only have been a hermit, and a chia, whose seed was used by the Indians for food. This was a place someone could live, perhaps indefinitely.

She could hardly contain herself. Rushing back out, she ducked under the trestles of frozen mountain. "I found something back here," she yelled. "It's beautiful!"

James gathered up the reins of Ellie's horse, and all the men led theirs to her.

"I don't think you can ride to the place," she said, "but I think the horses will fit."

Single file, they followed her though the passage. It was plain to see that even if a man stumbled onto the first of the entrances, he would have a hard time finding the second. The optical illusion presented by the narrow edge of lava across the black wall made it look like a dead end.

One by one they stepped out onto the sunken green island. For some reason the lava had flowed around this area. It formed a stark and beautiful contrast to the foreboding walls and deadly shelves that made up the Malpais.

"You did good, Ellie girl." James grinned. "I wouldn't have believed it."

Julian studied the map. "This must be the place," he said. He folded the map and stuck it back in his shirt. "Jumpy Suthers knew about this place. That's his cabin over there. He was with the men transporting the gold, and when they ran into trouble, he brought them here. He made the map here just in case."

"I'm not sure there's many people who could find it even with the map," Joe said.

James swiveled his head around. "Where is Zac?"

"He's back outside," Julian said, "rubbing out our tracks."

On the west side of the island, a gentle slope of black rock stretched from the grassy floor to the top of the wall. It was a gradual incline and one that looked smooth enough for a horse to walk on. A chilled rampart of black ground, it was a bubble that at one time might have threatened the island, but now was frozen in time.

James began to walk his horse up the incline. "I wonder how far a man can see from the edge of this place," he said.

"I'm not sure how stable that is for the horse," Joe called out.

"He's been with me this far," James called out. "He might as well see for himself too."

The animal stamped at the black rock, unsure of his footing. Suddenly, the ground beneath the horse began to splinter. The animal reared, and James held the reins. Coming down and landing hard on the rock, the hooves of the horse broke through.

"Hey!" James yelled.

They watched as James fell through the hole in the rock.

CHAPTER 37

+ + + + + + +

ELLIE SCREAMED AS JAMES'S HORSE backed up from the hole and clattered back down the rocky shelf.

Joe grabbed Julian. "You go get Zac. I'll climb up there."

Skipping up onto the ledge of black rock, Joe ran toward the hole. There were so many things about this place that a man didn't know. What might appear to be one thing on the surface could be something else in a matter of inches. Stopping close to the tear in the rock, Joe got down on his knees and inched his way forward. The crack had separated the rock, and from looking at it, Joe could see that the thing was brittle and little more than several inches thick. This entire shelf of lava had been only a bubble of gas.

Getting on his belly, he crawled closer. He hadn't noticed before, but Ellie was right behind him. "Can you hear anything?" Her voice was breaking.

"I do hear something," Joe said. He edged himself closer. He could hear a moaning sound coming up from under the surface of the rock. "Don't come any closer. I'll get up there, and I don't think we need to put any more weight on this thing."

"All right, but please hurry. Oh, Lord."

Joe inched his way forward. The crack in the rock was close to five feet long and the width of the break measured about four feet. The edges were rough and broken. Very carefully, Joe put his head next to the hole.

Joe could hear James moaning. He looked back at Ellie. "I can hear him. He sounds like he's in pain, but he's still alive."

"Thank God."

Julian had found Zac, and together they climbed to a position behind Ellie. "Do we have any rope?" Joe asked. "Anything at all?"

"I just have short pieces of rawhide," Zac said. "Not enough to do any good here."

"There might be something in Jumpy's cabin," Julian said. "I'll have a look."

Scooting down the black rocky mantle, Julian ran for the cabin. The place had been built under a ledge, which formed its roof and two sides of the cabin. Two small, narrow windows faced them on either side of the door. Julian forced it open with his shoulder, and it swung wide.

Jumpy had never been much for neatness, and the small light that came in through the open door and two windows didn't offer much help. A rough-cut table lay on its side and two chairs were piled in a corner. There were two narrow beds with mattresses that appeared to be stuffed with hay or straw and a cupboard next to a black lava wall.

Julian opened the cupboard. A few cans of food still sat on the shelf, along with a number of cups and plates and crockery. There was no sign of rope.

Making his way to the black rocky wall in the rear of the cabin, Julian got down on his knees and began to feel his way into the inky darkness. There was storage space here, a place that Jumpy had obviously used. It would have been an easy location to kick something out of the way, something a man didn't find frequent use for. He groped under the rock, swinging his hand back and forth and slashing with his fingers. He came out with several boxes, then felt something. It was a rope.

Pulling it out, he tucked part of it under the stump of his arm and reeled the remainder in. Gathering it up, he slung it over his shoulder and raced out of the cabin. He stepped lightly over the rocky shelf and soon scooted up next to Zac and Joe.

Grabbing one end of the rope, Zac tied it around his waist. "Joe, you hitch this other end to the dun back there and, Julian, I need you to find me a torch."

A short while later, Joe had the rope in position, and Julian had found a serviceable torch. The thing was a large stick wrapped with cloth and soaked with some coal oil he found in the cabin. He held the torch under his left stump and struck a match with his thumbnail. The torch burst into flame.

"Okay," Zac said. "Back up the dun and take up the slack. One of you will have to hold on and ease me down—the other ought to be right here to hear what I say."

"I'll handle the rope down there," Joe stated.

They could all hear James's continued moaning. The man was in obvious pain, but he was still conscious. Zac looked over at Ellie. "Don't you worry about him. We'll get him out."

Zac positioned himself over the opening and signaled to Joe. With that, he dropped into the yawning darkness.

The flicker of flame from the torch lit up the chamber ceiling. Overhead, he could hear Julian shouting out instructions. "Lower," Julian cried out. "Take him lower."

There were no footholds and nothing to hang on to. Suspended by the rope, Zac felt like a spider on the end of a web. He held out the torch and looked down.

James was spread out over the rocks some fifty feet below, his left leg twisted behind the right. The ground was littered with rocks of all size and description. That James had managed to survive the fall was a miracle in itself. "Hang on, James, I'm coming."

"It hurts like the dickens," James said hoarsely.

Zac heard Julian continue to shout instructions to Joe. The flame on the torch started to flicker and flare, rippling in a slight breeze. There was obviously an entrance to this place, and from the direction of the breeze, Zac could tell it was south of them. Perhaps there would be an easier way of getting James out than having to drag him up through that hole in the roof.

Moments later, Zac's toes hit the floor of the cave. He crammed the end of the torch in some rocks and untied the rope. Looking up, he yelled to Julian, "Haul it up. You better send down some splints and bandages. I think he's got a broken leg."

Stepping over to James, he bent down and inspected his older brother's legs and arms.

"I'm sorry about this," James said. "I didn't mean to be a nuisance or cause you any annoyance."

"Oh, you're not causing us any trouble. You know us boys, one less Cobb don't mean spit where we're concerned." He looked up. "But you better save your regrets for that lady of yours up there. She's careworn and more than a little agitated."

"I can imagine."

"You're a lucky man."

"How is that?"

"You might have hit your head and broke up these rocks something bad."

James coughed out a laugh.

Zac looked over the interior of the cave. What air there was came from the south, but it was what lay to the north of them that shocked him. There on the floor of the cave was what looked like a congealed sheet of green ice. It gave off the appearance of mint jelly, and the surrounding lower portion of the wall seemed to be covered with it. The tips of the black rocks on the floor poked out of the green ice like black bubbles in a huge bowl of tapioca pudding. He stood up and, picking up the torch, held it out. "You ever seen anything like that?"

"No, I haven't," James noted. "What could it be?"

"I think I'll go have a look-see." He turned back to James and gave off a slight grin. "Now, don't you go anywhere. I wouldn't want to have to go looking for you."

James chuckled. "I'll be right here when you get back."

Stepping over to the strange substance, Zac bent down and felt it. "It's ice," he called out to James, "green ice."

"Ice?"

"That's right, coldest stuff you ever felt." Moving over to the walls, he felt along the edges. "There's ice all over these walls, and all of it with this greenish color."

Looking up, he saw Julian begin to lower the bundle of bandages and splints. He stepped back over to James and held the torch up. "You notice something else peculiar to this place? It's like no cave I've ever seen before. It's rounded on the top and curved at the sides."

James looked around, wincing in pain. "I've seen something like this on an island I paid a visit to in the South Seas. This isn't a cave at all—it's a tube, a lava tube."

"A lava tube?"

"That's right. The molten lava forms a river of superheated rock. What was on the surface cooled faster than the hotter material underneath. By the time the entire river emptied itself into that lake of rock they call the Malpais, the tube would remain standing. This thing might go back for miles."

"I take back what I said about that education of yours. It just might be useful for some real living, after all."

Zac took the bundle from where it dangled over his head and untied it. He then signaled to Julian. "We got it," he yelled. "Send down some blankets and a bedroll. It's cold down here."

"I hadn't noticed before," James said. "But it is cold."

Zac squatted down next to him. "All right, that left leg of yours appears to be pretty broke up. I hope you don't mind walking with a cane?"

"Just so I can walk down the aisle. Besides, I might look more distinguished with a polished hickory stick."

"Fine. If we're going to get you fixed up at all, I'm going to have to set that leg. I'm not going to kid you—this is going to hurt like blazes. Your left arm appears broke too, but not as bad as this leg."

Zac untied the kerchief from around his throat and handed it to

James. "You can knot this up and stick it in your mouth, or you can just hang on and scream your lungs out. You're going to do one or the other, though. There ain't no easy way around it. Strong, brave men keel dead away."

"I think I'd prefer to scream," James said. "You know me. I like my voice to be heard."

"Well, it will be."

Zac lifted up James's right leg and pushed it aside. As he straightened out the left leg, James erupted in a chilling shriek.

"Now, that wasn't so bad, was it? Considering how we haven't even started yet."

"Zac, you must have the worst bedside manner of any person I've ever seen."

Zac grinned. "That's why I'm invited to more hangings that healings."

"I can understand that completely."

He took hold of James's ankle and put his foot next to the man's hips for leverage. "You ready to go?" Zac asked.

"I suppose." James held back his head and began to speak in a slow, deliberate tone. " 'Sunset and evening star and one clear call for me, and may there be no moaning of the bar when I put out to sea.' "

"Now how can I put you in pain when you're quoting Tennyson?"

"I was hoping you might feel that way. 'Twilight and evening bell and after that the dark, and may there be no sadness of farewell when I embark.' "

Zac heaved back on James's ankle and a roar of pain shot through the dark tube. The bellow sounded like it would shake the walls and ceiling down, and then James passed out.

It was sometime later when Zac finished with the splints on his brother's leg. He then worked on setting James's arm. It was much easier with the man unconscious, not having to look at or listen to his pain. He picked up the bedroll they had sent down and spread it over the senseless James.

Julian leaned his head down through the crack. "You all right down there?"

"We're fine. He may not wake up for a while."

"What did you do, hit him like you did me last night?"

"No, setting that leg of his is more than enough pain for one man in this lifetime," Zac yelled out. "I'm going to take the torch and walk this cave a ways. There just may be an easier way of getting him out of here.

So, you keep your head through that crack and listen for him. He may wake up before I get back."

"I got somebody else that wants that job," Julian barked.

Zac heard Ellie's voice. "Is he all right?"

"He better get used to riding or being drug or carried for a while. He's not going to do much walking for many a moon."

Zac picked up the torch and began walking down the length of the tube toward the place where he thought the fresh air was coming from. The sides were strange colors, not black as he would have expected. Gray and orange stripes ran down them to the floor.

He held the torch up higher. The tube seemed to flatten out. What had been a fifty-foot-high ceiling twenty yards behind him was now thirty. Overhead, he could see that the roof was indeed a sheet of paralyzed lava. That would be the most fragile part of the tube, as they had discovered. A good shaking from an earthquake would send the roof crashing down, filling up the entire tube and turning it into a mass of stony debris. It was a thought that chilled him to the bone.

As he moved forward, he came upon another portion of the tube filled with the green ice. It was a primeval rink of frozen ooze, having never been exposed to the light. Like something out of the arctic tundra, the glimmering green ice winked at the flaming torch Zac held overhead.

He lowered the torch. There was a light ahead of him. He didn't want the flame interfering with what he might be seeing. His heart beat faster. Maybe there was another way out.

A few minutes more of walking showed additional light until, after only thirty or forty yards, he could see the bright rays of the sun. He stepped out into a pool of the frozen discharge. Boulders were mixed with the substance, frozen solidly into the floor. There had been a cave-in, and the roof and a third of the side of the tube had given way. He climbed his way toward the light.

Soon Zac was standing on the outside of the tube in the bright sunshine. He could see yet another valley in the middle of the Malpais. There were trees scattered over the lava-strewn ground, and in the distance there was a patch of grass. Beyond that, he could see what appeared to be a cinder cone. The cabin would be north of him, just over the rocks. He began to climb. The rocks were steep here, black carbuncles of abscessed chilled stone. Getting James up this thing might be a problem.

A short while later, Zac stood on the wall of lava that made up the roof of the cabin. He waved his arms and began to whistle.

The group took some time in assembling a stretcher and making a litter. This would be better than pulling James back up through the crack in the tube. They struggled through the opening Zac had found. Holding up several torches, each of them stared in disbelief at the green ice that covered the floor of the opening.

"There's more down near James," Zac said.

"This is what Jumpy wrote about on the map," Julian said. "I couldn't figure it out then, but now it makes sense."

"What was that?" Joe asked.

"The green black gold." He pointed out a spot on the map.

They walked a short while before they spotted James. He lay in the darkness, awake and staring at the opening in the ceiling. Ellie rushed over to him, dropping to her knees. "I was so worried about you." She clutched his right hand.

James began speaking in a low tone. " 'For tho' from out our bourne of time and place the flood may bear me far, I hope to see my pilot face to face when I have crossed the bar.' "

Ellie looked back at Zac, a distressed expression on her face.

"Oh, he's all right," Zac said. "He was just finishing a line from Tennyson.

She looked down at James. "Don't scare me that way."

"I'm sorry." James grimaced with the words. "I was just finishing what Zac and I started before the lights went out on me."

Julian had wandered down the tube. They could see his torch about twenty yards away, flooding the darkness with a soft glimmer of flame. "I found it!" he yelled.

"Found what?" Joe asked.

"Come and see."

Zac handed his torch to Ellie. "You better wait here with him. It might be better if you told him a bedtime story so he doesn't scare you with more of that poetry of his."

Zac caught up with Joe and his dim light, and soon they stood beside Julian, listening to him count. There stacked in groups of three were barrels, each marked with the word "flour."

"I count a hundred and forty-seven," Julian said.

"You plan on opening a bakery out here?" Joe asked.

"No, that's the treasure. The emperor's men transported the gold in barrels of flour, and in the end that's what did them in."

"Why would that be a problem?" Joe asked. "Sounds pretty smart to me."

"It might have been all right, but they let a few ex-Johnny Rebs join up with them for protection from the Mescalero. The way Jumpy told it, those fellas came aboard the wagon train here in New Mexico and thought it looked mighty strange for armed guards to be standing over flour. When they finally decided to kill the guards, Jumpy threw in with them and they brought the shipment here."

"What happened to the others?" Zac asked.

"Jumpy says they were all killed—some together, a few one at a time over the next year. As far as he knew, he was the only one left, and he'd been in on the shipment from the start."

He stepped over to one of the closest barrels and handed Zac his torch. Pulling out his knife, he stuck it beneath the lid and pushed down. The wooden keg popped open, sending up a shower of white powder.

Reaching his fist down into the flour and then bringing it up, he shook the white substance to the floor. There in his hand was a fistful of Mexican gold coins.

CHAPTER 38

+ + + + + + +

IT TOOK THE GROUP the better part of an hour to carry James out of the tube and into the relatively warm sunlight. The air still had a cool touch in it but not the chill of the ice cave. Zac looked up the steep incline that led out of the small valley. "I'm not sure we should move him up that thing, at least not today. I'd suggest we just build him a fire right here and cook some food and something hot for him to drink."

James was weary and it showed. He turned his head toward Ellie. "That sounds glorious to me."

"I thought you might think so," Zac replied. Looking at Ellie, he said, "He's in a lot of pain."

"I'll go back for some supplies," Joe offered. "If we decide to sleep here, we can get the bedrolls later."

"You better bring Pablo back with you," Zac said. "The little feller's been alone for a while, and if he's not scared, he's bored."

"I'll do that."

Piles of broken rocky rubble were strewn over the ground. The entrance to the tube that had been fractured at this point was a mass of gray, sun-bleached rock cascading down into the entrance of the hollow cavern, a tumble of confusion with scattered samples of brush growing on top at various intervals. The plant life in the area consisted of hardy breeds, refusing to give in to the most austere conditions. They showed no sign of taking over, only of making their presence known.

Around one side of the small valley was a sheer wall. It rose twenty feet or more from the pile of rubble, and Zac could see small trees on top with brush peeking over the side. This valley had obviously been an extension of the lava tube that had long since collapsed. The mess of confusion left in its wake was enough to give any man an idea of what might happen to people or animals trapped underneath. There would be no escape. There was no way a man could get out and no possibility that people could dig anyone out of the debris. The rock-strewn ground they now stood on had once been the roof of that part of the tube.

Zac noticed Julian surveying the wreckage. "It's a good thing the place that friend Jumpy of yours wrote about isn't under our feet now."

"I was just thinking the same thing."

Zac got to his feet. "I'll take a look around. Why don't you stay with Ellie and James here."

Julian nodded.

Zac looked down at the two lovers. "Will you be all right?"

"We'll be fine," Ellie said. "Joe ought to be back soon."

James closed his eyes. The man was played out by the pain.

"I just want to make sure this place will be all right to start a fire in—somewhere we can't be seen."

"I understand," Ellie said. "You go ahead."

Zac stumbled his way over and through the rocky maelstrom. It was quite a stretch to even get to the part of the wall he wanted to climb. Reaching the sheer gray embankment on the west side, he wedged his boots into the crack and lifted himself up. For Julian, with one arm, this would have been a hard climb. Even as it was, it took both hands and some scurrying on Zac's part to get him over the side.

He lifted himself up off the wall. The Malpais stretched out before him, a tangled mass of black tumbled rock with ponderosa pines growing in the cracks and brush scattered over the surface. To the west of him was a slope that led up a cinder cone. Aspen were growing on its side, a smattering of gold and yellow dotted on top of the gray-and-black surface. From the top of the cone a man might get a good view—certainly of the valley where James lay and probably of the cabin as well.

Zac began his climb to the top. The rocks were broken. Some appeared to be fine ash, powdered down to a gray sand. At other places there were weird shapes of fossilized lava, skeletons of the long-ago eruption. One spot in particular caught his eye. A mound of frozen lava stood some seven feet high, bending over. It appeared for all the world to be an ancient monster turning to feed on some poor creature. A small arch formed the neck, and a massive puddle at the bottom displayed the profile of the head of the beast, locked forever in a feeding frenzy.

The trees were tall but scattered. They bent themselves in various directions according to the pressure of the rocks they sat on. Some were twisted and others pointed straight, but few were aimed directly at the sky above them.

The slope of the hill broke up into a carpet of fist-sized stones. They were uniform in size and layered the ground in a dull gray mixed with black and white speckles. A lone prickly pear cactus made its stand in the middle of the rocks, green with bright orange bulbs. It reminded Zac of himself, refusing to give in, standing alone, with sharp spines to ward off any unsuspecting intruder. For a man to survive, he had to be willing to go it alone.

Rounding the backside of the cone, he saw the edge of a large pit. The rim of the slide was some two hundred feet high at the sides. Sand and dirt dropped off at a forty-five degree angle, giving the thing the appearance of a colossal sandbox where the childlike giant had dug out the center to allow his toys a free fall down the slopes to the bottom of the hole below. Scattered trees grew along the slide, and inside the middle of the crater, around its rim, was a ledge of rippled rock.

Then something made him hit the ground. He saw movement and a flash of sunlight. There along the ledge, he could see a man prowling the rocks. The man was obviously carrying a rifle and the glare of the sunlight off the weapon had caught Zac's attention.

Zac rolled over behind one of the aspens and got to his feet. He scampered over the rocks to a spot where there was cover. Moving quickly, he made his way up the top of the hill. He was on the ledge, a little more than a hundred yards from where he had seen the man. He dropped to the ground and lay still.

Looking behind him, he could see James, Julian, and Ellie. Even from here a man could make out Julian. The man was hard to miss, having only one arm. Looking over, he could see the small island of green and the horses. Joe had taken Pablo over there, and the two of them were carrying supplies over the lava wall from the rear of the cabin.

This would be a perfect place for a man to see everything and an ideal location for a shooter to work his way around into position. It wouldn't be Escobar, but it just might be the hunter he'd been tracking, the man who had killed Chupta.

Zac edged over. If the man was taking his time and watching the movement in the valley, he would be coming in Zac's direction any moment now. Zac knew enough about the man to know he would be careful and a handful to deal with.

Suddenly, Zac saw him, carrying a Winchester rifle and wearing his distinctive sheepskin vest. The Winchester wouldn't have near the range of Zac's own Sharps, but that was something he didn't have with him just now. All he had was the Colt on his hip and the Greener knife at his side. Zac knew he was outgunned. He couldn't afford to get into a shooting battle, not here and not now.

Just from watching the man, Zac could see he was a shootist. He moved over the rocks like a big cat, keeping his eyes fixed on the valley

Zac had just come from, fastened on the sight of Julian in the distance.

Zac was up above him now, just over what might pass for a trail on the edge of the big slide. He'd have to time his jump just right. He had no hankering to go down that thing. From this height, a man would fall for a long time before he hit bottom.

The man moved cautiously and then Zac leaped. He was about six feet above the man when he jumped. Zac landed on him with boots out, knocking him to the ground.

The man sprang up, his rifle still in his hand. "You!" he said. As he swung the rifle in Zac's direction, Zac lashed out with a kick that sent the gun spinning off into space above the great slide.

Dropping his hand down to the pistol tied at his side, the man started his draw. Zac reached out and took hold of his vest, rolling back and kicking him into the air. The man hit the ground with a thud, and Zac jumped to attention. His revolver had landed some six feet away, and he got to his feet looking for it. "Why don't you just shoot me now?" he asked.

"That would be your style," Zac said. "You're a backshooter, and the man you killed yesterday was my friend."

The man grinned. "He died real easy, just one shot."

"That's because you didn't have to face him. Now, though, you have to take me on. Let's just see how easy you have it."

"Frank Gordon don't back down from no man, no time." Gordon drew his knife and began to circle. "You know I could have killed you and that boy real easy like some days back."

Zac drew out the Greener. "Killing easy is what you do best, isn't it?"

The man flashed his knife at Zac, sending him jumping back.

"You just watch out," Gordon said. "We wouldn't want you to fall."

With that, he rushed at Zac, and the two men locked knives above the hilt, grabbing at each other's wrists. The man was slightly older, but strong as an ox. Zac twisted his arms, sending a sweaty ooze onto the palms of his hand. He could smell the man, a pungent aroma of unwashed flesh mixed with woodsmoke. The two of them balanced on the edge of the great slide, moving from side to side to get leverage. Zac could feel the soft sand under his feet. Pressing his boots down made it give way slightly.

Lifting his boot, he curled it around Gordon's ankle and pulled forward with all of his might. Gordon's eyes bulged, and he held fast to Zac as he tumbled over backward.

Both men hit the top of the sandy slide and began to totter and then roll down the loose rock. Over and over they fell, arms and hands still locked in combat. Like two rag dolls thrown from the door of a moving train, they somersaulted down the sandy cone of gray pumice. Their speed picked up, slamming them into rocks that protruded above the surface, and then Gordon let go.

Zac slid for some way on his back, grappling to find a hold, a hold on anything. He spun with his feet pointing downhill, the force of the slide turning him from side to side. Spotting a small tree, he grabbed for it. The thing jerked him to a sudden stop, dust rising all around him.

Zac coughed and blinked back the dirt in his face. Sitting up in the soft surface, he looked down the hill. There on the bottom, Gordon lay spread out. He wasn't moving.

Zac stumbled to his feet, sinking into the soft pumice up to his knees. Awkwardly, he began to clamor down the cone. The thing was a sand pile, a gigantic heap of leftover earth. He skipped and half ran, bounding down the slope and shaking his feet and legs from it as he went.

Reaching the bottom, he stepped over to Gordon. The man lay on his belly, collapsed in a sprawling position with arms and legs pointing at all four corners of the compass. Reaching under Gordon with the tip of his boot, Zac turned him over.

Gordon's eyes were wide open, his own knife buried up to the hilt in his chest. It wasn't the way he'd planned it, but Gordon was done for. Zac tapped his holster. It was a miracle, but the Colt was still there, the hammer tied in place by the rawhide thong.

Zac looked up the side of the gray cone. Either one or both of them could have been killed coming down that thing, but he was alive, and the man called Frank Gordon was dead. Zac didn't believe in luck. A prepared man who used his head made his own luck. There were many who said he lived a "charmed" life, but Zac knew it was more than that. He had a purpose, and when his purpose was over, he'd be gone. A man needed a purpose.

Slowly, he made his way over the rocks at the bottom of the great chasm, and then he began his climb back to the high valley that led to the opening in the tube. It took him some time. Scaling the small collection of rugged debris, he finally stood on top of the area surrounding the cavern. James was still lying on the litter, but the rest of the people were gone. Not a soul remained.

That's odd, Zac thought. Searching the area around the wall, he found a spot he could climb down. He reached the ground and made his way to James. The man was sleeping. They had covered him with the bedroll, and he didn't seem to have a care in the world. Zac stooped down beside him and shook him softly. "Where is everybody?"

James's eyes blinked open. "What?"

"Where did everybody go? Did they all just up and leave you?" Zac could tell this was the first time James had opened his eyes since his departure. Perhaps they just thought he needed the rest and didn't have the heart to wake him. Even so, he couldn't imagine Ellie leaving.

James was just as amazed at being left alone. "I don't know where they went. I didn't see them go."

"I took care of that feller who's been trailing you."

"The one who killed Chupta?"

Zac nodded.

"Why was he following us?"

"I figured him to be working for that federal agent we met in Santa Fe. They like to have fall-back plans, and that feller must have been his."

James shook his head. "Why send us to get Julian, only to have him killed?"

"The Secret Service is interested in only one thing," Zac said, "and that's making sure this gold doesn't fall into Escobars hands. They wanted to send us down there just to get Julian out so that bunch could kill him. I guess they figured that with that brother of ours dead, they wouldn't have to worry about Escobar. This last feller here was out to make sure the job was done. They work that way."

"That's dirty business," James said.

Zac patted his head. "You go back to sleep. I'll find them. Don't worry about it. They couldn't have gone very far. I just saw them a short time ago, back from the top of that hill up there."

He walked over to the opening in the tube and, cupping his hands over his mouth, he called out, "Hello! Joe? Julian? Ellie? Pablo? You in there?"

There was no answer from the tube, only silence. They might be back where the flour barrels were, their curiosity getting the best of them. Or they could be back at the cabin. At least he could call down from the crack over there. It was close to the flour barrels below.

Zac climbed up the rugged rocks north of the small valley and stepped out onto the wall. The horses were there, feeding in the pasture. The saddles and blankets lay on the rocks close to them. Pablo had done his job. He was getting so good at saddling and unsaddling horses that he wanted to do it for everybody. Zac smiled. *Once a man knows what he's good at, he wants to keep doing it,* he thought.

Zac walked around the wall. He would go to the crack in the tube's roof and yell down. If they were looking over the barrels down below, they would be able to hear him from there. The wall of molten fire must have poured out of the side of the lava tube, creating an eddy of rock that formed the wall Zac was standing on. It circled the area, protecting the small island of greenery.

Zac stepped gingerly out onto the tube. He had no idea how fragile the area might be. They had been lucky the horse hadn't collapsed the entire structure. If that had happened, the place would have looked like the rocky ground James was lying on. Stepping several feet away from the crack, he got down on his knees and crept forward. He lowered his head to the fracture. "Hello the hole. You there?" There was nothing but silence.

Zac turned and looked back at the cabin. He would try there next. Perhaps they had all gone for a walk over the Malpais. The place was a wonder. It had sights that very few people had seen, and the temptation may have been too great to pass up. Still, that didn't explain Ellie's absence from James. There seemed to be no greater draw on the woman's life than that brother of his.

Minutes later, he walked up to the door of the cabin and pushed it open.

A deep voice sounded from inside the dark cabin. "Come in, señor. We are glad to see you."

Zac stepped inside. There on the two beds sat Joe, Julian, Ellie, and Pablo. A large Mexican in polished boots with a large drooping mustache sat in the chair facing the door.

Pablo's eyes fastened on Zac the second he stepped through the door. This was a lost boy in a world he knew little about. He looked like a kitten in a room full of boa constrictors—shy, frightened, and alone in a crowd. He inched off the bed and stepped quickly to Zac, clamping his arms around Zac's thighs. Zac put his arm around the boy. "It's all right, son," Zac said. "You'll be fine."

Around the room were men with drawn revolvers, two of them the Mexican soldiers he had seen in the bar in Silver City. The one with the bandaged hand recognized him right away. Zac could see it by the look of surprise on the man's face. He nudged the man next to him, the second man Zac had seen in the bar, but the two of them remained silent.

The man in the chair got to his feet. "I am General Escobar, and these are some of my compadres. We have followed all of you for quite some distance."

"This is the beloved husband of the lady you met in Santa Fe," Joe said sarcastically to Zac. "You might not remember, but her and her daughter are the ones whose lives we saved in Mescalero territory."

"And we are most grateful for that, which is why we will make your deaths as quick and painless as possible." He said the words with icicles hanging on each one, matter-of-factly and without one ounce of emotion.

"The general here is quite the man of honor," Julian added.

"How did you find us?" Zac asked.

Escobar laughed. "Quite by accident, I assure you, señor. We found a gringo this morning. My second in command was going to kill the man." Escobar laughed again. "This would have been a foolish thing, since we discovered we were not competitors, but associates. We would have made fools of ourselves."

Zac watched the tall blonde narrow his eyes and lift his chin. Zac assumed Escobar had been talking about him, and he could see the notion of calling any of his ideas foolish did not sit too well with the man.

"It seems he simply wanted to kill your brother here, but we want something much more," Escobar said. "This man Gordon said he had seen you while walking over the Malpais. He should be here any time now. He will do his business and then we will do ours. He will not be in our way, and we will not be in his."

"Perhaps we should all wait for him then," Zac said. "We wouldn't want you to deprive him of his pleasure." Zac pulled out his pipe. He wanted to show a matter-of-fact ease with the men to stifle any suspicion they might have.

"Ve should kill them now." The tall man with the blond mustache stepped out of the corner of the room. The man was all business and it showed. "There is no need to vait." He pointed to one of the men beside the door. "Take this man's gun."

The man beside the door pulled Zac's revolver from his holster and stuck it in his belt.

Zac watched Escobar. The major was a very proper but also very abrasive type, and Zac could see the general didn't much care for the idea of the man giving out orders in front of him. Zac saw a quick flash of irritation in the general's eyes, even though he tried his best to hide it.

"Allow me to introduce you," Escobar said. "This is Major Manfried Hess, my segundo, second in command."

Zac tipped the edge of his hat with his fingers. "Pleased to meet you, Major. It must be nice for the general here to have a military man watching out for him."

"Perhaps the major is right," Escobar said. He said the words, but Zac could tell there was an undercurrent of resentment attached to them. "We shouldn't delay ourselves over something that will happen eventually."

"I think you're wasting your bullets, General," Zac said. "My brother Julian over there has an interest in that gold of yours, but the rest of us want no part of it. Never have had any interest in the stuff."

"This is easy for you to say now, with our guns on you, señor. But if you had no concern in this matter, you would not be here."

"Our involvement is strictly a family matter." Zac lit his pipe and then poked the stem in Julian's direction. "We figured we owed it to our mother to try and pull our brother's fat outta the fire."

"Your brother is a mercenary and a murderer. He hires his gun out to the highest bidder, and this time he picked the wrong employer."

"It would seem so," Zac said. He looked down at Pablo and put his hand on the boy's head. "You plan on killing the youngster too?"

Escobar frowned, the top of his mustache pushing up against his nose. "We do not kill children."

Zac puffed on his pipe. "Then what about the woman. Do you kill women?"

Escobar stepped toward Zac. He was a man who didn't like being put in a corner, even by his own relatively skewed sense of morality. "We do not kill women or children. We leave all such things to French dictators and the lackeys they hire to do their dirty work."

"Let me kill him, General," Morales spoke up.

Escobar grinned. "You see, I have no lack of volunteers here."

A sly smile crossed Zac's face. "You might ask your man here how he came to have that hand of his bandaged. It's a colorful story."

Escobar wasn't about to be distracted. His gaze remained on Zac. Morales drifted back into a corner of the room, staring at Zac with hatred in his eyes.

"You might be interested in seeing the cave," Joe spoke up.

"Sí," Escobar said. "This would be a very intriguing thing to see. I think we would be very amused."

"Why don't you let us show you, then?" Zac said.

He held Pablo close as they stepped out the door. The Apache was standing by the horses. The man had evidently kept the recent arrivals out of sight beyond the wall until Zac had gone inside the cabin. Now, the animals were all bunched together at the base of the black sloped rock that made up the roof of the tube.

Zac pulled the boy aside. "You stay close to me, and when I tell you, you do exactly what I say. Is that understood?"

"Sí, señor. I understand."

CHAPTER 39

+ + + + + + +

THE GROUP ASSEMBLED outside the cabin, Escobar's men following with guns drawn. Zac held Pablo close as they walked to where the wall poured itself into the valley.

"Major Hess," Escobar vocalized his order in a crisp, assertive manner. "You, Paco, and Morales climb with the prisoners. We will keep them in our gunsights."

Zac cast a glance in the direction of the Apache scout and then spoke to Escobar. "You better have some torches ready," Zac said. "You ought to have your man over there join us too. The stuff down there is quite a sight, just where it lays."

Hess spoke up, always the proper military man. "That is not necessary. Utant should stay where he is. He is under orders, watching the horses."

Zac could see that the idea of the German doing the thinking was not something Escobar took well to—and that was something Zac counted on.

Escobar brushed his mustache aside. "I do not think that is necessary, Major. The horses are going nowhere, and neither are these people." He waved at Utant. "Come, bring some torches and join us. The horses can take care of themselves."

Hess and the two men began their climb. They scurried up the rocks, anxious to get to the top. Zac helped Julian up the first leg of the wall. Joe and Pablo climbed beside them. "You know, this may be it for the Cobb family," Zac said.

"I know," Julian replied, "and it's all because of me. I find that a hard thing. I don't mind bearing up with the count for my own sins, but I hadn't figured on taking you all down with me."

"Wrongdoing throws a wide lasso."

"I've found that out," Julian said, "maybe too late."

"Maybe not."

"You got something in mind?"

"Yes, I do."

Julian looked back at Zac while the man helped wedge his foot in a crack. "You were right about me last night," he said. "I always looked after myself best. Never gave much thought to what might come to other folks. Even at home, I took pride in being the one Pa had to tend to and the one Mama cried over. I guess a black sheep in a white flock always gets more attention, and I suppose I've lived a long time in a small world. There was only space in there for one, and I figured that ought to be me. The last time I ever did anything for anybody else was at Gettysburg, and it cost me dear. I s'pose after that and the time in that Yankee prison, I figured Julian Cobb better get what was comin' to him on his own. I turned all hard inside—hard and cold."

"Why are you telling me this?"

"Well, that knock on the head that took away my memory for a while did something to me. It not only made me to forget the things I'd done, but it made me pass by the thinking that took me there. For most folks, having a blank mind might be a fearful thing, but for me I s'pose it was a way to start over."

"With what you've done, starting over's going to be hard. There's things that have to be paid for."

"I know there is. I figured, though, I'd best start with people that know me best. I ain't never said this to anyone before, and it shames me to say it now."

"What's that?" Zac asked.

"I reckon I'm asking for you to forgive me." He shook his head, as if disbelieving what was coming out of his own mouth. "I'd feel a whole lot better about whatever happens if I knew you forgave me."

Zac climbed up beside him and gave him a boost. Climbing up the wall was difficult with one arm, and for some very strange reason it felt good to Zac to be the one helping Julian. "I'm not sure I can do that. Maybe I can someday, but saying it now would just be words. You'll have to let me think on it."

Julian nodded at him. "I can understand that. I still can't bring myself to figure on putting my past behind me. I've taken things that didn't belong to me and killed men who didn't deserve to die. I know God forgives me, but He's had a whole lot more practice at doing that than I have. I suppose just having you think on the matter makes it so I can die in peace if I have to."

"I don't plan on doing any dying just yet," Zac said, "and I don't think you should either."

"How you figure?"

"When we get down in that lava tube, you just hold back some. Don't go too deep in the thing. When we get in there, if we get to those barrels, you better be ready to light a shuck and fast."

They both watched as Joe climbed out onto the wall. The men below them were climbing, right behind Ellie and Pablo. Some stood on the ground, giving them cover while their compadres climbed the wall behind Zac and Julian. Moments later, Julian and Zac stumbled out on the top of the lava wall. Hess and his men had moved down the wall with guns drawn. Hopefully they couldn't overhear everything that was being said.

Zac pulled Joe aside. "When we get down there, stay on the entrance side of the tube and be ready to run for all you're worth."

Joe nodded.

Hess, Morales, and Paco inched up a little closer. They held their guns on the brothers. Ellie and Pablo climbed up closer while Escobar and the rest of the men followed behind them.

"Well, Major, it looks like you're about to get your spit-and-polished army," Julian said. "That ought to make you plenty proud, murdering innocent folks to get what you want."

"You are not innocent."

"Maybe not, but the boy and the woman are and my brother down there with the broken leg's never fired a gun in anger in his life."

"They vill not die."

"Let's face it, Major," Zac said. "Anybody going down into that cave is never coming out. You know that, and so do we."

"Ve vill leave the woman and boy outside with your brother."

"We appreciate that," Joe said. "I wouldn't want them to watch us die."

"Of course," Zac said, "the general may have something of his own to say about that."

Hess turned back and watched as Escobar climbed up with the other men. "He vill not know until ve get into the cave. I vill go last and leave the three of them behind when I go in. There is no place they can run to anyway."

Zac worked hard to make sure the smile he felt on the inside didn't show. Hess had to be certain this was his own idea.

It took the entire group a short time before they gathered around the bedroll that James was lying on.

Zac stooped down next to him and patted him on the shoulder. "You all right?"

"This leg of mine hurts like blazes."

Zac looked up at Escobar. "Well, it's going to hurt for a while yet. We're going down in the tube. We'll be showing the general and his men here just what it was that we found down there. Will you be all right until we get back?"

"I'll be fine. Don't worry about me."

Zac patted his shoulder again. "That's fine. I love you, James."

The expression of love was strange coming from Zac, and James's eyes showed his surprise. He seemed at a loss for words, and just mouthed the words, "I love you."

Zac stood up. "All right, we're ready. I think you're in for a sight to behold."

They made their way over the rocks to the icy cave below them. True to his word, Hess held Pablo and Ellie back as the rest of the men went on ahead. Escobar seemed anxious. He climbed down first.

Zac tugged on Hess's sleeve. "Can I have a few words with the boy here? He's an orphan and has kind of attached himself to me. He's gonna be real scared unless I can at least talk to him a bit."

Hess seemed reluctant, but the sight of Pablo's big watery eyes caused him to give in. "Yes, but hurry up. I don't want the general to see you."

Zac nodded and pulled Pablo aside. Stooping down next to the boy, he held his shoulders with both hands and spoke in low soft tones. "Listen to me real careful, pardner. Our lives will all depend on you doing just exactly what I say. Can I count on you to do that?"

"Sí, señor."

"When we go down into that cave and get out of sight, I want you to go back to those horses. You'll have to move fast. Get over that wall and down to them."

Pablo eyes were riveted on Zac.

"You've got to stampede all those horses up to where that crack on the roof is. Get them running and keep them circling up there for as long as you can. That big popgun of your daddy's is put away in my saddlebags. You can use that. Just put the fear of God into those animals and get them up that rise fast. Can you do that?"

"Sí, señor, I can do that."

Zac ran his hand through the boy's hair. "I'm depending on you—all of us are."

Zac stood up and walked to where Hess was standing. "Okay, we better go and show your general just what's he's got for all the trouble he's put you men through."

They started their climb down to where the rest of the men were standing. Zac only hoped that with all the excitement, Escobar wouldn't notice that two of his captives were missing. Leaving Ellie with James would be a risk. Zac knew that. The woman's absence was an easy thing to take notice of. He just didn't think he could risk the chance of having her in there, in case anything went wrong. He prayed that somehow God would put blinders on Escobar.

Escobar seemed distracted by the green ice that hung along the sides of the wall. The frozen ooze was an amazing sight to any man, and it had quite an impact on the general and his men.

"It's quite a sight," Zac said. "Isn't it?"

"This place is a wonder," Escobar agreed.

"You better have your men light their torches. There's more ahead and there's something very special." Zac was doing everything he could to create a sense of excitement about what Escobar couldn't see.

Zac watched as the general cast a passing glance up the pile of rocks they had just climbed over. "Your man Gordon ought to be here directly. Maybe you shouldn't let him see what I'm about to show you." Zac hoped that notion would hurry the man along.

"Yes, then we had better go."

Zac breathed a sigh of relief as Escobar signaled a man with a torch into the tube. They followed him as the man led the way. The other men lit their torches, and the interior of the tube flickered with the soft, fluttering light. The tube seemed to glow with life. The gray- and orange-striped walls pulsated with dancing shadows as the group walked forward.

It would take the boy some time to climb up the wall and then back down the other side. Then Pablo would have to hunt down the pistol. But when the shots sounded, Zac would know that it was time for all of them to run. They wouldn't have much time, and they would have to get beyond the lights the men were carrying. Even then, the entire hill might come down on them along with the rest.

The rocks on the floor of the tube were a tumbled mass. Some were fist size and others peeked their heads up in sharp pointed tips, looking like an ice field in the northern oceans. Zac worked at trying to see any kind of pattern where they would be safe to run in the dark. The only place he could see was the area next to the east wall of the tube. There the rocks were small. They piled down gently from the wall and were layered about three feet from the pile of rocks they were now stepping over. Zac caught Joe's eye and motioned slightly with his chin down at the path. Joe nodded. He couldn't be quite sure if Joe understood exactly what he was pointing out or what he had in mind, but the man had a quick mind, Zac knew that.

The group shuffled through the rocks. Escobar was in front, and Zac edged his way up to a spot behind him. "This cave's been here a long time," Zac said. "If Julian hadn't found that map, we'd have never found this place."

"You say this thing is just up ahead of us?"

"Not too much farther. We didn't check it over for booby traps, though. I know if I was going to leave something like that down here, I sure would've found a way to make anybody who found it pay." The last thing Zac wanted was for the man to spot the barrels and decide to shoot them on the spot. If he could place a little doubt in Escobar's mind, it might give Pablo enough time.

Escobar stopped and looked back. "Where are the woman and the boy?"

Hess stood to attention. "I allowed them to stay with the wounded man. They would slow us down here, and they can go nowhere up there. The rocks are much too steep for them even to climb."

Zac could see the answer irritated Escobar. He quickly pointed up ahead into the darkness. "The treasure is just ahead, just in front of that ice up there."

The thought snapped Escobar's mind back to finding the gold. He looked up at the ceiling and saw the slight tear in the roof. "What is that?"

"That's another entrance," Zac said. "That's how we found the place. It's hard to get up and down there, though, and when we went looking we found the entrance back there."

"I would hate to be lowered down through that," Escobar said.

"It's a plenty scary ride," Zac responded.

They had left some of the bandages on the floor where James had fallen, and Escobar spotted them at once. "What is this?" he asked.

"This is where I set James's leg. He broke it coming down from the roof up there. Like I said, it's a scary ride."

Escobar nodded an acknowledgment and moved on past the spot, waving the torch in front of him. The green ice on the walls blinked and the light from the torches made the slippery surface shine. An odd frozen liquid, it coated the rocks and washed the floor with a ghostly light.

"It's just up ahead," Zac said.

Gingerly, Escobar stepped over the ice. The rest of the men bunched themselves across the tube, each anxious to see the treasure. Zac hoped Pablo wouldn't get to the horses too early. The timing had to be right—

too late and they would in all likelihood be shot, too early and they would be buried along with Escobar and his men.

Moving over the ice, they spotted the first stack of barrels. "We can go ahead and shoot them now," Hess said.

Escobar held his hand up. "Not now. This place may have some traps set for us. What better way to lose the trail to the gold than to kill the prisoners before we touch it for ourselves."

Hess's eyes narrowed. He stood straight, his gun drawn.

Joe interrupted the conversation. "I wouldn't do any shooting down here. You don't know what these walls would do."

Zac liked that. Any doubt that could be planted into these men's heads would serve them well. It might even stop them from shooting when the brothers began to run. "I suppose you can never tell about that," he said. "As brittle as these walls are, you might never come out." He could see the thought was taking shape in Escobar's head.

The general turned to his troops. "There will be no shooting here," he said. "The man might be correct."

"He just wants to live longer," Hess added.

"Maybe so," Zac said, "but being safe never hurt anybody."

"Put your weapons away," Escobar said. "We have more than enough men to hold them with just our knives."

Slowly, the men began to plant their revolvers back in their holsters and take out their knives. Escobar motioned to the first set of barrels. "You three men go over and open them up."

"We'll need a knife," Zac said. "Might be best if we open them. You can never tell what those people did to them."

Escobar studied the situation. Lifting a knife from his belt, he tossed it to Julian. "We'll let your brother do it. He only needs one hand."

The three brothers moved to the flour barrels, and Julian pried the first one open. Wedging the knife between the stays, he popped it open. The flour spilled onto the floor, cascading a drift of white powder that spread over the icy floor and exposing a number of bags. Zac picked up one of the sacks and tossed it at the feet of the gathered group. The bag broke open on the rocks. Glittering gold coins spun and rolled on the green ice, winking and coming to life in the light of the flickering torches. They were hypnotic. Each man stared intently as the money danced and skittered over the ice. Several bent down to pick them up, and Paco and Morales got down on all fours to scrape coins toward them.

"There's a lot more where that came from," Zac said, "a lot more."

Julian moved to the second barrel and repeated the same procedure. This time the bags were bulky. Julian tossed one to Joe, who bounced it in his hands and then opened it up. "You better come take a look at this," he said. "It's not gold."

Escobar's eyes lit up like candles on a birthday cake. He walked over next to Joe and took the bag from his hands. Dipping his hand into the small canvas bag, he pulled up a fist full of glittering polished jewels. He held up the torch for a better look. Cold diamonds sparkled and mixed with the warm glow of red rubies and the green luster of emeralds. "This is amazing," he said.

Zac could see the lust for wealth dancing in the man's eyes, replacing the visions of patriotism that had been there before.

"I'll show you something even more amazing," Julian said. With the quickness of a striking rattler, Julian spun around, clamping the stub of his left arm around Escobar and planting the sharp blade next to the man's throat. "You make a move, even to swallow, and this green ice here is gonna be colored with your red blood."

Hess and the men quickly drew their revolvers.

"I wouldn't do that," Joe said. "At this point your general has a lot more to lose than we do."

"You better talk to them," Julian snarled. He pushed the blade of the knife slightly into the soft flesh of the man's neck. "Show them the error of their ways."

"Don't shoot!" Escobar ground the words out of his throat. "Do as they say. They are going nowhere."

"That's smart," Julian growled. "If we're going to die here, you are too. 'Course, you'll do it more slowly, your life leaking out all over this floor."

"Now," Zac said, "y'all lay your guns down on the ground. Then your knives."

Slowly, one by one, the men complied.

"Now, step over here behind the flour barrels," Zac said.

The men moved deliberately, each one stepping cautiously over the icy floor.

"Better take their lights," Julian said. "A little time in the dark might make them think a little clearer."

"Ve vill find you wherever you go," Hess said. "And the gold vill be here with us." He handed his torch to Joe.

"You're right about one thing," Zac said. "You'll be here with the gold, all right."

Zac and Joe picked up the weapons, sticking them down into their belts. They backed up as the men took their places behind the barrels.

Julian relaxed his grip on Escobar and, taking the bag, shoved him in the direction of his men.

"You men sit down," Zac said. "You might as well get comfortable."

The brothers backed up, Zac looking overhead at the tear in the roof. Then they heard the shot.

The brothers moved back quickly. Just moments later, they heard the sound of the horses overhead. The hoofbeats rang across the hollow tube, like an avalanche of living rocks along the side of a hill. The rapping of the lava roof made it seem as if they were on the inside of a brass kettledrum, and then it happened. The tear in the roof began to widen and shards of lava tumbled to the floor of the cave.

"That's it, boys," Zac said. "Let's get out of here."

Turning, the three brothers ran headlong toward the opening of the tube. They stumbled in the direction of the path Zac had spotted and ran along the wall.

Behind them in the darkness, they could hear the roar of exploding rock. The tube was coming down; soon it would be plummeting down all around them. They ran faster, paying little attention to the ground. The light from the flickering torches barely illuminated the floor in front of them—their feet hitting the surface at the same time as the dim torchlight.

Dust belched out from the tube behind them, a choking smog of loose dirt along with shards of flying, splintered black obsidian. The force of the rock bit into their backsides, tiny arrows of debris embedding themselves into their clothes and clouds of dust choking their nostrils and filling their hair.

Moments later, they stumbled into the faint sunlight. The room was filled with the dust of the collapsing tube, and overhead the roof shook.

They scrambled up the rocks, taking the boulders two at a time and cramming their feet into the cracks while they heaved themselves up toward the dim sunlight. Stumbling out onto the charred valley, they lay on the ground, coughing and wheezing. Joe got to his feet and lurched up the hill into the fresh air.

Zac stood up and, reaching down, pulled Julian up behind him.

"What happened?" Julian asked.

"I sent the boy around to stampede the horses up on that roof," Zac said.

"We could have been down there," Julian said.

Zac chuckled and began to dust himself off. "I guess I hadn't worked out the plan all the way."

"I'd say you hadn't. Seems to me you figured out how to bury those men and us along with them."

"I liked your plan better," Zac sputtered.

Julian put his arm around Zac. "We just might work well together, after all."

"We might. I been thinking about what you asked me to do."

Julian looked into Zac's eyes. "Forgive me?"

"Yes."

"I understand if you can't do that."

"I do forgive you. Do you forgive me?"

"For what?"

"I've always been the self-righteous sort. I've seen it as my job to right the wrongs. I'm not sure if I was more bothered, though, by the things you did or by the fact that you were my brother. But I was wrong about you," Zac said.

"How's that?"

"Joe said you'd changed, and I wouldn't believe him. You have changed."

"I'm just sorry I had to wait so long to do it. A man gets so used to the ditch he's walking in, he can't see the road beside it."

"You didn't answer me," Zac said. "Do you forgive me for my bull-headedness and blind hatred? What you've done are things the law is responsible for. You don't have to own up for your life with me."

"I forgive you."

"Good." Zac hugged his brother.

CHAPTER 40

+ + + + + + +

THE WIND BLEW UP a small dust devil, and it swirled along the street in Santa Fe, kicking up debris against the hotel restaurant window. The brothers sat at dinner with Ellie and her father. They listened to the rapping on the glass from the passing pint-sized tornado. James had his leg propped up on a chair and his arm in a sling. Ellie was by his side, hanging on to his good arm.

Zac stood outside the window with Pablo and his aunt. The woman nervously rung a small lace handkerchief. She already had six children but seemed anxious to care for her orphaned nephew. Her full dress billowed in the stiff wind.

Zac stooped down and put his hands on the boy's shoulders, looking him straight in the eye. "You gonna be all right here?"

Pablo nodded. "Sí, señor, I be okay."

"You pulled our fat out of the fire back in the Malpais. You know that, don't you?"

The boy's eyes shone.

"You handled yourself like a man, and I expect you to do the same now with your aunt here." Zac could see the puzzled look on the boy's face. "A boy only has today and yesterday, but a man has to look to tomorrow. You spend your time worrying about what you can't change and you'll stay a boy. You start thinking about tomorrow and what you're going to be, and you'll be a man. You understand that?"

"I think so. Will you be proud of me, señor?"

Zac pulled him close and hugged him. "I'm proud of you right now, son. Couldn't be any prouder if you were my very own." He pushed him back slightly, once again looking into his eyes. "Now, you got yourself a passel of stories to tell those cousins of yours, and you got yourself a job to do, tomorrow and the day after that."

Zac got to his feet. "This boy's going to be quite a help to you. He can be counted on."

The woman nodded and held the lace to her eyes.

Zac tossled Pablo's hair with his right hand. "We'll meet again, I'm sure. Meantime, you just grow up and take care of your aunt and your cousins."

Pablo nodded, and Zac turned and walked into the hotel.

"I do love the beauty of the West," James said. "But I'm not sure it agrees with my life and limbs."

"This wasn't your typical walk in the park," Joe said.

"Ellie and I will be going back East in three days. I'm anxious for my daughter to meet her." He patted Ellie's hand on the table. "A girl needs a mother, someone to build softness into her."

"You're looking plenty soft to me right now," Joe said.

"I have bruises in places I never knew existed before. One thing I am grateful for, however. I won't have to ride another mile on that horse."

Zac slipped into a chair at the table and poured a cup of coffee.

"Well, just make sure you send us all a wedding invitation," Joe said. "You'll have to time it with Zac here. From Texas, Karen and I will be traveling to both sides of the country it seems, going to Cobb weddings."

"You will have plenty of notice," Ellie said. "A girl dreams about that day her whole life and starts planning it at about the age of seven."

"The doctor says it will take me a few months until I can walk down an aisle, even with a cane. I wouldn't want people to think Ellie here is receiving damaged goods."

Zac sipped his coffee and looked over at Julian. "And what about you? Have you made any plans yet?"

"Well, I won't be robbing any more banks, if that's what you're wondering about."

Oscar cleared his throat. "Your brother and I will be going into business together, right here in Santa Fe."

"Business?" Zac said. "Business with Julian ain't healthy very often."

"I think this one will do quite proper," Oscar responded. "I found us a place in the square over there where we could open up a fair-sized store. I got me enough money of my own to buy the place, but this brother of yours here is putting up the funds to stock the shelves."

"What do you know about shopkeeping?" Zac asked Julian.

Julian grinned. "I know it's something a one-armed, half-blind man can do."

"Papa can teach him everything he needs to know, from buying to stocking to selling." She curled her arm around James. "Supplies and sundries are something Papa knows as well as James knows poetry."

"Well, one thing's for certain sure," Zac said. "You won't have to worry about protection. I pity the man who comes in and tries to hold you gents up."

"Nothing that ever happens out here is all that cut and dry," Julian said.

Ellie nodded her head and stirred her coffee. "In my years of travel I thought I'd seen it all, but these last few weeks have shown me different. One thing still troubles me, though—those Mexican soldiers we found buried at that fort. What happened to them? If they were poisoned, who did it?"

Zac slowly sipped his coffee. "I figure it had to be the doing of that lone gunman who followed us. He seemed to have a vested interest in making sure he got to Julian here, and I don't reckon he had any love for anyone who might have gotten in his way. If we never made it to Mexico, it would have suited him just fine. Without that escort, your chances weren't all that good."

Suddenly, Zac looked toward the door. The entire group turned to see who had just stepped in. Making his way to the table from across the room was the federal agent Michael Delemarian. The man wore a black suit and string tie. His hair was plastered down and parted in the middle, and he looked for all the world like a man heading off to a party, his face smeared with a sheepish smile. Carrying a document in his hand, he strode up to their table.

"Good evening, folks," he said. "I trust you're feeling rested after your trip."

"What do you want?" Joe asked.

"I made arrangements with your brother Julian this morning and conveyed to him the government's promises that I spoke to you all about before you left town. I'm here to deliver on them." He laid the document on the table. "This is the promised presidential pardon." Taking out another slip of paper, he laid it on top of the pardon. "And this is the reward voucher. You can cash it at the bank."

Zac picked up the two pieces of paper, and after looking them over, he passed them to Julian.

Delemarian stuck his hands in his pockets and, grinning, rocked back and forth. "All I need from you is the map, as promised."

"I have that," Julian said.

"You have the map on you?" Delemarian asked.

"That's the safest place."

Julian looked over at Zac, who was sitting at the end of the table. "You mind letting me out? What I've got for him, I need to deliver personally."

"Of course you realize," Delemarian said, "this pardon of yours covers all crimes you've committed in the past. It wouldn't affect any future criminal activity."

Zac scooted over and got up from his chair. "And how about you?" he asked. "Does that paper cover your crimes?"

Delemarian blinked, taken aback by the question. "I'm not sure I understand."

"You know," Zac said. "Hiring men to kill this brother of mine."

"Under the circumstances, the government is quite pleased with the outcome. We have what we wanted, a stable Mexico."

"You just do your job, don't you?" Zac said. "It makes no difference who gets killed or who you use to do it, just as long as you get what you're after."

The man swallowed. "I suppose that's right."

"No," Zac said. "That's true, but it ain't right. You dress better than most of the thieves and killers I chase and put away, but inside you're no different."

"I'm sorry you feel that way, Mr. Cobb, and I'm sorry you don't have more loyalty to your government."

Julian pulled the map from his pocket and handed it over to the man. "I think you'll find this place with no trouble," he said.

Zac gawked at Julian. He was amazed at how calm he seemed on the outside, a passive tranquillity written all over his face.

Delemarian's eyes lit up as he opened the map. It shook slightly in his hands from excitement. "This is wonderful. And you saw the treasure there?"

"Yes, we did," Julian said. "Mountains of gold and jewels."

"Fine, fine." The man folded the map and slid it into his coat pocket. "Then I think our business here is concluded."

"Not quite," Julian said. "I have one more thing for you."

Delemarian smiled.

Rearing back, Julian launched a haymaker that caught the man on the chin, knocking him onto a table full of diners and their plates. He slid along the surface of the table, spilling drinks and splashing gravy.

The people at the table scattered, overturning chairs as they ran. Every head in the place turned to watch the commotion, and several men haltingly got to their feet.

Julian stepped over and, clamping his hand on the man's shirt, drug him off the table. He stood him up. "That's a little something coming from me." He shook him by the shirt, then steadied him upright. "I will be living in Santa Fe, and if I were you, I'd ask for a reassignment. Take my advice, ask for one tomorrow. If I see you on the street, I'll shoot you on sight. Am I making myself understood?"

Delemarian timidly nodded.

Julian released him and, stepping back, brushed bread crumbs from the man's coat. "Fine, then we understand each other." He flicked off a couple of string beans that had clung to his jacket from one of the diner's plates. "We wouldn't want you all messed up on the train, now would we?"

Pivoting on his heels, Delemarian scrambled out.

Julian turned and retook his seat.

"I wish I could have done that," James said.

Joe smirked at Ellie. "You see what kind of a scrapper you're getting here? You're gonna have to work hard to keep him outta trouble, all this bad Cobb blood racing through his veins."

She laughed. "That's a chance I'll have to take."

Joe looked over at Julian. "They'll never be able to dig that gold up from what's left of that tube."

"No, but it would be pure fun to watch them try," Julian beamed.

"You just be careful," Zac said. "That man will have the law watching you like a hawk. They just might make things a bit uncomfortable for you."

"I doubt that. It's been my experience that a man of great wealth and property has little to fear from the local law."

Zac pointed to the voucher. "You don't expect that to carry you through, do you?"

"No, as a matter of fact, I'm splitting that up between the four of you." He smiled at Ellie. "I'm giving the lady her share, too."

"Then how—"

Julian held his hand up, stopping Zac in midsentence. Reaching into his coat pocket, he pulled out a canvas bag the size of two clinched fists. He laid it on the table and unwrapped the rawhide strap holding it shut. Cautiously, he spilled out part of the contents, a glittering array of precious stones, diamonds, emeralds, and rubies. "I did keep the bag Escobar was so taken with."

The group hunched over the table, spellbound by the sight of the polished jewels.

Zac took a few stones from the pile. "I'll sell some of these here in Santa Fe," Zac said."Pablo and his aunt could use some help. And I'll take the rest to Chupta's family."

Julian picked out two large diamonds, handing one to Zac and the other to James. "I figure these will look better on the fingers of a couple of brides I know about than locked in some government vault. One government stealing from another never made much sense to me, not when something like this could be put to better use."